# PRAISE FOR *A CURSE OF GOLD*

"Magic and mayhem, rogues and romance—*A Curse of Gold* dazzles with all this and more. A spellbinding adventure from start to finish!"

Sarah Glenn Marsh, author of the Reign of the Fallen series

# A CURSE

~ OF ~

# GOLD

ANNIE SULLIVAN

BLINK

*To the best friends I could ask for:*

*Alicia, Anna, Amy, Brynn, Carolyn, Christina, Elizabeth, Emily, Julia, Kristin, Liz, Mackenzie, Marija, Mary, Michele, Nikki, Rachelle, Rose, Savannah, Vinaya, Vivian, and Whitney*

# CHAPTER 1

⟫⟫⟫⟫⟫⟫⟫⟫❀⟪⟪⟪⟪⟪⟪⟪⟪⟪

The last thing I want to do today is turn someone to gold.

But as I pull on my gloves and take one last look in the mirror, I'm not afraid of what will happen if I do.

I smooth down the blue fabric of my dress and run my fingers along the swirled silver threads running through it. I chose this color because Royce will be wearing blue at today's ceremony reinstating him as a captain in the Royal Armada.

I'm amazed at how well the dress fits. I finally found a tailor who was willing to take my measurements and touch my golden skin. He'd had a cursed grandmother—he knows curses aren't contagious.

Now I just have to convince everyone else. And that starts by not wearing a veil for my first major public appearance since recovering my father's cursed gold.

I tuck a few stray hairs back into the golden braid fashioned across the top of my head. Just behind it nestles a silver crown made up of twisted and climbing filigree roses. It had been my mother's first crown. Each rose once held a ruby at the center, burrowed into the metal, but those spots are empty now; the stones were sold off long ago to keep the palace from running out of money, though my father hadn't been able to bear parting with the crown itself.

I straighten it one last time, ignoring the way the metal weighs down my head more than the veils ever did, and go over the faded words inked onto the crumpled pages of King Kalisrov's journal, which I'd found in the library with the other historical documents.

*Never appear in public without a crown*, the tiny script reads. That had been his top rule, as it showed everyone who was in charge.

I read on. *You should be so comfortable in your crown you are able to sleep in it with no discomfort.*

I scoff. I've barely mastered keeping the thing on my head. But as I look away from the fraying pages to the mirror, I can't help but wonder if he's right. Will the nobles respect me more now that I'm wearing one?

There's only one way to find out, so I throw my shoulders back and head out the door toward the great hall.

Already a crowd has gathered beneath the gleaming chandeliers that swing above the aisle leading to two thrones. The nobles bow as I pass. But I hear mumbles about me not wearing a veil and how they always knew I was gold through and through. I tune them out and bustle past, concentrating on not letting my head dip low enough to let my crown slip. Wearing the crown instead of hiding my face is just one small step to show them I won't be a ghost in the shadows anymore—that my father and I are here to rule.

But I see the judgment in their eyes each time their gaze flicks up toward me. They don't think I can do it. Or they don't want me to. Because they still believe a cursed person is a ruined person. They assume I'm going to infect the kingdom and make it weaker than my father already did when he asked for the ability to turn everything he touched to gold.

I ignore them and straighten my shoulders as I arrive at the throne next to my father's. My throne is smaller than my father's, and the wooden seat isn't comfortable for more than a few moments. I try unsuccessfully not to fidget. I cross and uncross my legs. Wasn't one a sign of hostility and one of welcoming? If I'd had tutors when I was younger, I would know. But they'd all left after my father turned me to gold when I was seven.

Despite what the nobles think, I'm trying very hard to educate myself and be the ruler Lagonia deserves, but there is still so much to study—and most of the month I've been back has been spent caring for my father, hiring new guards, and learning how to run a palace. I've only been able to sneak in a few books on the subject—like King Kalisrov's journal. I just pray it's enough to get me through today.

Past the dais, Lady Lucar looks down her nose at me as I switch my legs back and forth trying to figure out what to do with them. I settle for crossing them at the ankles and shoot Lady Lucar the most regal look I can manage. She looks away quickly, so either my aloof air of power is coming across . . . or she believes the rumor that says I can turn people to gold simply by looking at them.

Trumpets sound, echoing through the domed ceiling of the hall before reverberating back down. My father, King Midas, appears in the doorway. He's shaved the scruffy beard he'd grown while I was gone, exposing the skin around his once strong jaw. Wrinkles have taken up residence under his eyes and across his forehead. He looks like a man twice his age, a leftover side effect of being cursed by Dionysus, and another reminder of why the nobles don't want us to rule.

He's flanked by his new advisor, Tilner, who was hired on Royce's recommendation. He'd been Royce's father's most trusted steward before he'd been sent away after Royce's father was cursed, ruining the Denes family and leading people to attack the house and attempt to burn it to the ground.

My father and I had worked to hire him together. It had been our first joint venture. The first time we'd worked on anything together since the day his unthinking embrace made me a golden statue.

It had been difficult for both of us. He'd trusted my uncle Pheus as his advisor, and my father was still reeling from the revelation Pheus had helped Captain Skulls steal his gold, a betrayal that led to my uncle's death.

Tilner shadows my father down the aisle. He has a way of disappearing from view behind his king but is always there to offer a steadying arm whenever needed—an arm I had hoped my father wouldn't need.

I thought bringing back the cursed objects my father turned to gold would make him stronger—and he had received an initial boost of strength when they were reunited. But he's still tethered to that infernal treasure, still looks to the tower that once again holds it, more than at me. And the gold still drains him, siphoning away his strength.

He takes my hand as he reaches the dais. I help him settle into his seat. His eyes meet mine for a brief moment before sliding past them to the tower once more.

I squeeze his hand, bringing his gaze back to me, knowing he's trying just as hard as I am to be the leader Lagonia needs.

His eyes move to the crown on my head, eliciting a small smile, and I wonder if I remind him of my mother.

He gives my hand a weak squeeze in return before turning back to the room.

"Bring forth the candidate, Royce Denes," he says. His voice barely reaches the nearest chandelier.

The tall doors swing open to reveal Royce, his strong jaw set resolutely as he steps forward. As he strides forward, his sturdy form takes up all the space my father seemed unable to fill. He holds his hat under his left arm, right above his sword hilt, while his right arm rests stiffly against his side. Behind him, his crew waits in two lines. Together, they press forward.

As they near, sunlight glints off the golden threads woven through Royce's coat. But that's nothing compared to the gleam of the golden tassels perched on each of his shoulders.

I straighten my shoulders. I'd purposefully requested Royce wear a jacket with gold on it, to show that the monarchy wasn't afraid of it anymore, that the metallic sheen doesn't make us recoil in fear.

But I barely notice the gold because my heart leaps when I see Royce's bright blue eyes. He's gotten a haircut since I last saw him. Gone are the long blond locks that the sea breeze would drag across his temples. He looks more refined now. Tamer.

We've barely seen each other this past month. I've been busy helping my father run the palace, and Royce has been training to rejoin the armada.

And now he'll be leaving for three months on his ship's maiden voyage.

I swallow, remembering that wise Queen Teragram wrote that there is no ocean that can separate love, for it is a feeling and not a location. If she could survive ruling a kingdom under siege for two years while her husband was off at war, then I can survive three short months without Royce.

It's what rulers do.

That thought steels me as Royce takes a knee before my father, lowering his head. Strands of hair fall forward. My fingers itch to swipe them back, so I instead run them along the thin necklace tucked under the high collar of my dress. The necklace consists of a string of pearls with one sunrise tellin seashell as a pendant. Royce grabbed it for me from the lair of the Temptresses of Triton, siren-like women who were once Triton's lovers but who now lure men to their deaths with their enchanted voices and a trove of treasures.

Royce could've grabbed any item he'd wanted from their trove, but he'd grabbed only this, saying the rays on the front reminded him of me, of the sunrise on the outside and strength on the inside.

My father is supposed to stand to say his next words, but he doesn't. "Do you pledge your loyalty, fidelity, and life to the kingdom of Lagonia, its rightful ruler, and those under their protection?" His voice is weak, and I doubt Royce can hear them. But he answers as though he has.

"I do," Royce's voice rings out. It echoes through the hall in a way my father's never will.

"Do you pledge to protect Lagonia and her allies?"

"I do." His voice sounds deeper now. It's been so long since I've heard it. And something in me reacts to it. My pulse quickens.

"Do you pledge to uphold the honor of all Lagonians as you sail the seas?"

"I do."

"Do you pledge to uphold all Lagonian laws?"

"I do."

"And do you pledge to serve and follow the commands of those outranking you?"

"I do."

"For services rendered to your crown and kingdom"—my father pauses to take a breath—"I hereby promote you to full rank of captain in my armada." He takes another shaky breath. "And I offer you my personal thanks." I can't tell if he pauses to let that sink in or if he's having trouble getting the words out. "Rise."

Royce stands and steps forward, offering my father the hat from under his arm. My father tries to stand. To save him the embarrassment of having Tilner wrench him up in front of everyone, I leap out of my seat—careful not to lose my crown—and take the hat.

Lady Lucar scoffs at the breach in decorum. Though it's worth it because there's a flash of something in Royce's eyes as my fingers touch his hand. But he quickly steadies his face.

I ceremoniously place the hat on his head, and he steps back.

"Have you a loyal crew you wish sworn in at this time?" I ask.

Royce bows and steps aside, gesturing to the men lined up behind him.

They all take a step forward and kneel as Royce had done. Rhat, Royce's first mate, is at the head of one line. I barely recognize him in his blue-and-white uniform. The last time I saw him, he was shoeless and wearing an open vest. Not to mention his hair. His head is shaved except for a long black ponytail, but he's pulled it up into a bun for the occasion.

I can't decide if my cousin Hettie will like him more in his uniform or not.

I spot several other sailors I recognize, like Phipps, among those kneeling. Phipps looks older than I remember. More bags under his eyes. Ever since his identical twin brother, Thipps, died saving me, I've worried he'll lose some of his infectious joy. I'll have to find time to check in with him before the ship sets sail.

"Do you pledge your loyalty, fidelity, and life to the kingdom of Lagonia, its rightful ruler, and those under their protection?"

"We do." Their voices resound through the hall like a chorus.

"Do you also pledge to follow Captain Royce Denes as he fights for the honor and protection of Lagonia?" I ask.

"We do."

"Then rise," I say, "as sailors of the Royal Armada."

Cheers erupt through the hall. The men shake each other's hands and spread through the crowd to be greeted by family while members of the aristocracy keep to their own corners of the room and servants hurry to uncover all the platters of food on the tables lining the walls. I can already smell the delicious scent of the buttered honey rolls piled next to towers of different types of seafood packed in ice.

Royce has already been swallowed by the crowd by the time I turn to look where he'd been standing. I try not to let the disappointment show as I shift back to my father.

"Go," he says, waving his hand, "enjoy the feast."

I take my seat next to him and grasp his hand. "My place is here with you."

"Tilner will take care of me. Go congratulate the captain on my behalf." He offers me the largest smile he can, which is really no more than a slight upturn at the edges.

As if saying his name summoned him, Tilner appears at my father's side. He stands there silently, watching the crowd, waiting until he is needed.

"Go," my father repeats.

I bite my lip. This might be the last chance I get to talk to Royce before he sets sail. I give my father's hand one last squeeze and head down the dais steps.

Phipps appears before me, a wide smile on his face. It's the kind of smile that tugs so far up at the ends that I'm not sure his lips could go any wider, and it hints that he's probably up to something. But I don't care if he steals all the gold chandeliers; I'm glad to see him smiling again. Although I can't help but notice the tightness around his eyes and the hollowness of his cheeks.

"Hello." He bows awkwardly, his large ears sticking out even more as his hair sweeps forward.

"Phipps." I offer him my hand. "How have you been?"

"Oh, good, good," he says, pumping my hand up and down.

From behind him, a short figure peeks out.

Phipps motions behind him, and the person steps forward. "I'd like you to meet my younger brother, Lenny."

Lenny looks to be about thirteen or fourteen and has the same lopsided grin accented by lips that are just a little too big for his face. Scraggily hair down to his shoulders does nothing to hide ears as big as his brother's.

"I didn't know you had another sibling," I say.

"Well"—Phipps ducks his eyes—"my maw didn't think he

was ready to go to sea, but with . . . with . . ." He trails off, as if having trouble getting the words out.

Lenny gently nudges Phipps's shoulder and nods encouragingly.

Phipps laughs nervously and swallows. He nods down at his brother, and after a few moments his smile returns, though it seems forced. "It was finally time for him to get his sea legs."

Lenny bows rigidly at the waist, and I notice one of his coat arms swing forward, empty.

Phipps notices where my gaze has gone. "He was born a little differently."

Lenny grabs Phipps's elbow, tugging on his brother's sleeve without taking his bright eyes from me.

"Oh, and he can't speak." He then holds his hands up defensively. "But don't you think for a minute he can't hold his own. One time, Thipps and I were backed into a corner by these guys who thought we'd cheated them at a game of Lavender Luck, and Lenny showed up out of nowhere and took all three of the guys down."

Lenny nods proudly, standing a little straighter.

"Oh, and he makes a great lookout," Phipps continues. "He's got eyes like a hawk. Nothing escapes his notice." He leans in closer, his eyebrows rising upward. "He can even get secrets out of a person with just a look."

"I'm sure he'll be a wonderful addition to the Royal Armada," I say.

"Oh, he will," Phipps answers. "I've really taken him under my wing. Taught him everything I know." He throws his chest out and his shoulders back as though I should be pinning a medal on him.

I laugh. "If you've taken him under your wing, I expect you've already got some scheme dreamed up."

Lenny winks at me, his grin getting wider.

"That means yes," Phipps supplies.

"Just make sure you don't get rich too quick," I supply. "That doesn't always turn out well."

Phipps waves his hand dismissively. "Oh, we'll be rich for years to come."

I eye him. Now I really am worried he is going to try to steal the chandeliers. And he might not look who's standing beneath before cutting them down. On our recent voyage, he and his twin brother, Thipps, were renowned for how quickly they could come up with some money-making scheme.

Phipps eyes the crowd around us and then leans in closer. "It's not often the likes of me is invited to the palace, so I'm going to find a rich woman here to marry."

Lenny vigorously nods.

I laugh. "Good luck with that."

Lenny nudges his brother again.

Phipps swats him away. "I'll ask her." He clears his throat and leans in again, his eyes shifting around nervously as though it would be disastrous to be overheard. "Are there any you'd recommend? Ones with heavy pockets?"

I cast my eyes around the room.

I spot Lady Alyona. She's only a few years older than me and has one of those angelic faces that makes you believe she's the sweetest person in the room. But she's not. She was the first one to openly suggest Hettie was in on her father's plot to overthrow my father. She'd suggested Hettie be locked up until we could

11

ascertain her loyalty. Hettie had pulled her sword and nearly chased Lady Alyona from the hall before we stopped her.

I'd like to see that snake get a little of what's coming to her.

Lady Alyona is surrounded by her gaggle of other rich ladies, who hang on every word she says.

It's probably not the nicest thing I've ever done, but I point Phipps directly toward her. "She's very rich."

Phipps's mouth curls upward, and he gives me a miniature salute before waltzing off.

Lenny at least has the courtesy to offer another bow.

I catch the boy's gaze when he straightens, and Phipps was right; there is something intense in his eyes. Something that makes you feel truly seen for the first time in a long while. Something that hints Lenny has spent his whole life observing those around him and knows more than he lets on.

As a result, I can't help but ask, "How is Phipps really doing?" I keep my voice low even though Phipps is searching for a way to interrupt the circle of women and not paying us any attention.

Lenny's eyes follow my own. They linger on his brother, making me wonder if their mother's agreeing to send Lenny out wasn't so much his need to get his sea legs but instead her wanting her son watching over his brother after a devastating loss.

When Lenny finally looks back at me, he gives me sort of a twisted half smile, noncommittally moving his head side to side.

"Good days and bad days?" I venture.

Lenny nods.

My stomach clenches. I wish there was something I could do to ease the boys' pain. My head shouts that if I'd been a better leader, Thipps wouldn't have died in the first place. I close my eyes and shake the thought away. You can't change the past. Only the future. Queen Teragram had written that as well. And that is what I am going to do as I lead Lagonia.

I lightly rest my hand on Lenny's boney shoulder. "I'm sorry about Thipps. If there's anything I can do for you or your family, let me know."

Lenny offers a small smile in answer.

"And keep an eye on Phipps for me," I say.

He winks and then nods to where Phipps has somehow managed to weasel his way into the women's circle.

I laugh. "You better go help him."

Lenny raises his eyebrows and nods as if he's used to having to assist his brother in many similar situations. And I'm sure he has—I just pray he can help him get through the loss of Thipps.

I leave Phipps to his brother as I duck through the crowd, looking for Royce again.

Instead, I find Rhat gathering his meal. He's actually taken one of the decorative silver platters and piled it with different cuisines. Pastries with flaky crusts filled with honey-roasted nuts rest atop lightly browned fish fillets. Purple octopus tentacles dangle over the side, and every free spot is filled with grapes or olives in a variety of colors.

He always has had an interesting appetite.

"Princess." Rhat bows without losing a single olive from the platter. I wish I was half so good at keeping my crown steady on my head.

I sigh. I've told him at least four times to call me Kora, like he did on ship, but he never does. I think only a direct order from Royce would get him to stop using my title.

"Do you know where Hettie is?" he asks. He scans the room, and I know if she'd been here, he would've already found her.

She didn't come. She didn't want the prying eyes of the kingdom, the eyes of Lady Lucar and Lady Alyona, constantly judging her, looking for hints she really was part of the gold theft—that she wanted to be the next queen.

My cousin has been avoiding all appearances since the incident with Lady Alyona. She's even been avoiding me.

Hettie has taken up sword fighting instead, practicing with the guards and with Rhat. It seems to help. Some.

Though I worry about her. Especially since Rhat will be leaving with Royce in the morning. I don't want Hettie to turn into the same outcast I once was, when rumors stalking me down hallways controlled my entire existence.

I want her to talk to me, but I can't force it. Every time I find time to check in on her, she's either out practicing or pretends she's sleeping. But that doesn't hide the sniffles and sobs I sometimes catch before I knock.

"She's not here," I say to Rhat.

A flash of disappointment streaks across his face. We both thought that if anything could get her out of her room, it would be the reinstatement ceremony.

He groans. "She'll return when she's ready."

I softly touch his arm. "She will. We'll make sure of it. I'll watch over her while you're gone." I resolve to check on her more often once Rhat leaves, to show her she doesn't need to keep everything locked inside.

Although I half suspect she might attempt to sneak onto Rhat's ship before it leaves. And I'm not sure I'd stop her if that's what she wants, if that's what she thinks would help. I myself have wanted to escape from prying eyes on more than one occasion since being back.

He nods. "Thank you."

"Have you seen Royce?" I ask.

Rhat cranes his neck around. He motions his head to the right. "He's talking to some noble or another. I'm sure he'll be grateful if you rescue him."

I head in the direction he indicated and find Royce surrounded by a crowd of nobles in their finery. Red jackets imprinted with black. Green jackets patterned with blue wave designs. Dresses in reds and pinks and whites, each with a stitched design, swirl around Royce.

His head whips back and forth as they scramble to get his attention. One clasps his shoulder and asks his opinion on weather conditions for merchant ships. Another lady forces her hand into his, waiting for him to kiss it as she asks if he'll attend her dinner party next week. As if she didn't already know he is leaving tomorrow.

I clear my throat.

Royce's eyes meet mine over the crowd. He visibly relaxes.

There's grumbling as he excuses himself from the group.

He takes my hand and kisses it, sending a tingling up my arm. "Princess."

I can't help but smile.

I tug Royce toward the balcony doors overlooking one of the small courtyards, not caring what the crowd thinks of our abrupt departure.

The balcony is tucked away so no one can see out onto it, and it's deserted as I suspected it would be. None of the nobles want to risk missing any gossip or not being seen in their finery by the crowds.

Royce loosens his shirt collar and takes off his jacket, tossing it onto the balcony ledge. "It was like fighting off ten Temptresses at once in there. Everyone wanted to get their claws in me."

"Sick of being a captain already?" I tease.

Royce rolls his eyes and sits on the ledge, next to the jacket. "I've been at sea so long I've forgotten what it's like back on land."

I sit down beside him. "Well, you'll have three months free of those people."

A silence falls between us as the reality he's leaving sets in. I duck my head.

"It'll only be three months," he says quietly. "It'll pass quickly." He wraps his arm around me, and I rest my head on his shoulder, breathing in his scent. He doesn't smell like the open ocean anymore. Just like soap and freshly laundered clothes.

"Are you sure?" I don't risk raising my head to look at him. I'm not asking if it'll pass quickly. I'm asking if it'll only be three months. Which he clearly senses.

I've seen the way he stiffens around the nobles, the way he walks quickly through the palace, the way he tries to avoid drawing too much attention to himself.

He takes one of my hands in his. "I feel out of place here . . . I'm not used to all the eyes staring at me. It's not like that at sea."

My heart sinks. I've been dreading hearing those words since I asked my father to reinstate him.

He pulls my cheek up to look at him. "But Kora, if you can face it, then so can I."

"Are you sure you want to, that you want this to be your life?"

He takes my hands in his. "Kora . . ." He cuts off as a strange screeching noise slices through the air.

I stare out over the balcony railing into the dusty courtyard clogged with carriages and horses from the nobles who'd come to watch the ceremony. Several horses throw their heads back and others stamp their feet as something glints off their bridles.

A red light sparks near the closed gates built into the palace wall. It's too red and too erratic for a lantern.

I'm just about to ask Royce what it is when the front gates burst apart, a jumbled mess of melted and twisted metal where the lock had been. Hinges squeal as the remaining fragments are ripped from their moorings and tossed into the courtyard. They clatter to the ground, sending horses reeling.

Carriage drivers leap from their seats, but instead of running to calm their animals, they scatter into the shadows.

A burly man waltzes through where the gate once was. Behind him, something moves in the shadows.

The man takes a quick look around, but just as the flame of his body had drawn my eye, the slight glow of early morning sunlight hitting my golden skin draws his.

"There she is." The man points a finger as red as burning coal at me. "Kill her."

# CHAPTER 2

꙳꙳꙳꙳꙳꙳꙳꙳꙳❀꙳꙳꙳꙳꙳꙳꙳꙳

B ehind the man, a group of satyrs rushes in. The hairy half-human, half-goat creatures stand at least a foot taller than any person I've ever seen. And it's hard to see any of their human-ity between the thick coating of dark hair that covers their bodies and the twisted horns shooting out of their heads.

Two satyrs separate from the group, leaping over carriages and launching into the palace walls while the man leads the rest against the guards streaming down the palace steps. He melts the sword of the nearest guard with his bare hand while his other hand reaches up and burns through the guard's armor as if it isn't even there. The guard's gurgled cry cuts off as the man scorches through his throat.

I swallow down vomit.

"Get back," Royce cries, pulling me away from the ledge. The satyrs make quick work of slamming their human-like fingers tipped with pointed claws into the palace walls and climbing toward us. Marble shatters as the claws latch into the balcony railing and the creatures heave themselves over.

Their hooves make a terrifying clack against the floor as they advance, and the stench of dirt and matted hair becomes overwhelming.

Royce pulls his sword, and I skitter behind him, weaponless.

One satyr snarls, revealing jagged black teeth as it clambers toward Royce.

The other one huffs through its wide nostrils and runs toward me, head bent low so I fear I'll be impaled by its horns. I duck out of the way as the horns rake through the wall at my back instead, sending shards of stone clattering down around me.

I scramble across the debris toward the other side of the balcony.

Over the pounding of my heart, I hear Royce's sword clang again and again against the satyr's sharp nails as it blocks his blows.

The second satyr turns quickly and swipes at me. Sharp claws catch on my skirt, ripping the fabric as I lurch to the side. My crown clatters to the floor just before I smash into the balcony. I land on my stomach, and pain radiates through my ribs and arms.

It takes a moment for me to get air back into my lungs, but I'm already crawling. Because there, a few paces in front of me, is Royce's jacket. The gold tassels on the shoulders gleam encouragingly, but as I scramble toward it, a rough hand closes around my ankle, dragging me backward.

I scream and grope at the balcony floor, hoping to catch on some crack, some hole, anything to give me leverage against the creature's hold. I find nothing.

The satyr whips me backward, flinging me into the wall, and I land in a heap on my hands and knees. I curl into myself. My lungs ache so much I can barely catch my breath, but something tells me to move.

Move or die.

I throw myself to the side, rolling away just as the satyr

pounces where my body had been. It lets out a nasty snort and turns after me.

But I don't stop. I crawl across the debris, not caring that jagged wreckage punctures straight through the thin fabric of my gloves and digs into the skin inside.

Just as my fingers close around the jacket fabric, the satyr's hooves land on either side of me, shaking the entire balcony. I roll over, clutching the jacket to my chest like a shield, and I whip off a glove.

The satyr snarls down at me, sending spittle against my face. It raises a claw, ready to strike.

I fumble with the jacket without taking my eyes from the satyr's. Where is that tassle?

A claw strikes forward.

*There.*

A chill passes through me as I absorb the gold from one of the tassels—an ability I developed after my father failed to cleanse everything he'd turned to gold after the god Dionysus cursed him.

My hand snakes out, wrapping around the satyr's ankle. Before I can even feel the coarse hair poke my skin, the creature turns to gold, its claws inches from my chest.

I fall back against the balcony floor and let out a sigh that sends an ache through my chest. But I don't have time to register the pain. I turn just in time to see Royce pull his blade from a satyr's throat. The creature collapses to its knees and falls face-first onto the floor. Black blood leaks from its wound.

"Are you okay?" Royce asks, rushing over.

I nod, and he helps pull me carefully from underneath the metallic satyr. I wince at the movement. I'm going to be covered in bruises and scratches tomorrow, and my ribs feel like they're on fire.

I lean out over the balcony, my back groaning in protest. The man from the courtyard is nowhere to be seen. Only a trail of dead guards, some of them still smoldering, remain.

"We have to stop that man," I say. "He's in the palace." I pick up the jacket and rush back toward the great hall with Royce at my heels.

Sucking in air through the pain, I cry out, "Guards, secure the hall," just as the doors at the far end of the room crash open, a hole blazing through the wood.

A guard's lifeless body flies inside. I can only watch as it crashes into a row of chairs still set up from the ceremony and sends them scattering. The body is followed by the fiery man. His eyes scan the room as more satyrs stream in behind him.

"Leave the king," he says. "We only want the golden girl."

Screaming starts as the man burns a hole through the chest of a guard who rushes to stop him. Nobles in their festive finery become a blur as they push and shove, fighting to make it to the exits. Chairs clatter to the floor. Shoes lie discarded. Fabric rips.

Some make it out the door, and some are caught by satyrs trying to get to me. My heart almost stops at the sight of two nobles being thrown into the air as a satyr rushes forward.

Tables of food are overturned. Hooves scrape across the floor. Platters crash. And the screams get louder. More tortured.

A person is thrown into one of the chandeliers, causing it to fall and send shards of glass in all directions.

I try to cry out a warning, but it's too late.

Bodies lay tangled amid the twisted metal. Lady Lucar's is one of them. Her eyes stare unblinking at the hole in the ceiling, as if she's judging it even in death. A tiny trail of blood spills from her mouth.

I swallow, but it does nothing to stop the sickening feeling radiating from my insides as chaos swirls around me.

Royce's crew and the guards do their best to hold back the satyrs, but no one can stop the intruder as he burns through everything in his path.

The man is tall, with veins that stand out in the muscles of his arms. He's entirely bald, making his face look round. Small eyes are recessed behind a hooked nose. His lips are pale, but maybe that's because his skin has an underlying reddish tinge, as if a fire continuously burns underneath.

Royce rushes to stop him, managing to inflict a cut along the man's arm on his first swing. Blood bubbles out, boiling as it touches the man's skin. Royce's sword is just as red, but not from blood. It looks as if it's been stuck in a forge.

The man catches Royce's sword on the second swing. He melts through the metal while leering at Royce. The tip of the sword soon breaks off and clatters to the floor.

Royce stumbles back, staring at the hilt of his near-useless weapon. The man lunges at him. Royce dodges out of the way.

He's out of options.

I race toward the man, ripping off my other glove as I go.

I frantically flip around Royce's jacket until I find another tassel. Royce sees me coming as he pivots—he knows what I'm doing. He dodges the man's next strike, landing with his back to me. The man's next blow knocks the sword hilt from Royce's hand, and Royce falls to the ground.

The man laughs and saunters over to him.

I absorb the gold and rush forward, shoving my hand against

the man's arm and watching as he's frozen in a casing of gleaming gold.

The instant relief of having gold exit my body is replaced by fire, as though my hand has been blasted by an open flame. I tear it away from the man and shake it until the pain subsides, but I can already feel a palm-sized blister bubbling up.

Royce climbs to his feet, his chest heaving.

Rhat rushes over. At some point, he lost his jacket and shirt. Or maybe it was just easier for him to fight without them. "Are you both okay?" He tosses Royce and me swords. I turn to check on my father. He's still on his throne. Several guards surround him and Tilner. He's safe for now.

I move to follow Royce and Rhat, but a sound makes me pause.

It starts out like hissing. My eyes search for the source of the noise as it grows louder, turning into an odd plopping sound.

Suddenly, gold melts off the intruder and pools on the floor.

I stare, open-mouthed. How is this possible?

I leap back as the man emerges unscathed.

He smirks at me as his boots squelch into the still-steaming metal. "You didn't think Dionysus would send just anyone to kill the golden girl, did you?" he asks. "Or that you were the most powerful creature he could create?" His eyes are wide, wild— probably as wide as mine.

Other creatures? I'd always known Dionysus entered into bets with others, but I never thought he went around creating people with powers on a whim. People who clearly answer to him and who now want me dead.

"Kora," a weak voice calls from behind me. My father. "Look out."

Without another option, I swipe my sword at the man as he lunges closer.

He grabs the middle of the blade and melts off the tip.

Still clutching the hilt of my sword, I scramble backward. My heart races. I cast around for any weapon I can grab. My hands itch for gold, but I know it won't work any better a second time.

Behind the man, the melted gold has spread out like a lake. A useless lake.

And I can't help but think that's what I'll look like if he gets his hands on me.

He lumbers closer.

I look over my shoulder. I refuse to lead him closer to my father, so I back myself toward one of the walls lined with tables full of untouched food.

I take even steps backward, keeping my eyes on the man as he approaches.

I knock into a table. Platters rattle.

"Now it's time to melt you down too." He grins.

I lunge for the nearest tower of chipped ice packed underneath tiers of crab and shrimp.

I heave the ice at the man and steam erupts, shrouding him from view. He cries out and tries to wave away the cloud.

"Melt this!" another voice cries behind him. As the steam disappears, a sword shoots through the man's chest. Two daggers follow it on either side.

The man looks down, shocked. The sword's metal ripples and drips away where it touches his skin, and the protruding blade clatters to the floor.

The rest of the sword rips free, creating a large opening, and the skin around it singes, filling the air with the putrid scent of burning flesh.

The man's eyes roll up, and he collapses. The dagger hilts in his back melt into pools between his shoulder blades, and the rubies that had been set in one slide off and clink to the floor.

Hettie stands behind the man, the sword hilt in her hand misshapen from the heat of the man's body.

"Hettie." I pull her into a hug. "Thank you."

She's thinner than the last time I saw her, and paler too. Her auburn hair is pulled into a braid, and she's wearing her fencing clothes.

"I heard the screaming," she says. "There are dead guards all over the palace. What's going on?"

"Dionysus sent them," I say, "but I have no idea why."

As we turn toward the center of the room, Phipps pulls his sword from the last satyr still standing.

The entire floor is littered with bodies. Black blood swirls unnaturally with crimson. My stomach crawls at the sight. How could this have happened?

"They were after her," a nobleman whispers. The sound echoes through the nearly silent hall.

"What did they want with her?" someone else says.

The room goes completely quiet.

Slowly, I realize everyone's gazes have landed on me.

# CHAPTER 3

ﾟ)ﾟ)ﾟ)ﾟ)ﾟ)ﾟ)⊛(٤(٤(٤(٤(٤(٤(

S he's cursed." Lord Lucar pushes through the crowd, his eyes wide and his gaze frantic. His smooth black hair sticks out at all angles, and a smear of blood stains his cheek. "My wife is dead! She's dead. And it's all because of her. She'll kill us all."

Whispers start again around the room. They weave between the nobles and servants, who all no longer care who they're gossiping with. They slowly drown out the moans and crying as others search around the room for loved ones. They even draw in the people staring listlessly at the ceiling in an attempt to avoid looking at the carnage.

"Princess Kora just helped save you all." Royce moves through the crowd to stand in front of me, to protect me. His sword still drips globs of black blood.

I put my arm on his and give a nod as I step in front of him. This isn't his ship where people will listen to him and disperse back to their duties when he gives a command. This is the palace, where people listen only to those who outrank them. At least they're supposed to, but I can feel the energy in the room turning against me.

I move to straighten the crown on my head—as King Kalisrov would've done to draw attention to the power symbol—only to realize I'd left it out on the balcony after it fell off.

I drop my hand, scrambling for what to say that won't scare them more while also letting them know I have some idea of what's going on and how to handle it. I only wish I *did* know how to handle it.

I throw back my shoulders and say with as much authority as I can muster, "Dionysus sent these men."

Grumbling spreads around the room. I have to talk even louder to be heard. "And I'm going to find out why so it doesn't happen again."

Lord Lucar's eyes are wild. "He was after *you.*" He jams an accusatory finger in my direction. "We should just get rid of you. You and your family have brought nothing but curses down on us. It's time we had a real ruler." His voice cracks as the pain of his loss bursts through.

His words cut into me as sharp as any satyr's claw, but I set my jaw and refuse to look away. Because if I do, I'm afraid I'll lose control of the room entirely. I think the only thing saving us from a full-on revolt is the fact everyone is too scared and worn out to fight anymore.

Plus, most of the people holding swords answer to me.

I clear my throat. "For now, we need to tend to the wounded and search the palace to make sure no other satyrs remain. We'll increase the number of guards as we investigate."

I close my eyes and do a quick check of the gold up in the tower, using my ability to sense its location. Thankfully, all the pieces are still present. So if that wasn't the motivation for his attack, what was? And what did he want with me?

Across the room, Tilner moves forward and starts directing the still-standing guards where to take the injured.

As the attention of the room shifts, Royce, Rhat, and Hettie circle around me.

Rhat shoots Hettie a reserved smile, but she stands there stoically.

"What did you do to make Dionysus so mad?" Royce asks.

I shrug. "I have no idea." I've been stuck in the palace for the last month. I haven't had time to make anyone angry.

Royce eyes the crowd of nobles. "They're not going to be happy unless we give them some answers."

I nod. Even I don't feel safe behind the palace walls anymore. "How do we find Dionysus?"

"You don't," my father's voice cuts in as he hobbles closer. "I tried to locate Dionysus when you were turned to gold." He takes a steadying breath. "He only appears when he wants to be found."

"We know he wants Kora," Hettie says. "Why can't we use her as bait or something? Wouldn't he appear then?"

Royce shakes his head. "As much as I want to know what he wants with her," he says, his eyes meeting mine, "I don't think drawing him here is a good idea. More people could die."

I nod. He's right. I look around the room, at the floor slick with blood. We can't risk letting Dionysus or his henchmen return. But we need answers, and we need them now.

I scan Royce's face, hoping he has some sort of plan, even though I know he would've already shared it. I shift my gaze to Rhat, who's chewing on the inside of his cheek, and Hettie, who's staring at the floor. They're all as at a loss as I am.

I mentally go over every book and journal I've read since arriving home, praying there's something that tells me what to do. But nothing stands out. Sure, the twin queens Esor and

Ayaniv had been betrayed by their head guard and imprisoned. And Queen Teragram had written about how to survive a siege, but I'd come across nothing about a single attack orchestrated by a god. And not just any god. Dionysus.

I'm about to sigh and say we should head to the library to look for any books or ancient scrolls that could help when my gaze lands on the window and the mountains that loom in the distance. The mountains I'd always hated because the Great Oracle—the renown knower of all—was rumored to live there. The same Oracle who'd made the prophecy about my father becoming king and having a prosperous rule, a prophecy that eventually led to my father making a choice that doomed me to live as a golden girl.

"The Great Oracle." The words come out shakier than I'd meant them to. If anyone has answers, it will be her.

"We tried sending men to her back when . . ." My father trails off. "They never found her cave."

Nearby, Tilner whips his head around. He clears his throat and steps forward. "If I may, I'm quite fond of studying history." His eyebrows scrunch in concern. "I studied all the literature I could about the Oracle as well. She's a particular favorite of mine."

I stare intently at him. I'd given him a tour of the palace when he first arrived, and he spent half the trip telling me about the man who'd carved the columns in the front entryway. He knows more about my home than I ever will . . . maybe he knows more about my past too.

I lean in closer as he speaks again. "From what I've discovered, the path to the Oracle isn't always straight. Nor is it always there."

My eyebrows shoot up in surprise. "What do you mean it isn't always there?"

Tilner continues. "When I arrived here, I couldn't help myself from interviewing several of the soldiers your father sent to find the Oracle. Some of them could see the pathway and some of them couldn't. And even the ones who could see the pathway remember facing certain . . . challenges along the way, but none of them could recall what they were. And none of those men were able to find the Oracle."

I exhale. "So you're saying we won't be able to find her?"

He shrugs. "There are cases where she's been found, but I've been unable to find any links between those accounts. And none of them detail how she was found."

Royce sighs. "That's not a lot to go on."

I tightly wrap my arms across my chest. He's right. It's not a lot to go on. But as I stare at the mangled bodies around us, I wonder what choice we have. "It might be the best option we have," I say. "She could tell us what Dionysus wants and how to stop him."

"That sounds like a terrible plan," Hettie exclaims. "You're just going to roam around the mountains and hope you stumble across her cave? What happens if you get lost or get eaten by some creature? What if Dionysus shows up while you're gone?"

I rub my temples. I don't want to leave the palace so defenseless, but how much worse will it be if we're not ready with a way to defeat Dionysus when he does show up? "Hopefully Dionysus won't attack if I'm not here, and hopefully the Oracle can tell us what he's after."

"That's if you even find her, remember," Hettie groans.

"Why don't you stay here with Rhat and my father and work

on plans to fortify the palace in case Dionysus does show up, while Royce and I look for the Oracle? Either we'll find a way to get to Dionysus first or be ready when he comes." Plus, I wanted her here in case Lord Lucar tried anything.

"Fine," Hettie says. "But don't blame me when you get eaten."

Tilner nods. "I can continue my search for other options while you try to find the Oracle." He stares off into space as though he's already mentally preparing a list of books to read.

"Thank you, Tilner." I gaze out the window again.

The sun sits low in the sky, not even close to midday. For some reason, I expected it to be higher. But it's only been a few hours or so since I woke up, even if it feels like years. My consolation is that it's still early enough to make it to the mountain today. Because I can't risk Dionysus sending anyone else to attack the palace once he realizes his plan failed.

"We'll leave immediately," I say.

Leaving my father and Tilner to see to the cleanup of the main hall, I hurry to change.

My new maid, Kattrina, helps me into a pair of light trousers and a dark shirt. I pull on a hooded cloak and short, thick gloves. At least I'd had enough foresight to have traveling clothes made after my last adventure.

"Are you nervous?" Kattrina asks after I tell her about our quest. "I've heard oracles can be unpredictable."

I nod. But it's not just nerves. As much as the thought of seeking her out makes my stomach turn, I'm more afraid she won't be able to help us. And every moment we go without answers is another moment the kingdom is in danger, a danger my powers can't protect it from.

I only hope my powers will help us in the mountains, because

31

who knows what we'll face up there. I don't like going in without knowing what we'll encounter or without any sort of map to prevent us from becoming lost in the mountains forever.

Prince Ikkin had written that you should never go into battle without first knowing the lay of the land, so you know not only the conditions but also where the enemy may hide, waiting to ambush you.

His journal didn't say anything about when you were already at war. And Dionysus had brought the battle to my front gate—no, through my front gate and straight into the main hall, where bodies lay still warm from life.

Royce and I would just have to be prepared for anything—because I had no idea what beasts we'd encounter if we didn't get answers from the Oracle.

Then again, what will we encounter if we do?

By the time I join Royce in the courtyard, he's already mounted his horse. I stare up at the horse the stable master chose for me. It's a dark mare slightly smaller than Royce's mount. I approach it slowly.

Animals don't always have the best reaction to my skin.

The mare stomps her hoof but doesn't run away, and I let her sniff my gloved hand for a few moments before I mount. It's been a long time since I've been on a horse, and it takes me a few moments to gain my balance. I'm not even sure what happened to my previous horse. I'd stopped riding her the day my skin turned to gold ten years ago.

I notice with the smallest bit of relief that Royce doesn't look as comfortable on his horse as he does at the helm of his ship, so at least I'm not alone in my fears.

No one has come to see us off. But I do spot Kattrina waving from my balcony as Royce urges his stallion forward.

We speed out through the town. Faces whirl by. I keep my head down, hood pulled tight. Eventually the clatter of hooves on stone fades into the thick thud of hooves against packed dirt as we leave the city behind. Green fields surround us.

Butterflies with yellow-and-red-striped wings dance above tall, swaying grass. Small white flowers with faded pink centers grow in patches along the edge of the road. A hawk soars over us, casting a momentary shadow amidst the sunshine. In the distance, a sea of trees creates a moat around the great mountains.

I'd stop to enjoy the beauty if the kingdom wasn't at risk.

Royce falls in next to me as we ride toward the thick copse of trees that swallows the road.

I'm thankful for the protection from the sun as the canopy swallows us. I wish I could let down my hood and release all the heat that's built up.

But I know better than that.

Last time my hood came off, Royce's superstitious crew tried to throw me overboard, and then I was chased by pirates on the Island of Lost Souls when they saw my golden skin. No, I didn't have positive experiences whenever I took my hood off outside the palace.

I'm called back into the present by a bird calling out. Everything else is still. Sunlight flits between the trees, making the shadows dance and come alive—and making it impossible to see what they hide. The dark shapes reach out to me before curling back inward like a crooked finger beckoning me closer. I tighten my grip on my reins and look away.

The quietness of the woods suffocates me. I feel if I don't

break the silence, I'll start convincing myself there's something in the bushes.

I move my horse closer to Royce's.

"I've never been this close to the mountains," I say.

Royce smiles. "Me neither."

"I hope we find some answers." I sigh. "If we don't, I'll be dethroned before I make it back to the palace."

"No, you won't." He moves his horse so it is a hand's breadth from mine.

"They wouldn't even listen to me, Royce." I throw up my hands, and then quickly regret that decision and return them to the reins. "The only reason they didn't run me out of the palace is because you were standing there with a sword. If Dionysus attacks again, we'll lose everything."

Maybe I was foolish to think I could rule. I'd thought it would come naturally, that I'd be good at it—or at the very least that I could read and learn what I needed in order to help fix Lagonia.

But nothing I'd read could fix this. Not the documents outlining how cities like ancient Aijiram were built. Not the treaties between Orfland and Lagonia. And none of the journals kept by our past rulers.

I'd only succeeded in putting my people in more danger.

"You're not going to lose everything." Royce steers his horse so his leg is touching mine as we ride. "You're a great leader. You're willing to face down the Great Oracle for them."

"Only because I'm the one putting them in peril," I point out.

"You're protecting them," he replies. "If it wasn't Dionysus coming after you, it would be some other power-hungry person hoping to take over the throne. There will always be threats, but you're willing to face them. Don't forget that. Everyone wants a leader who fights for them."

"They want a leader who wins those fights," I reply.

"We haven't lost one yet," he counters.

"We haven't gone up against Dionysus before," I say.

His brow scrunches. He pulls one hand free from my reins, examining the golden skin visible in the gap between my sleeve and glove. "Haven't you been facing him your entire life?" He gives my hand a squeeze, "If anyone can beat him, it's you. You know the power of words, of how they can be twisted. If anyone can think of a way to outthink him, it's you. And when you do, the nobles will see how powerful you are."

He sounds so confident, and I can't help but wonder, would the nobles accept me if I stopped Dionysus? If I show them I can defeat the very god who'd placed the curse—the curse they all think is bringing the kingdom down—then maybe, just maybe they will see me as capable of ruling, of leading them.

Stronger than the god who cursed my father. Stronger than the curse itself. Strong enough to rule.

The thought energizes me, and I offer Royce a small smile.

"Don't worry. You'll show them you're a great leader. It'll just take a little time. But I'll be with you every step of the way."

His bright blue eyes are darker in the shade of the forest, more mysterious, and they draw me toward them.

His hand is on my cheek before I even realize how close I'm leaning toward him.

But his hand drops suddenly. He tenses.

Then something hard smashes into me from behind, sending searing pain through my body.

# CHAPTER 4

𝕯 efore I know what's happening, I land facedown with a thud
on the ground. My shoulders throb.

My horse stamps around me, sending up a cloud of dust.
I cough and choke, trying to roll out of the way before I get
crushed.

I throw myself to the side and tumble into a large rock,
which must be what knocked me to the ground.

"Get her saddlebags," a voice calls as I fight to get air back
into my lungs.

"There's nothing of value in there," Royce calls.

I'm about to rise to my feet when I realize it's probably safer
on the ground where no one can see my face. I've learned what
greedy men will do to get to the girl with golden skin—the one
who can turn things to gold.

Judging by the number of feet I hear scuffling around in the
undergrowth, we're far outnumbered. Worse, rough hands pull
me to my feet, gripping the arm that still throbs from breaking
my fall.

"Well," says a bearded man, "what about her? Is she valuable?"
His dirty fingernails dig into my arm. I bite my lip to keep from
crying out. My hood is still pulled low, and I hang my head as

far as I can. My heart is beating too fast for me to take calm, collected breaths.

"Get off your horse, drop your sword, and toss over your purse, and we'll let her go," the man says.

"No," Royce replies.

"No?" the man repeats as though no one has ever refused him before.

I try to judge from the heavy breathing behind me how many men there are. I think I hear four, but I can't be sure.

The large rock is still at my feet, but the bearded man is holding me too tightly. I doubt I'll be able to grab it before he reacts. Which means the only weapon I have left is the one that I really don't want to use.

With my free hand, I rip back my hood.

A patch of sunlight reflects off my golden skin. The man's instant recoil is exactly what I need. He loosens his grip, and I duck down for the rock. He grabs for me once more, but by the time he pulls me back I use his momentum to pull me up, smashing the rock into his chin along the way. He goes down in a heap.

I turn as three other men leap into action. Swords and daggers are drawn, including Royce's.

"Take one step closer and I'll turn you to gold," I shout, removing a glove.

The men backtrack and fall over themselves to get away. A man drops from the tree above us, arrows dribbling from his quiver as he stumbles after his friends. For a few moments, the only sound is them crashing through the undergrowth as they disappear into the forest.

For once I'm glad for the rumors about me.

"Are you okay?" Royce asks, getting off his horse and rushing to my side.

"I'm fine," I reply, ignoring the tightness in my side every time I move. I collect my horse from the side of the path.

"Are you sure?" Royce steps closer and pulls my face up to look at him. "I know you've already used your powers several times today—"

I lean into his chest. He knows I hate the way the metal always feels when I absorb it. "It's not as bad as it used to be."

His hand rubs up and down my back.

I want to stay there, to enjoy this moment with him in the woods like any normal couple would do. But we aren't a normal couple.

I pull away from him. "We should go before those thieves decide I might be more valuable than dangerous."

Royce nods and helps me climb back onto my horse.

I inhale sharply when I land astride it. I can only imagine how riding will feel, but I know we have to keep moving, so I dig my heels into the mare's sides as Royce mounts up next to me.

Eventually we cut through the tree line and Mount Yellek races above our heads.

"There." Royce points to a small, rocky path twisting up the side. One that looks far too steep for the horses to take.

We tie the horses off at the base of the trail and begin our ascent.

The sun beats down on us from above as small rocks threaten our balance from below. Thin weeds push through the rocks and sway in the wind racing down the mountain.

After making it up a rocky incline, sheer white cliffs press against my right side. On my left, a thin patch of grass leads to a steep drop-off as we climb ever higher. Even the slightest breeze tugging at me makes me tense. I keep one hand on the cliff wall to maintain my balance.

I grew up locked away in the palace. I've explored all of its towers, so I'm not exactly afraid of heights. But I am afraid of falling to my death. Especially after what happened on the balcony with my uncle, when he fell to his death trying to kill my father and me. I'd nearly fallen with him.

I close my eyes as the memory surfaces. He'd said I was as cursed as my father and that he should've been king. He'd charged at me, knocking us both over the crumbling balcony railing. I can still remember the air surging to claim me, the panic that rose in my throat, the way my stomach seemed to plummet inside me in the same way my body was about to do.

"Do you need a break?" Royce's voice shatters the memory.

I press against the cool rock and into the small bit of shade the overhang above us offers. I take a few steadying breaths.

The forest is laid out at the foot of the mountain. I can just make out the fields past it. Maybe the speck I see past all that is the palace—I can't tell from this distance.

But it's the reminder I need to push off the rock and keep going. Because I can't let Dionysus destroy my people. So I follow Royce up the path.

"Kora," Royce calls, "over here."

I climb over a pile of fallen rocks, and as I round the corner, the path diverges in several directions. Royce stands in front of a signpost up ahead but doesn't move in any direction.

"What's wrong?" I ask, coming up beside him.

He points to the faded lettering etched into the weathered wood.

> If it's the Oracle you seek,
> You are very near.
> You can only choose one path.
> All others disappear.

"This must be what Tilner meant." I'd been hoping he was wrong, that there'd only be one path leading directly to the Oracle.

Royce's brow furrows in concentration. "If I had to guess, we probably only get one shot at picking the right way."

I stare down the three paths. They look identical: gray pebble pathways leading toward jagged boulders that block the rest of the trail from view. I run my fingers through my hair, catching them in my braid.

How are we ever supposed to know which path to choose?

I scan for anything that might make one route look different from another. A flower, a bird, a breeze.

Anything.

But they're all as still as the landscapes woven into the palace tapestries.

I swallow. I know how much rides on this decision. I stare more intently at each path. As I do, small wooden signs appear at the base of each pathway.

I move toward the first. In the same jagged lettering as the other sign, it reads:

> Wisdom can be given out
> For a certain price.
> But do not take a single step
> If it's not worth your life.

It is worth my life, I think. And my father's. But I move toward the next sign.

Changing fate is hard indeed,
But it can be done.
Look not to the past you've trod,
But to the future that you've won.

I definitely want to change things, but something about the wording scares me. I move to the final sign.

Picking your path is not easy;
It may puzzle your mind.
Choose this one if you're ready,
To seek what you can't find.

I run my hands through my hair—through where my crown should be—and press against my scalp, where a headache is forming from trying to make sense of these riddles.

I turn back toward Royce. He's busy studying the other riddles.

"If she doesn't want anyone to find her, why does she even have signs?" I say when he finally lifts his gaze. Any of these could lead to her.

"Which one sounds the truest to you?" Royce asks.

I go over the signs again, ignoring the pounding coursing through my head. Something in me says to go for the first one. I need wisdom no matter the cost.

"That's what I was thinking too," Royce says after I reply.

We move to the base of the path and stand there a moment,

shoulder to shoulder. I can't think about what happens if we take this pathway and end up being wrong.

I won't think about it.

"Remember," Royce says, holding his hand out to me, "we're in this together."

I slide my hand into his.

With a deep breath, we step forward. We haven't even taken two steps when the other pathways and their signs melt away, disappearing from view.

Our path is sealed.

## CHAPTER 5

꙳꙳꙳꙳꙳꙳꙳꙳@꙳꙳꙳꙳꙳꙳꙳꙳

After nearly an hour of walking, the path hasn't changed. I can't even be sure we're actually moving. I swear I've kicked the same pebble at least three times now. Not to mention I'm pretty sure the same breeze washes over us at exactly the same moment over and over again when we pass the small rock overhang. Even the tufts of grass sticking out of the gravel are starting to look the same—five blades pointing straight up and three blades bent to the side. I shake my head clear and take a deep breath. We've only just started. I can't let the mountain get to me, because we could be here for days. Still, I kick the pebble again and send it reeling down the mountainside.

As we pass beneath the now-familiar rock ledge, the same breeze comes tearing toward us, tangling my cloak around my legs and trying to trip me up. I rip my cloak free and try to enjoy the last of the breeze. At least it provides a little relief from the heat. Sweat drips from my brow. Even my hands are sweating inside my gloves. I clench them into fists and keep going.

The next time we pass the overhang, it's only been a few minutes.

Royce's shoulders slump, and he turns back to face me. "We're going in circles, aren't we?"

My throat is too dry to respond—not to mention I don't want to say the word out loud.

Royce scans his jacket, pulling a loose thread until it unravels a length or two. He rips it free and ties it to a small plant sheltering beneath the overhang, which has three small white bulbous flowers bobbing in the breeze. He ties the string around the middle one. "Now we'll know for sure," he says.

He offers me his hand as we move forward. We each take deliberate steps, both afraid our suspicions will be confirmed.

My heart drops when I see the pebble I've kicked down the mountain countless times appear on the path before me once more.

And then the overhang comes into view. Three white bulbous flowers nod eagerly in greeting. And on the middle one is a string.

I stop in my tracks, trying to convince myself the string isn't there. But I can't deny the fact.

Royce pulls it free from the plant and lets it float down the mountainside. We both stand there, watching it disappear on the perfectly timed breeze that again whips my cloak around my body. Only this time, it feels like it's trying to pull me over the edge too, after the string.

I kick my legs free and cross my arms.

I'm ready to tell Royce we should give up, that we must've chosen wrong. That I chose wrong.

Then I think about what that means. It means going back with no answers. It means abandoning Lagonia to Dionysus. It means giving up on my people. And I can't give up—not with so much at stake.

I charge forward.

"Kora," Royce calls behind me.

But I don't stop. Because I can't. I'll walk this path until my legs give out. Or until I find that Oracle. Or until I think of a better plan. I just can't go back.

"Kora, wait," he calls again.

I don't wait. I keep going, and just as I round the next bend, the sound hits me first. Water. And lots of it.

I skid to a stop at the bank of a wide river. The water is an opaque, icy color except where white rapids toss into the air like horse manes as they collide with sharp rocks. It's so unlike the deep, steady blues of the ocean that I can't help but take a step back, lest I be sucked into the tumult.

Even still, I release a breath. This is the first different thing we've seen on this path, the first thing that doesn't make me feel like we picked the wrong direction.

Royce's boots crunch to a stop at the edge of the water as he comes up next to me. As he stops, another small signpost appears.

The same small letters slowly scrawl across the wood.

> If true wisdom
> Is what you seek,
> Learn if your mind
> Is strong or weak.

"What do you think that means?" I ask Royce. Before he can answer, the sign changes before our eyes.

> Take the cup
> And press it to your lip.

All it will take
Is just one sip.

He examines the sign before pulling out something from behind it. "This was hanging on the back." He holds a small cup fashioned out of clay.

We both look from the cup to the water.

My stomach feels about as calm as the rapids spilling ever forward. And I can't imagine what I'll feel like once I drink some of that water. But since it's clear we don't have a choice, I swipe the cup from Royce's hand and dip it into the water.

Royce stops me before the cup touches my lips. His eyebrows scrunch together. "Are you sure about this?"

"What other choice do we have?" I ask.

"What if it's poison?" he says. "It could be a test to see if we drink it."

I stare at the sign. "It says to take a sip. We have to chance it."

Royce reaches for the cup, and I know he's offering to do this. But I can't let him. Before I can rethink my decision, I tip the cup toward my mouth.

I don't even know if I actually swallow any of the water, because my lips go numb the instant the liquid touches them, and I've lost all feeling in my teeth and tongue. I can't even tell if my mouth is open or closed. I sputter to produce any sound, to cry out for help, but when I move my hands to my mouth, I discover my jaw hangs open, useless.

The numbness slowly spreads. It seeps through my throat and across my shoulders, like it's erasing my body as it goes, making it impossible to feel anything other than a cold, empty void. It spreads through my chest, heading to my lungs. I try to take a breath, to do anything that might stall the chill. But my body doesn't respond. I can't gag or choke. My arms lose sensation. Then my legs. And lastly, my heart. Curses always save that for last.

It's like being turned to gold all over again—the same iciness that clings to your soul and bleeds through it.

My eyes meet Royce's, and then I'm collapsing forward. His arms reach out, catching me before I plunge headfirst into the river.

My eyes close, and when I open them again, Royce leans over me. I'm lying on the riverbank, jagged rocks pressed into my back. The water continues to rage, tossing thick waves into the air where water collides with rock in its race down the mountain.

"Are you okay?" Royce asks.

It's odd. All feeling has returned to my body. I raise an arm to be sure. And that's when I see it.

I bolt upright.

My skin isn't gold anymore.

I stare closer, certain what I'm seeing is a trick of the light. But no—that's a freckle. And that's skin. Skin that doesn't look like liquid gold melted around it.

"Royce, my skin—" I stare up at him in amazement.

His eyes look just as wide as mine must be.

"I think the water cured you," he says, a smile spreading across his face.

I turn my arm back and forth in the light, looking at skin that's always been mine and yet seems so foreign. My fingers are the same length. My wrists the same width. And yet, I don't recognize them.

Royce draws my gaze to him by cupping a hand against my

cheek. "You look beautiful. More beautiful than I ever could've imagined."

Then he's kissing me, lips pressed firmly against mine. His hand wraps around my back, pulling me closer to him, anchoring me to him—a silent promise he'll never let go.

Warmth spreads through me, erasing any memories of the chill the water brought.

Royce slowly pulls away. "If the water cured you, I bet it would cure your father too. We can take some of it to him, and everything will go back to normal. It'll be like the curse never happened. Dionysus will have no reason to come after you then." He takes my hands, wrapping his own around them. "Then you and I can be together—like we were always meant to be."

He pulls me to my feet, fills the cup with water, and leads me back the way we came. I stumble over rocks as I fight to keep up with the pace he's set. I want to call to him to slow down, but every time he turns around, there's this wild grin on his face that makes me falter. He looks so happy, giddy even.

It's a side of him I never thought existed, especially thinking back to all those times I thought him rigid and unfeeling when I'd first met him on the *Swanflight*.

But maybe this is how someone is supposed to feel after they've finally broken a curse and have nothing else to worry about.

Then why don't I feel it too?

Slowly, I drag my feet against the ground, sending loose rocks scattering away.

"What's wrong?" Royce asks, his smile never faltering as he slows and turns to face me.

"This is too perfect—too easy. What about the Oracle?"

Royce cocks his head to the side. Then some sort of realization dawns on his face. He pulls me closer to him. "I know after all you've been through that it's hard to believe good things can happen. But they can, and you deserve to be happy. To not have to fight for something for once." He pulls me to his chest, wrapping me in a hug. "It's okay to believe you're cured."

I shake my head and push him away. "We're missing something." Nothing is ever this easy—especially when it comes to my life. And I can't believe *he* thinks it could be this easy.

I keep Royce at an arm's length. "I'm going back to the river to see if we missed something."

Royce shakes his head. "You won't find anything back there. Everything we need is right here." He points to the cup and the water jostling around inside. "I'm right here." He reaches toward me, but I scamper backward.

His smile drops. "I thought you wanted me. I thought you wanted us."

Heat rises in my cheeks. "I do, but this just seems—"

He scoffs, cutting me off. "Can't you just believe something good can happen to you once in your life?"

I open my mouth and close it again. I want to believe. I want to think positively. But this is all too unbelievable. "There's no harm in double checking."

He waves his hand dismissively. "Go check the river. Just know I won't be waiting here when you get back."

I take a step backward as though he's slapped me. There's a threat to his words and a tone I've never heard from him before. A tone I never thought he'd use.

"You can't mean that," I manage. I reach out to him, but he recoils as though I am a snake.

His face stills. "I'm giving up a lot to be with you. Do you think I like being locked away in that palace like you've always been? Do you want me to go back to sea?"

"No, Royce—" I stammer, but he cuts me off.

"Everything you want is right here." He gestures around himself. "You have your skin back, we can cure your father, and I'm right here."

"What about Dionysus?" I plead.

"Once we cure your father, what could Dionysus want with any of you? Besides, your father will be strong enough to take care of everything. You won't have to worry about the kingdom. You can step aside."

"Step aside? These are my people," I say. Even if they don't want me to rule, I am still their ruler. I still need to protect them. "Dionysus was after me. I can't leave them open to his attacks."

Royce slowly shakes his head, sending a few blond strands out of place. "Kora, they don't want you to lead."

I balk in amazement and blink to fight back tears that have sprung in the corners of my eyes. "You said I was a good leader—" The words are hollow, and they mirror the hollowness spreading inside me.

"Now you might be, since you're not cursed anymore." He moves forward and takes one of my hands in his. "I'm telling you we can finally have it all now."

I withdraw my hand from his. "No"—I shake my head—"we can't."

"Kora," he pleads, "don't be like this."

"I'm going back to the water. You can come or not." I turn on my heels before he can see any tears slip down my cheeks.

I march with my shoulders straight back toward the river, not giving him the satisfaction of knowing he's affected me.

In the distance, I hear his footfalls receding back down the mountain.

I hang my head and wipe a tear from the corner of my eye.

What happened to him? What happened to us?

Is there even an us anymore? The thought slides through me, breaking something loose inside me. I try to stare back down the path, but too many tears clog my vision.

Had I really been unreasonable to ask to inspect the river again? I wipe at my tears and scan the banks, but nothing happens. The rapids rage on, and no signposts appear. Everything else is eerily quiet. No birds chatter. No bugs flit by. Not even the wind blows.

There's nothing here.

I was foolish to insist on coming back here. And now I've lost Royce in the process.

I close my eyes to try and stop the tears, but it doesn't help. I kick at the rocks at my feet, but as I do, I lose my footing. Rocks shift beneath me. I fight to stay upright. My arms fly outward, but I'm already falling forward. Straight toward the river.

I hit the surface, and icy water swallows me, sending a shock through my body. My skin turns to ice. My lungs seize shut. I can't breathe. I can't move.

I try to struggle to the surface, but my arms won't respond. The current whips me away from the shore, and then it drags me down, down, down, until I can't even see the surface.

My lungs continue to burn as the rest of my body goes numb.

Inky darkness clouds my vision, and everything goes black.

# CHAPTER 6

§§§§§§§§❀❀❀❀❀❀❀

When I open my eyes, I'm slumped against Royce's chest.
"You came back for me," I mumble.

"What?" he says. "We haven't moved." His eyebrows scrunch inward, and his eyes scan my face.

The clay cup falls from my hand and smashes into pieces on the rocks. Immediately, the raging river shrinks back down into a crossable stream.

Royce slowly lowers me to the ground.

My body feels frozen.

But not wet.

"What happened?" I ask. I stare down at my arm. My skin is as gold as it ever was.

Royce shakes his head. "You took a sip and collapsed. But you were only out a moment or two."

"A moment or two?" I puzzle. "But—" I stare down at my golden skin, and I'm relieved that it's gold once more. Because that's normal. That's how it should be.

And as I shake my head to clear away the remnants of the vision, I realize I'm not the same girl who once wanted the golden hue of my skin to fade faster than a sunburn. I'm the girl who wants to save her kingdom. And maybe I don't understand everything the vision meant, but I at least know that.

"Are you feeling okay?" Royce asks.

The numbness recedes slowly, and I let Royce pull me to my feet.

Where the river had once raged, clear water trickles gently around gray rocks, and larger stones grow out of the water, creating a perfect pathway.

"I feel better than ever," I finally reply to Royce once I take in this new path. Whatever had happened in that vision, I proved I wasn't giving up. "Let's keep going."

I jump onto the first stone jutting out of the water. I wait to see if the pace of the water quickens or if the river will expand, but nothing happens. Then, I hop across the stones the rest of the way and turn to face Royce on the other side.

He's standing there with a puzzled look on his face. "Are you sure we should be moving on?" He scrutinizes the sign. "I'm not sure we've passed any test yet."

If I had any doubts I was back in reality, they're gone now. Because this is the Royce I know. The one who questions and thinks things through. The one who's always pondering what could be ahead and if we're prepared to face it. The one who's always willing to look deeper.

"I—I had a vision," I say, "after I drank the water. It said—" I look away, not wanting to remember what he'd said to me during it.

"Was it bad?" he asks.

I nod. "Although I think it was supposed to be good. I didn't have gold skin anymore, and the vision tried to tempt me to go back to the palace."

"But you didn't," Royce says. "And I wouldn't let you." He

shoots me a smile that makes my heart remember this is my Royce.

After that, he doesn't hesitate before leaping easily across the rocks.

We continue forward. But we don't walk far before we find a cave waiting for us. As we near the entrance, two lit torches appear on either side of the jagged opening. The flames snap and crackle.

Something like hope leaps in my chest. Could this be the Oracle? Finally?

But as we get closer, another signpost materializes.

> The most valuable thing
> You must soon find.
> Now figure out what
> You can't leave behind.

I groan. Another test.

Or maybe it's not a test. Maybe it's a series of unending obstacles the Oracle created to prevent people from ever making it to her.

Either way, I don't have a choice. It's forward or failure.

Royce and I take the torches and venture inside.

Cool dampness surrounds us, reminding me of the smell of earth after it rains. Our shuffling footsteps echoing off the walls is the only sound.

The glow from our torches reflects off giant damp stalagmites and stalactites that grow at odd angles all over the cave. They distort our reflections as we move past. We stick close to one another, and I pray this isn't some sort of maze. I have no desire to get stuck in these dark depths.

Ahead, there's a light. But it's not the soft light of day. There's something off about the illumination; it's a little too golden.

We slow our approach as we near a bend in the tunnel. When we peer around the curve, our jaws drop.

A lit room bigger than the palace's main hall is packed floor to ceiling with more treasures than the Temptresses had when we once raided their trove. Golden thrones. Bejeweled crowns. Rubies the size of my fist. Everywhere I look, a treasure more ornate than the last rests.

Royce and I gawk as we stumble forward.

A golden peacock, its tail spread wide behind it, sits atop a table whose entire surface is made of emerald. Where feathers should be, thousands of gemstones rest in a blue-and-green pattern. Past that is a sculpture as big as any fountain back home. It's made of a diamond surface that's meant to represent a pond. Several swans made from glistening pearls float upon it, their necks intertwined.

The room stretches on and on. I think I even spot a ship made entirely of gold buried under statues dripping in diamonds and clustered with crystals.

"Everything in here is valuable," Royce breathes. "How are we ever supposed to choose?"

"We need to think like the Oracle," I say as I peer under tables and over stacks searching for anything that stands out from everything else. "What would she value?"

"Time? The future? The past?" Royce picks up a gold platter, looking at his reflection before tossing it back into the pile. "I can't imagine any of this stuff holds the same value to an immortal being who can see all things."

He's right. Besides, any of these things could have different value based on who you ask.

There's another sign at the far end of the cave where the tunnel continues. I move toward it and read:

Decide what you value
And take it in hand.
Then venture forward
To see where you land.

I go over the words again and again. Since my father was cursed by Dionysus using his words against him, I've always thought I'd be better at figuring out riddles, that when needed I'd be able to figure out all the ways words could be twisted to have different meanings and results.

This sign makes it sound like I have to choose what I find most valuable. But the first sign had also hinted I should take the one thing I wouldn't want to leave behind. I scan the items. Is there something here I couldn't live without?

"Maybe it's water or food," I say, scanning a table laden down with silver dishes. "Humans can't live without that." But there's nothing edible on the table.

"Breath?" Royce ventures. "Can't live without that either."

"How are we supposed to hold that in our hands?" I ask.

He cups his hands, blowing into them before sealing them quickly together.

I eye his hands, but it just doesn't feel right. "But what about everything else we need to live. Like a heartbeat? Like blood? There are so many things besides breath."

He releases his hands and points at me knowingly, a smile spreading across his face. "See, this is why I brought you along. You're full of good thoughts."

I laugh. "I'm pretty sure it was me who made you come."

He steps closer, looping his fingers through mine. "You didn't make me do anything. I would've come no matter what." He leans his forehead down against mine.

I've just closed my eyes, relaxing against him, when he gasps and pulls back.

"That's it. I've got it," he says.

"Got what?" I say, opening my eyes to find a gleam in his.

"I know the answer," he says. He brings our clasped hands up between us. "It's you. You're the most valuable thing in the room to me."

I can't help the smile that slides across my face or the feeling of elation that lights up my heart. And after the vision I had and coming back to find my real Royce, I know deep down that he's right. I don't need any of these treasures. I simply need him.

I give his hand a squeeze. "How come I didn't think of that?"

"I can't let you have all the good ideas," he replies, smiling.

And while I would love to stand there staring at him, at the way his eyes hold mine, I know we need to keep moving. I give his hand one last squeeze. "Ready to test your theory?"

He nods, and hand in hand, we approach the sign and walk past it into the tunnel.

Our torches cast small puddles of light around us as we move onward. We don't let go of each other's hand, and the warmth of his fingers around mine is welcome in the cold of the cave.

The path starts to slant downward, and an odd plunking noise sounds every so often. Weird, rippling shadows appear on the wall ahead of us, and the tunnel opens up into a wide cavern with yet another sign waiting for us.

> From crystal's end
> Drink one single drop.
> But touch flesh to the lake,
> Your journey will stop.

I groan and rub my forehead. These signs are only making my headache worse. If the Oracle doesn't want to be found, she shouldn't have a pathway to her cave.

Royce and I step forward into the vaulted space. Unlike the cavern filled with gold, this one is filled with pristine crystals. They grow like sharp daggers from the cavern walls. Some are long and slender while others sit like squat shrubs against the ground. Still others have fallen from their bases, laying either whole or in shattered pieces along the sandy cave floor.

The sand slopes down toward a round lake. In the center of the lake, a giant crystal hangs from the roof of the cavern. Every few seconds, water drips and falls into the lake, creating a giant ripple that cascades across the water and laps onto the shore.

"So I guess that's the crystal we're supposed to drink from," Royce says.

"How are we supposed to get out there if we can't touch the water?" I ask.

But my words cut off as the tunnel we walked through seals in with dirt. I scan the rest of the cavern. There's no other way out. Great. Now we're stuck here until we can figure out how to get to the center of a lake we can't touch.

We decide to go opposite ways around the lake. Using my torch, I prowl along the edges looking for anything resembling a boat. Too bad I can't go back for the gold one I saw in the last cavern.

My feet crunch over ground-up crystal fragments as I move along the shore. But there's nothing hiding behind the towering crystals except more crystals. The only other thing I see is my golden reflection sliding across the fragmented surfaces to stare back at me.

"Find anything?" Royce asks from the other side of the lake.

"No," I call back. "Nothing." I kick at the bits at my feet as the large crystal continues to send droplets careening into the water below.

After circling the lake twice, Royce and I collapse near where we entered. He grabs a handful of crystal shards in his hands as we think. The unending plunk of droplets echoes continually off the walls.

*Plunk.*

*Plunk.*

*Plunk.*

"Maybe we could knock the main crystal down somehow?" he says.

"But we don't know how deep the lake is. It could sink," I counter with a heavy sigh.

*Plunk.*

"Do you think there are enough crystals that we could throw them into the lake and pile them up enough to walk on?"

"I doubt it," Royce says. "Besides, there are only a few broken ones. It would take ages to get the rest free."

"We've got ages," I reply. Next to me, my torch burns lower and lower, signaling we may be trapped in darkness for all those ages. I swallow down the panic that rises at that thought. I have to find a way back to my father, my people, before Dionysus tries anything else.

"What if we hollowed out one of the crystals?" he asks. "Maybe there's one long enough that we could use it as a sort of channel to catch the water from the crystal."

It's a good thought, but as we both stare around the cavern, it's clear no crystal is long enough to reach the middle of the wide lake.

We fall back into silence.

*Plunk.*

"That sound is going to drive me insane," I say, covering my ears.

Royce pulls me against his chest, careful of the gold on his jacket. "Don't worry. If anyone can get us out of here, it's you. You've spent years thinking about how Dionysus weaves words. You can figure this out."

I stare at the ripples on the water's surface as they jump up and down.

I go over the sign's words again and again. Drink from the end of the crystal. Don't touch the lake.

I bite my lip. I've still got nothing.

Royce has picked up a shard of crystal about the size of his forearm and is turning it over in his hands, running his finger along the crack zigzagging across the outside. He brings it close to his face.

"Anything?" I ask, leaning in closer, trying to see any secrets the glassy crystal might hold. "Another riddle? A map?"

He shakes his head and lets it fall away. He absently drills the end of the crystal into the ground over and over again.

But it drills a thought into my mind right along with it, and I jolt forward.

"What is it?" Royce asks.

"The sign never said that crystal." I say, pointing to the one in the center of the lake. "Why not any crystal?"

His eyes shoot to mine. "It's worth a shot."

I pull him to his feet, and we move to the edge of the lake.

Together, we drag a thin crystal to the edge of the lake. Royce insists on going first as I dip the end into the water and then hold the crystal high enough for a drop to fall into his mouth.

Then Royce does the same for me. The moment the water touches my tongue, the cave rumbles, revealing an opening at the other end.

"Another test down," Royce says, a triumphant smile spreading across his face.

"Hopefully it's the last," I reply as we make our way down into the new tunnel. But the moment we step into the tunnel, the walls disappear and light flares up around us.

We're standing outside on another pathway with high mountain peaks ahead of us in the distance. A fierce wind wraps around us. It tugs at my cloak, pulling me toward a small gravel path. A path that leads to another cave.

"There." I point. Could this be the Oracle's cave at last?

My heart thuds in my chest. I blame it on everything we've been through and not on meeting the woman whose prophecy led to my father becoming king—and ultimately to him being cursed.

The entrance to the cave is tall enough that neither of us have to duck. Tiny purple flowers bob their heads on either side of the entrance as the wind catches them.

Darkness hangs like a curtain just inside the cave. I swallow. Fear roots me to the mountain.

Maybe we shouldn't have come. Maybe the Oracle is no better than the god who gave my father The Touch. Maybe she just likes to manipulate lives and make people miserable too. Maybe I'm next on her list.

My throat is dry as I look to Royce. "Do you think that's it?"

He shrugs. "When it comes to the Oracle, who knows."

His body is tense, and his hand rests on his sword hilt.

"Maybe I should go in alone," I say. Dionysus's search for me is why we are here, after all.

Before he can reply, a voice calls, "Both of you, come in. I've been expecting you."

My blood runs cold as Royce and I look at each other before turning to the entrance of the Oracle's cave. The Oracle I've feared my whole life.

My stomach feels as if a river rages through it. The only thing worse are my thoughts. Maybe we shouldn't have come. Maybe the Oracle will simply kill us. Maybe she'll make some prophecy about me that will ruin my life—just like she did to my father.

There's only one way to find out. And I have to risk it to save Lagonia.

We step into the cave.

As soon as we cross the threshold, all traces of the wind stop tugging at us.

The walls of the cave are smooth and cold. It smells similar to rich, fresh earth, like the palace garden in springtime. Long, carved columns rush up toward the ceiling as we make our way through a short entryway that guides us to a much wider, deeper area. As we walk, I notice levels of concentric circles make up the floor of the cave. Heavy stones jut out of the sides of the circular layers, offering an uneven staircase that leads to the center where a woman sits crossed-legged next to a fire.

Billows of smoke shoot up through an opening at the top of the cave.

Oddly, the cave doesn't smell of smoke at all.

The woman's hand streaks out, gesturing us forward. She's more petite than I expected, with a frame as thin and short as that of a child.

The wrinkles on the dark skin of her face look like a rose from above, deep crevices striking out in a circular pattern around her face. Bracelets line her thin arms from her wrist to her elbow while a thick shawl slumps over her shoulders. But as we get closer, it's her eyes mine keep going to. They're entirely black and darker than any night I've ever seen, and yet, there's a vastness about them, like gazing into a starless sky. It's not so much staring into two orbs as it is staring through them to the endless landscape beyond. The harder I look, the deeper I see, each passing moment promising that if I just probe a little longer, I'll discover something—some secret, some truth—hidden there amongst all that darkness.

The woman's cracked lips move slowly, breaking my gaze. "Welcome, my children." Her voice is ageless as it rings out softly and yet loud enough to absorb as it passes through me, somehow managing to reach to my very bones, to the very core of my being.

I quickly lower my head, afraid to look in her eyes once more, as we make our way down the stone staircase. "You knew we were coming?"

She weaves her hand through the smoke in front of her, causing it to spin and twist upon itself. "I know many things, Princess." When we reach the center, she gestures for us to sit on the side of the fire opposite her. "Although you took much longer than expected for someone with so great a need. It's only when one truly needs it that I allow my cave to appear."

"So it didn't matter which path we took?" Royce asks, eyeing her sideways.

She laughs. "Of course it mattered." A sly smile slides across her lips. "All paths have different destinations. Some just lead to them faster and some lead to them not at all."

Royce and I share a look.

She wags a thin finger at us. "You have fallen into the trap many humans do. You assumed the signposts and the scenarios you encountered were meant to test who you are."

"So they're not?" I ask reluctantly, wondering what the point was then.

"The signposts foreshadow what may be to come, and if you cannot overcome those small challenges now, there is little hope you will in the future. So my guidance would be useless."

"So those are things we're going to face in the future?" Royce asks, perplexed.

"Yes. No. Not exactly. Perhaps," the Oracle replies, steepling her hands. "There are many answers to that question. And the final one always depends on what choices you will make when the time comes. But by passing through those trials, I now know with more certainty which path you are headed toward, and you've proved yourself worthy, that your need was so great you'd give up anything to get it—something you may well need to remember in the future." She stares at me as she says the last part.

I look away, unable to meet her gaze. I tell myself it's because of her eyes, the way I can see myself in them. A blink of gold amongst all that darkness. But it's also because of the shiver in my spine at the memory of the vision I'd experienced by the river. The one where my skin was no longer gold and Royce left me behind.

If I continue down whatever path the Oracle spoke of, what will I lose in the process? Royce? My powers? My kingdom?

Some part of me shouts to leave, to get out of there before her words tie me to a future I don't want. And yet, I can't leave. Not without answers.

The Oracle continues. "You see, you first proved to me you wouldn't give up on your country no matter how many times you walked in circles. You took the same path you'd taken before, one you knew wouldn't end well, and walked it despite knowing what waited for you at the end. Then, you showed me you wouldn't put yourself and your wants and needs above your goal when you had that vision offering you everything you could have wanted. Next, you showed me you wouldn't give up on each other, that you would carry each other through anything, especially when the other may not be able to carry themself. Finally, I tested your minds. For where your path may lead, you'll need your wits. You'll need to find solutions others can't, to see the pathways through words, through truth and untruth."

"Dionysus," I breathe. He is the greatest at wordplay, the trickiest one at weaving words into offers that sound like good deals but are actually thinly veiled conquests on his part.

The Oracle's lips thin, but she doesn't respond.

"He's why we're here," I start. "Why is Dionysus, the god who gave my father The Touch, after me?" I venture.

The Oracle again motions for us to sit, and Royce and I settle in on the other side of the fire.

The smoke eases so that we can see the Oracle more clearly. She stares at us, her hands resting on her knees.

"The god you seek to know about is very powerful." Her words are slow, but they wind toward me, causing me to lean closer to hear her. "Very powerful," she repeats absently. "But I wonder why you do not ask what you really need to know."

I scrunch my brow. I have no idea what she's talking about. "What should we be asking?"

Her eyes hold the reflection of the flames dancing back and forth. "You won't fare well against the tongue trickster, Dionysus, if you don't get your words under you now."

I think again. "How do we cure my father?"

The Oracle shakes her head. "Only Dionysus can undo that magic, since any other option is currently out of the reach of mere mortals."

I drop her gaze and stare into the flames. Orange tendrils spiral around, burning through the dry, cracked wood already blackened by the blaze. My eyes shoot up, the memory of the man who could burn through things fresh in my mind.

"Then can you tell us how to stop Dionysus?"

A small smile flickers across the Oracle's lips. "A more fruitful question. But first we must understand the god you wish to defeat. To understand one's past is to understand their present. And there is much of Dionysus's history that still afflicts him today." She twists her arms in front of her, and the flames send out even more smoke, which she twirls until it balls up in front of her. An image appears in the collected haze. Small shapes that mirror what's in the ball reflect in her glassy eyes, which have taken on the white hue of the smoke.

"In the beginning, when Olympus was first made, there were many gods. Zeus, Hera, Poseidon, Demeter, Athena, Apollo, Artemis, Ares, Aphrodite, Hephaestus, Hermes, and our very own Dionysus." Figures swirl to vivid life in the smoke. Some are tall and lean, others are shorter and softer. Some men have long beards and some women have luscious locks streaming over their shoulders. Each wears a plain white tunic that gleams brighter than any sunbeam I've ever seen. The largest figure holds on to a lightning bolt and laughs boldly and can only be Zeus. He has bright blue eyes and tanned skin. If he'd been standing before me in person, he'd be taller than my father. A curly beard spills down his chest, and even though his hair is white, he doesn't look old. There's something timeless about his wrinkleless skin.

I marvel and lean in closer, inspecting each god and goddess in turn. They're oddly beautiful. Each one shimmers in the light, like the sun catching the tip of a wave. They move with more grace than I could ever muster as they converse with each other.

Only one figure stands apart from the others. He's hard to make out in the smoky shadows.

The Oracle continues. "But Dionysus is not like the other Olympians. He was the last and was born of a mortal mother."

The scene in the ball shifts, swirling to focus on Zeus, who shrinks down, donning a human disguise that somehow does little to hide the bravado with which he carries himself. He swaggers forward and presses his lips against a smaller figure, a woman with dark, wavy hair that hangs loosely down her back. The smoke grays and expands, revealing a new image. The woman's belly now extends far out from her body, heavy with child. She beams upward, looking toward the sky. But another woman appears above her.

Hera.

Her brown hair and eyes stand out against the white smoke filtering around the scene.

She and Zeus stare down at the pregnant woman. Their arms fly accusingly at one another, though I can't hear what they say. Eventually, Zeus storms off, his cheeks a ruddy shade.

Hera glares after him before looking down to the woman cradling her stomach. A sickening smile stretches across Hera's face, and with one last look in the direction Zeus took, Hera dashes off.

"Hera was jealous," the Oracle continues as the image shows a hooded Hera in front of the entrance to a dark cave. The opening stretches so high it could swallow any mountain I've ever seen. "She planned to release the Titans from Tartarus to destroy the woman's child, but she wasn't strong enough. Yet she tricked Zeus into thinking she had." Hera transforms into a tall, monstrous figure and appears before the pregnant woman.

"Zeus rushed in to stop what he thought was a Titan bent on destroying his unborn child."

Zeus grapples with the Titan, sending lightning bolts flying in all directions. But one of the lightning bolts strikes the woman.

Hera laughs, shrinking back into her form to reveal she hadn't released a Titan after all.

Zeus rushes over to the woman's side and kneels next to her, but her head sags backward when he lifts it. He cries out toward the sky with a roar so loud it shakes the world itself.

"Zeus saved the woman's child by sewing it into his own leg to continue growing," the Oracle adds. "Giving the child the moniker 'twice-born' when it finally burst forth from his skin. Zeus knew he had to keep the child safe from Hera. So he created an island, one that would go where Hera hadn't been powerful enough to travel—Tartarus, the dark abyss where the

Titans wait entrapped. All day, his island would travel across the ocean where Zeus's brother Poseidon would protect it, and at night, it would sink beneath the waves and reappear in the depths of Tartarus."

Royce's eyes go wide. "You're saying Dionysus lives on Jipper?"

The Oracle nods.

Royce and I share a look. We'd always wanted to sail to find the mysterious island that rose and sunk into the sea.

"Dionysus was supposed to be the last of the twelve Olympians, but he was never allowed there, making him bitter and jealous. He resented the other gods—even Zeus because his father had effectively made him an outcast by banishing him to live on an island instead of punishing Hera. That's why he's not only the god of chaos but of misfits—it's why he creates the creatures he does. He's formed an army by giving humans his own version of being born twice—of being remade with more powers. Because that's what he wants more than anything: more powers—enough to control Olympus itself."

"Is that why he's after me?" I ask. "Does he think I belong to him, that I'm one of his creatures?"

The Oracle shakes her head. "I'm afraid it's much more complicated than that." She waves her hand again, wiping the images in the smoke away. Then, slowly, another figure appears. It climbs up the very mountain we'd just climbed, becoming clearer and clearer as the figure ducks inside the Oracle's cave.

The Oracle sits inside the cave, much as we found her.

Her eyes look up toward the stranger. "Welcome, Dionysus."

Dionysus pulls back his hood. At first, a young man stands there with a thin walking stick, but then he transforms into an older man—one about my father's age. He's average height with a stocky yet solid build. His curly brown beard matches his thick eyebrows.

He doesn't look at all like I expect him to. He doesn't have a twisted smile that's sickening to look at or big, bulging eyes that track my every move. He has plump cheeks and an easy smile.

His walking stick has transformed into a staff, one covered in twisted vines and fat grapes. He leans on it as he lumbers down toward the center of the cave. "You're not as hard to find as I thought you'd be."

The Oracle smiles. "Perhaps I wanted to be found."

"I hear I'm not the only one looking for you."

The Oracle stares into the flames. "Too many of the gods wish to make use of my power and knowledge." Her eyes flick back up. "You included."

Dionysus spreads his hands wide. "I suspect you knew that when you let me in, so you also know why I've come."

It isn't a question, but the Oracle nods. "You want me to enter into a bet with you. In exchange, you're going to offer to set up a series of tests for me so that I can control who finds the way to my cave."

He nods. "Exactly. You'll finally be rid of all those mortals and gods seeking you out, the ones who've spent centuries hounding you, not giving you a moment of peace."

"And I wouldn't even have to win," the Oracle says coolly.

"Exactly," Dionysus says. "Instead of having to win, you get what you would've won upfront for simply agreeing to my little wager. It's that simple. Enter into one bet with me and get what you've always wanted in return."

"Are you so sure of yourself, Dionysus, that you would enter into a bet with one who can see time itself?"

"I've never lost one yet," Dionysus says, crossing his hands over his chest.

"Name the terms of this bet."

Dionysus rubs his hands together. "I bet that I will prove your next prophecy false." He licks his lips. "If I win, you'll hand over your power to me so that I can know everything you know about the past, present, and future."

The Oracle steels her face. "I know the knowledge you seek. Every night you travel to Tartarus. You have spent many years searching for a way to free the Titans there in order to have revenge on Hera and the gods who've mistreated you. You seek the memory I hold within of how to release the Titans."

Dionysus's face sours, his lips thinning into a tight line. "Will you enter into the bet or not?"

The Oracle clasps her hands behind her back. "I have no desire to see the Titans released, to relive the destruction and death they once caused." Her eyes flash white and she inhales sharply, as if she's lost in a painful memory. "But I will enter into this bet with you, under one condition." She stares into the flames for a long time. "Neither you nor one you command can kill the one the prophecy is about."

"Agreed."

The Oracle stands. "Then we have our bet."

Dionysus bows. "Then I very much look forward to your next prophecy."

The crackling of the fire breaks my gaze from the smoke as it dissipates. The cave comes into focus around me once more as the vision fades.

"The next prophecy I made was about your father becoming king," the Oracle says as her eyes take on their dark hue once more.

"But he became king," I reply. "So Dionysus didn't win the bet. Is that why he's mad?"

She shakes her head. "The entire prophecy was that your father would not only be made king, but that he would also have a prosperous rule."

My shoulders slump forward. "So Dionysus is going to win because my father's rule has—" It's hard to say the words. "Because his rule has destroyed the country."

The Oracle's lips thin. "Dionysus has not won yet. He only wins when King Midas's rule ends. Until then, there is still time for your father to turn his rule around and bring the country to prosperity."

Royce straightens. "So if Dionysus finds a way to kill the king right now, he would win the bet since the kingdom is still struggling?"

The Oracle nods. "He cannot kill King Midas. But he wants to kill you, Princess, in hopes it weakens your father."

Her words course through me like ice, as my father's cursed gold once did, chilling my insides and making me numb to the world. My pulse pounds in my ears, drowning out all sound. My mouth opens and closes, searching for something to say, anything that could make this better.

But there's nothing. Dionysus wants me dead. And if he succeeds, he might just shatter the little progress my father has made over the past month since his gold returned. He could send my father into a downward spiral he'll never recover from. And then Dionysus would win the bet. He'd have all the knowledge he'd need to free the Titans. And in his quest to destroy the other gods, he might just destroy the world.

The smoke in the cave is suffocating. My throat is dry and my head continues to pound. I can't even swallow. I force my eyes to meet the Oracle's, to be swallowed by those black abysses. She sits watching me, her hands resting easily in her lap as if she doesn't have a care in the world.

"We have to find a way to stop Dionysus," Royce says, his gaze flashing to mine. His eyebrows are scrunched in concern as he searches my face.

The Oracle's eyes flash white. "You must be very careful. Your actions have already set new paths in motion, for Dionysus has learned the man he sent to kill you has failed. He's now using his island to speed around the world, gathering all the humans he's remade with new powers. He's on course to attack Lagonia in five days with the army he's created." She sucks in a breath and shivers. Her eyes darken, and when she looks at me, sadness mars her features.

"If Dionysus reaches Lagonia's shores," she says, "he will win, and many will die."

I shake my head, trying to make sense of her words. That can't be possible. That can't be the only outcome.

But before I can voice that thought, she draws my eyes to the haze in front of her. In it, an image of the palace appears. Between wisps of smoke and charred boulders, bodies litter the ground. Royce runs forward into the fray. He sneaks behind boulders and dashes across open expanses. He has a cut on his forehead and another on his arm, and I watch as he shouts to someone behind him and then runs forward, sword at the ready. But a column of fire blasts into him, blowing him backward.

He hits the ground hard and rolls toward the palace steps as the flames cut off. He lies unmoving as smoke curls away from his charred body. Then Hettie appears, sword in hand and hair flying. She charges at a figure whose body is made entirely of metal. Where arms should be, swords wait at the ready. Hettie swings again and again at the creature, but even when she does hit him, it does no damage. Sweat dots her brow as she moves forward again, determined to not let the man get any closer to the palace behind her. But as she moves, the ground beneath her heaves unnaturally. She stumbles, and that's when it happens: twin swords slice through her chest. They rest there for a heartbeat before ripping free, leaving Hettie to collapse to her knees. She falls forward, and her eyes stare blankly, reflecting the flames as they take over the palace walls before engulfing the entire image.

"No," I gasp as the image disappears. I fall forward and clutch my chest. I struggle to suck in air. Heat flushes my cheeks, and I can't get thoughts to stay in my mind. "That can't be true."

"What can't be true?" Royce asks, wrapping his arm around my shoulder and pulling me closer.

Before I can answer, before I can even attempt to voice the words and describe the images I so desperately want to erase from my memory, the Oracle's gaze finds mine. "That vision is for you alone to carry."

I shake my head. I can't carry that.

"It'll be okay," Royce whispers, kissing the top of my head.

But he's so wrong. It's not okay. I just watched him die. I just watched my entire world be ripped apart, and it feels like it took a piece of me with it. My whole chest aches as though I've just run up the mountain.

I shake my head. "There has to be something we can do to stop that." But less than one week? How can we stop him in so little time? How can we stop him at all? He's a god. And he's going to kill us all.

"You must prevent him from reaching your shores," the Oracle says.

"Then we'll take the fight to him," Royce says, his voice hard and unforgiving as his arm tightens around me. "How can we find Dionysus?"

"Where anything can be found. Right where it wants to be."

Her answer is as confusing as the thoughts racing around my mind. Five days to find Dionysus. Five days to stop him. Or I lose everything. How could this have happened?

I stare at the Oracle, at the woman who's been toying with lives since before I was even born. Is this just another one of her manipulations, her way of altering my life again? Will I end up cursed like my father if I follow her path?

But what happens if I don't?

The image of Royce's burned body flashes through my mind. I shake it away. I can't risk that happening. Especially as something tells me the Oracle truly doesn't want the Titans released anymore than I do—nor does she want to lose her power to Dionysus.

And that means we truly only have a handful of days to stop Dionysus.

"And where does this man want to be?" Royce asks. "Is he on Jipper? How do we find it?"

The Oracle turns her eyes to him. "He's no man. He's an immortal, free to go virtually wherever he wants whenever he wants. He is never in one place long, and even when he is, mortals often cannot easily reach him."

"Then you mean you don't know how we can find him?" My voice is hollow as I sink back in dismay, the image of those swords plummeting into Hettie's flesh replaying over and over again in mind.

"There is one who could take you to him . . ." The old woman trails off, focused on something in the flames before her. "But I'm not sure if you'll wish to follow where that path leads." The fire crackles, and small embers sizzle out.

I find myself holding my breath as a hush falls over the cave. Not even the shadows seem to move.

"Where does it lead?" I whisper, both needing and fearing the answer.

"To Poseidon."

"Poseidon, ruler of the seas?" Royce exclaims.

"Yes." The Oracle's lips purse together. "But many dangers await that path."

"Like what?" I say, my stomach coiling inward.

But it isn't the Oracle who answers.

"Triton," Royce says, looking intensely into the flames.

"What?" I ask, my heart skipping a beat. That can't be true. I swing my gaze toward the flames. But all I see are the tendrils of blue and orange dancing together until they peak in a yellow tip.

"Nobody gets to Poseidon without going through Triton first," Royce says. "Triton is his messenger."

My throat goes dry. The smoke from the fire irritates my eyes as I blink over and over again, trying to find some way that the words he said don't mean what I think they mean.

"We can't find Triton," I sputter.

Images of the Temptresses of Triton flash through my memory. Human women spurned by Triton. When he grew tired of them, he changed them into sea witches so that no other man could have them. I'd faced them just a month before. They were women who'd become part of the sea, fluid beings bent on revenge against all men. During the fight to escape, I'd killed one, and that wouldn't exactly put me in Triton's good graces.

In fact, I'm probably the last human he wants to see.

Smoke swirls around my head, as jumbled as both my thoughts and my stomach. I cough and try to fan it away. It was foolish to come here. We're as good as dead if we seek out Triton. And everyone in Lagonia is as good as dead if we let Dionysus reach our shores. There's no way to win.

I get to my feet and pace back and forth, running my fingers through my hair. The Oracle had clearly known this all along. And yet, she'd led us to believe there was a way to find Dionysus, a way to stop him.

She and Royce continue to sit, staring into the fire, at something I am unable to see. And I can't take it anymore. I can't take her secrets and her visions and her manipulations. I take off toward the entrance. I just need a moment to think—to clear my head.

The cave's heavy darkness leaves me as soon as I step across the threshold. It feels like I've been in there for hours. My muscles are cramped, and my eyes sting. Not to mention it still hurts to breathe.

The world seems bigger after being in the cramped cave. I close my eyes and let the breeze wash over me, sucking in a deep breath.

"Why do you run away so quickly?" the Oracle asks.

My eyes snap open. How did she move so swiftly and silently?

She props herself up with a walking stick. And yet she looks solid, as if despite her age, she needs no manmade object to keep her upright.

"Triton won't help me. He'll kill me. I'm sure you know that." I can't hide the bitterness that seeps into my voice.

"There are many possible endings to that story." She stretches her arms wide, indicating the scenery around us, but I can't find her meaning.

I cross my arms tight across my chest and stare down at her petite frame. "So we won't die if we face Triton?"

"I tell no one of their death—just as I cannot see my own." The Oracle smiles, an almost grandmotherly smile. "He's an elusive friend I've yet to invite in." Her eyes find mine, and it feels like they hold the soul of the world in them. And I worry if I keep looking, I'll never be able to look away. "It's why you mustn't speak of what I showed you to your friend or your cousin, for I find that if you tell mortals of their deaths, it only hastens them all the more."

I dig the tip of my shoe into the dirt at my feet for a distraction, for anything to get the image of Royce lying there from my mind, and I swallow down the lump forming in my throat.

"So much pain inside you." The Oracle shakes her head.

She should know. Most of it is her fault—hers and Dionysus's. She's the one who entered into a bet with him that put the whole world at risk, not to mention the prophecy that ruined my father's life.

I swipe away a tear that threatens to slip unbidden down my cheek.

"Your path is not an easy one," she says, lightly resting her hand on my arm and drawing my gaze back toward hers. "Being a leader requires tough decisions and sacrifices that others aren't required to make."

Her gaze is so intense it burns right through me. Yet it doesn't focus on any one part of me, and I realize in that moment that she's blind—at least to the things I can see. But something else hides in her eyes that wasn't there before. Sadness? Sympathy? It's hard to tell. But whatever it is, it causes the tension in my shoulders to loosen as I wonder what kind of life she's had.

"I cannot tell you how your journey ends," she continues. "That depends on the choices both you and Dionysus make. All I can tell you is to remember what you encountered on this mountain, and trust the path you've been shown." She gives my arm a squeeze and then turns back to her cave.

I clear my throat, finding my voice. "What path?"

She turns back and pauses. "The one you were shown."

"Shown when?"

But the Oracle doesn't answer. She disappears into the cave. Sighing, I move to follow her, to demand answers, but Royce emerges, smacking right into me. He grasps my shoulder to keep me from falling backward.

Once I'm stable, he releases me. "The Oracle showed me the way to Triton's fortress in the flames of the fire."

I drop my gaze. Is this the path the Oracle meant? She'd said to trust it. But how can I? Not when it leads to Triton.

"How can we go there?" I say. "Triton's not going to invite us in and give us a tour of his gardens. He's going to attack us with things worse than Temptresses."

Royce presses his hands against my upper arms. "Are you not

even going to try? The Kora I know marched into the Temptresses' lair unafraid."

"That Kora had no idea what was waiting for her. This Kora does," I say.

"That's just it," he replies. "I was thinking about something the Oracle said, about how we'd have to take the same path again—like the first challenge. I think she means we have to find Triton and his Temptresses. We have to walk that path again."

"We almost died last time," I say.

"But we didn't," he counters.

I stare at him, at the way his lips turn up ever so slightly at the edges. At the freckle that hides just below his left ear. I place my hand against his cheek and rub my thumb against the skin weathered by the sea. I can't lose him.

And if Dionysus reaches our shores, I will.

I close my eyes and take a deep breath, leaning against him. He wraps his arms around me, holding me close.

So much is riding on each decision. The Oracle had made that very clear. But the only path I have, the only one I know has a chance of saving Royce and Hettie and all of Lagonia, is the one that leads to Triton.

Royce and I have taken on pirates, an island of cutthroats, and my uncle's plot to take over the kingdom. Maybe together we really can find a way to convince Triton to let us see Poseidon. No, I will convince Triton to let us see his father because I'm not losing the ones I love.

Didn't King Kalisrov's journal say a good leader should be able to talk their way to any resolution by reading the situation and the people involved? And my people need me to lead them to safety right now.

I pull away from Royce, straightening.

"So are we going to find Triton?" he asks, the breeze ruffling his hair, reminding me of all our times aboard his ship.

I stare down the mountain and out past the fields to where the sea is indistinguishable against the sky. To where my people—and now my future—are waiting. To where I have no other choice if I want to save them all.

"Yes."

# CHAPTER 8

The ride back to the palace is uneventful. The setting sun turns the fields gold as we ride through them. I half-heartedly think about hiding in them, about disappearing. But I can't turn back now, no matter what lies ahead—even Triton.

It's fully dark by the time we ride through the palace gates and dismount. And I let out a sigh of relief to see that the palace hasn't already been engulfed in flames like in my vision.

"I'll get back to the ship," Royce says. "We'll leave as soon as you're ready."

I nod and watch as he disappears into the darkness.

Kattrina's waiting at the steps for me, and I wonder how long she's been sitting there.

"Did you find out anything useful?" she asks as she takes my cloak once we're inside.

"We found out who we need to find first," I reply. "Triton."

She gasps, clutching my cloak to her chest.

Tilner appears and bows. He looks like he wants to ask me a thousand questions about the Oracle, but he waits instead for me to speak.

"I'll be leaving on Captain Royce's ship as soon as I pack," I say. "I'm not sure how long I'll be gone." I tell him about the meeting with the Oracle and how we're off to find Triton and

Poseidon. And how we only have a matter of days until Dionysus will reach our shores.

He purses his lips. "Be very careful. Poseidon is not known for his love of humans. There are varying accounts as to why." He taps his lips with his forefinger, thinking. "And be wary of Triton. He's Poseidon's son and messenger, but he hasn't been spotted in centuries. I hope you'll be able to find him." He wrings his hands.

"Just keep researching," I say, putting my hand on his shoulder. "Find any way you can to fortify the palace against an attack." I detail what the Oracle said would happen if Dionysus reached our shores.

He bows and moves off to inform my father of our plans.

Kattrina falls into line behind me as I head up the steps to my room. "Are you sure Triton's the only way?" she asks once I throw open the door to my room.

I turn to face her. "This was the only way the Oracle could foresee."

Kattrina nods to herself. But her hands shake as she helps me pack. No sooner have we closed the lid on my trunk than Hettie slinks into the room.

She has a bag of clothes slung over her shoulder, and her hair fizzles in every direction.

I close my eyes against that image of swords ripping into her and take a deep breath. She's alive. And it's my job to keep her that way.

"I'm coming with you," she states.

"Okay," I reply. I figure she'll find some way on board anyway, and right now, I want her close.

"Now, listen here." Hettie tightens the grip on her bag. "I'm not going to stay in this palace one moment longer, and if you're going after Dionysus—" She stops, realization dawning in her eyes. "I can come?"

"Yes." After all, Hettie helped us fight the Temptresses last time around. Without her, I may not have made it out alive.

"Good." Hettie loosens her posture. "When do we leave?"

"I've just finished packing," I say, indicating the closed trunk.

We head down to the courtyard together. A small cart waits for us.

Rhat is relaxing across the back of the cart while Tilner stands at attention next to it holding on to my father's elbow.

Rhat sits up when he sees us, his bald head reflecting the torchlight.

"Where's Royce?" Hettie asks.

"He's already on the ship," Rhat replies. "He sent me to make sure you both get transported down without any incidents."

I half wonder if he came up to make sure Hettie would come.

Hettie tosses her bag in the back and climbs up next to Rhat.

Two servants arrive, carrying my trunk. While they're busy loading it, I find a moment alone with Tilner.

"I'll take care of your father while you're away," Tilner says quietly.

I nod. And while the last time I'd left the kingdom, I'd come back to a traitor running things, that is one fear I don't have now.

"I don't want anyone near the tower with the gold until I return," I say.

"Your father holds the only key, and I will guard it—and him—with my life," Tilner says.

"Thank you," I reply.

"I wish you a safe journey," Tilner says. "And a swift return." Then he leans forward hesitantly, "And—if I may, when you return and the threat to the kingdom has passed, I would so much enjoy chronicling your encounter with the Oracle."

"Of course," I say, noting the visible excitement in his eyes.

Next, I find my father. His hand reaches out unsteadily for mine. "Are you sure you should do this?"

I nod. I won't let Dionysus destroy our kingdom. Not without a fight.

My father pulls me into a hug. I feel tears land on the top of my head. "Promise me you'll come back to me alive."

I nod again, not trusting my voice.

"And if you'd visit me from time to time, to let me know you're okay—"

"Of course," I manage. My connection with the gold had allowed me to visit the palace in a ghostly form when I'd been away before. And using that same connection again, I could keep him updated on where we are and how we're going to stop Dionysus.

We share one long look before I tear my gaze away and climb into the cart.

Rhat clicks the reins, and the horses jump forward.

I swallow the lump in my throat as the city comes into view through the gates. I'm not spellbound like I was last time I rode out headed for a ship. The heights of the palace walls and the storefronts we pass don't hold my interest. I'm focused solely on the vessel in the distance. Its mast sways above the rooftops.

It is not unlike the *Swanflight* I traveled in before. The main deck spreads to the bow of the ship while the helm rests on a raised deck at the back of the ship. Rigging tangles the area above the decks, and sails hang deflated.

I search the deck as we board for the streak of blue indicating an officer's uniform. I find Royce at the stern of the ship.

"How do we find Triton?" I ask as the last of the ropes tying us to shore are pulled in.

"We sail to the middle of the sea."

"And then what?"

"We look for his palace."

"You don't know where it is?"

"The map I saw in the fire was a little hazy, but I know generally where we're heading,"

I'm about to say that it seems crazy to trust a map he saw in a fire, but in our last journey Royce never questioned my ability to sense the gold we sought. "So what do we do once we find the palace?"

"We wait and see if he wants to talk to us or attack us."

"Let's hope he's more interested in talking than his Temptresses were," I say.

"You could always just turn Triton to gold. He might be interested in talking after you turn him back."

I nod. I pray it doesn't come to that, but I'll do whatever it takes to prevent the vision the Oracle showed me from coming true.

"Will there be any dancing tonight to appease Triton, like we had before?" I ask as a distraction.

Royce shakes his head. "I doubt that'll make much difference to Triton now. I feel like he already knows we're coming. There's not a single ship on this ocean he doesn't know about." He sighs. "I should get back to the helm. It's always tricky getting out of the harbor at night."

"Of course." I watch him walk away. I know this isn't the

maiden voyage he envisioned for his new ship. My father should've been there to send the ship off with his blessing. Crowds of people should've lined the dock.

With a heavy breath, I sidle up to the nearest railing and watch the cliffs flow past as we round the coast. No seabirds dip up and down in our wake. Instead, they're all safely tucked away in the crevices in the cliff for the night.

My heart holds none of the excitement I'd felt the first time I'd sailed out of the harbor. It beats faster and faster at the thought of Dionysus not just destroying Lagonia, but—if he releases the Titans—the world. And we only have five days to stop him.

After a short time, the coastline disappears completely. White-tipped waves become the boat's only companion. I stall for time, not wanting to venture down into my cabin where Hettie is no doubt trying to fight off seasickness. I don't want to be in the middle of that mess—again. I take off my gloves and let my fingers play in the wind, praying that it will carry us swiftly to Triton.

As I stand there, Phipps slides up next to me.

"I wanted to thank you for setting me up with Lady Alyona," he says, a smile playing about his lips. His ears stick out from underneath his untrimmed hair, highlighting the one golden hoop earring dangling out of his lobe. The first time I'd boarded the *Swanflight*, I'd nearly run away after seeing that earring, after discovering all the places gold could hide out in the world. I don't even flinch this time.

"Should I be expecting a wedding soon?" I pull my glove back on.

Phipps's smile gets even wider. "Well, see, at first, she

wouldn't even talk to me. She kept trying to hide behind the flock of women around her. But once those satyrs attacked, she was hiding right behind me. She clung to my arm." He points to a spot. "I saved her life." He folds his hands across his chest. "I'm expecting her to be waiting for me when we get back."

I pat his shoulder. "I'm happy for you, Phipps."

I have no idea if she'll actually be waiting for him or not, and I actually hope she's not because Phipps deserves better. But there is no harm in letting him dream.

"How's Lenny doing?"

"The kid's a natural." He waves his hand to where Lenny is climbing in the rigging. He's wearing a loose short-sleeved shirt that displays his missing arm. As he dangles off the rigging, the breeze tangles through his hair and ruffles his shirt.

"He really does look like a natural up there," I say.

Phipps beams. "The kid's always wanted to go to sea."

"Did his arm stop him?"

Phipps nods. "Nobody would take him. They all thought he couldn't do it. Even our own maw never really thought he could do it. She never really took to him like Thipps and I did. The kid followed us around from the moment he could crawl." He stares across the rigging to where Lenny leans into the wind, legs firmly wrapped in the ropes and a smile on his face as he lets his arm wave out to his side, almost as if he was soaring along. "He's why Thipps and I were so good at making a spectacle, because if people were looking at us, they weren't looking at him—weren't making fun of him.

"Thipps and I had been hopping from ship to ship and crew to crew looking for the perfect ship for him to join with us, to get him away from our maw and out into the world, when we found it here with Captain Royce. And after—after—well, it was just the right time to bring it up with the captain."

"Royce has always been good at looking past appearances and seeing the value inside," I say.

Phipps nods.

"You're a great brother," I say, "and Lenny's lucky to have you."

Phipps laughs. "I'd say I'm lucky to have him. He keeps me in line when he has to. He always gets this look in his eyes when an idea is too outlandish."

I can't imagine what either of them considers too outlandish. And I'm almost tempted to ask when Hettie shoves her way up from below decks. She doesn't look happy as she heads straight for me. And all I can imagine is that we're going to have a replay of what happened last time she was on a ship. I give her plenty of room so she can access the railing and empty her stomach.

Instead she marches right up to me, no hints of green coloring her skin.

"I thought we were supposed to have dancing tonight. Rhat was telling me about it since I missed it last time." She stares around the ship, looking for the grand party she's missing.

"Royce didn't seem to think it would make a difference with Triton," I say. "I don't think there'll be dancing."

"Oh no." Hettie squares her shoulders, her features taking on a hard edge. "There *will* be dancing. This is my first night outside the palace since my father died. My first night without every single person staring at me, wondering if I was in on his plot. We are going to dance tonight!"

I let her go. This is the most she's talked to me since her father died. I don't want to make things more difficult.

She stomps across the deck. "Rhat!" she shrieks as she goes. "Rhat!"

Rhat comes tumbling out from below deck, sword in hand. "What—what is it?" He spins in circles, as if expecting an attack to come from somewhere.

"Put that away," Hettie says, now a perfect vision of calm. "We're going to dance."

Her screeching has attracted half the crew, who now mill aimlessly about the deck.

Rhat looks up to Royce at the helm.

Royce shrugs. "Fine, go ahead and dance. I suppose it can't do any harm."

Hettie waits with her arms crossed as sailors fetch instruments.

When they return, she pulls Rhat close and they sway across the deck. She rests her head on his shoulder, relaxing for the first time in weeks.

I look up toward Royce. He's staring at me. Both of us waiting for the other to take one step forward.

Before either of us do, Phipps nudges me in my side. "How about another dance, Princess? I've got to be honest. I don't really remember the last time."

"All right." I let him pull me forward and start spinning me around. Sadly, he's not much better of a dancer sober than he was drunk. We stumble around the deck, kept on our feet by the sailors around us who push us back toward the center every time we veer off track.

"Triton loves a good party," Phipps says.

"I just hope he loves your dancing," I mutter as we crash into the railing. Wood bites into my side.

Phipps laughs. "I've always heard the rowdier the dancing, the smoother Triton makes the seas."

I smile through the ache in my side. I suppose the bruise forming will be worth it to have smooth seas. It'll go nicely with all the welts from the satyr attack, anyway.

"Lenny didn't believe me when I said I danced with a princess." Phipps tries to pull me back toward the center of the ring of sailors, but I resist. Our dancing has been rowdy enough, and my side can't take another impact.

"I'll sit this one out," I say as a new song starts up.

Phipps skids to a stop and turns to look at me. Then he turns back toward the makeshift dance floor as if trying to puzzle out what went wrong. Slowly his eyes lift, and he spots Royce coming down the steps from the helm.

He glances back at me with a knowing nod. He whistles along with the music as he dances himself back to the center of the deck, where he loops an arm around Lenny and starts spinning him around.

I take a few steps away from the railing.

Royce is headed straight for me. He dodges around Hettie and Rhat.

He's only a few steps away when suddenly the whole ship jerks to the side.

I crash back into the railing, and Royce plows into it next to me, his eyes wide.

We hold on to the balustrade as the ship steadies itself.

Around the deck, sailors are lying in piles. The musicians have stopped playing.

The only sound is the deck's creaks as the ship creeps forward.

Night air clings around us.

"Do you think it was a reef?" I ask Royce.

He shakes his head. "Not this far out."

I turn and stare into the dark water. At first, I think I see the reflection of my gold skin shining back at me. But something is off. It's too big.

A shape rises out of the ocean, water draining as it breaks through. A golden eye greets me.

I stumble away from the deck just as the scream goes up.

"Sea monster!"

# CHAPTER 9

〉〉〉〉〉〉〉〉●〈〈〈〈〈〈〈〈

The golden eye is attached to a body about twice my height with a mouth like that of the illustrated crocodiles I've seen in my copy of *Captain Corelli's Account of the Sea*—except this one's mouth opens side to side and not up and down. The entire creature is completely covered in green scales. Talon-like claws accent the ends of what look like webbed wings on either side of its body. Multiple bones are visible through the thin webbing and race through the fin-like wings and come out as spikes at each end. The creature uses its claws to hook into the boat and drag itself upward, revealing a serpent-like tail with another webbed area at the end, like a nightmarish mermaid fin.

I stagger away from the railing as the beast's jaws snap at me. Teeth with green algae at the base come for me over and over again. I roll backward to avoid them.

Somewhere a bell is ringing, and someone's shouting for all hands on deck.

The creature pulls itself over the railing and flops onto the deck mere feet from me. Water puddles all around it as the ship groans and tilts slightly under the weight. The creature screeches, sending its jaws to either side, and rancid breath, like the rotting corpse of a beached whale, washes over me. I don't have time to gag because a long tongue shoots out. Straight toward me.

A blade meets it in the air, knocking it away without so much as breaking the surface.

"You picked the wrong ship," Hettie says. She tosses her hair back and readies for another attack. "I've been waiting for a fight like this."

Her eyes sparkle dangerously, and a smile creeps across her face.

I scramble backward and get to my feet as men rush forward.

"Move out of the way, Hettie," I call. I won't let a sea beast get her any more than a metal man.

She doesn't obey.

The beast turns, using its tail to send men flying in all directions. Hettie dives under the strike, trapping herself against the railing with the beast staring right at her.

She doesn't seem to realize the danger. Or maybe she just doesn't care.

"Come and get me," she screams, throwing her arms wide. There's a wildness in her eyes as she swings her sword again and again at the creature's snout.

The beast snaps forward. Hettie deflects the blow, but it costs her. Her feet slip in the water, and she lands with a thud on her side, her sword clattering just out of reach.

The creature rears upward.

"Hettie!" Rhat screams. He rushes forward, aiming a knife at the beast's exposed back. He drills the knife against the beast, but the blade only skims across the scales.

The creature uses one of its wings to knock Rhat away, and he flies into the deck.

Hettie lets out a strangled cry as she grabs her sword and climbs to her feet. She moves toward Rhat, but the monster's claws squeeze around her arm, biting into her skin. She screams as the beast lifts her into the air and tosses her as if she weighs nothing at all.

My heart stops as her body soars straight into one of the sails. She slides down the fabric and lands unmoving on the deck.

"No," I whisper, my heart skipping a beat.

The beast thrashes around, its one eye twitching back and forth like it's searching for something. It lands on me sitting several lengths away, frozen in place, and slides forward.

As men rush to meet it, I crawl across the deck toward Hettie and flip her onto her back. She moans but doesn't open her eyes as I cradle her head. Blood pours out of three deep lacerations on her arm. "Hettie," I say over and over again.

"Is it dead?" she groans, cracking open her eyes.

Someone lets out a horrifying scream, answering her question.

I glance to where the creature has moved farther across the deck, its claws leaving deep grooves in the wood. Men encircle it on all sides. Royce shouts something about trying to aim between the scales. But the few men who aren't swatted away by the tail or the wings have no more luck piercing its side than Rhat did.

Royce nearly misses being impaled by one of the spikes jutting out of the wing. He tries to drive his blade through the webbing, but the creature's tail shoots around, knocking him off his feet.

He lands in a mixture of water and blood. Several bodies lie unmoving on the deck. I can't bear to look too closely.

"Help me up," Hettie snaps. She tries to get up but doesn't make it more than a few inches. "I'm going to kill it. I'm going to show it—"

"Stay down," I say. "You're in no condition to help."

Her face is ashen, and she winces with each movement as I prop her against the nearest mast. "Stay here," I say. "I'll be right back."

At least I hope I will.

I rush toward the fray, careful not to slip on the wet deck. Wood splinters as the creature digs its claws into the deck and swats at more men with its tail. Part of the railing is knocked into the water.

I pick up a sword that lays discarded on the deck and rush forward. I scan the men, looking for what I need. Royce is on the other side of the creature. I spot Phipps. He'll do.

Before I can move toward him, Hettie's voice echoes in my ears.

"Come and face me."

She's barely standing, having propped herself against the mast.

I half want to turn her to gold just to keep her out of the fight. But I don't have time to even contemplate that because the creature flips around again. Its eye lands on me once more, and it scrambles toward me with renewed vigor, knocking men aside as it thrashes to get to me.

I backtrack, knowing my sword will have no effect.

"Phipps," I call, not taking my eyes from where the creature approaches, "have a rope tied near the hole in the railing ready for me."

"A rope?"

"I have a plan. Just have it ready."

I don't wait to see if he obeys. I whip around, hoping to dodge around the mast and lead the beast back toward the opening in the railing. But I've misjudged where I am on the ship. I run right into the main mast. I turn just in time to see the beast propel itself closer. Its jaws open wide.

They snap around me.

I suck in a breath, knowing the pain will start any moment. Nothing happens.

I look down only to discover the monster's jaws are stuck in the mast on either side of me. It fights to rip its teeth free from the wood, claws digging in above me and sending splinters down as it fights to liberate itself. I duck down through the jaws and rush back toward the rail opening, ripping off my gloves as I go.

Phipps is already positioned. He's unwound some length of rope from a peg and has it puddled in his arms.

"Princess," he cries.

Behind me, a wet thud signals the creature has freed itself. Each swish of its tail and plunk of its claws digging into the deck signal it's getting closer and closer. And I need that rope in my hands before I can complete my plan.

"Phipps, the rope," I yell as I race ahead. He holds out the end as I skid to a stop in front of him.

I grab it from his hands and wrap it around my arm as many times as I can.

"It's coming," Phipps screeches.

I turn. The beast is nearly on me. "Get down," I shout. My hand crashes into the side of Phipps's face, sending him spiraling to the deck.

"Kora!" Royce's scream shatters through the night.

I ignore him and hold my ground as the creature leaps at me, jaws open wide.

Not yet.

Not yet.

When the beast is mere inches away, I let myself fall backward through the opening in the railing. I throw one hand up in the air, and it glides across the creature's belly, instantly turning it to gold as the beast soars forward through the gap. The body splashes into the water, sinking into the depths at the same time I crash into the side of the ship.

I barely keep my grip on the rope. Again and again, my body bangs into the ship's hull. I whip my other arm around to help distribute the weight.

"Kora." Royce's head appears over the side of the ship. Relief floods his features when he sees me hanging there. In an instant, the rope tugs upward, pulling me with it.

I land like a caught fish on the deck, and my whole side burns.

"Are you all right?" Royce asks.

I nod and force myself to my feet. "Where's Hettie?"

Royce points toward the mast, and I head straight over.

Rhat is already there arguing with Hettie, telling her she needs to stay still. He forces her to sit on the deck. "We should get those cuts on her arm sewn up soon," he says. "They're bleeding a lot."

"I can do it," I say.

"I'll carry her downstairs," Rhat supplies.

"Why is everyone always talking about me like I'm not right here?" Hettie murmurs. She rolls her head to the side so she's staring up at the three of us clustered around her. Dark circles have taken up residence under her eyes, and her hair is matted and limp.

"If you two can handle this," Royce says, "I'm going to see to the other injured."

We nod as he dashes off toward the nearest man lying on the deck.

Then another cry goes up.

"Lenny? Where's Lenny?"

Phipps runs frantically across the deck. "Where's Lenny? Bang on something, Lenny, if you can hear me."

The ship stills for one heartbeat. Then two.

Suddenly, at the end of the ship, a pile of debris shifts. A pair of legs appear as the entire pile crashes to the side and Lenny appears.

"Oh, Lenny." Phipps visibly relaxes and lets out a strangled laugh. His usual smile returns. But it's more strained than it was before, showing just how much Thipps's death has affected him. I know what he was imagining in those moments.

Lenny maneuvers himself from the pile to where Phipps stands with his hands still shaking. Lenny's usual smile has been replaced with a scrunched brow as he looks up at his brother.

Phipps has his eyes tightly shut while his hands continue to tremble. Lenny takes one of those hands, unfurling the clenched fist so he can rest the palm on his own shoulder. Then he places his hand on Phipps's shoulder.

Finally, Phipps opens his eyes, but tears dot the corners. "I'm concentrating on you," Phipps says, his voice cracking. "I'm concentrating."

Lenny takes an overly deep breath and moves his hand down toward Phipps's chest, toward his lungs. His eyes stare intently at his brother.

"One deep breath in," Phipps replies while sucking in air.

"One deep breath out." He clenches his eyes shut again. His chest rises and falls more softly. Eventually, his hands slip off Lenny's shoulders, and he opens his eyes.

"I'm— I'm okay now." He pulls his brother into a hug and gives him a kiss on the top of the head.

I turn back to Hettie, feeling I've intruded on something I wasn't meant to see.

Before Hettie can protest, Rhat scoops her up and gently carries her downstairs. He cradles her like my father used to carry the roses he picked from the palace rose garden, the ones he grew in memory of my mother. I pray he lulls her to sleep. Otherwise, I'm in for a rough time sewing her arm up.

꙳꙳꙳꙳꙳꙳꙳꙳꙳꙳꙳꙳◈꙳꙳꙳꙳꙳꙳꙳꙳꙳꙳꙳꙳꙳

# CHAPTER 10

H ettie doesn't fall asleep.

She screams into my ear as I lean closer to start on the second cut.

"I'm going as fast as I can," I mutter. I slide the needle into her arm.

She inhales sharply and bites down on a cloth while sitting on the bed we share. She stomps her feet on the floor, rattling the cup of herbs Rhat supplied for the pain and to help her sleep. So far, it isn't having any effect.

It would be easier if Rhat were here, but with so many injured, he is needed elsewhere.

Hettie takes deep inhales and exhales.

"At least it's not your sword arm," I supply.

She glares at me.

"Okay, okay." I search for another topic to distract her with, but I don't know what to say—and what might set her off.

"How are you doing?" I ask, eyes downcast, the scene of Lenny and Phipps playing out in my mind.

She sucks in a breath and clamps her eyes shut as I finish sealing up the wound. She rips the cloth from her mouth. "I have three large gashes. How do you think I'm doing?"

My needle pauses. "I meant after—after—"

"I'm fine," she snaps.

"Hettie, if I could've saved your father—"

"I said I'm fine."

I swallow down the rest of my words. How am I ever going to reconnect with her if she won't let me mention what happened?

I pass the needle through the base of the third cut, the deepest one. "I'm here if you ever want to talk about it."

She bites back a cry. "I don't want to talk about it. Ever. He's gone. That's all there is to it."

"Hettie—"

"No, Kora." Her words are slightly slurred. The herbs must be kicking in. "All that's left to do now is to kill the one who caused all this. I'm going to kill Dionysus, no matter what. That's all I have left. He took everything from me."

I pull away from her. "You have Rhat, you have me, you have—"

"No." Her words are more forceful. She sways, and I have to shoot out an arm to keep her upright. She flings my hand away drunkenly and jabs a finger into my chest. "You're the one who doesn't understand. Even if your father had died back when you two weren't speaking, you'd still be Lagonia's princess. You'd still have a place there. I have nothing. I'm just the leftover daughter of the king's traitorous brother."

"Oh, Hettie," I say. "You'll always have a place at the palace with me."

"Doing what?"

I stall. "You could be my advisor."

Her face darkens. "I can't do that. I can't do what he did. I don't need any more comparisons to him."

"I wasn't trying to compare you to him," I say softly. "I'm trying to show that I trust your judgment."

She scoffs, but it turns into a yawn. "The only thing I'm good at is fighting." Her head swings to the side. She stares down at her injury. "At least, I used to be good at it. Not anymore."

No wonder she was so reckless with the creature.

I take her hand. "Hettie, you're a great fighter."

"No, I'm not. I should've been able to kill that sea monster." Her eyes shoot up, suddenly finding clarity. "How can I kill Dionysus if I can't even kill his creatures?"

"It took all of us to defeat it," I supply. "It's okay to have help. We're in this together." I squeeze her hand.

She rips away. Her lips press together and her nostrils flare. "I don't need your pity. I don't need any more of that. Just give me the needle and get out. I'll finish the last cut myself." She reaches shakily for the needle.

I hold it out of her reach.

She tilts forward to grab it, but instead passes out on the bed and starts to snore.

I sigh, rubbing my temples.

I adjust her body so she's resting comfortably. Then I finish sewing up the final cut.

I shake my head and slip from the room. Even if I could sleep with the snoring, I need time to process everything Hettie threw at me.

I sink against the door once I close it. What could I have done to make her feel like she has a place at the palace? What can I still do? And will her need for revenge continue to cloud her judgment?

I rub my eyes with my palms.

It's too much to figure out now.

Besides, I owe it to the men on board the ship to check on them.

The stairs creak as I make my way up to the main deck. All the blood has been washed away, and a rope is tied across the missing section of railing. Phipps sweeps the bits of broken wood out through the opening as Lenny mops around behind him.

Phipps gives me a small smile as I approach, all signs of his earlier breakdown gone. Except for how tightly he clings to the broom. His knuckles are white. And the tension around his eyes doesn't seem to lessen either.

"I hope I didn't hurt you when I pushed you to the ground," I say.

He stops his sweeping and leans on the broom. "Just my coin purse," he says, pointing to his ear. The same ear that hours before held a gold hoop earring. That jewelry is now a murky silver color.

"I'm sorry," I say. "I needed gold and didn't have many options."

"I'm not complaining," he says. "You did save all our lives, but I'm sure you'll find a way to repay me." A familiar gleam begins to grow in his eyes, but after witnessing what I did between him and Lenny, I wonder how much of it is real and how much is a front he's putting up to hide his pain, to seem like his old rascally self.

Either way, I encourage it. "I'm sure I will."

"I would've been happy with a gold sea monster. That thing was so heavy, it would've been worth a fortune."

"Exactly," I reply. "I didn't know how much it would weigh

once I turned it to gold. I was afraid it would sink us. That's why I had to lead it off the ship."

Phipps lets out an exaggerated sigh. "Fine. But next time you turn a sea monster to gold that's not big enough to sink the ship, it's all mine."

"Deal," I say.

"Although," Phipps continues, "I have been thinking of other ways you could repay me right now." His smile seems more genuine now, and his eyes not so tight.

"Go on," I say, hoping his scheme is something I can actually agree to.

"I couldn't help but notice your golden fingernails." He stares at me expectantly, like I should've already worked out his angle.

I stare back blankly.

He sighs and throws up his arms like I'm an idiot for not knowing what he's getting at. "Clearly they can't be easy to cut. Gold is hard stuff, you know." He takes my hand, drawing it to his chest. "I'm volunteering my services to help you cut your nails. Of course," he says, "as my fee, I would simply keep the clippings." He nods his head as though the movement will convince me to do the same.

I look down at his hand holding mine. His own nails are all broken and uneven. Not to mention the loads of dirt trapped under them. You'd think with all the water he's around on a ship that he'd find some to clean up with.

"Phipps—" I extricate my hand from his. "I don't mean to disappoint you, but my nails don't grow."

His smile drops.

"They haven't since—since I was turned to gold."

His brow furrows. He stares down at the deck.

"But"—his eyes shoot up at my words—"if they do grow, you'll be the first person I call. And if you think of any more schem—ways I can pay you back, you're welcome to come tell me."

"Okay," he says. He points to his temple. "I'm already working on ideas."

"Good," I reply. Maybe it will distract him from everything else.

"Ahem." Someone clears their throat behind me. "Shouldn't you be sweeping?"

"Yes, Captain," Phipps says. He ducks his head and keeps sweeping curls of wood into the ocean.

I slowly turn to face Royce. Dark circles have taken up residence under his eyes, giving his cheeks a more hollow appearance despite the scruff starting to show.

"Oh, Royce." I relax against him—careful not to touch the gold on his jacket.

"How's Hettie?" he asks.

"Physically, she'll heal. But the things she said to me when I tried to ask how she's really doing—"

His grip tightens around me. "A parent's death is never easy."

I nod numbly. I'd been so young when my mother died. I remember her as one remembers a ghost. She flits through my memories, but I don't know what's real and what's not.

I think about what Hettie said, about if my father had died while he and I weren't on speaking terms. How would that affect me? I'd still be angry and sad. I'd weep for all the times we could've had together. All the things we couldn't share. All the things I would have wanted to tell him.

It must be similar with Hettie. She and her father weren't

on the best of terms. Yet, she had loved him, had done what she could to make him proud. And now she feels like she has no one.

I have to work to change that, to show how wanted she is. I add that to the list of things I need to do to actually be a leader. And a friend.

But I have immediate things to deal with. I pull back from Royce and stare into his eyes, which continue to hold so much warmth.

"Who do you think sent the creature?" I say.

"I think it was Triton," he says.

"Not Dionysus?"

He shrugs. "Triton controls things of the sea, and he probably knows we're coming. And there was nothing about that monster that suggested it was once human, like the Oracle said Dionysus's creatures were."

I stare out at the waves, only their white peaks visible in the moonlight. "So do you think there'll be more?"

He doesn't answer, and I swing my gaze back toward him. He shrugs. "I honestly don't know. But we should be ready for anything at any time. I plan to give the crew more battle training as soon as I can and will have extra men stationed on lookout duty."

"How is the crew?" I ask.

Royce clasps his arms behind his back. "Two are fighting for their lives. We should know more in the morning. One will lose a leg. The rest have cuts and bruises and a broken rib here or there."

I swallow.

"It would've been worse if you hadn't done what you did." His shoulders soften and he takes my hand in his. "Are you sure you're okay using your power this much?"

"I have to be." I shiver and wrap my arms around my chest as night air drifts in. It brings with it the icy feeling of absorbing gold. I hadn't even hesitated this time to reach out to the gold. I don't know if I should be proud or terrified. I'm too tired to decide.

He nods ever so slightly. He's worried—I can tell.

I lean against the railing and stare down at the waves tossing their manes against the ship. Every time I blink, I think I see another golden eye in the water.

I have no idea if Triton will send more monsters after us. Or what he'll do when he finds out what I did to this one. If we had any chance of him helping us before, I may have just ruined it for good.

Royce pulls me back to his chest and holds me there while he tilts his head down against mine and I stare down at the waves—frightened by what I'll see.

"At least we'll finally get to see Jipper," he says.

"If Triton helps us," I remind him.

"We'll make him help us, and then we'll sail for the island of legends, where streams run clearer than any water you've ever seen." He throws his arm out wide as if he's envisioning the scene before him. "We'll be revered among seafarers everywhere as the ones who found Jipper—the island most of the world wouldn't even admit existed."

"Is that what you want?" I ask. "To be the greatest seafarer alive?"

He shrugs, once again wrapping his arm around my waist. "What I want is to be wherever you are." He kisses the side of my neck, sending a shiver through me. "Land or sea, everywhere is an adventure with you. And I want to spend a lifetime discovering every place with you."

"You might not feel the same after we actually discover what lives on Jipper."

"Oh, I don't know," he says. "Compared to the Island of Lost Souls, it could be a nice break. At least we know there won't be any pirates."

I laugh. "I guess that's one thing we can look forward to."

We fall into contented silence as the gentle rocking of the boat sways us back and forth. We stay that way until a gurgling sound slices through the night.

Royce tenses at the noise. Then, all around us, the ocean heaves.

We stumble apart to keep our balance as the ship sways and steadies.

Royce rushes to the railing just as Rhat rushes up from below decks.

"What was that?" he shouts.

Men pour out from below, ready to face the new threat. Blades gleam in the moonlight while the men adjust their stances.

Everyone waits as the noise continues to get closer.

Braver sailors venture toward the railing, scanning the black waves for any sign of what's coming.

I search for a weapon, but I don't see anything littering the deck. I'm about to run downstairs for one when Royce cries out.

"There." He points out into the darkness.

Thick green tendrils race across the top of the waves. They weave and slither over, under, and atop one another, intertwining across the water.

Snakes. Thousands of them.

They wriggle over the top of the water at an unnatural speed as they head straight for the ship.

"There's more on this side," Phipps calls out from the other side of the deck.

"Swords at the ready," Royce says. "Stay by the rails. Try to keep them from coming aboard. And prepare the cannons."

Men position themselves all around the railing while others rush off to get the cannons ready to fire.

Cannonballs clink and powder floats through the air.

But as the mass vaults forward, there's something strange about it. They can't possibly be snakes, or if they are, they're the longest ones I've ever seen.

I squint, trying to get a better look. Unending strands of green dip up and down at even intervals. Snakes don't naturally move like that.

As it gets closer, it becomes clear it's not thousands of slithering reptiles. It's endless strands of seaweed weaving over each other as they race to reach us.

The ship sways violently as the plants encircle us, but they don't rush up and over the edge like I expect them to. They wrap around the base of the ship instead.

That's when the cracking starts.

The swirls of seaweed wind tighter and tighter around the ship. The hull's boards groan and bow outward before snapping.

The ship lurches downward. Swords clatter to the deck as men drop them to stay on their feet. The ship starts to tilt to the side as a long crack rips down the middle of the ship.

The entire deck comes alive as men scream and scramble to leap away from the growing rupture.

"The ship's going to sink," Royce yells. "Get to the longboats!"

The words aren't even out of his mouth before the seaweed tentacles find their way over the railing and go straight for the four longboats, wrapping them up and squeezing until more cracking signals their demise.

"What are we going to do?" Rhat says.

Royce's eyes slide from his to mine. They scan around blankly. And I realize for the first time that Royce doesn't have an answer.

Men scramble for the swords they dropped and are attacking the vines crawling across the deck, but the ship is nearly covered.

"Go get Hettie," I tell Rhat. "She's asleep."

Rhat rushes off.

I turn to Royce and the crew. "If we're going to end up in the water, we need to be prepared as best as we can be. We should start ripping off doors—anything big enough to float on."

"Yes," Royce nods, "and ropes to bind things together."

Just as he says the words, seaweed laces around his ankles. One minute he's standing there, and the next, he's gone.

He disappears over the edge of the ship with a splash.

I scream his name and rush toward the railing. That's when I feel something slimy, wet, and cold clamp around my skin.

Seaweed attaches itself to my foot like a leech. It twists its way over my ankles and up toward my calves.

With a yank, I clatter to the deck, slip over the edge of the boat, and disappear into the water.

The chill leaks into my bones and instantly shuts down my body.

Bubbles swirl all around me. I fling my arms around and try to fight to the surface, but there's nothing but seaweed in all directions. It curls around my arms and loops over my shoulders. It races to wrap me up just as the gold always did in my nightmares.

My lungs shudder, and they begin to burn. My throat clenches together, begging me to open my mouth, to find air somewhere. Even my stomach begins to revolt, as if vomiting would at least force me to unseal my lips.

The last of the bubbles escape from the corners of my mouth.

My head pounds, and my eyes close.

There's a light in the distance. It's the aura of the cursed gold back in the castle. It gleams invitingly—reminding me of everything I left behind, everything I have to protect.

I force my eyes open.

I refuse to give up.

I give my arms one final thrash and kick as hard as I can.

For a moment, I break through the surface. I gulp in air through the pieces of seaweed plastered to my face. Through the slits, I spy the ship in tatters. Its broken halves already dip below the waterline.

No. No. No.

"Hettie," I scream. "Royce, where are you? Rhat? Phipps?" I can't see anyone else in the water.

I try to fight toward the wreckage, to find them, to find something we can float on, something that hasn't been shattered. But the seaweed won't let me through. My arms slap uselessly against it instead of propelling me through the waves.

I spin around, trying again to find anything, anyone. The dark night presses in tighter around me. There's no one there. Just me and the endless black sea.

A familiar sensation flits through me as the seaweed tightens its grip on my ankles, wrenching me back under in a spray of bubbles.

I fight and kick and pull at the green vines. But this time I'm pulled deeper faster and faster.

My golden hair spiraling around above me is the last thing I see before the darkness of the sea swallows me whole.

# CHAPTER 11

𝔇𝔇𝔇𝔇𝔇𝔇𝔇𝔇𝔇𝔇𝔇❀𝔈𝔈𝔈𝔈𝔈𝔈𝔈𝔈𝔈𝔈𝔈

P ainful light fills my vision as I open my eyes.

I blink. I'm lying atop something coarse and uncomfortable while water gently laps at me from all sides.

I sit up to see a hazy sunrise in the distance while maze-like corals spread out below me. Down the way, I spot another crumpled figure.

Royce.

I crawl across the rough coral and flip him over.

He groans and opens his eyes. "Kora?"

"Yes, I'm here," I say.

Groggily, he sits up. "And where exactly is 'here'?"

"I'm not sure." I help pull him to his feet.

We're standing atop some sort of coral reef. Green, mossy-looking ones near the surface squelch under my feet, and fiery red corals jut out of the water like twisted antlers. Huge sea fans breathe up and down beneath the waves.

Small fish swim around and through the holes in the reef.

But as I turn, it's what inside the circular reef that makes me stop cold.

A watery palace shooting out of the surface of the ocean. Running water forms every wall, turning whatever lies behind it into shrouded shapes. Tall turrets stretch high into the air.

The thick coral reef rings it in. Inside the reef, sharks swim in lazy circles. The small whisper of their fins breaking the surface at odd intervals is the only sound until someone behind me shouts, "I'm drowning! I'm drowning!"

It's Hettie. Her hair floats around her as she struggles at the surface.

Cocoons of seaweed unravel all around her to reveal different crew members. Rhat is already rushing to pull Hettie from the surf as Phipps helps another injured man onto the coral.

Lenny pops up next. He hooks his arm over the coral and pulls himself up.

Phipps is there immediately. He pulls a bit of seaweed from Lenny's hair and pats him on the shoulder. A look I can't understand passes between them, but Phipps seems to relax slightly after seeing it.

As soon as the last man arrives, we study the distance from the reef to the palace. The water that had seemed calm before appears to be growing darker by the minute. Or maybe it's my imagination that the waves are getting closer and closer to our feet. Not to mention the sharks.

"How do we get over there?" Hettie asks, cradling her arm as she eyes the palace. "Assuming we actually want to get over there."

"I'm not sure we have a choice," Rhat replies.

No sooner are the words out of his mouth than an arch forms in one of the watery walls. Water speeds around it without dripping into the opening. From the base of the gap water spouts up, forming a bridge between the palace and the reef. The bridge hardens, turning to ice.

We all share a look.

Rhat tests it with his foot. It creaks but holds his weight. He starts slowly across, gliding one foot in front of the other, and appears to never take his full weight from the ice.

Royce tells the crew to wait on the coral while he and I follow.

Despite her injured arm, Hettie charges up after us. I figure it's better not to argue with her.

Beneath the bridge, the sharks' fins drag against the underside, sending ice chunks melting into the ocean. It sounds like claws digging into prey.

I ignore the sound and concentrate on my footing and only release my breath once we're all safely across.

We enter through the gap in the wall and find ourselves in a high-ceilinged room. Other watery walls cut it off from other parts of the palace. Colored algae in deep reds and greens crisscross back and forth to form an intricate rug on the floor.

Chairs made out of coral and seashells line the edge of a table made of driftwood. It's more intricate and beautiful than the driftwood that ends up on the shores near the palace, and someone has painted scenes across it. Some show small yellow-and-orange fish swimming along. Others show palm trees guarding their beaches as waves wash ashore.

Those aren't the only paintings in the room. Seascapes are plastered all over the wall using what I can only assume are live starfish to anchor them in place. I lean in to get a closer look and jump back as a real stingray swims through one of the walls and disappears into the ceiling, showing off its gill slits as it swims above us.

"Wow," I whisper. I stop myself before I reach up toward it.

Across the room, Hettie is sticking her hand in and out of the wall, marveling each time it comes back out.

"Welcome," a voice echoes across the room.

I freeze, suddenly as cold as the floor of ice beneath us.

Slowly, I turn. At the other end of the room is a tall man.

He doesn't look older than about twenty. He has high cheekbones balanced by full lips that pout forward slightly as though offering an open invitation to kiss them. His tan skin goes nicely with his dark hair, which is weighed down by a twisted coral crown.

It can only be Triton.

He wears loose pants and no shirt. He saunters forward, showcasing the muscles of his sculpted abdomen.

Hettie's mouth drops open, but she quickly snaps it shut.

It's not hard to see why he was able to convince so many women to become his Temptresses. He has bright eyes that are balanced by a mischievous grin spreading across his face. There's an air of mystery to him, something that hints at him knowing something you don't, of having explored all of the places people long to go.

A few months ago, I would've been drunk on that kind of charm. But Aris had that same air about him when he pretended to court me. He'd lured me in with all the places he'd seen. And I know how that ended up—lied to, hurt, and deceived into thinking he valued me, when he actually was working with Captain Skulls in hopes of harnessing my powers for his own means.

I square my shoulders.

"I'm Prince Triton, son of Poseidon, Prince of the Tides, Sovereign of the Sea, Commander of the Currents, more courageous than any sea creature," he continues. He leans against one of the walls and smirks as he looks us over. His eyes linger on me, and one eyebrow shoots up inquisitively. His smirk seems to falter just a bit, but I'm too far away to know for sure. "I see you've invited yourselves in."

"There was an opening in the—"

He holds up a hand, silencing me. "I allowed you to enter. Now we'll see if you leave alive. Follow me." Without waiting, he turns and heads into the room behind him.

Royce's eyes glance toward mine. I read the warning there. He and Rhat go first.

I wish I had a sword, a dagger, anything. At least Royce has gold on his coat if I really need it.

No footsteps sound as we walk across the room.

The next room is even more magnificent. The ceiling soars farther upward. Another algae rug runs the length of the room until it ends at the foot of what can only be considered a throne.

The throne gurgles upward out of the floor and is made from the same water as the walls. Jets of water spray up behind it to give it height and grandeur.

It reminds me a little too much of the swan fountain back in the palace garden for my taste.

Triton picks a small yellow fish out of one arm of the throne and tosses it through the wall before plopping down on the seat, reclining so that his feet hang over the other arm.

He twirls his finger through the watery arm now supporting his torso, sending ripples across the surface as he continues to study us.

"Why have you brought us here?" Royce finally asks.

Triton's eyebrow shoots up. "And here I was thinking you

were looking for me." He stretches back and rests his hands behind his head, leaving his midsection on display.

"We were," I say, stepping up next to Royce.

Triton's eyes narrow as they land on me.

"We need—" I start to say.

Triton holds up a hand, cutting me off. "No."

I swallow.

Triton slowly brings his legs back down to the floor and leans forward. "You and I have unfinished business."

My heart feels like it's been turned to gold in my chest. Thankfully, I manage to keep a straight face. "What would that be?"

Triton's smirk returns. He snaps his fingers.

Out of the floor on either side of his throne, two shapes rise from the water. They take on the shapes of women. Watery women.

The Temptresses.

# CHAPTER 12

The Temptresses stand there regal as any queen. Their bodies are as fluid as the walls around us, their hair flowing like waterfalls over their shoulders. They remain the most graceful and deadly creatures I've ever seen.

I hold my breath. I had hoped with the Temptresses' lair being so far away that they wouldn't be here.

Despite her injured arm, Hettie slides out her sword, a wide grin on her face. "Oh, good, I could use the earrings that match the necklace I got from them last time."

I hold her back. We don't want to go into battle unless we have to. And we don't have any fire to kill the Temptresses like we did last time.

Plus, Royce and Rhat will be susceptible to their siren-like voices.

I'm casting around for anything we can use to protect ourselves when I realize the Temptresses haven't moved.

The taller one stares at me and clenches her hands into fists. Then she turns toward Triton.

"You summoned us," she says bitterly.

"Bring it," he says.

The Temptresses dive through the wall. A few moments later, they reappear carrying the body of the sea monster I'd turned to gold and place it on the floor between us and the throne. Triton has to stand to see us over it.

"I don't think I need to ask which one of you did this." All traces of a smirk have disappeared from his face as his stormy eyes meet mine. "Change him back. Now." His voice is just as icy as his monster.

Something strange drags my attention away from his glare. All around us, bubbles appear in the waves of the walls, racing upward.

Boiling. The water around us is boiling.

Triton's cheeks have gone a muddy red.

"If I change him back, you'll just send him after us again," I say.

"If you don't turn him back," Triton replies, "my Temptresses will have some new playthings." His nods toward Rhat and Royce.

The Temptresses display horrid, toothless smiles. One solidifies so that legs appear. She takes a step toward Rhat, but Triton calls her back with a hook of his finger.

"Not yet," he says.

She lets out something akin to a hiss.

"Tell us how to find Dionysus, the god that gave my father The Touch, and restore our ship. Then I'll turn your sea monster back."

"He's not a monster," Triton says, looking down at the creature. Something softens in his features for a brief moment before his face resumes its rigid mask as he turns back to us. But the walls have stopped boiling. "And if you're looking for Dionysus, you're really looking for Jipper."

"We know that," Royce says.

"Then you should know it's impossible for humans to find."

He scoffs. "In fact, it's near impossible for almost any god to find. It rises out of the water with the sun, races more rapidly across the water than any ship can sail during the day, and then sinks back into the water when the sun sets. The only gods who can reach it are my father, myself, and Dionysus."

I bite my cheek. Only three gods can reach it? And only one doesn't currently wish me harm. Though if Triton knows how to find Jipper, maybe I can leverage that and avoid having to bring Poseidon into it at all.

"I'll turn your—your creature back," I say, "if you help us get to Jipper."

Triton stares down at me, his face darkening. "No."

I somehow manage to contain my sigh. King Kalisrov had written to always keep a level face when negotiating. He'd also said it was better to always be the one receiving offers instead of making them, that doing so gave you the appearance of being the one in power. But I've already messed that part up. Now all I have going for me is that I still have something Triton wants—a position King Kalisrov said to use to your best possible advantage.

"Then get us an audience with your father." It is an easy trade to get the introduction to Poseidon we came for. And it might be our only hope of finding a way to reach Jipper now.

Triton scoffs. "You, a human, want to meet with my father?" He stares down his nose at us. "My father hates humans, or haven't you heard?"

"But a good word from you would help us," Royce ventures.

Triton crosses his arms across his chest. "Doubtful. My father and I are not on good terms."

"That's not hard to imagine," Hettie mutters under her breath.

Though not quietly enough.

Triton's eyes narrow in on her, and my stomach tightens as I try to search for anything I can say to salvage the situation. But Triton's next words surprise me.

"No, it's not hard to imagine," he agrees, his eyes flashing sharply as the watery walls begin to boil again. "Because my father is a vengeful, unforgiving barnacle who cares more about his precious sea creatures than his own son. In fact, the only being he probably hates more than you humans is me. That's why he imprisoned me in this"—he gestures wildly around toward the room—"this pathetic oceanic cell instead of letting me back out in the ocean where I belong." He drops his arms and glares at us, his chest heaving. "So, no, I won't be putting in a good word because my father doesn't want to hear from me, and I want nothing to do with him."

I stand speechless. Imprisoned here? I certainly wasn't expecting that.

I sneak a glance at Royce. Sweat drips down his forehead from the heat radiating from the bubbling walls, but the tilt of his brow shows me he's worried. We need to calm Triton down. Fast.

"What if we could negotiate with your father for your freedom?" I blurt out.

"Kora," Hettie hisses, but I ignore her, not taking my eyes from Triton.

It's the only thing I could think of that would get us an audience with Poseidon and maybe get Triton to calm down. And if the god of the ocean truly hates humans, maybe we will need to negotiate for Triton's freedom and gain his help instead.

Triton rolls his eyes. "I just told you my father hates humans.

What part of you thinks me sending humans to him will put me back in his good graces?"

I fiddle with my fingers, thinking. There was certainly nothing in the books I'd read on how to approach a situation like this. But if I don't answer soon, I'll have missed our shot.

I stare at Triton. What could I possibly say to convince him to let me see his father—a father that hates humans?

Finally, I offer him the only thing I have. The thing that makes me different—that makes me who I am.

"I'm not like other humans," I say. "Look at me. I have golden skin, and thanks to Dionysus, I have the power to turn things to gold. With just one look, your father will see that I'm different, that I've dealt with gods before and not only come out alive, but come out the better for it, the more powerful for it. He'll see the other gods thought I was worth noticing before, and he'll see I'm worth dealing with now." I hate invoking Dionysus and making it seem like I sought him out and asked for what happened to me, but it's all I have to convince Triton I'm different.

Triton scoffs. "You humans know nothing of the gods. My father hates Dionysus slightly less than he hates me, so he certainly won't welcome one of his creatures."

Something like hope blossoms in my chest. I'd thought when the Oracle said Poseidon protected Jipper at Zeus's request that I'd have to find a way around the truth, to steer clear of the fact we wanted to stop Dionysus when we asked for his help finding Jipper. But if Poseidon is at odds with Dionysus, that changes everything.

"What if"—I take a deep breath—"what if your father knew we were seeking out Dionysus to get revenge?"

The words hang in the air as Triton studies me. Sweat drips down my arm and pools in my gloves.

But if I'm not mistaken, the walls are starting to dim to a simmer instead of a rolling boil.

"How exactly do you plan to get revenge on Dionysus?" he asks. "He's a god."

"That's for me to deal with," I reply. "I just need your father's help getting there."

Triton clenches his jaw. "You really think you can go up against my father and win?"

I swallow, but nod.

Triton raises an eyebrow. "Fine. I'll send you to my father. But if I have to resurrect you after he drowns you just so you can turn my creature back, I'm going to be very unhappy. And don't forget you're negotiating for my freedom too, because on the off chance my father lets you escape with your lives, it doesn't mean I will if you don't come back with what I want to hear."

Despite his words, relief floods through me.

And Triton wastes no time motioning us forward. "The sooner you leave, the sooner I am able to go free." He steps yet closer and waves his hand for the two Temptresses to follow him. "Only two of you can go, however."

"Why?" Hettie asks. She eyes him suspiciously, her hand glued to her sword hilt.

"As I said," Triton intones, "I can't leave, and the Temptresses can only carry one person each."

Royce and I step forward at the same time, and he gives me a reassuring nod.

A slight smile spreads across one of the Temptress's faces, and a chill runs through my body. Maybe I should've thought this through more. The Temptresses are known for trying to drown men.

"Maybe Hettie and I should go," I whisper to Royce.

He shakes his head.

I turn my attention to Triton. "How do we know they won't drown us the first chance they get?"

"They won't."

"They tried to drown my friend." Royce gestures to Rhat, who for his part looks relieved he's not one of the people going with the Temptresses.

Triton lets out an exasperated sigh. "What they do in their cove is up to them, but outside of that, they obey me. And I still need you to release Grax." He points to the sea monster.

His answer isn't as reassuring as I wanted, but it is all we have to go on.

The Temptresses move toward us.

I stiffen. Royce does the same beside me.

"I'd hold my breath if I were you," Triton says.

The Temptress's watery form blurs in front of me. Fluid arms surround my torso. Water sinks into my clothes.

"Missed us, did you?" the Temptress whispers into my ear. Her voice sounds like a wave sliding ashore in the dark.

I refuse to look away from her. "Don't make me do to you what I did to your friend."

She scoffs. "I don't see any fire now."

Then, without warning, the world jolts as the Temptress flings me toward the wall. I barely have time to suck in a breath before we emerge into the ocean. Warm water floods around us. Bubbles speed by as the Temptress jets downward.

Royce and the Temptress carrying him appear next to us.

The light of the surface disappears. Murky water filters in around us. Several glowing fish whirl past as the Temptresses speed by.

We're moving faster than I could ever swim, but it's not fast enough. The farther down we go, the more the ache in my lungs spreads. They tighten, begging to breathe, to cough, to do anything to get air in. The Temptress tightens her arms around me, making my chest sting even more.

Are they trying to drown us after all?

My throat burns. Every second brings with it renewed heat in my chest. It's so dark around me, I can't tell if I'm losing consciousness or not.

Then, light leaks upward from the bottom of the sea. It's dim at first, like the first rays of the sun peeking over the far horizon. It grows larger and larger until another castle appears.

It's so mesmerizing I almost forget about the ache in my chest.

Millions of tiny pearls form the wall of the castle. Around the castle, a coral reef grows taller than any hedge at the palace. Striped fish dart in and out of the porous holes. Eels laze in and out of small crevices. They retreat as we zip over the top and stop at the front door.

The Temptresses shove us inside. "We'll wait here."

I land with a thud on a floor crafted entirely of gleaming pearls. I cough and sputter as I stare at the golden reflection distorted in their round frames. The sensation of cool air rushing into my lungs overpowers every other feeling; I almost don't even register the pain in my knees.

Next to me, Royce gasps for breath. He shakes water from his hair as he rises to his feet. He bends over me. "Are you okay?"

I nod and let him help me stand. I shove back some of my golden hair that's plastered to my face. "I thought they were going to kill us."

"Me too."

A large room spreads out before us. I hold my hands up against the light emanating from the chandeliers. But they aren't ordinary chandeliers. Golden octopuses dangle from the ceiling, each tentacle supporting a torch.

Furniture similar to what Triton had in his palace lines the room. Long driftwood logs bolted into the wall support rows of odd objects. Goblets, necklaces, and spoons all mingle together on the shelves.

"King Poseidon will see you now," a voice calls across the hall.

I look for the source of the voice amongst the sea of white pearls but see nothing.

"Follow me," the voice adds.

I look to Royce. He shrugs.

"How can we follow you if we can't see you?" I question.

There's a tiny sigh. "I'm down here."

Squinting, I spot a cream-colored clamshell.

"You can talk?" It looks like any other clam I've seen.

"Always kind and generous, King Poseidon has gifted me with the ability and sent me, one of the smallest of his sea creatures, to be the one to summon you to his presence so that you may know how little he thinks of you." With each word, the clam's upper and lower shells open and close in time with its words.

I bend down to get a closer look.

The clam snaps at me. "Your kind eats enough of mine," it

says. "You're to follow me, not eat me, or King Poseidon will end you where you stand."

"I'm sorry. I wasn't going to eat you," I reply, straightening.

"I do not accept your apology, and neither will King Poseidon. Now come. King Poseidon loves to drown humans, and we mustn't keep him waiting." The clam hops across the pearls toward another room without waiting to see if we'll follow.

My eyes jump to Royce's, and despite all the water around us, my throat feels raspy as I swallow.

Royce takes my hand, giving it a squeeze. "We're going to be all right. We can do this."

I try to give him a reassuring smile, and try to believe he's right, that we'll somehow get through this alive. But we don't have a plan. We don't even have a way to keep Poseidon from drowning us. I'd used my skin, my powers, to convince Triton it was enough to make me different. But as the clam leads on, the sinking feeling growing in my stomach says that won't be enough to convince Poseidon.

We'll have to come up with something though, because as the clam moves forward, the wall where we'd entered solidifies in place.

There's no way out now.

And that thought sends my heart jumping just as erratically as the little clam does, counting down the moments until we come face to face with Poseidon.

# CHAPTER 13

৶৶৶৶৶৶৶৶৶৶◉᠅᠅᠅᠅᠅᠅᠅᠅᠅᠅᠅

R oyce doesn't let go of my hand as we pass silently through room after room until we reach one with walls made of glass. For a moment, I think we're about to step into the open ocean itself because thousands of fish swim behind each one, giving the impression they'll suck me into their world if I venture too close.

Every fish is different—from tiny half-orange, half-purple ones to oblong, shimmery green parrotfish. Large sharks haze in and out of view toward the top while sea turtles laze around at the bottom like rocks.

And part of me does want to get sucked into that world, to get out of here as quickly as I can. But we're at the bottom of the sea, and I'll drown just as quickly out there as I just might in here once Poseidon arrives.

At least here, there's still a chance I can save my kingdom. So I steel my shoulders as the clam comes to a halt, and I fix my gaze down past the cases of fish running the lengths of the room to where a dais with two empty thrones wait.

Conch shells comprise the larger of the two thrones. The shells fan out above the head of the throne like cream-and-pink-colored sunrays.

The other throne is made of sunrise tellin seashells—the

same type of seashell on my necklace from Royce. The dainty shells match the colors of the conch shells without their same bulkiness. Their smoothness reflects the light, making the throne appear softer than it probably is. I don't see how the shells could bear the weight of a puffer fish, let alone a human or god. I crushed those same shells underfoot walking on the beach as a child.

But my theory is proven wrong when two figures appear and sit on the thrones. The first is a wisp of a woman with long blue hair that moves as though it floats through water, even though there's no water around her. Her skin is paler than the pearls on the floor or the ones that pile atop one another to form the crown on her head. Her wide-set eyes take in the entire room as she rests her hands daintily on her lap. The dress she wears is made up of multicolored scales that catch the light with each move she makes and change the hue of the dress.

The woman might not look so diminutive if it weren't for the figure next to her.

Poseidon.

I go rigid as he hefts himself onto the larger of the two thrones.

His face stretches far to either side, balancing out his wide shoulders. His chest is entirely bare, showing hardened muscles beneath a cloak draped over his shoulders. Jagged shark teeth line every edge of the cloak, clinking together as he moves. But the thing that draws my attention most is the blue iridescent trident in his hand. It stretches taller than he is, ending in three sharp points.

His crown consists of five live seahorses interspersed with starfish holding themselves regally above his dark hair. The seahorses' tails curl around a thin gold circlet, and their snouts point upward like trumpets.

Beneath them, Poseidon's eyes catch my attention. There's something odd about them. The longer I stare, the harder it is to figure out. It's like they're changing, altering, as if made of moving water that pulsates with the tide.

I try to think how to greet him. Bowing? Or is that too human?

Thankfully, the clam at my feet hops forward. It clears its throat, or at least makes a noise resembling the sound. "I present the most honorable King Poseidon, King of the Ocean, Ruler of the Seas, stronger than the tides and controller of the trident, and his wife, Queen Amphitrite, Queen of the Ocean, Countess of Coral, more amiable than an angelfish and wiser than the waves themselves."

I decide to risk curtseying, so I step forward and present myself. When I rise, I say, "I'm Princess Kora of Lagonia, and I present Captain—"

"Your names are of no importance to me," Poseidon interjects, "just as you are of no importance to me, land princess." He spits out the last two words as if they were poison. "Now, as you drown, you can tell me why my son has sent you to defile my palace." As he says the words, he twirls his finger and water begins to gurgle upward from the floor. It slowly covers my feet, creeping closer and closer to my ankles.

My eyes jump to Royce's as my heart leaps into my throat. Poseidon's going to kill us.

Royce splashes toward where we entered, and I race after him. We skid to a stop as the entrance seals itself, becoming a solid wall full of fish like all the others. Royce presses against it with both hands, but all it does is send ripples through the room.

He tries ramming his shoulder into it but bounces off.

I run to another part of the wall and shove against it again and again. The fish cluster in closer in reponse, as if they don't want to miss the show. But no matter how many times I try, the wall is impenetrable.

"Temptresses," I scream, pounding on the wall in the hopes they'll hear me. But if they do, they don't appear.

"Oh, I love it when they struggle," Poseidon says, relaxing back in his throne.

I stagger back and scan the room, but there's no other opening. Even the one Posiedon had entered through is gone. I run my hand through my hair as I try to think, but my heart is thudding so loudly I can barely concentrate over the sound.

Added to that is a small voice chanting, "Drown. Drown. Drown."

I spot the clam's shells opening and closing in time with the words, and I resist the urge to kick it. I don't have time to waste because the water is already at my calves. And I'm quickly running out of ideas.

I consider trying to turn Poseidon to gold, but I doubt he'll let me close enough, and even if he did, I can't guarantee that'll stop the water rising. The only weapon I have left is my words.

"We've come because we're trying to stop—" I try to say, but Poseidon cuts me off.

He leers forward in his throne. "I don't care what you're trying to stop. I asked why Triton sent you here. He always wants something from me, and one of the few delights I have left beside my ocean is denying him what he wants. So tell me"—he creaks back in his chair—"what is it he's after this time?"

"Triton sent us to negotiate his freedom," I say, trying not to think about the fact that if I don't negotiate for that, I'm equally as dead back at his palace as I might soon be here. "But it's because we're trying to reach—"

"Ha!" Poseidon cancels me out again with his booming voice. "If I wanted to grant him his freedom, he would stand before me and not you. His request is denied, and I'll show him what happens to those he sends to make requests of me on his behalf."

The water rises closer to my thighs as seconds tick by.

Royce trudges through the water to join me. "If you gave him another chance—" he starts to say, but Poseidon cuts him off with a sharp glare.

"He's been imprisoned for unforgivable crimes against the ocean, and I will not release him. What he did . . ." Poseidon trails off and clenches his hands around the arms of his throne, splintering several seashells under the pressure as his face turns as red as the fiery coral in his courtyard.

I bite my cheek as I risk a glance at Royce. Worry stains his brow as he purses his lips. I know he must be wondering what I'm wondering: What could Triton have done that's so terrible, that could incite such hatred in his own father?

Something ignites inside me. Humans. Poseidon hates humans. And the Temptresses, the ones Triton created, were once humans. That has to be it.

"The Temptresses—" I say, turning back to Poseidon as the water laps at the top of my thighs. "We know how to destroy them."

"Don't even mention those creatures again," Poseidon snaps. "Those things are the least of his treason, but they're another reason he shouldn't be set free. For I'll not have him polluting my ocean with more of his mistakes—with more of those humans bringing their hatred down into my seas with them." He bristles, making the sharks' teeth trimming his cloak gleam brighter. "In fact, I should imprison my son longer for what I went through with Zeus as a result of Triton creating his little playthings. My own brother accused me of trying to steal his humans. As if I'd *want* any of you disgusting little creatures in my ocean." His words get louder and louder, and his body rises with it. He bolts upright from his throne, and the fish in the walls scatter toward the far end as he points the trident's prongs at us. "All you humans do is pollute, pollute, pollute. You litter your sunken ships across my sea floor. You send your dead away in boats to rot in my waters. You even threw Medusa's head into my waters, turning countless fish to stone and causing even more to be eaten by those disgusting snakes on her head as they wiggled free to grow into more gorgons. You—you—" He leans in closer, and the water rises more rapidly, swirling up around my torso before heading straight for my collarbones. "Your kind is a plague that infects my waters, and you should stay on the land where Zeus put you."

His wife gently puts an arm on his until he drops heavily back onto his throne.

"Why don't you turn the Temptresses back into humans and set them free?" Royce ventures. "That would take care of the problem."

I nod encouragingly, hoping maybe that would redeem Triton even a little in his father's eyes. Because if we don't figure out a way to do that soon, we're not going to make it. The water is already twirling around my throat. Soon, I'll have to swim to stay above it.

Poseidon's lips tighten. "Because it's not my magic that made them Temptresses. It's Dionysus's. Because Triton couldn't be trusted to take one simple message to that—to that cursed island of his without entering into a bet that nearly cost me *my* ocean." Poseidon's arms shake from gripping the throne so tightly. "And my worthless son should be grateful I let him live anywhere close to my waters. So your plea is denied, and your sentence is death for daring to trespass here."

The water surges upward, and Royce and I tumble around as we shoot toward the ceiling. My hands slam into the top, and I kick to stay above the waterline.

"Hold on," Royce shouts as he pounds at the ceiling. But it has no effect. He cries out and pounds harder.

I join him, smashing my hands against the wall until they go numb. Still, it doesn't give.

The water continues upward, lapping at the edges of my lips as it hastens to fill the final few inches. I press my face up against the ceiling and gulp in air while I still can, all the while, my mind swirling, refusing to believe it's going to end this way, that Dionysus will win.

Dionysus.

Triton had said Poseidon hated him too, and Poseidon had all but confirmed it moments ago. It's what I'd been trying to tell him about when he'd cut me off earlier.

"We're trying to destroy Dionysus," I cry as the water swallows my head. Bubbles escape my lips as I thrash beneath the water.

Royce's hair fans out around him as he continues to struggle, to slam his fist into the ceiling.

And just when I think it's over, there's a loud whooshing noise, and I plummet downward. I land on the hard pearl floor gasping for breath as the rest of the water drains around me.

Next to me, Royce coughs, emptying his lungs as he climbs to his feet.

"You're trying to destroy Dionysus?" Poseidon questions.

"Yes," I reply, sucking in air as I struggle to my knees before rising to my feet.

"Why?"

"He . . . he"—it takes me a moment to catch my breath—"he means to destroy my kingdom and release the Titans." I relate what the Oracle told me about Dionysus making a bet to win her knowledge, a bet he is very close to winning. "So you see," I say, a new line of thought forming in my mind, "that means more ships sinking into your sea and more dead bodies clogging the waves—your waves—if the world goes to war."

Poseidon relaxes back into his throne and steeples his fingers under his chin, resting his trident in the crook of his arm. "I'd heard rumors Dionysus was looking for knowledge about Tartarus, but I thought those had died out centuries ago—that Zeus had put an end to it."

He drums his fingers against the shaft of the trident, clearly thinking for a moment. "I promised my brother I would keep his child safe and allow his island safe passage on my ocean. But that was before I knew what he'd become and how he'd use that island as a haven for the humans he twists into his own creations. And as much as I wanted to destroy his island after what my son did, I couldn't without risking Zeus's wrath, but"—his eyes take on a darker tone, like a storm at sea—"that doesn't mean I couldn't help you find your way there to do the job. But what makes you think you're a match for him?"

"She has powers," Royce offers. "She can turn things to gold."

Poseidon waves his words away. "You think that makes you more powerful than the one who gave you that power? Foolish human." He strangles his fingers around his trident.

My chest tightens, knowing we're mere moments from water filling the room again if we can't come up with an answer, with some bit of knowledge that will convince him I can go up against Dionysus and win.

That's it. Knowledge. Or more precisely, wisdom.

"We passed the Oracle's tests to gain an audience with her," I say. "She wouldn't have sent us onward, guided us here to you, if she didn't see that a favorable outcome was possible because she doesn't want the Titans freed anymore than you do." Maybe that was stretching the truth a little. The Oracle had never said as much, but I needed to believe it was true as much for my own benefit as for convincing Poseidon.

Poseidon absently runs his thumb up and down his trident.

"It won't be long until Dionysus comes after you with those Titans," Royce prompts, pushing back several hairs plastered across his face.

I hold my breath, waiting, as my eyes search Poseidon's face for any sign our words have swayed him.

Slowly, a twisted grin crosses his face, displaying gleaming teeth that remind me far too much of a shark's. "Who better to destroy Dionysus than one of his deceitful schemes finally come back to haunt him?" He pounds his fists against the arms of his throne. "I'll get him out of my ocean at last."

I exhale. But my relief is short lived because that's only half our battle. If we don't get Triton's freedom, it doesn't matter if Poseidon lets us go. But I don't know how to broach the subject without setting Poseidon off again.

"So you'll lead us to Jipper?" Royce asks.

Poseidon scoffs. "I don't take humans anywhere, but"—he wags his finger—"I know exactly who can take you there— someone who needs to learn a little humility of his own, someone who if he wants to continually cohort with your kind can finally see what it's like to be ruled by you. Triton."

My stomach drops, and I share a look with Royce. We both know Triton won't go anywhere unless his freedom is part of the deal.

"Will you let him go free if he leads us there?" I ask.

"No." Poseidon's voice booms around the room.

Queen Amphitrite again places her hand on her husband's, but this time she speaks as well. "Let's not be too hasty. Let's hear them out." Her voice is high and melodic, like seashells clinking together against the shore.

They both turn their attention to us expectantly. But I can't think of anything to say.

"Perhaps Triton could prove himself," Royce supplies, and I shoot him a grateful look.

"How do you propose he do that?" Queen Amphitrite replies, once more resting her hands lightly in her lap.

"He could prove he's changed," Royce says. "That he's learned his lesson by leading us to Jipper and resisting entering into another bet. He'd be doing his part to take down Dionysus and make amends for the harm he caused you."

"Yes," I add, thoughts filling my head. "And surely making him travel with poor, helpless humans is enough of a punishment—enough to earn him his freedom."

Poseidon's brow scrunches, and his eyes are as unreadable as the ocean at twilight.

"Not to mention this might be your best chance at stopping Dionysus and teaching your son the lesson he deserves." I let the words hang in the air between us as Poseidon tosses his trident from hand to hand.

Finally, he nods slowly. "If he leads you to Jipper and manages to stay out of trouble, I'll let him go free. But I'll be watching, and if he doesn't prove himself or if he gets into trouble or enters into any bets, my retribution will be swift."

Royce and I both nod.

Poseidon slouches against the back of his throne. "Now leave before I change my mind, and never return here." He clangs his trident against the ground and the doorway we'd entered through reopens.

The clam looks tight-lipped as it turns and hops back toward the entrance, once again expecting us to follow. I linger a moment, taking a breath and trying to absorb everything that just happened. But I don't stay long because what I'd thought had been walls holding back the fish had really been some sort of magic. With a flick of Poseidon's trident, the water swooshes inward, washing over the dais and filling up the room. It splashes together from both sides like curtains being drawn across. As the first portions collide, they form a barrier between Poseidon and us.

More and more waves crash together, slowly making their way toward where Royce and I stand. The freed fish huddle in groups and stare at me.

"Come on," Royce says, pulling me from the room as the water whooshes closer.

The clam leads us back the way we'd come, and I cast a quick glance over my shoulder. Behind us, the throne room is entirely filled with water. It didn't even cross my mind that Poseidon had probably only created a momentary air pocket for our sakes.

The next room we pass through fills with water the instant we exit over the threshold into the next one.

"Sadly, you may leave," the clam says. It's led us to the front of the palace. Outside, the ocean fills the doorway that's opened there. Through it, I spot the two Temptresses waiting. They're chasing and terrorizing the fish in the coral gardens, but when they spy us in the entryway, they swim over and wait with their arms crossed.

"Swim out whenever you're ready," one of them says.

"As stated, King Poseidon kindly requests that you never return here," the clam adds. "And if you do, you will be drowned. Now you must leave."

Water seeps in through the walls.

"Let's go," Royce says. He grabs my hand and pulls me toward the Temptresses. I suck in a breath right before we break into the ocean.

"I hope you had a pleasant visit," one of the Temptresses says, swimming toward me with no rush. She circles around me once before twirling around to face me. "Because Triton doesn't like bad news."

Her arms wrap around me, and we speed toward the surface. I can't tell if the sudden lurch of my stomach is from the change in direction or from the Temptress's words.

# CHAPTER 14

I collapse against Triton's floor gasping for breath. The Temptresses had taken their sweet time dodging the guardian sharks and bursting through the waterfall walls.

Before I can recover my breath, a face appears above me.

"Am I free to go?" Triton asks, cocking one eyebrow.

I shove off the floor and rise to my knees. Next to me, Royce sputters and sits up.

Hettie and Rhat wait on the far side of the room. Hettie looks paler than when we'd left. She's still cradling her injured arm against her stomach while the other doesn't seem to have left her sword hilt.

Rhat looks as ready to leave as I feel. He jumps every time a sea creature glides through the watery walls.

Triton apparently has no idea what personal space is—or manners—because I get an eyeful of his sculpted abdomen as I struggle to my feet.

"Well?" he asks when I'm upright. "Am I free or not?"

I want to hate him, and yet, I find I can't. As arrogant and self-centered as he is, I know what it's like to be trapped behind walls. I can't help but feel his haughtiness is a side effect of his confined life rather than the reason for his imprisonment.

Swallowing down my annoyance, I choose my words carefully. "You will be."

Triton's eyebrow drops back down. "What do you mean, 'will'?"

"Your father put conditions on your release," Royce says, having gotten to his feet.

"What conditions?" Triton paces the length of the floor, his bare feet slapping against it.

"You're to accompany us to see Dionysus," Royce explains. "You're supposed to lead us to Jipper, stay out of trouble, and prove to your father that you deserve a second chance."

"He's coming with us?" Hettie blurts out. "No, no way. Not after he sent that thing after us."

Triton stops pacing and stares, eyes wide. "You had already killed one of my Temptresses, and you were sailing right for me. What else was I supposed to do?"

"Talk to us," Hettie says.

"I don't make a habit of talking with liars." He pointedly looks at Royce. "I only allowed you to come so you could turn Grax back."

"Liars?" Royce says. "We haven't lied about anything."

Triton scoffs. "Do you honestly think I'd ever believe my father would want me to go back to Jipper? He would never allow it."

"It's the truth," I say.

"You're lying. He would never—" He spins around toward the Temptresses, looking for support.

One of them shrugs as though she doesn't know what to say, and the other nods. "We heard your father say as much."

The watery walls around the room begin to boil again.

Through them, a spiky black sea urchin flies in. Triton catches it in his bare hand, only to toss it right back through the wall.

He turns on us. "I bet he thought it was funny, didn't he? He knows I can't go there." He storms over to his throne and sits down, jiggling his knee up and down. He stays there a few moments, brow creased in thought, before hopping up again. "I'd rather stay here and rot."

"Your father offered you that option," Royce says. "You can either help us or you can stay imprisoned forever."

"He didn't offer me a choice," Triton shoots back. "He knew I'd never take his offer. Dionysus and I aren't on the best of terms."

"Our hope is you could go there and show your father that you've changed," I say, keeping my voice even. As much I as I don't want Triton and his moodiness lurking on the journey, he's the best and now only chance I have of saving the kingdom.

He focuses his eyes on me. "Why do you think Dionysus gave your father the power to turn everything to gold? Do you think he really wanted to help your father? That he was just some benevolent traveler who swooped in to save your impoverished country?" He shakes his head. "He knows how humans react to power. He knew exactly what the power would do to your father, how it would destroy his life. And he wanted it to happen. He enjoyed watching it happen." Triton hunches his shoulders forward, shaking his head. "If he knows why you are coming, and that I was responsible for getting you there, he'll curse me before I even set foot on his cursed island. So turn Grax back"—he waves vaguely at the sea creature still frozen in the middle of the room—"and then get out."

I steady myself, pulling on the diplomacy skills I'd read

about—the ones I'd been trying unsuccessfully to model back at the palace. "With your knowledge of the way Dionysus thinks and our skills," I say as I gesture to Royce, Rhat, and Hettie, "we can find a way to defeat him. And you can win your freedom."

Triton rubs his temples. "The only way to beat him is to play his games. I've played his games before." He lifts his eyes up again to take in the group. "When I was younger and more foolish, I loved to play his games. Each one was a personal challenge."

Hettie rolls her eyes but thankfully keeps any thoughts to herself.

"After every game, I kept telling myself I understood his thinking better, so I'd beat him next time. I kept betting more and more. When I had nothing left, I bet him my father's ocean. Can you imagine what would have happened if I'd lost?"

"How did you beat him?" Hettie questions.

"I didn't. That's how I ended up here." Triton looks away, staring through the walls to something only he can see. The sea urchin bursts through the wall again. Triton catches it, tossing it up and down in his palm before pitching it back out the wall again. "My father had to save me. I'd bet Dionysus that I could keep his island from rising with the sun the next morning. My father is the ruler of the ocean, and as his son, the ocean also listens to me. I was sure I could stop it from rising.

"So the next morning, I wove a seaweed net over the spot where the island would rise out of the waves. I placed a layer of sand atop it to be sure nothing would get through. But the island kept rising. I used up all my strength holding the water in place, trying to make it solid so the island couldn't pass through.

"But I wasn't strong enough. The peak broke through, and

just as it did, my father showed up. With a wave of his trident, the island sunk back down.

"Dionysus claimed he'd won, that the island had risen. My father argued that only the tip broke through and not the entire island. After hours of shouting, Dionysus didn't so much let me go as my father dragged me away and locked me in here."

We all stare at each other, not sure what to say.

Royce clears his throat. "Poseidon did mention that you aren't allowed to make any deals with Dionysus if you do come with us."

Triton grunts. "I won't be going." The urchin makes a third appearance. Triton fiddles with the spikes, rolling the thing over and over again in his palms like Royce used to do with a coin from his father's cursed pile of gold. He looks like a sullen child.

And I know the longer he wallows in self-pity, the less likely he is to agree—not to mention every moment he spends moping is another moment Dionysus could be advancing his plans against Lagonia.

I move around the golden sea creature and stride up the steps to Triton's throne. I put my arm on his shoulder, pushing him backward. "Listen—you can either stay here alone for eternity with some bitter Temptresses and your sea monster. Or you can be part of our adventure and win your freedom."

He looks down at my hand like he hadn't expected me to be solid and real. Or maybe he's surprised he hasn't turned to gold at my touch.

"I know what it does to a person to be locked up," I continue. "I know that you're going to retreat deeper and deeper into your mind until you can't find your way out. Is that what you want?" I take my hand away and straighten, letting my words sink in before I go on. "Is that how you want to fade from memory? As just another individual bested by Dionysus? Or do you want to be the one to finally bring him down? To pay him back for all those times you lost?" I feel a little guilty using that against him, but my kingdom's counting on me. "We're offering you the best chance at that, and your only chance at freedom. I doubt your father will ever give you this chance again." I lower my voice, going in for the strongest emotional appeal I can think of. "Prove him wrong. Prove you can do what he thought you couldn't."

I pray I've found the right angle as I stare down at him, waiting for his response.

He doesn't meet my gaze. He looks younger, more unsure than I thought possible for him. He studies the ocean, distorted outside the watery walls.

I bite the inside of my cheek, waiting.

Just when I think he's never going to answer, without looking at me, he tosses the urchin back through the wall and says, "Even if I wanted to go, there's no way to get you there too."

"Why not?" I ask.

"Zeus made the island nearly impossible to reach even for a god—and nearly impossible to leave. If anyone came for his son, Zeus wanted to be able to capture them there." He straightens. "It's an island that moves faster than anything else in the ocean. No ship can anchor to it without being ripped apart at that speed. No land creature and none of my father's sea creatures can move fast enough to catch it—even Grax struggles, and he's the fastest creature in the ocean. Even the waves I create to catch it barely reach it. I have to perfectly time my leap onto the island. Not to mention, if I can somehow propel you along with me, you'll all die when the wave crashes into the island." He throws up his hands. "And, if anything were to happen to me, you'd be stranded in the middle of the ocean when you tried to leave."

Triton falls back and crosses his arms.

I stare back toward the others. They're all looking to me. Because I'm supposed to be the one leading them. But nothing I read prepared me for trying to reach an uncatchable island.

And if no land or sea creature can make the journey, then how?

Air.

A creature that could fly.

I whip back around toward Triton, something Poseidon said tugging at my mind. "When was the last time you visited your half-siblings?"

〉〉〉〉〉〉〉〉〉〉◉〈〈〈〈〈〈〈〈〈〈〈

# CHAPTER 15

No," Triton says. "It's just as dangerous to go there as it is to go to Jipper."

"But it could work?" I ask, hope cautiously welling within me.

He waves his hand around. "In theory."

"And they'd be able to get us off the island too."

Hettie clears her throat. "Care to let the rest of us in on this plan?"

"Pegasi," I say. "They're winged horses created from the sea."

"But do you know what else you need to birth a pegasus?" Triton cuts in.

"Gorgon blood," I reply.

"Exactly," Triton says. "Gorgons, with their scaly bodies and heads full of snakes. Gorgons, where if you look them in the eyes, you turn to stone." He shakes his head. "Even after a gorgon itself is dead, if one of those snakes bites you—you'll die."

"Charming," Hettie mutters.

"But," I counter, "I've read that Panacea's potion would cure a bite or someone who has been turned to stone." When I was turned back from being a golden statue as a child, I read about transformations and cures and every magical thing I could think of in hopes I could find a way to make my skin the way it once was. I spent a lot of time reading about gorgons, like Medusa, since they turn people to stone. I thought if Panacea could cure that, maybe her potion would work for me."

Triton rolls his eyes. "No one knows where Panacea keeps her potion. And I doubt we'd be able to find it in time. Once someone is bitten, they have only a few days at the most."

"What about Hebe's cup?" I add. Hebe was cupbearer to the gods. Any mortal who drank from one of her cups would be brought back to health. I'd seen pictures of a crystal-clear chalice with the different faces of the gods and goddesses circling it.

Triton rubs his temples and looks at me sidelong. "She is located where no mortal—or punished demigod like yours truly—can set foot."

"Perhaps the Oracle—" I start to say.

"No," Triton proclaims. "You can see that it's impossible. Turn Grax back and leave me in peace."

I cross my arms over my chest. I refuse to give up.

"If someone gets bitten," I say, my eyes shooting up to find his, "I could turn them to gold to stop the poison from killing them until we could find the cure." Of course, I'd do everything I could to prevent that from happening, but it's the solution I need to get Triton to take us there.

Triton arches one eyebrow. "You really want me to take you to Gorgon Island, where hundreds of these creatures are slithering around waiting to trap victims in their muddy ponds?"

"Yes!"

"Humans are more foolish than I thought," Triton mutters. But he looks up at me. "Fine, I'll take you to Gorgon Island—but if you die, that's on you. I'm only going so I can get out of this prison." He waves his hand. "Now change Grax back so we can be on our way."

I nearly fall off the throne steps, I'm so relieved.

I dash down and rip off my glove as I approach the sea monster. Only then do I hesitate. "I need your assurance it won't attack us as soon as I turn it back."

Triton rolls his eyes. "You humans are all so untrusting."

"He did try to kill us," Hettie chimes in, gesturing to her arm.

Triton waves his hand. Water shoots out of the wall and wraps around Hettie's arm.

She screams, trying to swat it away.

Then, just as quickly as it came, it drops away into the floor and disappears.

Hettie yanks at her sleeve, pulling it up to reveal perfectly healed skin. She gapes at Triton.

"You can heal injuries?" Rhat marvels, looking at Hettie's arm.

Triton shrugs. "Only things caused by the sea or its creatures." He waves his hand. "And you'll find all your other men have been healed from whatever injuries they had. Now release Grax."

All eyes land on me. I take a steadying breath and reach forward. Instantly, my insides go cold. Every limb tingles. The gold flings itself around inside me, but that's nothing compared to what the sea monster does.

It whips its tail around, nearly missing me as I duck under it. The beast stares right at me, its one eye unblinking. Then it lunges forward.

I scream and duck, hand at the ready so I can turn the creature back into a statue. But it doesn't leap straight onto me like I'm expecting.

It leaps over me. I turn to see it has pinned Triton to his throne, and the creature's long tongue lolls out, sliding up and down Triton's face.

"Off, off," Triton says, laughing.

"It's his *pet?*" Hettie says, making some sort of accompanying gagging noise.

The creature rubs its snout against Triton's leg. Triton absently scratches its head before he hops down the steps. "Are we going or not?"

He strides past us toward the entryway.

I transfer the gold to a nearby seashell and slip it into my pocket to give to Phipps later.

Outside, the rest of the crew waits on the reef.

Triton hesitates a moment, unsure what will happen when he crosses over the threshold. But he squares his shoulders and plunges forward onto the bridge.

Once out of the palace, his confidence grows. He raises his arms up, watching the breeze blow across his arms. He smiles and saunters over to the reef.

Grax bursts through the palace wall, sending water in every direction. Triton stands on the reef, eyes closed, enjoying the moment.

"Who's this?" Phipps asks.

He and Lenny must've been playing some sort of game they just invented, because Phipps has another sailor bent over on all fours acting as a table while he scatters little pieces of coral and takes bets on which side will land upward.

At our appearance, Lenny sweeps the coral bits into a pile and Phipps whips them away into his pocket.

Triton's eyes snap open. "I am Prince Triton, son of Poseidon, Prince of the Tides, Sovereign of the Sea, Commander of the Currents, more courageous than any sea creature." His eyes narrow, and he looks down his nose. "And I don't care who you are."

Phipps scoffs and puffs out his chest. "I'm Phipps, King of Games, Swindler of Secrets, Sovereign of Schemes—"

Triton turns to me, incredulous, and cuts him off. "This is the crew you brought to go up against Dionysus?"

"They're worth ten men each," Royce supplies.

"Cute," Triton scoffs. "You brought men to a fight of gods. Let see how that turns out for you."

I swallow, knowing he's right. That I could be leading these men to their deaths. But if I don't at least try to fight, the vision the Oracle showed me will come true. And I can't let Lagonia be destroyed—or the world. Besides, I'm still clinging to the idea that what I'd said to Poseidon is true—the Oracle sent us here because we could win.

"How long will it take to get to Dionysus?" I ask Triton to show I'm not backing down.

Triton shrugs and stares out over the horizon. "It's about a two-day walk to Gorgon Island."

"Walk?" Hettie asks. She stares out over the waves like she's missing some obvious path.

Triton peers down at her as if he smelled something rank. "You don't expect me to ride in one of your human ships, do you? Prince Triton, son of Poseidon, Prince of the Tides, Sovereign of the Sea, Commander of the Currents, more courageous than any sea creature, does not ride over the ocean in a boat."

"What about those waves you were talking about?" I ask. "Couldn't we ride on one of them to save time?" I stare up at the sun. We have less than four days until Dionysus arrives at the shores of Lagonia with an army at his back.

"I had a hard enough time not drowning you in my seaweed. Not to mention the rocky shoreline that stretches for miles around the island. Walking is much easier." He waves his hands, and the waves part, forming a watery staircase leading down into the depths of the ocean.

Without waiting for the rest of us, Triton ambles down the staircase.

I sigh and start down the steps into the ocean's abyss.

# CHAPTER 16

>>>>>>>>>>>◉《《《《《《《《《《

When we finally reach the bottom of the stairs, my legs ache. It felt like we were descending for hours.

And though I'd never been scared of the ocean, looking down into the distorted depths and seeing dark shadows and blurry outlines made my skin crawl the whole way down. Not to mention I'm still dripping wet from my journey to Poseidon's palace, and it'll take hours to dry off in the darkness at the bottom of the ocean. If I dry at all.

The salty smell is so overwhelming, I'm surprised salt crystals aren't falling around me like snow.

Sand squelches beneath my feet as I survey the scene. Some sort of air bubble has cleared a decent amount of space on the ocean floor. Blackness presses around us as the ocean looms overhead, blocking out any view of the surface. There's an eerie silence, as if the water swallows all the noises we make. Little ripples appear where fish and other larger creatures touch the edges of the air pocket.

Rocks and bits of coral twist up from the ocean floor. They're covered in patches of algae and other slimy-looking substances. Bright purple and green sea fans lay deflated along the reefs.

I used to find fans like those washed up when my mother and I would walk along Lagonia's shores. Only the ones we found were tattered and small. These fans are easily longer than one of my arms.

But they look so odd the way they cling to the now-dry reef.

Triton extricates himself from where he was lounging on a big chunk of coral and comes over. "What took you so long?" He stretches, putting his entire abdomen on display.

"There were a lot of steps," I say.

"Well, then—" Triton snaps his fingers, and the stairs turn into a slide.

The crew slips and tumbles down the slide, landing in a heap on the sand.

Triton smiles widely.

Somehow the flickering reflection of the water manages to highlight the grooves between each of his abs. I can't tell if that was by chance or if he had something to do with it.

"Ugh." Hettie extricates herself from the pile and pushes past him.

"What's her problem?" Triton asks, finally dropping his outstretched arms.

My eyes follow her path as she leans over to inspect a tall sea fan and a red starfish that rests beneath its crumpled form.

"She's dealing with a lot right now," I say.

Triton huffs. "That's what all the human women I meet say." But then his eyes focus on mine. "Except for you, that is. You're different."

I force the scowl forming on my lips into a thin smile, reminding myself that we need him. Not to mention he could easily remove the air bubble around us at any time.

"Can you just lead the way?" I ask. I wrap my arms around me for warmth and falter backward, right into Royce's chest.

"Is there a problem over here?" Royce asks, his body rigid and his voice as commanding as if he were standing on the bow of his ship.

"No problem," Triton says. "I was just thinking Princess Kora must not appreciate being soaking wet." He waves a finger and my clothes instantly dry out.

But something in the way the water drains off me jerks me forward, and I collide with Triton, catching myself on his bare chest.

"Better now?" he asks, flashing a wide smirk at me before slowly lifting his gaze to meet Royce's.

I shove off him, tucking stray hairs behind my ear to keep from socking the grin right off his face.

Royce strides forward. "Keep your hands off of her."

I throw out my hand, stopping him before he can swing the hand he's balled into a fist. He won't fare well against a god.

Triton smirks at the sight of me holding back Royce. "She fell into me," he says as he lifts his hands in feigned innocence.

"It was your powers," Royce throws back, jabbing a finger in Triton's direction.

He shrugs and then crosses his arms, leaving his arm muscles on display. "Powers are unpredictable, but I guess you wouldn't know that since you don't have any."

"Enough!" I shout. "If we're going to travel together, then we're setting some rules."

Triton tosses his head back, flinging loose hair away from his face. "I'm not so good with rules, or did you forget why my father locked me up?"

I ignore his words. "Well, you're going to abide by these or you won't get your freedom."

"Don't forget that you need me," Triton snaps.

"We need each other," I shoot back. "This only works if we all get along."

"I'm not interested in getting along. I'm interested in getting you to Jipper as quickly as possible so I can go do whatever I want, wherever I want."

"Well, if we come to blows," I say, "then I doubt any of us will make it to Jipper. So from now on, you keep your hands off of us. Got it?"

He throws his arms up. "Fine, have it your way." But a gleam shines in his eyes, and the edges of his lips perk up.

The next thing I know, Royce jerks around as the water dries off of him like it did me. Only Triton uses more force, and Royce spins out of control, landing in the sand at Triton's feet.

"Still finding your sea legs, Captain? Or just trying to bow down and give me the respect I deserve?" Triton quips.

"Triton," I scold as Royce closes his eyes for a moment, taking a deep breath and collecting himself.

Triton throws up his hands again. "I didn't touch him, did I?"

"No using powers on us either. Understand?" I clarify.

Triton rolls his eyes. "You humans are no fun."

I stare him down. "Triton, do we have an understanding or not?"

"Fine," he growls. "Let's just get moving so I don't have to be around you a moment longer than necessary." His eyes rove down to Royce. "That's if your captain is done playing in the sand."

Royce rises to his feet, briskly brushing off the sand clinging to his clothes. His lips are tight, and his eyes are fixated on Triton's. "Lead the way."

Without taking his eyes from Royce, Triton flicks his fingers and the coral he'd been sitting on splits in half, creating a pathway through it.

Triton's eyes move to mine for a half second before he turns toward the pathway. "Welcome to my kingdom. Do try not to ruin anything while you're down here."

An eel falls out of one of the holes in the coral and flops around in the sand. Triton twirls his finger around and a jet of water shoots out, whipping the eel into the water above our heads.

I take Royce's hand as we move after Triton. "Are you okay?"

"The sooner we're rid of him, the better," he says.

And I nod in agreement. "Thanks for keeping your cool back there."

He offers me half a smile. "Thanks for holding me back. You probably saved me from ending up in the sand a lot faster than I did."

I stare up ahead to where Triton is twirling water around in intricate patterns as he walks. "I doubt he'd fight fair even if he didn't use his powers."

"Let's just hope we don't have to find out."

"Agreed," I say, resting my head against his shoulder. But I don't keep it there long because the ridged sand makes walking uneven, and we haven't gone far before my slippers are full of coarse, damp sand. I drop Royce's hand to pull them off and then carry them, and the others do the same behind me.

"Nothing like your toes in the sand," Rhat says as he helps Hettie with her shoes. "Back in the Polliosaian Islands, there's sand everywhere. The smoothest sand you'll ever find. And on the eve of a new year, everyone goes out to the beach to leave footprints. If the first wave at midnight washes over your foot-prints, it's supposed to be a good year."

As Rhat continues to tell Hettie more traditions she'll have to look forward to when they visit the islands together someday, Triton sneaks a glance to see if I'm watching his watery display.

I ignore him, slipping my hand back into Royce's and keeping my gaze on my feet.

The next thing I know, Royce pitches forward, nearly face-planting into the sand.

"Careful there, Captain," Triton calls over his shoulder. "Looks like I missed a piece of coral."

"Looks more like you're not as powerful as you think," Hettie shoots back at Triton, "if you can't even move a little rock."

Triton huffs and continues walking as though he hadn't heard her words, but I can't help but notice the water patterns he's making get bigger and start changing from dark blue to nearly purple before fading to a light-green color.

"Just ignore him," Royce says as he gets to his feet. "He wants us to get upset about it, and I won't give him the satisfaction. He'll tire of his little games soon enough when he sees they have no effect."

"Or he'll just try harder," Hettie mutters.

I'm honestly not sure who's right—Royce or Hettie. All I do know is that this is going to be a very, very long journey if Triton keeps pushing the limits of the rules we'd laid out.

Triton pushes us hard, not showing a bit of exhaustion him-self, while the rest of us sweat and stagger our way through the sand for hours on end. While the sand appears to rise upward, cushioning Triton's every step, for me it feels like it is trying to erode me from the bottom up. It grinds into my feet and splatters upward, rubbing my skin raw where my legs brush against each other.

Not to mention trudging through the uneven sand has done nothing for the bruises I received from the satyr attack and falling off my horse. What I wouldn't give to be back in my soft bed at the palace. Or even just to stop and rest for a moment.

But Triton doesn't show any signs of stopping. He whistles an unfamiliar tune accented by our heavy breathing as we huff along behind him.

Eventually even Rhat, the most sure-footed of us all, begins to sway on his feet.

Royce holds up his hand. "Enough, Triton. We should rest for the night."

"*Prince* Triton," Triton corrects. "And I forgot how weak you humans are. But fine. We'll stop."

The men let out a sigh of relief before dropping like flies into the sand to rest. Even Phipps is too exhausted to make any jokes or remarks as he plops down next to Lenny.

Lenny leans his head on his brother's stomach, reminding me how young he truly is.

"I'm going to make sure all the men get settled," Royce says.

I nod, too tired to answer. I collapse where I stand and set about running my hands over the grainy sand, beginning to even out an area underneath an outcropping of rock to sleep. As much as I don't want any more sand grinding into my skin, I'd sleep just about anywhere right now.

I've just got a nice rectangle-looking area smoothed over when an unwanted voice chimes in.

"What are you doing?" Triton asks, stretching his hands high to grab on to the outcropping so he can lean forward, once again no doubt trying to highlight his toned midsection.

"I thought it would be easier to sleep if the sand weren't so lumpy," I say, sitting back on my knees and swooping back several strands of golden hair. I suppose it was too much to hope Triton would settle down somewhere for the night and leave us in peace. He's like a puppy with his constant need for attention and entertainment. Only puppies aren't vengeful and unpredictable when they don't get their way.

Triton swings his arms down and crosses them across his chest. "Huh. I didn't think humans enjoyed sleeping in sand."

"We don't," I state, fighting to keep my tone even. "But we'll make do."

I'm hoping now that he's gotten his answers, he'll leave so I can go to sleep. But of course he doesn't.

He stands there watching me as I go back to evening out the sand.

"Is there something else you wanted?" I say after a few moments.

"I just wanted to see how you humans do it before I showed you a better way."

"By all means." I hold in a sigh and gesture to the sand, assuming he'll wave his hand and even it out in one fell swoop. Anything to get him to go away faster.

But when he twirls his finger around, the sand before me doesn't shift. Instead, there's a watery explosion above me, and an entire sunken ship blasts into the air bubble. Men cry out and duck as the ship lands a mere arm's length from them.

Water rains off the wood, and a few crabs scuttle out of the crack that separates the ship into two halves. Triton waves his hand, and the boat dries out, groaning in protest as tendrils of water float from the wood to meld into the water above our heads.

It takes me a moment to realize it's Royce's ship. The one Triton sank to get us to his palace.

"You found our ship," I say, gaping.

A cheer goes up from the rest of the crew as they recognize it.

"I trust finding you a better place to sleep was an acceptable use of my power," he says. "Or should I send it back where I sunk it?"

I eye him. And I for the briefest second, I wonder for the first time if he's hiding a heart beneath all the muscles of his exposed abdomen. But the thought disappears as quickly as it came. Nothing I've learned of him so far suggests he has an ounce of kindness or thought for others inside him. He probably just wanted to show off his powers again.

"Thank you," I say, actually finding I don't have to force the words as much as I thought.

He waves me away. "Don't thank me. I just don't want to hear you all complaining after not being able to sleep on the sand. I know how grumpy you humans get when you don't sleep, and you're all already annoying enough as it is."

He refuses to meet my gaze as he says the words, inspecting his immaculate nail beds instead. And I take that as a dismissal.

I'm just grateful for a bed to sleep in, so I join the others as they move toward the ship to look for lost belongings and a place to rest.

I get there just as Phipps pulls Lenny into the hull amidst the mass of other sailors. "Hey, Lenny," he calls. "Do you think everything on this ship counts as sunken treasure on account of this ship being sunk under the sea?"

Lenny hangs his head and presses his hand to his face.

"Phipps," several sailors groan in unison as they climb over the jagged wood sticking out where the ship broke in half.

"Joking," Phipps cries out. "I was joking."

He slowly shakes his head and offers me a hand up. "Seems like no one can take a joke these days."

"They're just tired," I say, giving him a pat on his shoulder. "We all are."

He nods. "And on that note, I want to make sure we get some decent hammocks. Come on, Lenny." He and his brother disappear farther into the ship while I climb up a slanted staircase until I arrive at my old room.

The two chairs that had once formed a sitting area lay tumbled in a heap with my trunk against one wall. All the books that once lined the walls are scattered across the floor, and it smells musty. But it's so much better than sleeping on sand.

I set about dragging my trunk back to the foot of the bed and straightening out the pages of all the books that lay bent and torn. The books remind me of Tilner, which makes me remember my promise to visit my father.

I lie down on the bed and close my eyes, enjoying the feel of the mattress cradling my sore body. In the distance, the bright light of the gold beckons, and then I'm standing in the palace tower where all the golden objects my father turned to gold gleam invitingly.

My father sits in a chair near the gold, watching it glisten. He startles at my appearance, leaning back in the chair.

"Father." I move toward him quickly. I know I don't have much time in this ghostly form. "We've found Triton, and he's leading us to Dionysus."

I leave out the part about the gorgons. I don't need him to worry.

"We will find a way to stop him and his attack."

He raises his eyes to mine, then brings his hand up to my cheek as if he can touch me. "Be safe."

I swallow the lump in my throat. "I'll let you know if I discover any more information."

"Your mother would be so proud of you." There are tears in his eyes. "I'm so proud of you."

I offer him a small smile. Then, I'm closing my eyes and flying back to my body.

I jolt awake on the bed. But I've barely opened my eyes when Hettie bursts in, her eyes wide and a sour look on her face.

"I've been sent to summon you," she says.

"Summon me?" I ask, groaning as I extricate myself from the soft bed. "What's going on?"

"I can't even begin to explain it," Hettie says.

I freeze. "Are we under attack? Is something after us?" Dionysus? A sea monster? Poseidon? An endless list of possibilities scrolls through my mind. Has Grax attacked? Is the air bubble shrinking? Have the Temptresses shown up?

"You'll just have to see for yourself," Hettie says somberly.

My stomach clenches as we file out the door. She doesn't

lead us up to the deck or off the ship like I expect. She stops at Royce's cabin.

Air catches in my lungs, and all feelings of tiredness flee. Has something happened to Royce?

Before Hettie can open the door, I grab the handle and throw it open.

Inside, bright lights greet me. What had once been Royce's cabin now looks like a coral reef has exploded.

Glittering red-and-gold tapestries are held in place by deep maroon-colored starfish as they drape across the room, concealing every bookshelf. The desk has purple silk draped across it while a thick blue carpet stretches across the floor. All of Royce's books and tidily kept maps scrawled with notes in his own small handwriting now lay crumpled and discarded in a corner, seeping up water from the soggy carpet. Dark ink slowly swirls downward as the words begin to run and pool together.

The table that once held those maps is laden down with lit candelabras casting light down on plate after plate of food. What looks to be an old burgundy curtain with fringe dangling off the sides acts as a tablecloth. None of the place settings match, and a few have cracks.

The grandeur of the table distracts from the figure at the far end. Triton sits on a tall throne covered in barnacles. He sips from a silver goblet that has algae winding around its stem.

I step closer, and my feet sink into the wet rug, causing a puddle to ooze out behind me. And the scent of stale water permeates the room.

"Do you like it?" Triton says, raising his goblet and indicating the room. "I had some dolphins fetch these from a few nearby shipwrecks. It helps bring a little life into this dreary human vessel."

At that moment, Royce appears in the doorway, Rhat at his heels.

"Ah, Captain, you've made it," Triton says, throwing his arms out wide and causing dark liquid to slosh out of his cup.

Royce pushes into the room, his feet squishing onto the rug. His eyes go straight to the pile of ruined maps. And then he's staggering toward them. He kneels down, picking up fragments that rip apart where he touches them. "What have you done? I just laid these out to dry."

"I decorated for our feast," Triton says, waving his free hand around the room.

"A feast?" The veins in Royce's arms throb to the surface as he balls his fists. "You destroyed my maps to have a feast?"

Triton takes another sip from his glass and stares at Royce over the rim. "Yes—this is my first night out of that palace prison, and I've decided we're going to feast in celebration." He gestures for us to sit in the chairs around the table.

Royce slowly stands, his face growing redder by the moment and highlighting the indents in his cheeks from his clenched jaw.

I know Royce is doing his best to control his anger, but Triton's pushing it even for him.

I take a deep breath, remembering that it was King Kalisrov who said a leader should always be in control. And right now, I'm far from that, so I push forward.

All eyes land on me.

"I . . . I . . ." I can't think of what to say. I don't want to give in to Triton, but I'm afraid what will happen if we don't. How can I placate them all—especially someone as self-absorbed as Triton?

Then it strikes me. I knew someone who used to be exactly like Triton. I'd even compared Triton's air to the swagger he'd once had.

Aris.

An idea settles in my mind as I clear my throat and start again. "Royce, I know you need to go check in on the crew, but I'm sure the rest of us would enjoy a pleasant dinner."

Rhat stands there stone-faced as Hettie gapes at me like I've lost my mind, and she slowly shakes her head back and forth either in disbelief or in refusal to my proposal.

Royce's eyes meet mine, and I silently plead with him, giving him the slightest nod to let him know I've got this under control.

Not only do I want him to have some time away from Triton—as much as he probably wants it himself—but Triton will be more amenable to my plans without trying to one-up Royce at every opportunity.

Royce nods in return, turning back to Triton. "Yes, I'm afraid the crew needs me. If you'll excuse me." He doesn't wait for Triton to answer. He turns on his heels and strides out of the room.

"I didn't want him to stay anyway," Triton says loudly. His eyes dart to the seat on his left, and I realize there are four empty seats around the table. So even though he won't admit it, Triton must've been counting on Royce staying.

But that's what Hettie and Rhat are for. As much as they're not going to like it, they're part of my plan to appease Triton by having some of us join him so he doesn't feel ignored or slighted.

Because that's what would've set Aris off—being ignored and not being seen as the most powerful one in the room.

Not only did Aris revel in attention, in having others listen to the stories of his grand adventures—stories I had eaten up far too eagerly—he had even been rumored to throw lavish parties with incredibly exclusive guest lists. It was the appearance, the superiority those supposed events conveyed that Aris fed off. It gave him status. It gave him power.

And I can feed into Triton, can seemingly give into his demands, as long as it gets me the information I want. Because if he thinks he's in control, he might be looser with his words, as those assured of their own power often are. And if I can understand the way he thinks, perhaps I can not only prevent more of his outbursts—making it a more pleasant journey for everyone—but I can also glean information about Jipper from him.

And that's the only thing that makes dining with him palatable.

"Thank you for inviting us," I say to Triton through what I hope passes for a smile as I move closer to the table.

"I knew you'd join me," Triton says. "I've saved this seat for you, Princess." He points to the chair immediately to his right.

After I'm settled, I look to Rhat and Hettie. "Please join us," I say with emphasis on the word *please*. I send them pleading looks.

Hettie finally throws up her arms and stalks into the room. Rhat's clearly not about to leave her alone with the half-naked Triton, who's capable of anything, so he comes too.

"Eat, eat," Triton says. He stabs a rusty fork into a plump scallop and pops it into his mouth.

Besides the scallops, bowls overfilled with clams and mussels line the table while a chipped platter heaped with kelp acts as an edible centerpiece.

But as I stare at the food, I can't help picturing the clam that talked to me in Poseidon's palace. Maybe one of these is that clam. In fact, the more I stare at the mussels, the more it looks like one is opening and closing its shell, like it wants to tell me something or scream for help.

I tear my eyes away as Hettie speaks.

"If you're prince of the sea," she says, a disgusted look passing across her face, "aren't fish and clams and things your subjects?" She glances over the platters before swinging back to meet Triton's face.

I'd hoped she and Rhat would be too busy eating to ask questions—or to say anything really. So I bide my time, waiting for the moment I can jump into the conversation.

"Yes," Triton replies, prying the meat out of a clam and slurping it off the shell. "It's no different than humans eating all those land creatures."

"They aren't our subjects," Hettie replies.

"What subject wouldn't be willing to give his life up for the nourishment of his prince?"

"Ugh," Hettie says, but Triton's words don't stop her from spooning a mound of clams onto her plate. Next to her, Rhat does the same.

And I know this is my chance.

"Triton—" I begin.

"Prince Triton," he says, again emphasizing the word *prince*. Then he waves his hand, telling me I can continue.

I sigh, summoning all my diplomacy skills and what I can remember from Prince Ikkin's writings about knowing the terrain of upcoming battles. "*Prince* Triton, since you're one of the few powerful enough to go to Jipper, let alone make it out alive, what can you tell us of the island?"

As I scoop several seaweed strands onto my plate, I pray stroking his ego and giving him a chance to share his knowledge and stories will help, that he'll rise to the challenge and revel in having all attention on him.

He slips another piece of clam meat into his mouth before answering. "It's a small island, only a few miles in any direction. But it's dangerous to weak humans like yourselves. Just because I'm capable of surviving it, don't think you are."

"What makes it so dangerous?" I ask. I tear off a piece of seaweed and slip it into my mouth. It's slimy and salty and chewier than I expected. But that doesn't stop me from doing the same thing over and over again so Triton doesn't think I'm ungrateful for the food.

"Well . . ." Triton picks up a mussel and tips the shell toward his mouth before throwing it empty onto the table. "Dionysus likes to keep things interesting. There's a volcano that goes off whenever he wants it to, but honestly, that'll be the least of your worries."

I notice he doesn't include himself in the group that will have to face the island dangers, but I don't press it.

"You'll have to deal with some of his cursed creatures," he continues.

"Like what?" Hettie questions, slurping a strand of seaweed into her mouth.

Triton leans back, resting his feet on the table. "He's won a lot from other gods over the years, so any sort of creature could be lurking on the island.

"Oh, and rows and rows of grapes surround his house. He grows them to make wine. When you're passing through, don't eat the grapes. Some of them are poisoned. For that matter, don't drink the wine he offers you either."

"So no grapes, avoid his creatures, and hope the volcano doesn't go off," Hettie says. "That doesn't sound that hard."

Triton slides his feet off the table. "Those things are more dangerous than you think. And even if they weren't, they're meant to slow you down, if nothing else."

I shake my head. "Slow us down? Why would that matter?"

Triton rests his elbows on the table, leaning forward eagerly to tell his tale. "The island rises and sets with the sun. Any mortal still on the island when it sinks becomes bound to it. It's why Dionysus will try and get you drunk or ask you endless questions or give you an impossible task to complete." He flicks his hand around so one long finger points at his own chest. "Personally, I've never stayed on the island after sunset because it enters another realm—Tartarus—when it sinks. Dionysus certainly invited me enough times, and that's exactly why I refused."

"So do you think we can cross the island in one day?" Rhat asks.

Triton shrugs as he finishes what's on his plate. "I only have to get you there. The rest is your problem."

"Do you even have a heart?" Hettie asks, tossing an empty shell back onto her plate.

"Hettie," I hiss.

"No, it's all right," Triton says to me. "She's welcome to come put her ear right here"—he points to his bare chest—"and listen. She hasn't been able to stop staring anyway."

"Why you—" Hettie's words are cut off by Rhat's chair scraping across the floor as he stands.

Hettie has one hand strangling a dinner knife, and her other hand is twitching toward her sword.

I leap to my feet, drawing everyone's attention to me again. I run my hands through my hair. Managing Triton is like managing a country that's trying to do everything it can to cause a war despite having a treaty.

"That's enough, Triton," I say.

He leans back in his chair, flexing his arms back behind his head. "You're right. That is enough. I'm full." He pats his stomach. "Enough sitting for one night. There has to be some form of entertainment on this ship."

"I don't know," Hettie says, venom staining her voice. "We can't even dance without getting attacked by sea monsters."

Triton claps his hands together. "Excellent idea, land girl. Dancing. That's perfect. It's been ages since I've danced."

Before I can even think how to object, he strides out of the room.

"Great," I groan, sending Hettie an exasperated look. Now I have to go deal with that situation when all I want to do is go crawl into bed and go to sleep, like the rest of the men probably have. But I can't, because I'm sure Triton will have no qualms waking the men up to play music for him. And that will not go over well.

"Don't act like this is my fault." Hettie bolts out of her seat and plants her hands on the table, leaning over her plate toward me. "He does nothing but insult us all the time, and I'm not going to take it. You're the reason he's here, so from now on, you keep him away from me." As she shoves backward, her chair topples over with a clatter, and she doesn't bother righting it before she storms out.

"Hettie, wait," I try to call.

She doesn't turn back.

"It's probably best to let her have some time to cool off," Rhat says. "I'll talk to her."

I nod, but I doubt even his calming presence will have much effect on Hettie.

And as much as I want to go after her and smooth things out myself, I have to deal with Triton first. Because he's like Hettie was on our first voyage—with the addition of magic powers. There's no telling who he'll annoy to get what he wants.

Yet I have no idea how to deal with him or how to make things right with Hettie. I don't even know where to start— except to head after Triton, hoping I can stop him before he causes even more trouble.

〉〉〉〉〉〉〉〉〉〉❀〈〈〈〈〈〈〈〈〈〈〈

# CHAPTER 17

I hear Triton shouting before I even emerge on deck.

"Dancing," he calls.

When he spies me stumbling onto the deck, his smile widens. "Ah, you've come to join me." And somehow he gets louder, shouting across the ship, "The land princess and I wish to dance."

I skid to a stop, my stomach feeling like it did while staring at the mussels a few moments ago. "No, we're not—"

"Hello, musicians," he hollers over my objections. He meanders over toward the mast as if sailors might be hiding behind it. He nearly trips on one of the deep claw marks Grax left behind the deck.

"Your captain should really take better care of his ship," he says.

Before I can tell him his pet did that, he's already gone back to searching the deck for any sailors he can force into being musicians.

I scurry behind him, but just when I'm about to tell him there will be no dancing, he turns around and throws up his hands.

"Doesn't anyone on this ship know how to make music?"

"The sailors are most likely sleeping," I say, holding up a

hand to stop him while I go on. "And we will not be waking them up to play music."

"Fine," he replies.

The stern objection that had been forming on my lips dies. Fine? I'd been expecting him to argue. But at this point, I'm too tired to care why he's given in so easily. I just want to thank him and get out of there.

I'm opening my mouth to do just that when he snaps his fingers.

"Don't worry," he says, a wide, lopsided grin streaking across his face. "I fixed it."

A slow melody hums over the ship. It seems to come from all around us at once. The notes are low and long, accented by little clicks that almost sound like bubbles popping in a steady beat.

"What is that?" I ask.

"Seahorses singing through their trumpets. Magical, isn't it?" He sways back and forth, and his eyes twinkle as they stare down at me. They're misty blue—just like the ocean where the tide meets the shore—a swirl of blue and white melting together.

I clear my throat and look away. I don't need to be staring moonstruck into his eyes. He may be handsome, but I know better than anyone that real beauty is more than skin deep.

"Aren't you tired?" I venture.

Triton leans in close. "I don't need rest. I'm immortal."

But I barely hear his answer because his face waits inches from mine. His skin smells fresh and light, like the breeze that drifts in through my windows on a warm summer's day. The smell overwhelms my senses. I'm vaguely aware this must be how Triton lures women into becoming his Temptresses.

Something about the music, about his eyes, the way he smells, it all makes me want to lean forward and kiss him.

I pull back, stumbling away from him, the feeling fading the farther I move away. "What did you do to me?"

Confusion crosses his face as his brows narrow. Then some sort of realization must dawn because he crosses his arms and stares out toward the ocean around us. "I forgot about that. It's been a long time since anyone's visited."

"Forgot about what?" I say, my feelings still settling inside me.

His jaw tightens, and for a moment, I don't think he's going to answer. But without looking at me, he says, "That was Dionysus's magic. He made it so that if any woman falls in love with me, or I with her, she turns into a Temptress. His magic draws women to me. Once they're close, the magic takes over, heightening all their feelings, making them want to love me. And if they do love me—or I them—they become fully entranced and eventually turn into Temptresses. It's what I got for losing a bet against Dionysus, so you can see why I'm not eager to go back and face him again. Not that I have much else to lose at this point."

"So you didn't ask Dionysus to create the Temptresses for you?" I stare, wide-eyed. True, Poseidon had told me Dionysus's magic had a hand in making the Temptresses, but so much had been going on I didn't stop to think about it. I'd always just assumed Triton was a monster, turning ordinary women into sea witches out of spite when they no longer loved him. That's what the legend said.

"Not on purpose," he snaps, his gaze meeting mine. "But everyone assumes I did, so I might as well have."

"I just always thought—"

"You thought wrong—just like you humans always do." He

turns and stares back out toward the air bubble, his shoulders slumping forward. He waves his hand, silencing the music, plunging us into an eerie silence. "You can leave now. I'm no longer in the mood for dancing."

But I don't leave. For the first time, I look at him. Really look at him. Sure, he's attractive at first glance, but there's a tightness around his eyes that shouldn't be there on someone who appears so young. Not to mention the way his brow stays furrowed as he stares resolutely ahead and how he wraps his arms around his chest like he's holding himself together.

With his wall of confidence gone, he looks broken in a way I know all too well. And for the first time, I realize Triton and I might have more in common than I ever thought. People think he's monster, just like some people think that of me and my golden skin. And we both know what it's like to be caught in Dionysus's magic web and what it's like to have false rumors floating around about yourself. It isolates you, sets you apart. And in his case, it's made him bitter against the world.

I can't imagine what his life has been like—especially having Poseidon as a father—but I'm beginning to understand why he pushes people away. Because either people—like his own father—have pushed him away or they've gotten too close and been turned into Temptresses. He pushes them away before they can abandon him.

I can't imagine how lonely he must be. Or maybe I can. Didn't I feel the same way when I was turned to gold? I lost touch with my own father and everyone around me. I didn't let anyone in. But I turned things around, and maybe he can too. He just needs some help getting there.

"You know," I say, "if you gave humans a chance, you might find we're not so bad. Maybe you'd even find friends."

"You humans and your friendships," he scoffs. "They never last."

I rub my forehead. He certainly doesn't make this easy. And I'm wondering how I can possibly get through to him when he finally transfers his gaze to me.

"How many came for you?" he says.

"I don't know what you mean."

He takes a step toward me, lowering his voice. "You were trapped in your palace like I was. How many humans—how many of these friends—came to free you?"

"I wasn't—" I stammer. "I wasn't exactly locked inside. It only felt like a prison because everyone treated me like an outcast."

"So no one came to free you," he says with a little too much self-satisfaction, as if he's proving some point to himself.

And I realize he's comparing us—my time locked away with his—to prove that no one came for me just like no one ever came for him.

"My friends on the ship don't treat me like people back at the palace did," I say. "And now they're willing to risk their lives to help me go up against gorgons and Dionysus and anything else we're going to face. They care about me."

He turns back toward the railing, staring out into the dark ocean. "Are you sure they're not drawn to you for your powers? Humans love power. They're always trying to get more."

"Of course not," I say. "They love me for what's inside my heart, not what I look like or what I can offer them."

Triton scans the deck slowly before turning back to me. He gives me a skeptical look. "All the human women I've met have only ever been interested in what I look like—even before Dionysus's magic took hold." His head cocks to the side. "But then again, I've never met one who has so easily resisted the magic Dionysus instilled in me. Usually women are drooling at my feet. But not you." He moves closer in the darkness. "What makes you so different?"

I shrug. "I don't know. Maybe I'm used to his magic after living around it so long. Or maybe it's because I've already found someone I love. Someone who treats me with kindness. Someone who supports me. Someone who understands my past and what it did to me. Someone who listens to me."

Triton looks confused, so I add, "Royce doesn't make me feel like a prize he's adding to his collection. Nor does he throw himself at me and expect me to like him just because he's attractive."

"So you do find me attractive?"

I roll my eyes.

He throws his hands up defensively. "I was kidding," he says. "You're saying I actually need to get to know someone and not talk about myself all the time and how superior I am to them."

"That about covers it."

"But I am superior to them."

I bury my face in my hands.

"Here, watch this," he says.

He waves his hand and part of the air bubble collapses, stopping right at the edge of the ship's railing. He guides me to the railing.

I stare out into the dark water.

One giant eye appears before me.

I cry out and leap back as Grax's snout bursts through the bubble. He licks Triton's face until Triton shoves the beast back into the water. Grax hovers in front of us, his tongue lagging out the side of his mouth. He nudges the air bubble with his snout.

"Not now, buddy," Triton says. He pulls off a broken shard of wood from the railing and sends it shooting out into the water. Grax happily swims after it.

"That should keep him busy for a while."

"I've already seen your sea creature," I say.

"We're not here to see Grax," he says. He waves his hand over the water, and I gasp.

Dozens of luminescent fish surround us. The majority of their clear bodies are impossible to see. Only the illuminated parts are visible. Some have fins that glow yellow. Others have eyes that radiate bright blue. They sparkle in the water like fallen stars. One creature swims right past me and looks like a millipede swimming through the water. Another has tentacles longer than my hair.

"These are my father's favorites," Triton says. "He made it so that they live in the deepest parts of the ocean where land creatures would never see their beauty. Impressive, right?" He leans his back against the railing and crosses his arms, some of his cockiness returning at the chance to display his powers.

"It is impressive," I reply. "But there are people out there who might actually like you if you didn't have any powers at all. In fact, any person who wants me to use my powers isn't my friend. Once you figure that out, you might not feel so lonely, because a friend doesn't demand you use your powers for their benefit. Rather, a true friend would risk everything to help you. They check in on how you're feeling and do small acts of kindness just because they know they'll make you happy."

He sobers slightly. "You're the only one on this ship who's

been kind to me," he says. "No one else wanted to eat with me, and the others wouldn't have stayed if you hadn't made them."

"Well, if you tried a little harder—"

Before Triton can answer, Royce strides up behind us and clears his throat. "I heard you yelling, Prince Triton, and I've gathered my musicians if you'd still like to dance."

A couple sleepy-eyed men stand gathered behind Royce, and my heart softens at the sight. Royce has every right to hate Triton, and yet, here he is offering him this small kindness— which I hope Triton notices.

And I think I fall in love with Royce even more in that moment because Royce is doing this for me, to keep things civil with Triton, to make sure we can find a way to save Lagonia.

"I've— I've lost my desire to dance," Triton says. He shoots me a look I can't decipher. "In fact, this whole ship doesn't suit me. I'll be sleeping in the ocean. You can have your little cabin back, Captain. And I think you'll find your maps dry now. They weren't worth wasting my water on." Without another word, Triton steps onto a set of watery stairs that appear out of nowhere and heads toward the ocean floor.

"What was that about?" Royce asks after the water closes around Triton. "Here I try to accommodate him, and he up and leaves."

I can't stop the smallest bit of hope blossoming in my chest. "Give him time. I think he might come around. In fact, I think drying out your maps was his way of making amends without actually admitting he did anything wrong."

"If he doesn't come around, it's going to be a long journey," Royce says, slipping his hand into mine.

I nod, relaxing against Royce. He feels warm and solid and real amidst all this water, and I can't help relaxing against him.

"How did dinner go?"

I fill him in on the events, including both what Triton told us about Jipper and how Hettie stormed out.

"I hope you're not mad I had dinner with him," I add.

He gives me a half chuckle. "What? Just because that guy has more muscles—and mussels—than I've ever seen?"

I laugh, lifting my head.

"I knew you had things under control, that you wanted to eat with him for a reason. Besides," he continues, as he strokes the back of my head, "I trust you. I will always trust you." His eyes move from mine to my lips.

Then he's kissing me, pulling me tenderly against him. His lips are gentle but insistent as they part mine, begging for more of me. I respond. I kiss him back with an intensity that pulls me closer to him and sends sparks through my body, making me feel like lightning is striking down all around us. He entwines his fingers in my hair, not letting me go. The longer we kiss, the more I feel like I melt into him, that we could become part of the ocean around us, and I wouldn't even notice because he's the undertow and I'm helplessly caught in his grasp.

When we break apart, I'm breathless. I gasp as if the air bubble had collapsed and we had to swim back to surface.

He rests his head on mine. "We'll get through this. We just have to remember what we're doing this for."

I nod, trying to get my thoughts back in order.

I know what I'm doing this for. For Lagonia. For my father. For us. For moments like this.

But fighting with Hettie and dealing with Triton are more draining than I'd ever thought they'd be.

And we haven't even reached the island of gorgons yet.

>>>>>>>>>>◉<<<<<<<<<<<

$\mathcal{I}$ rise early the next morning, trying not to think about how we're one day closer to Dionysus reaching Lagonia's shores, how we only have three days left.

Hettie didn't say a word to me when she crawled into bed after me last night, and I don't think she'll feel up to sharing this morning either—so I sneak out before she wakes up.

The deck is deserted, probably because there's not much light to alert anyone the sun has risen. It's odd to arrive on deck and not feel a breeze tousling my hair or have the sea spray caressing my face. There's no comforting sound of waves crashing against the hull, assuring us we're moving forward. There's only a deafening silence that presses in from all sides.

"Mornings at sea are always so peaceful, aren't they?"

I turn to find Triton lying atop the ship's railing, staring at the ocean as light plays through the water above our heads. He's got one arm under his head and the other across his bare stomach.

"I've missed this—being out here *in* the ocean." He looks calmer than yesterday, as if being inside the sea instead of stuck in his palace has renewed him in some way. Like my father looks when he sits with his gold. "There's nothing like it."

"It's amazing," I reply, moving closer to him.

He sits up and turns toward the water, dangling his feet over the railing. "Even the breeze is gentlest in the morning, easing you into a new day."

"I used to love standing on my balcony, looking at the sea when the sun rose over it," I say. "It was the only time I felt free."

"How long were you locked away?" Triton asks.

"Ten years."

Triton laughs. "Try three hundred and sixteen."

"Three hundred?" I echo. "How did you stand it?"

"It wasn't so bad at first. I pulled ships toward my palace so that I had others to talk to, but soon I grew restless. In some ways, I became like Dionysus. I played games with the humans I drew to my palace. I offered them the riches of the Temptresses if they could complete impossible tasks. They always failed, and I was always left emptier inside because of it."

"You're not Dionysus, though you do understand him better than anyone," I say. "If we have any hope of getting him to tell us how to break my father's curse, it'll be because of your knowledge."

He looks away. "Don't make me out to be the hero. Dionysus is more likely to curse me on sight than to help us."

At that moment, a giant ball of kelp lands at Triton's feet.

Grax sticks his head through the air bubble.

The tangle of kelp squelches as Triton picks it up, oozing seawater over the deck. He heaves the mass far out into the ocean.

Grax leaps eagerly after it.

"To Grax, you're the hero," I venture, hoping to continue to edge him toward breaking away from the pains of his past.

"This is how I've entertained myself for three hundred years," he says, following Grax's path through the water with his eyes.

"Where did you find him?"

"My father created him for me as a gift when I was little."

Grax brings the mangled mess of kelp back and heaves it onto the deck. Triton does his best to shape it back into a ball before tossing it out again.

"Grax is the only one who never left me," he says. "Sort of like the friends you spoke about."

Before I can respond, he reaches for something resting by his side. "Here, I had Grax fetch this for you since I saw you didn't have one."

He hands me a small, rusty sword. "I thought you might need it for facing the gorgons."

I turn the blade over, inspecting it. Some sort of faded inscription lines the blade.

"Thank you," I say. "That was very kind of you." I guess he really did listen last night.

Triton starts to smile, but after a moment, his body tenses. "Good morning, Captain," he says, turning to face Royce.

I have no idea how Triton even heard him coming. Maybe spending all those years alone in a quiet, watery castle makes someone notice tiny sounds. Or maybe if someone's that lonely, they can hear anyone coming because they've become so used to listening for the sound.

"I see you didn't need a wakeup call this morning," Royce says, eyeing the sword in my hand but saying nothing.

"I always forget that you humans can't hear the rhythms of the sea," Triton says. "You could time your lives more accurately by them than the sun and stars. You'd be a better sailor if you could feel them."

"I take it you're ready to lead us to the gorgon's island, then?" Royce says.

"I'll eat my breakfast first," Triton says. "By the time your crew is assembled outside, I'll be done."

Several clams shoot out of the sea and land on the deck. They pile themselves in front of Triton. He picks up the largest and pries it open. "Look at that." His fingers delve into the shell and pull out an oblong pearl. He tosses it to me. "That's the first pearl I've found in three hundred years. Maybe luck is on our side."

As he strides across the deck, the clams bound after him.

The look of incredulity on Royce's face as the last clam hops down the steps to the sea floor after Triton makes me laugh.

Maybe we can survive this journey after all. Or at least survive Triton. Because a matching smile is spreading across Royce's face.

The second day of walking doesn't feel as strange as the first. I'm slowly getting used to the sky not being overhead and the lack of breeze. Although I still jump every time Grax swims above us, creating an ominous shadow.

Hettie still refuses to talk to me.

I try to pull her aside to talk, but she charges ahead of me without a word. She even surges past Triton. I'm about to call out to her to stop, but there's no point. She won't come back.

A heaviness settles over my heart. I'm finally making progress with Triton, but I'm somehow making things worse with her.

I sigh and watch a crab scuttle by, leaving a trail in the sand. Part of me wishes I could follow it wherever it is headed, but I can't. Instead, I keep my head down and keep walking, trying to think of a way to reach out to Hettie.

But by the time we stop for a break near midday, I haven't thought of anything to say to her. And she sits as far from me as she can.

Between us, Phipps and Lenny have a crab backed up against some coral.

"Don't let it escape, Lenny," Phipps says. "I'm starving." He dives toward the crab, but the creature scuttles into the sand beneath the coral and disappears.

"Triton take you," Phipps curses before going pale as he slowly realizes what he said.

Triton sits up from where he'd been lounging on a bed of coral, and everyone stills.

I hold my breath, not sure what to expect.

"I have no intention of taking that crab—or anything else anyone calls on me to take—anywhere," Triton says. "But it does seem like your mouth could use something to occupy it."

He wags his finger, and mounds of clams and mussels shift out of the sand at our feet. Triton's eyes land on mine for a moment, and I offer him a brief smile of thanks before he goes back to lounging around.

We break into groups and sit as we eat, and while the crew—especially Rhat—seems happy with the feast, something about eating seafood while under the sea still feels wrong to me.

"Not going to eat that, Princess?" Triton asks, strolling over and staring at the pile of oysters in front of me. "I can get you something else if you prefer."

"Thank you," I say. "I'm just not very hungry. I'm too worried about the gorgons." It's not entirely a lie. I am worried about them, but I'm also worried about how that seafood is going to settle in my stomach. "How far away are we?"

"Not far." He plops down in the sand next to me, letting his tall frame stretch out over the sand as he lies on his side. "My father imprisoned me very close so he could monitor both of us at the same time. He doesn't like gorgons any more than he likes humans. When they die, the snakes on their heads separate off and slither away into the ocean to colonize other islands. And they eat so many fish when they escape. We're just lucky that once they grow into full gorgons they can't live in water any-more. Their heavy tails would drag them straight to the bottom of the sea."

Royce leans around from my other side. "So what can you tell us about facing the gorgons?"

Triton smirks and summons some water, magically toss-ing it back and forth in his hands as he sits up. "First of all, don't face them. They turn whatever they look at to stone. Keep your eyes down. Or look through something that reflects things around you."

"There's a mirror in your cabin back on the ship," Royce says to me, "and one in the crew quarters. I think that's all we have on board. Maybe we could get those."

"Mirrors?" Phipps asks, the bit of oyster he was eating falling from his mouth. He goes pale and looks quickly to Lenny.

Lenny shakes his head at us, as if he's trying to tell us not to bring up mirrors. Though I'm not sure why.

"Mirrors break so easily," Phipps says hurriedly. "We shouldn't use them." He ducks his head and begins shoving food into his mouth again.

I open my mouth to ask why he doesn't like mirrors, to ask

what could be so frightening about them, but I figure he probably doesn't want to admit whatever it is in front of the rest of the crew.

I transfer my gaze to Lenny. His eyes have gone wide, and I can see the reflection of my gold skin in his pupils. I shrug, hoping he'll give me some sort of hint.

He stares even harder at me, tilting his chin down and looking up at me as if I'm missing something.

But I don't understand.

I used to hate mirrors because I didn't like my skin. I avoided them for years. But there's nothing different about the way Phipps looks. All he would see is his usual self.

Then it hits me.

Every time Phipps looks in the mirror, he's not just seeing his own reflection. He's seeing the ghost of his twin brother.

My heart breaks for him, and I fight to keep my voice steady as I change the subject. "Perseus used his shield."

Phipps relaxes slightly, sinking back into the sand as he shoves another handful of food into his mouth.

"My men aren't used to fighting with shields," Royce says, "and neither am I. They aren't practical to carry around and maneuver aboard a ship." Royce purses his lips. "But they might be our best option if we can find some." His eyes slowly drift to Triton.

"Why are you looking at me?" Triton asks.

"I thought you could use your powers to gather some shields from some nearby shipwrecks," Royce clarifies.

"Oh, now you want my powers again," he says.

But after a look from me, he clears his throat and sighs. "Fine. Sharks patrol the shipwrecks to keep other fish away. I'll ask some of them if they can find any shields inside."

We all sit quietly staring at Triton, waiting for him to act. But he just keeps tossing the ball of water back and forth, letting it squish against his hands, nearly coming apart as it stretches around his fingers before it reforms and slings back the other way.

"What?" he finally says when he notices us still staring.

"Are—are you going to talk to the sharks or something?" I prod.

"I already did." He points to his head. "One of them is having trouble fitting inside the tiny human-sized hole in the ship's deck, and he's waiting on his cousin to show up to help. The others are rummaging around as we speak."

"Oh," I reply. "I didn't realize . . ." I trail off.

He waves his hand dismissively. "You can go back to discussing how you are going to somehow not die on that island. It's going to be quite the spectacle. I might even watch."

"You're not coming?" I say.

The water splashes into the sand as Triton's eyes shoot up in surprise. "You thought I was joining you on that island?"

"I thought—" I simply assumed he was coming. "You're the only one who's faced them before, who knows what that island terrain is like. We could use your help."

But my attempt to flatter him and his ego goes nowhere.

Triton holds up his hands defensively. "I hate that island. I'll wait for you down here where it's safe."

"I guess you're not the all-powerful lord of the sea or whatever it was you said you were," Hettie challenges without bothering to turn around and face us from where she's sitting with Rhat.

"Listen," Triton says, "you don't know what it's like up there. It's smelly and desolate, and this fog emanates from these pools of—of—" He throws up his hands. "I don't even know what to call them. Mud is too clean for whatever is in there. Even the freshest ocean water takes hours to wash that smell off. The whole island is a death trap."

"If we die, you can't deliver us to Jipper and earn your freedom," I remind him.

"I don't know. My father might let me off on account of human foolishness."

"Or he'll think you led us to our death," Hettie throws back, finally turning to glare at him.

I can't decide if her comments are helping or hurting, and before I can make up my mind, shadows fall over her face. Then dark shapes burst through the air bubble and rain down around us, exploding into the sand.

Hettie screeches and ducks, curling into a ball in the sand. Men tumble over each other to get out of the way. Rhat dives just in time to avoid being crushed by one of the objects. He rolls away into the sand, landing in a crouch, eyes wide and chest heaving as he scans the area.

Dark objects continue to clink down all around us.

Royce throws himself atop me, covering me with his shoulders and forcing us both to land several feet away in the sand. I clutch against him, my hands circling around his back to hold him to me.

Over his shoulder, a dark shape hazes into view in the water above us. Then, droplets rain down as another object breaks through the bubble.

It's headed straight for Triton.

He's the only one who hasn't moved, sitting there as calm as a statue.

I'm about to scream for him to get out of the way when his hand shoots out and grabs the object, stopping it midfall.

A shield.

He inspects the circular edge, turning it over in his palm to reveal a crest with two waves crashing together over one center tower.

"Yes, these will do," he calls upward, and the rain of objects stops.

Hettie crouches on all fours, her hair dangling down over her face. "You did this?"

Triton tosses the shield onto the sand, where it clinks against another one. "You said you wanted shields."

"You could've warned us!" Hettie cries, scrambling to her feet. Rhat holds her back before she can even get close to our supposed benefactor.

Triton shrugs. "I told the sharks to drop them off. They aren't like octopuses, who can carry these things like those serving people you have. I didn't think they'd literally drop them through the opening, but sharks aren't the brightest."

"You could have killed us," Hettie steams, her cheeks taking on a red complexion. Rhat has his arms clamped tightly across her shoulders to hold her back as she tries to claw her way toward Triton.

Triton spreads his hands wide. "But I didn't. And now you have shields. So you're welcome."

Rhat leans down and whispers something into Hettie's ear. Her glare doesn't soften, but she stops struggling against him. She stomps off toward the edge of the air bubble, kicking several shields for good measure along the way.

Royce pulls me to my feet and starts inspecting the shields.

Some are round, others square. Some have crests with birds and spiders. Several have creatures I don't even have names for, with twisted heads and clawed wings. And many are too rusted to even make out what creatures are carved into the front.

I flip over the shield closest to me.

Where a shiny, unblemished underside should send back a distorted reflection of my face, a layer of rust clogs the effect.

I pick up another and another. They're all rusted on the back, thick patches of dark red crust clinging to the metal.

"Are any of them usable?" I ask.

Royce keeps searching. The crew jumps in. Phipps flips over shield after shield while Lenny moves along next to him, kicking the rejected ones toward the edge of the bubble. Hettie glares when he kicks one too close to where she's positioned herself to watch the scene. Lenny shrugs apologetically and keeps going.

By the time we've searched the hundred or so shields, only eight have a clean enough surface to send back a decent reflection.

Hettie finally pulls herself away from the edge and shoves through the crowd of sailors around us. She snatches up one of the good shields, scraping at a small patch of rust with her fingernail. "I'm taking this one."

Royce's eyes rove over the crew and then back down to the pile of useable shields. "We can't take the men onto the island without shields, so we'll have to leave most of the crew on the edge of the beach. We could leave four shields with them, and then you, Kora, Rhat, and I will take the other four onto the island."

I nod. Even though I'm pretty sure Prince Ikkin said a leader should stay away from the battle, protected—that they should be seen on the field as a sign of encouragement but not participate. But I can't do that. I'm the only one who can turn someone to gold if they get bitten.

"You can leave three shields with your men," Triton says, coming up and taking the shield with crest of waves crashing against a tower from the pile.

"You're coming?" I try to keep the hope from my voice.

He throws up his hands. "If you humans can barely survive some falling shields, if I want my freedom, I'll have to make sure you live long enough for me to get it." Several strands of seaweed shoot out from the ocean and tie themselves to either end of the handholds on the underside of the shield. Triton then hoists the shield onto his back, shiny side out, and uses the seaweed as makeshift straps to keep it there. "See—now you can see what's sneaking up behind us as I lead you across the island." He tilts back and forth for effect. "You're just lucky I can't be turned to stone. Otherwise I wouldn't be going anywhere near that place. But," he says as he climbs to his feet, "if you're foolish enough to want to, then we might as well get this over with."

With those words, the remains of our lunch bury themselves back into the sand.

Then Triton trudges off into the depths of the ocean, leading us straight toward an island full of gorgons.

CHAPTER 19

꣸꣸꣸꣸꣸꣸꣸꣸꣸꣸꣸❀꣺꣺꣺꣺꣺꣺꣺꣺꣺꣺꣺

The island looms large overhead. I can just make out the out-line of the rocky shore above us. Though we've been steadily climbing upward in the sand for the past hour or two, and I'm too out of breath to celebrate.

Even Hettie rests her hands on her knees and takes a few deep breaths as we gather at the base of the island.

I squint up through the sunlight filtering down around us. I haven't been this close to the surface—or the sun—in what feels like a lifetime.

"So here's the plan," Triton says, gathering us all around him. "If we can get a gorgon head or two, we'll just have to make it back with enough blood in them to drop into the sea." His face has lost his usual smirk. "The thing about gorgons is that they don't have a lot of blood in them to begin with, and you'll have to slice off the head because their necks are their thinnest, weakest point. If you manage to slice off a head, you'll have to turn it upside down quickly to prevent blood loss. Oh, and avoid looking it in the eye and avoid getting bitten by the snakes on its head."

My stomach rolls, but I try not to think about what we're about to attempt.

"We could stab our swords into the heads after we cut them off," Hettie says without the scorn I've come to expect. "Then we could carry them far enough away from our bodies so we wouldn't get bitten."

"That should work for carrying the head as long as the additional wounds aren't too deep," Triton says. "But as soon as you kill a gorgon, the snakes start separating from the scalp, leaving more holes for blood to escape. We'll have to move very quickly."

"Couldn't you use your powers to bring water with us?" Rhat asks. "Then we wouldn't have to carry the heads back."

Triton studies the surface above us. "It's worth a try, but it might not work. The water doesn't—it doesn't always react the same way when it's not part of the ocean itself. It doesn't have its full connection."

"It's still worth a try," Royce says.

"Then let's go," Hettie says.

"Wait," Phipps calls before dropping his voice to a whisper, as though the gorgons are right above us. "How are we supposed to avoid getting bitten?"

Triton closes his eyes as if pained and takes a deep, heavy breath. "Do whatever it is you do on a daily basis to not get bitten by your land creatures."

Phipps opens and then shuts his mouth. "Oh—okay."

With a twist of Triton's finger, another watery staircase appears. "Here we go."

Halfway up the stairs, a brown haze starts to clog the tunnel. It drifts down toward us, swirling around us like a ghost. It slides across my cheeks, down the bare skin on my hands, and then laces its way through my nostrils. The scent of rotten flesh mixed with the sharp scent of burnt hair floods through me. My nose feels like it's decaying just smelling it. Somewhere behind me, I hear someone vomit.

I shiver but force myself to keep climbing. I thought the sun would become brighter the closer we get to the surface, but it doesn't. The fog drowns out everything.

On the surface, dark rocks point up like fangs all along the shoreline and far out into the water. The water that pounds the coast has a layer of brown foam atop it—the same color as the cloudy fog around us. But the brown fog doesn't simply float on the water, it clings like oil to my skin.

"Welcome to Gorgon Island," Triton says.

Farther inland, loose rocks lead up to steep cliffs full of boulders. Boulders where anything could be hiding. I tighten my grip on my shield's handles. The rest of the island is swallowed by the fog.

Royce surveys the haze. "This looks as good a place as any to station the crew while we go inland."

"What should we do if we see a creature?" Phipps asks from where he's standing without a shield behind the rest of the men on a strip of brown sand beach.

"Don't look at anything but the water," Triton says. "If you have a shield, use it to see what's around. And if you hear one coming, swim a ways out. Gorgons can't swim."

"What do they sound like?" Phipps swallows.

"Hissing," Triton says. "Lots of hissing."

Phipps nods slowly, his hand on his sword hilt. He takes a few steps toward the water gurgling onto shore, motioning for Lenny to do the same. The men look frightened. Half stare at the ground, and half stare out to sea. No one wants to look into the brown fog we're about to enter.

We turn toward the dark mist. It creeps toward us, swirling around our feet and threatening to claim us. Bigger bits of brown dust and dirt float amidst the haze like stars unable to shine in such a toxic space.

I can't make out much in the murkiness besides some rock formations. I drop my eyes to the pebbles at my feet and run my hand along the back of my neck. My hair sticks to my skin and sweat runs down my spine. The island is hot, almost as if the fog itself gives off heat.

Next to me, Hettie's normally unruly hair has already started to deflate and stick to her forehead and cheeks.

"What are we waiting for?" She adjusts her grip on her shield and pulls out her sword.

"We should let Triton lead the way," I say.

She doesn't acknowledge my words.

At my side, Triton twirls his finger, summoning a pool of water to surround our feet.

"You can use the pool as another reflective surface," he says. "And if we're lucky, we can use it to make some pegasi."

Hettie trudges forward into the water without waiting. By some sort of magic, no ripples appear in the water.

We move slowly, all of us straining to hear hissing. I can't tell if the fog absorbs sound or if everything has gone quiet, like crickets do when something approaches.

Rhat and Royce both travel with their shields held high so they scan the reflected area around them.

I swallow and concentrate even harder on the water at my feet, finding it easier to look into than hoisting my heavy shield.

Although my eyes hurt from watching the world pass by upside down. Every shriveled shrub that comes into view sends my heart racing. I clutch my shield close to my chest and hold my sword out at the ready.

"Whoa," Royce cries, his hand shooting out to steady Triton, who's on the verge of teetering forward because one foot is submerged in a thick brown substance.

"I hate this island," Triton cries. He jerks backward over and over again without being able to free his foot.

"Here," Royce says, stepping forward to brace against Triton's side.

Together, they heave backward, and after a few tries, there's a wet sucking noise as Triton's foot slips free.

Both men stumble back, and Rhat puts up a hand to stop them.

"Thanks," Triton says to both with an acknowledging nod.

"What is that?" Rhat asks.

Before us, a bubbling, muddy pit is barely discernable from the rest of the landscape. Brown gas leaks out of it and clogs the air.

"Gorgons hunt around those pools," Triton says, "looking for things that get caught in them."

"What is there on this island for them to eat?" Rhat asks.

"There are a couple small animals, but mostly they eat each other," Triton says. "And anything stupid enough to come here, because as you can see, it's really hard to get out of these pools once you get stuck in one." He tries to shake the grime from his foot, but it doesn't come off.

I swallow, my throat dry. My tongue sticks to the top of my mouth. When I take in a deep breath, the scent of rotting, sweaty flesh is overwhelming. Every bubble that wriggles to the surface of the pool lets out another gust as we walk past.

Vomit crawls up my throat, and I gag it back down.

Then I hear the first hiss.

My body goes cold. The sweat sliding down my side sends chills racing across my skin.

In all this fog, it's impossible to tell where the sound is coming from.

*Hiss. Hiss. Hiss.*

Everyone stops moving.

*Hiss. Hiss. Hiss.*

The sound is all around.

"Get close," Royce whispers.

Everyone retreats to the center of the puddle. We stand in a circle with our backs to each other, each of us staring down or at our shields, waiting for a gorgon's reflection to appear.

Royce breathes heavily beside me.

The hissing gets louder, closer.

My heart hammers in my chest. I tighten my grip on my sword and raise my shield even higher, ready to cover my eyes.

"There!" Rhat cries.

I spin around to see the reflection of a gorgon lunging toward Rhat and Hettie.

The creature is easily taller than Rhat, with gray skin that looks like it could be made out of rock. The top part of the creature looks disturbingly human, minus the fingers that have been replaced with long claws. The bottom half is like a snake. Black rings circle around the thick tail at even intervals.

But the most frightening thing of all is the head.

Dozens of green snakes twist in all directions—some with small tongues diving in and out and others hissing and snapping their jaws, displaying sharp fangs. They curl around the gorgon's face and lash toward Hettie while she goes for the gorgon's midsection.

The creature lets out a terrifying screech that seems to echo off the fog around us, reverberating in our ears. I cry out and cover my ears. But the noise is already inside, bouncing around my skull, making me want to crumple into a ball and shake my head until the sound is gone.

Hettie's attack has done nothing, just as Triton warned.

In retaliation, the creature darts forward, arms out. Its claws splinter Rhat's sword as he brings it up for an attack, and Rhat splashes backward into the water to avoid the claws tearing through his stomach as well.

Royce moves forward to take his place. He advances backward, using his shield to guide him. He spins quickly, his sword screeching against the tough skin of the gorgon's arm before glancing off. While Royce readies his next blow, he doesn't see the gorgon's long tail whip around and wrap around his ankle.

"Royce!" I cry too late.

He jerks around, landing on his back.

The creature crouches over him. Right over his face. All the snakes stand on end and let out a screaming hiss as the gorgon's eyes let out some sort of light.

Royce shuts his eyes and tries to get his shield up for extra protection, but he doesn't move fast enough. Triton twists his hand and creates a barrier of water between Royce and the gorgon just to be safe.

The gorgon lashes her body around. Her tail crashes into Triton, sending him flying backward into the fog.

Royce has his shield up by the time the water above him splashes back down into the pool.

He swings his sword around wildly as the gorgon hunches over him again.

The gorgon raises her claws, but before she can strike, I stumble forward. My blade glances off her arm. She grabs it and presses downward, pushing my blade closer to Royce's chest.

The hissing snakes on her head snap inches from my ear.

"Keep your eyes closed," I shout as much for Royce as for me.

I drop my shield to grip the sword hilt with both hands, using all my strength to keep the blade from sinking another inch. I'm so focused on it, I don't see her other arm jerk straight toward me.

Hettie's shield knocks it away, and she quickly swipes at the creature's neck. But the creature pulls back, knocking me aside with its arm.

Jagged rocks cut into my back as I splash into the water beside Royce.

I roll over on my back so I'm not facing the gorgon, and I move to tell Royce to do the same. But his body is already rotating. Only, it's not a natural movement.

While Hettie and I were so focused on the gorgon's upper body, she'd been coiling her long tail around Royce, squeezing the life out of him. The tail's already up to his chest.

Royce takes ragged breaths. He's dropped his sword and shield and rips at the coils, trying to tear them from his body.

"Hang on, Royce," I scream, pulling at the tail. Thousands of tiny, dagger-sharp scales bite into my palms, ripping into my skin.

Rhat joins me, pulling at the coils, but he can't loosen them. They continue twisting Royce around and around as they choke the life from him.

Royce lets out a pained gasp as the tail closes around his neck. His face goes an awful shade of blue, like the water at the bottom of ocean we'd just left behind.

Rhat grabs Royce's sword from where he dropped it and leaps to his feet.

He and Hettie trade grunts as they ram their swords at the gorgon. Hettie ducks low, covering her face with her shield and going for the creature's neck, while Rhat wards off the gorgon's raging arms.

I shove my sword into the tail with no effect. I try to wedge it between the coils to pry them apart. When that fails, I try to get my sword between the scales, but they're too tightly packed.

"Triton, help me," I yell into the fog. But the god is nowhere to be seen.

Royce's face darkens even more as it disappears behind the last of the tail.

"No, no, no," I cry, dropping my sword. I dig my fingernails into the tail, barely noticing the scales ripping into my flesh. I claw at them until my fingers are covered in blood.

I grab my sword and climb to my feet, but without Triton to keep the puddle steady, I have to wait for the ripples to clear before I can make out the gorgon's shape.

One of her snakes nearly catches Hettie in the arm as she ducks out of the way and behind the gorgon.

I trudge forward, waving my sword to keep the creature's attention directed forward. I can't tell how close the beast is. The ripples make her close one moment and farther away the next.

I swing my sword upward and connect with nothing.

A rock flies from somewhere and crashes into the gorgon's head. The creature staggers to the side. Rock after rock hits her in the head. She shrieks as one snake goes limp and dangles down over her cheek. The other snakes grow frenzied, each trying to coil closer to her scalp for protection.

There's a sickening thwack from behind. Hettie's sword slices clear through the creature's neck, sending the head rolling.

"Don't look," Triton cries from somewhere.

I snap my eyes shut and back away from where I heard it land until Triton speaks.

"It's staring away from us," Triton says. I open my eyes to find him there with another rock in his hand.

Hettie impales the head on the end of her sword while I race to Royce. Rhat's already there. We fight to unwind him from the gorgon's grip.

When we finally unwind the last of the tail, he's not moving. His body rests lifelessly against the rocks, his skin a dusky purple color.

"Royce." I cup his face in my hands. "Royce." My voice rises unnaturally. A nauseous feeling starts in my stomach and crawls through my body with every second that passes. My breath catches in my throat.

Then there's a tiny inhale.

But not from me.

Royce's eyes flutter open. He struggles to take another breath.

"Royce!"

I collapse against him. He coughs, and I pull back.

He struggles to sit up, taking gulping breaths and cradling his ribs.

Then Hettie lets out a scream.

A burst of snakes explodes from the gorgon's severed head, slithering in all directions. There must be twenty of them.

Hettie kicks the skewered head free and starts slicing at the snakes around her ankles.

Royce and I rush to our feet, and I toss my sword to him, knowing he's better with it. I pick up Rhat's broken hilt and jab it into the middle sections of a few of the creatures while everyone else chops at the snakes, hacking into anything they can. Green flesh floats atop the water while a red stain inks into the puddle.

I crush one snake under my heel while Rhat slams his shield into another.

A snake rears up right behind Royce, fangs exposed and ready to bite. It shoots toward his calf, but a rock smashes into its head, crushing it.

My eyes jump to Triton. He picks up more rocks and launches them at the creatures with deadly accuracy.

Hettie brings her sword down with a reverberating clang, severing the head from the last wriggling snake. She takes big, gulping breaths. "That's gorgon blood, right?" She points to the water. "Where are the pegasi?"

Triton sighs. "I worried it wouldn't work. We'll have to drop a head directly into the ocean to meet all the necessary conditions." He stares at the head Hettie discarded. "But it might be better if we lure one closer to shore, because we'll need a new head."

"This one won't work?" Hettie looks down at the gorgon head surrounded by a pool of blood. When she stabs at it again and raises it up, eyes faced away from us, a few final drops of blood leak out, and then nothing.

Triton shakes his head.

Hettie slides the head off her sword with her foot. "All of that work wasted since we couldn't get the head back to the ocean in time," she mumbles.

I stare down at the water around us as it grows darker with

blood. Finally, I spot my shield and pluck it from the mess. The gorgon's tail must've hit it because it's bent in on itself.

Royce comes up next to me and strains his muscles as he tries to bend the shield back into its original shape, but it doesn't budge. He gives up with a grunt.

"Here, take mine," he says, handing me his from where he dropped it. Gorgon blood drips down the front of it.

"Royce—"

"I'd rather you have it," he says, cutting me off. "I fight better without it anyway."

I know he'll say anything he has to in order to get me to take the shield, so I slip my arm through the handles.

Triton separates some water from the pool and trickles it over the shield, rinsing off most of the blood. "We should head back to the shore. All this blood will attract other gorgons. One will probably follow us."

"Probably?" Hettie asks from where she's kicking snake bodies to be sure they're dead. "Didn't you think having this puddle of ocean would *probably* work? We shouldn't be retreating. We should be going out there and finding a gorgon so we can stop Dionysus."

"Maybe we should go back to the beach and regroup," Royce says, trying to defuse the tension.

"You're giving up?" Hettie cries.

"Hettie," I start, "we're covered in gorgon blood." Bits of it are splattered up and down her legs and arms while the rest of us are stained from rolling in the bloody water. "Rhat's sword is broken and one shield is crushed. We barely beat that creature fully armed."

"Fine," she says. She starts to stomp off in the direction we came from.

"Wait," I call, "we need to stick together."

But Hettie seems as bent as ever on ignoring my words, and before I can stop her, she disappears into the mist.

"Hettie," Rhat cries, but his voice is echoed by another one.

Hettie lets out a sound that I can only describe as absolute disgust.

We rush forward and find Hettie waist-deep in one of the mud pits. Splashes of gritty brown muck cover her arms, neck, and chin. She tries to struggle toward us, but the substance is thicker than honey—and looks stickier too. Chunks of rock sit on the surface, not yet having been swallowed by the sludge.

No waves appear as Hettie thrashes around. The pit almost manages to look like solid ground except where it creeps up around Hettie's waist, depositing gravelly bits on her shirt as she jerks up and down in the muck. When she finally manages to twist around, the look on her face is one of pure hatred.

Then her face pales.

It takes me a moment to realize why. A moment later I hear it. The hissing.

It reverberates through the air.

Then there is a sickening splash.

My body goes cold.

Without raising my eyes too far, I use my shield to see what's going on. I make out the torso of a gorgon pushing through the mud pit as if it were nothing more than water.

And it's headed straight for Hettie.

"Get out of there," Rhat shouts, his voice resounding louder than I've ever heard it. He kneels at the end of the pool and stretches his arm out to her. Her fingertips graze his, but they can't grab hold of each other.

My heart leaps into my throat, and I struggle to suck a breath in. My feet itch to move forward, to help somehow.

The gorgon is getting closer and closer.

Rhat moves to jump into the pool, but Triton holds him back. "If you get stuck, the gorgon will get you both before we can get you out."

Rhat shakes him off and kneels again. He stretches forth once more, his knees sinking into the edge of the pit, but he still fails to reach her. Hettie drops her shield into the muck and throws out her arm, straining against the unmoving goo.

The hissing gets more agitated, as if the snakes see their prey in sight and know a meal is coming.

And as Rhat fails again, a sinking feeling settles in my stomach. It'd been hard enough to get Triton's foot free. How much more force will it take to get Hettie out?

The hissing coils around my mind, creeping under my skin and through my veins, pulling tighter and tighter as the beast gets closer and closer. I find a rock on the ground and pitch it toward the gorgon, but without looking, the rock misses by an arm's length. I grab rock after rock, but the gorgon moves faster through the pit. Its sharp claws rise out of the pit, dripping sludge. They rake through the mud, propelling the gorgon forward even faster. It's closing in fast. Too fast.

Bile crawls up my throat as I imagine those claws digging into Hettie. I hurl another rock, but the creature stays focused on my cousin. On the prey that is trapped.

It opens its mouth and lets out a shriek, its claws nearly within striking distance. A few arm lengths away. A few seconds away.

My heart jolts. It takes a moment for it to start again. When it does, it pounds so loudly it almost drowns out the never-ending hissing, each beat a countdown echoing in my ears.

"Hurry," I cry, launching more rocks that end up swallowed by the muck.

Triton and Royce grab ahold of Rhat's arm and try to angle him toward Hettie. But Rhat keeps losing his footing on the edge of the pool, sending chunks of dirt into the mud. Royce and Triton fight to keep a grip on him as he nearly plummets face-first into the muck.

"Come on," Rhat roars frantically as he adjusts his feet.

I see the men working, making miniscule movements in the placements of their hands on Rhat. Each one trying to make sure he has the best grip despite the sweat clearly staining their palms. But they're not going to get Hettie out in time. The gorgon is too close. It's nearly there—each swish louder than the last.

Rhat loses his footing again.

"Try again," Hettie says, but her voice is forced. Her cheeks are bright red from the heat of the pit, and her hair sits limply on her head.

The gorgon's faint shadow falls over her.

She stills. She knows she can't turn around, but she can see the fear playing across our faces.

"Kora." Her voice is small, pleading. Her eyes search out mine. As she does so, her face becomes ghostly pale and her eyes widen.

The fear I see is crippling. I want to say something, to reassure her, but I feel as stuck as she is. All I can see is the gorgon's torso as it rises behind her.

She must see her own fear reflected in my face.

My heart clenches in my chest. This can't be happening. Not to Hettie. She's a fighter. She's always been able to get out of trouble. And I was supposed to save her from dying—from having the Oracle's vision come true.

I move to the edge of the pit. Bits of dirt crumble in under my feet. But my eyes aren't on them. They're on the gorgon's torso as it raises its sharp claw, readying for a killing blow.

I drag my gaze to Rhat. Tears stream down his face as he screams for Hettie to reach.

But no matter how hard she tries, she can't.

She seems to sense the blow coming. She steels her face.

"I love you," she whispers to Rhat as their fingertips brush each other.

Rhat cries out and tries to charge into the pit, but Royce and Triton pull him back before he falls headfirst into the mud.

The three men tumble backward.

I lock eyes with Hettie. But how can I watch her die? I drop to my knees, as they refuse to support me any longer. I want to melt into the puddle and disappear. And yet I can't look away as the gorgon's arm speeds forward.

Then an idea flashes through my mind, spurred on by the thought of a different puddle—the golden puddle Dionysus's henchman had left behind.

But I need gold. And I need it now.

Royce is too far away.

I bite my lip.

The seashell! The one I'd turned to gold after freeing Grax. The one I'd forgotten to give Phipps because so much else had been going on.

My hands tear at my pockets, fighting to get to the oblong

shape. My fingertips graze the metal, sending a surge through my body as I absorb the gold.

I shove my hand against the muddy pool, turning it instantly to gold. But was I fast enough?

My eyes jump up. The gorgon's claws falter a mere finger's breadth from Hettie's back as gold rears up all around the creature.

Hettie sucks in a tight breath as everything around her hardens.

Rhat's already on his feet and skidding across the golden pool before the gorgon gains its bearings.

"Duck," he yells at Hettie, who bends forward as he lops off the gorgon's head, spilling blood across the golden surface.

The rest of the gorgon's body slumps forward, nearly knocking into Hettie.

"Leave the gorgon's head," Triton says. "There's no use trying to get it back to shore. And if Kora changes the mud pit back, the snakes might sink in and get trapped in there."

Rhat kicks the head away and then makes it back to land. He manages to use the gold to lean far enough forward to get a grip on Hettie with one hand while Royce and Triton hold his other one.

"On three," I say, "I'll turn it back and you pull hard so Rhat doesn't get stuck too."

The others nod.

"One, two, three," I call. Then I press my hand back against the gold.

With a squelching, sucking sound, Royce and Triton pull back fast enough to keep Rhat from sinking into the pit, and he in turn pulls Hettie right along with him. They collapse in a pile while I grab a rock and transfer the gold. I stick it into my pocket and rise to my feet just as the others do.

Rhat wraps Hettie up in a tight hug, and she relaxes against him, tears slipping down her cheeks. She stays there a few long moments before she peels away from him and comes up to me, wrapping her arms around me. Her breath pulses hotly against my neck as she exhales. "I'm so sorry, Kora. Thank you."

She shudders against me, reaching up to wipe at the tears dotting her cheeks, but she only succeeds in smearing more goo across her face in the process.

"It's okay," I say, pulling her closer despite the heat radiating off her body. "We all want to find a way to get to Dionysus. And we'll find a way—together."

"We should get back," Triton says. "The sooner we get back to the ocean, the sooner we can get this crud off of us. Not to mention this pool of blood is probably what attracted that gorgon—and is now attracting every other creature on the island." He raises his hands up, separating the water from the blood and moving the pool over to a cleaner area.

Hettie pulls back slightly and nods down at me. And I think maybe things are finally going right. We may not have our gorgon head yet, but at least Hettie's talking to me. That's a start.

I smile up at her, dropping my arms. And that's when I feel it. Fangs biting into my ankle.

≫≫≫≫≫≫≫≫≫≫⊛⊰⊰⊰⊰⊰⊰⊰⊰⊰⊰⊰

# CHAPTER 20

I inhale sharply.

The fangs are like knives digging deeper into my skin, ripping through my flesh as they fight to break loose. But they don't break free. Searing heat shoots into my veins.

I force back a cry as the fangs finally release.

Concern washes across Hettie's face. "What's wrong?"

I look down, and a green snake slithers away from my feet. One of the snakes that escaped from the gorgon's head. One whose bite is fatal.

I swallow down the fear rising in my chest. Bitten. I couldn't have been bitten. But I feel blood trailing down my ankle, and my skin burns where the snake's fangs pierced. The heat doesn't just stop there, though. It rises through my body.

My eyes meet Hettie's, and I start to tell her what happened. But I hold in the words. I can't tell her.

Because the only one I can't save from a snake's poison is myself.

I stand there, the ever-increasing heat throbbing through my ankle. If I don't find Panacea or Hebe, I'm going to die.

Before I can think what to do, long hisses sound over my shoulder at uneven intervals. I don't have to look to know that not only are they close, there are a lot of them.

I find my voice. "Run."

Hettie nods and pulls me back toward the others. "Go, go," she calls.

We clump together in the pool as we run, but my ankle keeps giving out.

"Are you okay?" Royce asks, siding up to me as I trip forward for the fourth time.

My heart aches as I stare up at him. Not from the poison, but from the thought of being without him. Why hadn't I listened to Prince Ikkin's journal and stayed out of the battle?

*Because I'm not a good leader.* The thought slides through my mind. I shake it away. I chose this because I don't want to be that kind of leader. I want to be the kind that fights for my people, that protects them. That's what I was doing when I got bitten. And I wouldn't change that even now.

But how long did Triton say I had? A few days? Long enough to get us to Jipper. Long enough to save Lagonia. Or long enough to go after a cure. Just not long enough to do both.

A tangle of emotions steals through me at the realization. I shove them back down. Because it isn't a choice. Not to me. No matter what any journal or book says to the contrary, a good leader puts their people above themselves. I didn't have to read that to know it's true. I feel it with every fiber of my being, knowing I can't save myself and lose my people.

That's what a true leader is. And that's who I am. I'd give up anything for them.

That's when another realization settles over me. The Oracle had said the tests we'd faced in getting to her in some way mirrored what we would face in the future. And when I'd drunk from the water, I'd been faced with giving up everything—my golden skin, my powers, my relationship with Royce, even my very right to rule. Everything except my life. But those are the things that make up my life.

She knew I'd come here and get bitten. She was preparing me, testing me to see if I'd give up on my objective and take the easy way out or if I'd keep going, keep fighting to save Lagonia when it would result in losing everything I loved.

And I kept going then.

Something in that steels my resolve, ensuring me I'm making the right choice.

So as much as I want to tell Royce about the bite, I don't. I can't risk us losing even a single second arguing about possibly going for a cure. Because as the searing heat jets up from my ankle toward my knee, something tells me I'm going to need every second if I want to save Lagonia.

"I must've just twisted my ankle on a rock," I say, thankful I can keep my eyes on the pool of murky water.

"Stay close," he says. "Lean on me if you need to."

I nod. I've never lied to him like that before, and I can't tell if I'm imagining a funny taste in my mouth after saying the words.

"There are so many of them," Hettie yells.

Their tails flick small rocks to the side as they slither behind us, and the hissing becomes overwhelming the closer we get to the shore.

"What are we going to do?" Rhat asks. "Should we swim for it?"

I shake my head. That won't get us the blood we need, and we need that blood fast. As fast as we can get it.

But how can we face so many at once? Too bad we can't crush them all as easily as we did the snakes on their heads.

Or maybe we can.

"Keep leading them to the shore," I say. "I have an idea."

We quicken our pace and surge through the fog. The shore-line rears up ahead of us.

The crew leaps up at our appearance.

"Quick," I call, "everyone up the hills. We can crush the gorgons with those boulders if we can get them loose." With any luck, we'll crush the snakes on their heads right along with them.

Men start scrambling up the rocky slopes. Pebbles rain down in their paths as they fight upward toward the bigger boulders.

"Kora, come on." Royce holds his hand out to me as he dashes toward the cliffs.

I don't make it more than a few steps upward before pain sears through my ankle. I cry out and drop to my knees. I land on jagged rocks and inhale sharply as more pain blossoms.

Royce is there in an instant. "Are you okay?"

"Just my ankle," I manage. I stare up the incline, each loose rock looking like an obstacle. "I don't think I can make it up there."

"I'll carry you." Royce moves to pick me up, but I stop him.

"You'll barely be able to get up there yourself."

We both look to where the men are fighting their way upward, some sliding down when they lose their footing.

The hissing is getting closer and closer.

Royce glances toward the fog and then back up the hill, no doubt trying to calculate if he could get both of us up.

I bite my cheek, searching for a plan, another option.

"I'll stay with her," Triton says to my surprise. "I can signal your men when to release the boulders from here."

"You'll both be crushed when the rocks come down," Royce counters, his chest still heaving from jogging across the island.

Triton gestures to the water at his feet. "There is just enough here that I can turn it into an ice dome to protect us."

Behind us, rocks scatter as the thick gorgon bodies crush them under their immense weight and brush them aside with their tails.

Royce looks between Triton and me. "Are you sure about this?"

I don't see another option, and I want Royce as far from the gorgons as possible.

I nod. I slide off the shield he'd given me and hand it back to him. "Be careful."

He clenches his jaw but doesn't say anything else. He sprints toward the slope.

Triton helps me settle down into the rocks. "Thanks for staying with me," I say.

"That's what human friends do, right? Stick together?"

I smile up at him. "I think you might be catching on."

"Or maybe I didn't think anyone else would still go after Dionysus if you didn't make it, so it's in my own interest to stay." He gives me a teasing smile.

But his words settle over me. Would the others go on if I didn't make it? I'm not sure. I hope they would, but I had always planned on being the one going up against Dionysus. And I'm not sure how the others will fair against him.

All I can do is hope I last until I can face him. I have to.

"You'd best look toward the hill," Triton says, all his usual cockiness gone. "I'll give the signal to the crew when the gorgons are close enough."

I nod and stare back toward the rocky slope. Men wedge

themselves against boulders. Hettie and Rhat brace against a particularly large rock, pushing it back and forth to be sure it's loose enough to knock over. Lenny is lying wedged between the ground and a boulder, ready to shove it with his feet when the time comes.

They're all up there fighting for Lagonia, and I can't let them down. I brace myself against Triton and close my eyes.

The throbbing in my ankle wells up. My heart races faster, as if it knows it only has so many beats left. My breathing drowns out the sound of rocks crunching under twisting bodies as the gorgons slither closer.

Hissing presses in from nearly every side. It sends tingles through my skin and causes my hair to stand on end.

Triton goes still.

They're close. Sweat trickles down my back. I tense, waiting for his signal, waiting for the cascade of boulders.

Rocks scatter to my right then off to my left. They're too close.

"Triton," I whisper, not daring to open my eyes.

"Not yet."

The hissing twists through my body. It weaves through my veins and pulses under my skin.

I can only imagine that long claws are racing toward me. But I don't dare look.

Triton lets out a shrill whistle.

Then he's pulling me close. A gurgle of water signals the barrier going up. There's a sharp crack as it hardens into ice around us. My breath goes cold in my lungs.

There's a small sound, like the soft plinking of rain. Then the boulders come crashing down.

An endless thunder rumbles across the earth. The ground shakes beneath us, sending pebbles bouncing into the air.

A boulder crashes into our ice dome. I can't help opening my eyes at the sound of cracking ice. Shards rain down on my head, melting against the heat of my body. Above me, a slice is missing, revealing the hazy brown sky through splintered cracks.

Triton melts water from a different area to repair the crack as another boulder smashes into the side of the dome and glances off. The dome rattles.

I dig my fingers into the dirt as I fight to stay anchored to something. My breath comes out in white puffs. I swallow, my throat dry from the heat of the island and aching from the cold of our cave.

Gorgon shadows loom large through the cloudy ice. Some screech as boulders smash into them and they disappear from view. Others let out battle cries, their voices gurgling deeper before rising sharply over and over again.

I tuck in closer and closer to Triton as our ice dome keeps getting smaller and smaller as bits break off and Triton fills the cracks with water from other areas.

A gorgon circles around our dome and drags her claw along the ice. Her tail lashes into the side, sending a sickening groan through our shelter.

I don't know how much more the dome can take—and how long until the ice is so thin, I'll be able to see straight through it. Straight into the gorgon's eyes.

Despite the ice, sweat drips down Triton's forehead. He frantically waves his hands around again as the gorgon's tail smashes through.

We need a plan. I don't have a good sword. But I have small rocks. And I have my powers.

I grab the gold rock from my pocket.

"Next time the tail breaks through," I say, "don't fill up the crack."

"Are you crazy?" Triton's eyes are wild.

"Trust me."

A piercing screech fills the air. It's followed by a gorgon tail knocking away the top half of the dome.

Before I can rethink my plan, I dive through the opening and come eye to eye with a gorgon.

# CHAPTER 21

I'm not sure what I was expecting a gorgon's face to look like, but it's much more human than I imagined. There's an oval mouth, bigger than a normal human's, full of fanglike teeth. There are two slits for a nose and two round eyes.

Eyes that are now frozen.

I can't help but study them, wondering what they would've looked like if they'd been the last thing I ever saw. They're two blank circles, like unminted gold coins. There aren't any eyelids, and I wonder if gorgons can blink.

I pull my hand away from where I'd crashed into the gorgon. I duck around the body, careful not to touch it and reabsorb the gold.

Royce comes skidding down the hill screaming my name.

He cuts through snakes wiggling across the rocks as they escape from crushed gorgons.

Hettie and Rhat aren't far behind.

Triton climbs out of what's left of the dome and lets it melt. "Stay here. Let me check if it's safe."

He studies the battlefield, squinting into the fog.

"Did we get them all?" Hettie asks breathlessly as she slides down next to Royce.

Rhat holds up his shield so we can survey the scene behind us.

Triton roves around, stomping on a few escaped snakes and checking behind boulders. "It's all clear," he says. "There's one gorgon crushed over here whose head is sticking out." He kicks the head so the eyes face away from us.

Just as he does, a gorgon lunges out of the fog.

"Look out," I exclaim just as Rhat rips the shield away, cutting off my view. He heaves the shield with deadly accuracy. It spins through the air, slicing right into the gorgon's neck. The creature's head rips backward as the metal lodges into its throat. The head doesn't detach, but it's enough to send the beast crumpling to the ground.

"Nice shot," Triton says just as more hissing sounds farther inland.

"Let's grab a head and get out of here," Royce cries.

He signals for the men.

"Oh, come on," Phipps says, sliding down the mountain with Lenny at his heels. His eyes land on the golden gorgon. "This one's too big to carry too. Can't you ever turn a small creature to gold?"

"Maybe next time," I reply.

"Here's the head we can use," Triton calls, straightening from where a gorgon's body is crushed, leaving the shoulders and head exposed. Triton has again already turned the head away from us with his foot. But the snakes still attached to it are squirming, trying to snap at him.

"How are we going to get it into the water?" I stare toward the edge of the sea, about a ship's length away from us.

"I think I know someone who can help with that," Phipps says.

He pushes Triton to the side with great fanfare and makes sure Lenny is a few steps behind him.

He nods to Lenny, then he chops off the gorgon's head.

Before any snakes can escape, Phipps leaps out of the way and yells, "Now, Lenny."

Lenny takes a few running steps forward and kicks the gorgon's face. The head spirals into the air and drops down into the ocean with a satisfying plunk.

"Taught him to do that myself," Phipps said.

We all wait, watching where the head disappeared. The first things that surface are loose green snakes. They bolt off in all directions. Grax crashes to the surface within seconds. He starts chasing down the snakes one by one, slurping them up with a satisfied grin.

A giant gurgle of bubbles billows up where the head disappeared into the ocean. Shapes burst out of the water. Great winged shapes.

Pegasi.

They're a rich red color. Bloodred. And taller and wider than normal horses.

They fly in a circle above us before floating back to land.

The winged horses land regally on the ground, their black hooves clicking against the rocks. Somewhere around thirty of them prance around, picking their feet up to avoid the uneven rocks and shaking specks of dirt from their glorious hair.

But it's their wings that demand attention. Each is larger than I am tall, and every feather glints like the ocean water when the sun hits. The pegasi fold their wings against their bodies and stand there waiting—which is not something I want to be doing as the hissing echoes closer.

"We should grab them before they fly away," I call.

"No need," Triton says. "Pegasi belong to the one who created them."

Everyone looks to Lenny, but he and Phipps are hunched over another gorgon, whose forehead is barely visible beneath the rock that crushed the rest of its body. All the snakes have escaped the head.

But when Triton's words reach them, the brothers straighten.

A wide smile stretches across Lenny's face as the realization dawns. He and his brother share a look, then Phipps takes off, hooting and hollering toward the closest pegasus.

Lenny buries his head in a pegasus's hair while Phipps has his arms looped around its neck, kissing it over and over again.

Triton snorts and rolls his eyes. "They act like they've never seen a pegasus before."

"They haven't." Hettie, who's gotten a sword from someone, lobs off the head of an escaped snake and kicks its body away as she searches for more.

"They've seen me," Triton quips, leaning against the nearest pegasi. "And we're half-brothers." He stares down the creature. "Although, I think I got all the good looks in the family."

The pegasus snorts and turns its head away.

Somewhere rocks scatter.

"Hurry," Royce says, "before more gorgons show up or someone gets bitten."

I duck my head.

Phipps helps Lenny climb onto the closest pegasus, then heads to the next creature and clambers ungracefully on. He beams like a king from atop the proud beast, unable to stop himself from running his fingers through the creature's mane.

The other crew members quickly do the same, eager to

be away from the island. There's more than enough pegasi for everyone, and I assume the rest of the herd will follow when we take off.

I spend a few moments brushing my hand along the closest pegasus's nose. Pegasi may be magical creatures, but they look too similar to all the horses that used to rear when I got too close with my gold skin.

This pegasus doesn't seem bothered at all. It leans into my touch, nuzzling me. Its hair is soft and plush, almost like silk.

I pat it on the nose, and Royce helps me mount.

It's nothing like sitting atop a horse. This creature is wider, and it's harder to figure out where to put my legs because of the wings.

I wince as my ankle settles into place.

"Are you okay to fly? Do you want me to take a look?" Royce asks, noticing my distress.

His eyes are scrunched in concern, and his hand is so gentle where it rests on my knee, rubbing in small circles. His eyes are so kind, so full of concern—so full of love. Love I was just getting used to. Love I don't want to lose.

My resolve weakens, and the words are on the tip of my tongue. Maybe he and I could take these pegasi to look for Panacea. Triton could lead the others to Jipper. If he helped us with the pegasi, then maybe he'll stay and help them fight Dionysus in my place.

I close my eyes and take a deep breath.

I can't. There's no guarantee we'd even find Panacea anyway—especially without Triton. And Lagonia needs me. The vision of Royce and Hettie dying plays over again in my mind. I can't let Dionysus reach our shores. No matter the cost.

I open my eyes and take his hand, giving it a squeeze. "No, it's fine now."

More hissing cuts through the mist.

"We should hurry," I say.

The creases around his eyes soften, but before Royce lets go of my hand, a commotion draws our attention.

Triton sits astride one of the tallest creatures, and the pegasus is prancing back and forth beneath him, tossing its fiery mane from side to side.

"Oh, fine, I didn't mean what I said earlier," Triton finally admits. "You look very regal. Just stop prancing."

The pegasus keeps kicking its feet up.

"And you are also beautiful."

The pegasus gives its head one final, satisfied shake.

Triton looks up to see us watching. He immediately straightens, his cheeks reddening. "Just a little family misunderstanding."

The creature snorts.

Triton ignores him.

"Thank you," Royce says to Triton as he mounts his own pegasus, "for saving me back there and for helping Kora."

Triton gives Royce a brief nod. "Of course."

Royce offers a small smile in return.

Hissing sounds from several sides.

"Save the thank yous for later," Hettie says. "They're getting closer."

In response, Triton calls, "Lead us out, Lenny. Once everyone's above the clouds, I'll let you know what direction to go."

The pegasus's wings unfold and jut outward. Then the creature leaps into the air, big, swooping flaps blasting us all with wind.

The other pegasi quickly follow suit. I twine my fingers into my pegasus's mane and hold on tight. There's time for one breath, and then we're launching into the air.

After a few moments, we break through the smog of the island. Crisp, fresh air washes over me.

Others break through after me, leaving holes in the brown cloud below as we congregate above the island.

The view is magnificent in the midday sun. Sunlight glints off the water all the way toward the horizon, as though the entire sea is made of diamonds.

It's so much like the sunrises I used to watch from my palace balcony.

A lump rises in my throat at the prospect of never returning to Lagonia. Of never seeing my father again.

Tears leap to my eyes.

I close my eyes and take a big breath of the clean air, hoping it will help calm me.

"Is it your ankle?" Royce asks, bringing his pegasus close.

I discreetly wipe at the tears. "It's just so beautiful," I say.

He doesn't take his eyes from me. "It is."

I blush as I turn away to watch the sun sparkle on the ocean water. And I try to pretend that it's not glistening the same way on the tears falling even more forcefully down my cheeks.

# CHAPTER 22

》》》》》》》》》》◉《《《《《《《《《《《

F lying through the air is like nothing else in the world. It feels as though my entire body has been replaced with air. Cool wind tangles around me as I lean in close to the pegasus's neck. Every *thwap* of the creature's wings echoes the thunder of wings around me.

We're like a giant red cloud gliding through the sky. Some men cling to their mount's neck, eyes clamped shut while they mutter what might be prayers.

Others, like Phipps, have their arms thrown out wide, letting the wind run over them as they laugh. I half expect him to try standing on the pegasus's back next.

We head away from the gorgon island and fly out to sea, toward where Triton expects Jipper to surface. But we have a lot of distance to cover.

Eventually, the sun sets, turning the sky around us into an imitation of the sunrays imprinted on the seashell around my neck. Deep pinks and light reds drip around us, cradling us into the evening.

They're the same colors creeping up my leg. When the itching started around my bite, I'd taken a look. At first, I thought the maroon coloring on my skin might be a reflection of my pegasus's hair, but I can feel it in my body, a rising heat slowly pulsing outward. It clenches at my stomach and throbs through my head. Sweat dots my brow, only to be whipped away by the wind. If it weren't for the breeze, I'd be burning up.

I take slow, long breaths as pain sears through my chest. I focus on the horizon, on the darkening sky, as stars melt into view.

I count the stars over and over again to keep from closing my eyes, from letting the burst of fire that rises every time I close my eyes consume me.

But as calming as I find the stars, I know someone who doesn't enjoy their presence.

My eyes go to Royce, and I urge my pegasus closer to his.

He used to dream the stars would fall from the sky and turn into coins—the same coins that buried his father after he'd wished for a pile of money so big he'd never see the top of it.

"They can't hurt you," I say loud enough for him to hear me over the beating wings.

Royce extends his hand out to me.

I lean over to grab it, but my body seizes beneath me at the sudden movement. My head spins and my stomach tightens. Warmth curls through me.

I look at him, a small gasp escaping from my lips as pain paralyzes every inch of me.

One minute my legs are tucked around the pegasus, the next the world spirals around me and I'm falling.

Somewhere, someone is screaming.

The sea and sky blur together, one unending loop of twisted blue. Gusts tear through me, ripping my arms away and then flinging them back. My legs kick uselessly against the air. I fight to gain control of my body, of what's happening, but I can't fight the torrent of the wind.

I can't even scream as my breath gets ripped from my body. The ocean rears up below me, ready to swallow me.

I close my eyes, letting the poison's heat flood through me. Then I crash.

I expect the pain to be immeasurable, but the toxin dulls it. My chest contracts, and I realize I'm not drowning. I'm breathing. My eyes fly open.

Somehow, Royce caught me. He holds me tightly against him. "It's okay. I've got you," he says as his pegasus recovers from its steep dive by skimming its hooves across the water before arcing back upward.

I cling to Royce as we clear the dangers of the dark waves and bury my face against his chest, barely even noticing the gold buttons on his jacket as I try to steady myself and slow my rushing heartbeat.

He smells like the island, all dirt and mud, but beneath that, there are hints of the saltiness of the sea. I breathe it in, willing it to force back the nausea welling up in my stomach.

As the pegasus decelerates to a gentle hover, Royce pulls back to look down at me, his eyes quickly scanning my face. "Are you hurt?"

"I'm all right. Thank you," I say, taking a calming breath. "I must've— I must've gotten dizzy so high up."

"Is she okay?" Triton questions, the loud thundering of pegasi wings signaling his arrival along with Hettie and Rhat.

"She's all right," Royce confirms, and Triton visibly relaxes back against his pegasus while Hettie lets out a relieved sigh and shares a reassuring look with Rhat.

"Do you want to stop for the night?" Triton asks.

I shake my head. I can't let them stop. We barely have two

days before Dionysus reaches Lagonia. And I don't know how long I have. "No, I'm fine now. We should keep going as long as we need to tonight."

Triton studies me for a moment, and I think he'll see through my lies. But slowly, he nods. "All right. We'll keep going."

"Why don't you ride with me until we stop, then?" Royce says to me.

I nod. Not only do I not want to risk falling off again, but maybe this way I can save some energy by not having to focus on staying alert atop my pegasus. "Thank you."

"I'll always be here to catch you when you need it," Royce says, planting a gentle kiss on the side of my head. "And I'd carry you to the ends of the earth if you needed me to." Then he urges his pegasus higher as the others do the same to rejoin the herd thundering across the sky.

I release a breath and soften against him as we take our place amongst the cloud of pegasi, but the constant pounding of wings makes my head throb. I snuggle closer to Royce's chest, trying to drown out the noise by focusing on finding his scent again beneath the stench of the island. But the wind steals it from me, leaving me nothing to concentrate on besides each new blossom of pain caused by every jostle of our pegasus.

I fixate instead on keeping my arms locked around Royce as he cradles me, on how truly grateful I am to have found him, to have someone who's willing to catch me when I fall, to carry me onward when I need it most.

But that thought sends a sudden recollection spiraling through my mind—one that must have been jogged loose by Royce's words.

The Oracle tests.

Specifically, the one Royce figured out about picking out and carrying the most valuable thing you could find in the cave. The Oracle had said that test proved we'd carry each other when we couldn't carry ourselves. I hadn't thought she'd meant it literally, but as more pain snakes up from my ankle and bites its way into every muscle, I have a feeling I'm going need him to carry me a great deal more than I ever could have expected in the coming days.

And I know he'll do it, that he'll carry me anywhere, but I also know those moments I'll spend clinging to him—and this one right here—might be some of our last few close ones.

Tears prick at the corners of my eyes, but I blink them away. I chose this.

So I don't waste time. I melt into him, feeling every movement of his body, memorizing how my arms feel wrapped around him, enjoying just resting against him, wishing I never had to let go.

Still, it seems all too soon, all too unfair, when Triton calls, "I've created a sandbar over there with more weapons for those that lost theirs. We can rest there for the night."

Royce's pegasus touches down lightly on the sandbar. He slides off, holding me against him, and lays me gently onto the sand. He smooths back my tangled hair as I reluctantly release my grip on him.

"How are you feeling?"

"Fine." I force a smile and hope he doesn't hear the weakness in my voice.

"Are you sure you're okay?" he asks. "You look flush." His hand goes to my cheek.

I put my hand over his, pulling it away before he can feel the heat there. "Must be windburn."

Next to us, Phipps slides off his pegasus and helps Lenny down. Then he starts shouting orders, telling everyone to brush down the pegasi as best they can with their fingers. "I want their coats to shine. These guys need to be in top shape."

Royce rolls his eyes. "I better go deal with those two before the crew turns on them." He gives my hand a squeeze before heading toward Phipps.

As much as I want to call him back, to have him stay with me, I don't. I let him go.

Triton takes his spot, settling into the sand and staring out toward the dark waves lapping at the edge of our temporary oasis.

"Looks like you humans don't get sea legs or air legs under you easily," he jokes.

"Very funny," I say.

"I thought it was funny," Triton says. "And you would've too if you weren't in pain."

I sigh. Maybe yesterday I would've thought it was funny, would've seen that he was trying to be friendly. But right now, I'm just trying to hold myself together and upright while the rest of my body screams to curl up into a ball and wait for the pain to stop.

"If it's swollen, maybe I can wrap it in some water to cool it," he says.

"No," I reply, trying to hide the bite under the hem of my pants, but Triton's already sent a trail of water to lift up the edge.

"No objections, and don't say I'm breaking the rules," he says playfully. "This is one of those 'friends things' where they do kind things for each other. I think I am getting the hang of it.

Turns out all it takes is for me to do for you what I would do for me—well, what I would do for me if I had a weak, human body like . . ." He trails off and stills as his attention lands on his handiwork. Something shifts in his eyes. The usual light that plays there dims, and his smile sinks. His eyes drag to mine. "When did it happen?"

"After we helped Hettie." I don't meet his gaze. I busy myself fixing my hem over the anklet of water wrapped around my skin, the one that does bring a tiny cooling sensation with it.

"You know what this means?" His voice is still, unnatural.

I nod.

"It's not too late, Kora. We can take the pegasi and look for Panacea."

"No." I latch on to his arm, forcing him to meet my stare. "Dionysus will destroy Lagonia—maybe even the whole world if he frees the Titans. We have to go after him. We have to stop him. We only have two days until he reaches Lagonia."

"You only have a few days before that poison kills you. If you go after Dionysus, you'll die."

I look away. "I know."

"The others aren't going to agree to this."

I stiffen. "They can't know." My eyes drift to where Royce is helping some of the more frightened crew members off their pegasi. "Promise me." I pull my gaze back to Triton. "Promise me you won't tell them."

"Kora—"

"You know what it's like to rule. They don't. I have to do this for my kingdom. For them. I can't put my life above theirs."

Triton purses his lips and transfers his gaze out to the ocean.

He thinks for a long moment before he finally says, "All right. I promise."

I relax my grip on his arm. "Thank you."

There's a blankness to his face as he picks up a handful of sand, weighing it in his palm for a while before he speaks again. "You know"—he turns slowly to face me—"you were wrong about human friendship after all."

"How?" I ask.

"Because—" His voice breaks, and he pauses before starting again. "Because they do end. Because you're all made from sand and dust and fade away in the blink of an eye." He flings the sand as far as he can into the dark water, and if I'm not mistaken, tears glisten in the corners of his eyes as he turns back to confront me, his voice hoarse. "Why aren't you like the other humans I've met, who care more about themselves, about their own lives? Why don't you try to save yourself?"

I drop my gaze and swallow down the lump forming in my own throat. "I can't. My country is counting on me, and I might be the only one who can stop Dionysus. And I have to stop him at any cost."

He shakes his head, his loose hair tumbling forward to cover his eyes. "Do you really think you can beat him? He's the greatest trickster of all time. Even I couldn't beat him, remember?"

"I have to at least try," I say.

He pulls his knees in close to his chest, staring down between them toward the grooves his toes left in the sand. "Then I hope you beat him," he says. "I really hope you do."

The waves gently lap at the shore around us, filling in the silence.

But I don't have time for silence. Not anymore. I need every bit of information I can get out of him about facing Dionysus—not to mention something to take my mind off thinking about the pain throbbing up my leg.

"How many bets did you lose to him?" I ask.

He frowns. "More than I care to count. But there's one I wish I could take back more than all the others."

"The one where you bet your father's ocean?" I say.

"I regret that, but that's not the one."

"Which one, then?"

"The one I told you about the other night. About the Temptresses." He shakes his head. "Every day, I regret what happened to those women. I mean, I knew they'd become Temptresses if they fell in love with me, but I didn't know that Dionysus had made it so women would find me hard to resist and be tricked against their will, enamored to the point where if they weren't in love with me yet, they would be soon enough. I couldn't figure out why it was happening at first. But I tried to do what I could for them each time. I sent them away from the world, where I thought they couldn't do much harm."

"How exactly did he word the bet?" I ask.

"Let me think." Triton runs his hands through his hair. "I bet him I could make any human fall in love with me, and if I did, I could pick anything I wanted from his collection—from the things he'd won from the other gods and goddesses. But if I lost, he got to alter what happened if someone fell in love me, or me with them."

"So how'd you lose the bet?"

"Dionysus always has a trick up his sleeve. He brought a woman to his island. A dead woman. He told me to make her fall in love with me, which was impossible." He digs his toes into the sand. "Don't underestimate him. There's always a catch in his words, some loophole he'll slip through."

"So how do we beat him?" I ask, resisting the urge to rub my throbbing ankle.

Triton lies back, cradling his arms under his head. "I've been pondering that for three hundred years."

There's a low whining sound, and Grax shuffles out of the water, dropping a stick at Triton's feet.

Triton sits up and takes the piece of tangled driftwood, turning it over in his hands before launching it back out to sea for his pet to chase.

"I'm hoping to get close enough to turn him to gold."

Triton clasps his hands across his bent knees and shakes his head. "I've always heard that the creatures Dionysus curses can't use their powers against him."

I slump forward, a sinking feeling flooding through me. That had been the one plan I'd been counting on to work.

But if I couldn't do that, what could I do?

"There's got to be some way to weaken him or trap him. What about those bad grapes you mentioned?" I say.

"Dionysus is no fool. The only way to really weaken him would be to capture his staff—but don't count on that. He's never let me even touch it before. And only he can wield it anyway."

I weigh a handful of loose sand in my palm, letting it drain between my fingers. "We'll have to outsmart him, then."

"Good luck with that."

"Good luck with what?" Royce says, coming over and sitting down on my other side.

"Finding a way to outsmart Dionysus," Triton replies.

"There's got to be a bet or something he would take.

Something we could win." I pour the remaining sand from my hand back onto the shore and stare out at the dark waves. But no matter how long I sit there, I can't come up with anything Dionysus couldn't counter.

I bury my face in my hands.

"We'll think of something. We've got time," Royce says, rubbing his hand across my back. "Didn't we outsmart the Oracle's tests?"

I nod slowly, thinking back to the crystal challenge and how we'd had to read between what was written on the sign to figure out how to pass. Sure, we'd eventually figured it out, but we also weren't up against a god with near limitless powers.

"I bet I could outsmart him," Phipps says, plopping down in the sand, Lenny at his heels. "There's not a deal I can't get someone to make." Phipps's eyes swing to Triton and a familiar grin passes over his face. He nudges Lenny and then clears his throat. "Speaking of deals . . ." He straightens, looking at Triton. "It seems like you've got a lot of human junk littering the bottom of your beautiful ocean. If you wanted to just sweep it up in a wave and deposit it on land, I would take care of disposing of it for you. All those sunken ships and everything. We could clean the whole ocean right up together."

"You mean all those ships full of jewels and cases of gold and other goods that are just lying useless on the sands of my ocean?" Triton asks.

Phipps smiles widely, nodding along.

"Not a chance," Triton says.

"Just one ship?" Phipps ventures.

"I could cause barnacles to grow all over your face, you know," Triton says.

And while in the past I may have taken him at his word, I can tell by the upturn of his lips that he's joking.

Phipps waves his hands in defeat. "All right, all right. No ships." His eyes gleam. "How do you feel about pearls?"

"Phipps," Royce says, groaning in unison with the rest of us.

"Fine, tough crowd," Phipps says, shoving a clam into his mouth that Triton had just summoned for dinner. "No one understands that with Thipps gone, I've got to work twice as hard to pull off my business ventures. None of them have worked out since he—since he—"

Lenny nudges him, his brow furled. He nods toward the pegasi.

"No, Lenny, those are yours."

Lenny stares at him, motioning toward the winged horses once more before gesturing between himself and his brother.

"You'd really let me start a flying horse show with them?"

Lenny nods eagerly.

Phipps smiles down at Lenny, and I think I spot tears in his eyes as he pulls him close for a hug.

"Don't I have the best younger brother?" Phipps shouts. He holds his brother so tight he nearly strangles him. Lenny pushes against him with his legs to extricate himself.

Phipps laughs and releases him. "Things are finally looking up! In fact"—he cracks his knuckles—"I'm feeling so good, I bet I could convince Dionysus to part with all those treasures he's collected on Jipper. He's probably got better things than anyone." Phipps slaps his leg. "I could bet him I could identify real gold over that fool's gold faster than he could."

"He'd probably turn you into a statue while he figured out

which is which," Triton says. "He's always planned some way to win before he accepts a bet."

Phipps's smile falters a fraction. "That's not fair. He should have to win a bet without using magic. Otherwise, how are we supposed to beat him?"

"You're not," Triton declares. "But if you really want to find out if you can, you will at sunrise. That's when we'll get the signal for how to find Jipper."

"The signal?" Royce and I share a look.

"Oh, you'll see," Triton says.

And while the others start discussing what this mysterious signal could be, all I can do is think about how soon that means we'll reach Jipper. And about how I don't have a plan to defeat Dionysus once we get there.

>>>>>>>>>>❀《《《《《《《《《《《

# CHAPTER 23

While the rest of the crew sleeps, I toss and turn. Sand digs into my skin, eroding me from the outside while the poison dissolves me from the inside. When I can't lie down any longer, I roll to my side and try to rise. But my muscles don't want to respond.

A rushing pain spirals through my body, infecting my muscles and turning them almost to liquid. I fight against it, forcing my arms out from under me. I eventually make it to my feet. I wobble to where Triton stands on the beach, throwing another stick for Grax.

"You're up early," Triton says.

"It hurts too much to sleep." I risk a look at my ankle. The swelling has gone down, but what's taken its place is much worse. Green veins snake up my leg, as high up past my knee as I dare look.

My throat tightens. I roll down my pant leg and try not to think about what it means.

"Here." Triton pulls out something crumbled and lumpy from the pockets of his pants. "I had Grax fetch some snilloc kelp. It's used to help with fevers." He hands me slimy green pieces. "You chew it."

"Thanks." I shove the kelp into my mouth, trying not to gag on the salty juice as it slides down my throat.

Though as soon as the juice touches my stomach, the aching eases.

"Better?"

I nod.

"Are you sure you're up to facing Dionysus?"

"I have to be." I duck my head. "I just wish I had a plan."

Grax pops back out of the water, spraying us with droplets, and lets a long piece of driftwood covered in bite marks fall between us. I pick it up and fling it back into the ocean.

It floats there for a second before Grax surges out of the water, clamping his mouth around it. Only, he bites too hard and the wood shatters.

Grax looks around, confused, before diving under the water and disappearing.

"He breaks them all the time," Triton says. "But don't worry, he'll fetch another one. He always does."

Not moments later, Grax bursts through the waves and slides onto the beach. He drops another twisted piece of wood at Triton's feet.

Triton tosses it, using what I assume is his demigod power to make the wood disappear far across the waves.

"If only Grax could destroy Dionysus's staff like he does that wood," I say.

Triton digs his toes in the sand. "I wish. Grax isn't allowed on Jipper. He ate too many satyrs on his first visit. Dionysus said he'd kill Grax if he ever so much as grazed one of Jipper's rocks again."

Grax brings a partially chewed branch back and gnaws on

the end for a while as he curls up at Triton's feet. Triton leans forward and rubs his side.

"Even if we could get Grax on the island, Dionysus would never let him close to his staff. It rarely leaves his side, and he'll definitely have it in hand by the time you show up."

There's a loud crunch as Grax bites through his current stick. He lets out a whimper and looks to Triton as if he has another one hiding somewhere. Triton sighs. "If you want another one, you can get it." He motions to the waves.

Triton's words, combined with something Phipps said about magic last night, break through my mind. I whip toward him, sending my head throbbing again. "Do you think Grax could find a particular piece of driftwood—one shaped a certain way?"

Triton's brow scrunches inward. "I suppose he could."

"And could you have one of your sea creatures bring me a small piece of gold?"

He nods.

I can't tell if the heat I feel in my chest is the poison or hope burning for the first time. We'll have to act fast if we want this to work.

Triton looks at me like I've lost my mind as I tell him my plan. Maybe I have. But this is all I've been able to come up with.

"We can give it a shot," he says. "I'll get Grax. You wake the others. It's almost time to go."

I groan and rise to my feet, letting my vision settle before I edge forward.

I wake Hettie first since I know she'll be the hardest to stir, not to mention her groaning might rouse the others.

She swats at me when I shake her shoulders. "The sun's not even up yet."

"Come on, Hettie. We're facing Dionysus today, remember?" Rhat yawns and stretches awake beside her.

I touch Phipps and Lenny, who are sleeping back to back. "Better get the pegasi ready," I say. "It's almost time to go."

Lenny kicks Phipps when he scrunches inward and continues to sleep. After another kick, Phipps wakes up. "Fine, fine. I'll see to the pegasi." He wipes his eyes and goes to check on the herd, who have curled up with their wings around them to rest.

"Time to wake up, my beauties," Phipps calls, rubbing one on its head and another along its neck.

I smile through a streak of pain racing up my side. I find Royce tucked on the edge of the sandbar. He looks younger when he sleeps. Peaceful. I wish I could leave him in that world of dreams.

I kneel in the sand and ignore the ache in my muscles at the movement. Green veins peek out along my wrist right below my sleeve. I yank the fabric down, but it won't be long before they're visible all down my hand.

I gently touch Royce's shoulder. "It's time."

Sleep clouds his face, and he blinks a few times before recognition sets in. He smiles up at me. "Good morning." He sits up slowly, smoothing out his hair. "I guess today's the day."

I nod.

He gives me a hand as he stands. I look down to prevent him from seeing the pain across my face, but Royce gently pulls my chin toward him. "No matter what happens, remember we're in this together." His eyes hold mine as he strokes my jawline with his thumb.

Then his lips are on mine. His hand twines through my hair, pulling me closer. He tastes like the ocean. He tastes like freedom, like life itself. And I want more. I want to stay this way forever.

Heat rises through my body, and I'm afraid he'll feel it. That he'll know what I'm hiding.

I pull away, ducking my face. "We don't want to miss the signal."

He nods and pulls me back toward the pegasi.

"Remember not to ride them too hard," Phipps says to everyone as they mount. "And stay away from the wings. They don't like it when you bunch in too close to them."

"There's not much time," Triton calls. "We all need to be mounted and ready before the first sunrays touch the ocean."

"Watch their manes too," Phipps calls as he scrambles to his pegasus. "Don't tangle them too much. It's going to take a lot of brushing to fix."

"Is this the one I had yesterday?" Hettie asks from atop hers. "The one yesterday kept nipping at me."

"Then maybe you should be nicer to it," Phipps says.

Hettie scowls down at him.

Royce hops onto one of the pegasi and then pulls me up next to him. Thankfully, I'm in front of him, and he can't see the way my lips tremble as I fight to hold in a whimper. I clench my fingers into my palms.

I lean back into Royce, suddenly wanting nothing more than to slip off into the cool sand and lie there, but as the pain spreads, I'm starting to think I might never get up again if I lie down.

Triton moves his pegasus forward to the very edge of the sandbar. "The moment the light touches the water, look for a green flash. Then we fly as fast as we can in that direction. The island won't stop moving, so overshoot the landing. If you don't, you'll drop off the sharp edge of the island, straight into the water, in which case you'll have a hard time remounting. You'll never catch up."

We all wait, the cool night breeze ruffling the manes of our rides. The only sounds are the impatient stamping of hooves squishing into the sand. Even Phipps is quiet.

The sky lightens. A green flash sears at the base of the horizon.

"Now!" Triton cries.

All the pegasi swarm into the air.

Triton sets an unwieldy pace, forcing his pegasus to go faster than I thought possible. The wind tears through my body and forces tears to well from my eyes.

We speed over the ocean, and suddenly, there's a shape on the horizon. And it's getting closer.

An island.

Royce's grip tightens around me as he spots it.

"Jipper," he cries, giving me a squeeze around my waist. "We've found it. We've really found it."

The island speeds ahead of us. It moves quicker than any ship can travel, quicker than I've seen anything move.

"Faster," Triton calls.

Foam streams from our pegasus's mouth as its wings continue to thump up and down. Its legs fight against the current of the wind, pumping faster and faster.

A smooth shoreline comes into view. Trees roar up past it. Royce anchors me to him as we dip forward, aiming for the sand. The ground rears up at us. We're coming in so fast.

But the pegasus is having a hard time catching up with the island. The sandy beach seems to stay just out of reach. Hooves graze the top of the ocean, and Triton's words about ending up in the water rush through my ears.

Royce pulls upward, but we fall even farther behind the island.

The pegasus surges. Its hooves connect with the beach. It glances off but tries once more. At last, its hooves find traction. We clamber onto the beach, the pegasus jolting forward.

But something happens as soon as the pegasus makes it all the way onto the island. It's as if the island stops moving. But we are still moving at a breakneck speed.

We catapult into the trees. Royce and I vault forward as the creature tries to stop.

Trees and vines tangle around us, and a branch scrapes across my side. I crash through the underbrush, roll across the ground, and land on a pile of thick leaves. Lumps of dirt pile around my shoulders where they've dug into the ground.

I lift my head and try to orient myself.

For a moment, everything is fine. But then the pain sets in. My shoulders, my elbows, my thighs, my knees. They all burn.

I drag my arm out from where it's twisted under my body and struggle to my knees.

I can't force myself any higher. I wrap my arm around my stomach as my insides scorch. I'm glad I didn't eat breakfast because it would've come back up.

"Kora," Royce cries, crashing through the bushes. "Are you okay?"

I suck in a breath as the poison rips its way through me, peeling away another layer from my insides and incinerating it. I can't get any words out. It's a struggle just to stay upright.

He crouches before me. "What hurts the most?" He wipes at the dirt covering my cheeks, letting his fingers rest there.

"I'm okay," I finally manage to croak.

That's when we hear shouting from the beach. We freeze, sharing a look. Royce wraps his arm around me, hauling me up. He helps me climb over the fallen logs and tangle of vines that clog the jungle floor until we break through the tree line and onto the uneven sand. I sink in with each step, leaning even more into Royce to stay on my feet.

We push forward to find Phipps standing there trying to drag Triton off his pegasus.

Triton keeps dancing his mount backward out of Phipps's reach.

"What's going on?" Royce says.

"He's trying to steal one of Lenny's pegasi," Phipps says. "That pegasus belongs to Lenny, and if he's going to leave, he doesn't get to take it with him."

"You're leaving?" Royce asks, turning toward Triton.

Triton sits stoically, refusing to meet any of our gazes. "I've done my part. I got you to Jipper. Now I'm free to go."

"What?" I say, pushing off Royce and moving closer, my pain forgotten for a moment. "You can't leave. We need you."

"You're better off without me. Dionysus won't take kindly to finding me with you. Aim to the left of the volcano, and you'll find him. Stick to the trees so he doesn't see you coming. And remember to be off the island before the sun sets."

I shake my head, trying to make sense of his words. "I thought—" I try to figure out what to say to him. "I thought we were friends."

"You thought wrong," he snaps. "I told you friendships don't

251

last, and I've seen enough humans die during my years. I don't need to see any more."

"You could guide us through the island," I say. "You could help us."

He looks down. "It's better if I leave now."

"Better for you," Hettie says. "But then again, you only do what's in your best interest."

"I fulfilled my promise. I'm free."

"At least leave the pegasus," Phipps says.

The crew starts to circle around Triton, but we're wasting time on this battle when another one is waiting for us.

"Just let him take it," I say. "The sooner he leaves, the better. We should be saving our energy for Dionysus."

"But—" Phipps says.

"Just go," I say to Triton, pulling myself up as much as I can.

Triton's lips thin. He gives me one long look, then his pegasus vaults into the air, disappearing as the island moves onward.

I refuse to watch his path.

Instead, I focus on the island. I hadn't even realized you couldn't tell the island is moving once you set foot on it. The sky doesn't speed by. The wind doesn't howl. There are just some early morning clouds lazing by.

There's something eerie about the beach, though. It takes me a few moments to place why. There are no seagulls calling out, and the waves don't wash upon the shore, sending seashells clinking upward with each crash. The waves simply rest against the edge of the island without moving.

"We should get going," I say. "We need to be off the island as fast as we can." I limp back toward the trees, wincing with each step. If I can just make it to them, I can lean against a trunk.

Maybe the others won't notice the way my feet drag and my body sways unevenly.

Blood rushes in my ears so loudly I can't hear if the others are following or not. My chest feels extremely tight, as if my clothes have shrunk down into a snakeskin I can't shed, making it hard to get any breath in.

Above the canopy, a large volcano looms in the distance. If I can barely make it to the trees, I don't know how I'm going to make it all the way there, but I keep putting one foot in front of the other until Phipps's voice calls me back.

"What about the pegasi?" he says.

I slowly turn to face him. "We'll have to leave them here. We can't risk Dionysus seeing us coming." Although I have a sinking suspicion he already knows we're here, that there's nothing on his island he doesn't know about. Besides, I imagine as soon as the pegasi try to take off toward the volcano, they'll have to fight to keep up with the island again and so never be fast enough to fly us all the way to another part farther in.

Royce steps to my side. "Should we take everyone with us or leave some men here with the pegasi?"

I turn to answer him, but his face has gone white.

He pulls me toward him, twisting me toward the sunlight. "Kora, something's wrong with your neck."

Hettie moves forward to look. "Is it dirt?"

Royce rubs at it.

"Maybe she touched something when she landed in the jungle?" Rhat comes up. "We have some poisonous plants back on my home island. If you show me where you landed, I can take a look."

I push away from Royce and the crowd. "I'm fine."

The trees sway in and out of focus as I swing toward them. I wheeze as I fight to get closer. I just have to make it there.

The jungle hazes and blurs again.

I don't even realize I'm falling until my knees grind into the sand.

Royce is there in a second, kneeling in front of me. "Kora, your veins are turning green."

I take a deep breath. "I know."

"You know?" Hettie repeats, crouching down next to me.

I guess I knew I'd have to tell them at some point. At least we're already on Jipper.

"I—I was bitten on the gorgon's island."

"What?" Royce asks. Confusion plays across his face. His eyes meet mine. They look even more blue with the ocean at his back.

"I knew if I told you that you'd want to go after the cure." I drop my gaze. "And I couldn't abandon Lagonia like that."

Some sort of emotion plays across Royce's face. He shakes his head back and forth.

"I'm so sorry," I whisper. It's the only thing I can say.

"There's got to be something we can do," he says, his voice cracking.

I shake my head. "We go after Dionysus. That's *all* we can do."

Tears prick at the corners of his eyes.

"Please," I say. "You said you'd always trust me. Trust that I'm doing what I have to in order to save my people, to be the leader they need."

"You're already the leader they need," he says, his voice breaking. "You're the one willing to fight for them. To protect them. But, Kora, not this. Don't ask this of me." He blinks the tears away and closes his eyes. He looks like he's fighting something within himself.

Hettie rises on her knees, a determined look on her face. "Rhat and I will go after Triton. We'll make him take us to find Panacea."

"Even if you could locate him," I say, "you won't find Panacea in time."

"There's got to be something." Her lips quiver slightly as she fights the motion.

Rhat moves toward Hettie and puts his hand on her shoulder.

She shakes it off and jumps to her feet. "Dionysus can fix this. He has powers. We'll make him fix this."

The rest of the men stand stoically around us, eyes downcast.

There's no way Dionysus is going to cure me out of the kindness of his heart. But that small hope might be enough to keep her going for now.

"We got that no-good Triton to help us. We'll find a way to convince Dionysus." Her voice rises with every word, as if the energy she puts into it will be enough to make it come true.

"She's right," Royce says. "This isn't over yet. Leave the pegasi here. We all go after Dionysus." He lifts me delicately to my feet.

Then, he pulls me close, whispering into my ear. "I trust you—but I love you more. And I'm not losing you, no matter what." He leans back, meeting my gaze with a nod, solidifying his promise.

Then, before I can reply, he leads me toward the trees— toward where Dionysus waits.

CHAPTER 24

〉〉〉〉〉〉〉〉〉〉◉〈〈〈〈〈〈〈〈〈〈〈

The jungle is dark and quiet. Big, leafy ferns sag off the trees, waving their fronds at us, beckoning us farther in. Vines tangle overhead while tree roots intertwine under a carpet of decaying leaves. Strange half-moons of fungus grow in patches on the sides of trees, competing with the various white mushrooms that live in lines between thick green patches of moss.

The air feels moist, as though it's recently rained, and heat clings to me. Sweat slides down my skin and soaks through my shirt, competing with the poison-fed fever inside.

Ahead of me, Hettie's hair is matted to her neck as she moves forward to cut through the lush foliage. Only Rhat seems unaffected by the heat, but even he seems wary of the forest around us. He keeps casting glances deep into the jungle, where shadows jump around every time the breeze shakes the trees.

Triton said Dionysus had won things from many of the gods, and some of those catures live on this island. I have no idea what we might encounter. Or if I'll even have the strength to face any we do come across.

Royce keeps his hand under my arm and around my back so I remain upright. My feet persist in dragging behind me, barely able to keep moving. And I continue having to stop to catch my breath.

Royce rests me against a tree near a stream after I ask him to stop for a moment.

I let my head fall back against the trunk. My shirt clings to my back. My throat feels like an inferno.

"I'll get you some water," Royce says.

But before he can move, something rustles in the jungle.

I freeze.

"What was that?" Hettie whispers.

The sound of swords being drawn from their sheaths breaks the silence around us as the men prepare for whatever may be coming.

The leaves shake again.

No one breathes.

Out of the bushes shoots a bright purple bird. It's akin to the peacocks my father keeps in his garden with its tail of dark purple feathers dragging through the dirt behind it.

The bird lets out a few caws before hopping harmlessly into the undergrowth.

I sag into the tree in relief. Several ants crawl down the bark in a curving line before disappearing beneath the leaves.

"Hey," Phipps calls. "You should see this stream."

I straighten and stagger toward the water like the rest of the crew, drawn by the excitement in Phipps's voice.

A small stream not wider than an arm's length runs off into the jungle, water gurgling quietly.

Phipps dips his hand into the current. When his hand emerges, he's holding clear rocks. No, not rocks.

Diamonds.

I move closer, pain lacing each step, and stare into the clear water. Instead of stones and rocks clogging the bottom of the stream, diamonds line it. They tumble through the water, gathering in pockets and reflecting the sunlight.

Phipps scoops up handfuls and shoves them into anything he can find that can double as a pouch. "We're rich," he cries. "Lenny, come over here. I need your pockets."

I'd always heard rumors of the clearest, purest water being found on Jipper, but treasures like these are what drew men to the Temptresses. And that had been a trap.

"I don't like this," I say.

I scan the forest, but I don't see anything in the shadows.

The water in front of Phipps shimmers. An icy, diamond hand shoots out, grabbing Phipps's wrist. He screams as his skin slowly freezes over, taking on the same transparent hue as whatever it is that holds him. The sheen creeps slowly up his arm. He pulls backward, causing the creature to rise out of the water. At first, I think it's a Temptress, but as the water drains away, a hard shell remains. Her skin looks solid and comes together at jagged points, just like the diamonds in the stream.

"We need to get out of here," Rhat shouts. "She'll turn us all into diamonds."

Hettie and Royce react immediately. Royce brings his sword down on the creature's wrist. It ricochets off, leaving a chip in the blade. The creature doesn't flinch. Phipps's entire right arm is now a giant diamond. His eyes have gone dull, as if with each inch of his body that is consumed, more of his life is sucked out.

Lenny looks like he wants to tackle the woman, but another sailor holds him back.

Hettie aims her sword for the creature's throat, but she has no more success than Royce. The blade doesn't even chip its skin. Again and again, they hack, and soon, the tips of their sword blades turn clear and hard wherever they crash into the diamond woman's body.

The creature doesn't falter or move away. A glowing smile spreads across her face as the gleam creeps farther up Phipps's arm. And it's moving closer and closer to his heart.

I know what'll happen if it reaches there. Summoning what strength I can, I lurch ahead, not knowing if my plan will work after what happened with the man who melted through the gold back in the palace. But I have to try.

I crash into Royce. At first, he tries to shake me off, no doubt thinking I'm another assailant. I spin him around, searching his jacket for gold. I press my palm into a button. Cold power wells up inside me.

I brush past him, staggering forward. The woman doesn't care; her eyes haven't moved from Phipps.

I move as quickly as I can as my vision threatens to spin again. I jolt forward into her arm. I cry out as a prick of pain shoots through my finger, followed by the familiar depletion of energy as the gold drains from my body. There's a flash of golden and white light, and then I'm tumbling backward.

For a few moments, all I can see is swirling light, until the white glow is overtaken by gold. I blink it away. Slowly, the trees above me come into focus. Then, Royce's concerned face is above mine. His mouth is moving, but I can't make out what it is he's saying.

My head rolls to the side.

The creature is frozen, encased in gold. Phipps slumps forward. Rhat and Hettie pry Phipps's wrist loose from the creature's grip, but his arm remains diamond. The sound of it thudding against the ground is the first noise that crashes through my mind.

Royce grasps my shoulders, drawing my gaze back to him. "Are you okay? Kora, what's wrong?" he shouts over and over again.

There's a pricking sensation surging through my pointer finger. I bring it close to my face and spot a tiny dewdrop-shaped diamond patch on my skin. I tap my fingernail against it.

Royce grabs my finger and inspects it. "Can you stand?"

I nod, and he helps me to my feet, saying, "So that's what happens when two of Dionysus's gifted come into contact with each other."

"You think that's what she was?" I ask, trying to draw breath into lungs that feel smaller and smaller with each inhale.

Royce shrugs. "What else could she be?" He helps me over toward Phipps. "Triton did say he was gathering his creatures for the attack on Lagonia."

Rhat helps Phipps stand.

"It's not so bad," Phipps says. He tries to smile but fails.

"We'll find a way to fix this." I have no idea how, but I can't leave him without hope.

Lenny pops up beside me, inspecting the arm.

"No need to fix it," Phipps says. "I've got the world's greatest diamond arm." I can't tell if he's putting on a brave face for Lenny or if he's starting to come around to having a jewel limb.

"Can you keep going?" Rhat asks.

Phipps nods. He walks forward on his own but topples to the side as the weight of his arm drags him down. Rhat props him up again, letting Phipps lean on him for support.

Just as he does, another sound echoes through the jungle.

The golden creature crackles. Patches of diamond skin break through.

"She's coming back," Hettie calls. "She's turning the gold coating into diamonds."

The entire bottom half of the creature sparkles in the sun. A sound like shattering glass accompanies the return of her entire midsection to diamond skin.

"Run," Royce shouts.

Rhat drags Phipps away from the stream, and Royce wraps his arm around me, yanking me forward.

We crash through the undergrowth until we can no longer hear the fracturing sound of the creature restoring herself.

Royce collapses against the nearest tree while I lean on my knees, panting for breath. Sweat plasters Royce's hair to his forehead, and he wipes it away as he shoves off the tree.

"We need to keep moving. We're easy targets the longer we stand still," he says.

I know he's right, but my chest just keeps getting tighter and tighter. Every breath I take turns stale the moment it reaches my lungs, hot and unbearable until I have to cough the air out.

Royce's eyes keep flicking toward me. "Maybe we should rest a while longer," he backtracks.

"No," I force myself upward, ignoring my vision as it reels again before settling. "You're right. We have to keep going."

Rhat scampers up the nearest tree as if it were easier to climb than the rigging. "Volcano's that way." He slips back down and lands soundlessly on fallen palm fronds. "We're not far. It doesn't look like the island is very long."

I let Royce wrap his arm around me as we continue walking.

After a few moments, we both jolt to a stop as the jungle ends and a wide expanse of open land awaits.

Bright sunlight flares down around us. Golden grasses sway back and forth in the breeze. Several bugs buzz between the yellow-and-white flowers that grow in small clumps around the field.

"A field doesn't belong on an island like this," Rhat says. He squats down to examine the grass.

"I don't like it," Hettie says. "It's too open."

Off to our right, the base of the volcano rises like gnarled tree roots leading up to a wide mountain. There's no way we can go back around the other way.

"If it's the fastest route," I cough. "We have to take it."

Her eyes meet mine before drifting down to my neck, where I can feel the green veins have started creeping up my chin to stain my cheeks.

She swallows. "Okay." She keeps her shield on her back but pulls out her sword and ventures into the grass. It sways around her hips. She dips her sword into the tufts of grass, but nothing comes out.

Slowly, the rest of us make our way into the field. The grass is rougher than it looks. It whips against my clothes, trying to dig its way in.

There is a caw above the rustling of the grass.

"What was that?" Phipps asks, still leaning on Rhat.

"Just a bird," Royce says. "Probably like the one we saw before."

But the cawing gets louder. And the pitch is different. It's much higher than before.

We've only gone a few more steps when Phipps lets out a startled cry, and Royce pulls me forward.

"Please," a weak female voice says. "Please help me. The birds eat human flesh."

Sticking out barely above the grass is the head of a woman. Her blonde hair blends in seamlessly, and her green eyes frantically scan the skies. She's crouched low, hidden in the grass.

"Come with us," Phipps says at the same time Royce tells him to wait.

Phipps lets go of Rhat and reaches out with his good arm. As soon as he does, the field erupts around us. Dozens of blonde heads shoot out of the grass. All nearly identical.

A wicked grin spreads across the closest woman's face. Then her mouth opens and a screeching sound that makes me want to claw off my own ears comes out.

The woman's form vaults out of the brush, revealing a squat, fat body covered in feathers. Two broad wings spread wide as she swoops upward before diving straight toward us.

"Harpies," Royce cries just as the entire flock takes to the skies.

# CHAPTER 25

>>>>>>>>>>✿<<<<<<<<<<

The only thing that saves Phipps from the harpy heading straight for him is his diamond arm. He manages to raise it just in time, protecting his chest from the harpy's claws.

The birdwoman screeches away and takes aim for another attack.

All around the field, harpies launch toward sailors, talons extended. Several careen straight toward Rhat. He knocks one away with a swoop of his sword, but another sinks its claws into his shoulder from behind. Hettie's there in a second, leaping through the air, sword extended. She crashes into the bird's torso, ripping it open as she uses her own weight to pull her weapon down.

I can't see what happens next because a harpy dives low. Royce rips his sword free and swipes it back and forth to keep the monster at bay. Up close, the face that had appeared so human has more birdlike features. Two lips pucker outward like a tiny beak above a narrow chin. And beady eyes stare out from behind eyelashes that look more like feathers than hair.

The harpy plunges lower, aiming for my head. I grab the new sword Triton supplied for me when gathering new weapons after Gorgon Island and swat the feathered beast away. My sword clangs metallically against its talons, glancing off. I don't have any force behind my blows. It's hard enough just lifting my blade into the air.

The harpy must know I'm an easy target. Its beady eyes focus in on me again and again, and its rough feathers brush against the top of my head as I duck out of the way.

Royce manages to cut into the birdwoman's wing as it swoops by. The creature crashes into the grass, staining it with blood and feathers. It cries out as it hops around with one wing before the noise is cut off with a gurgle as Royce stabs it through the chest.

But a sound rises above it.

"Lenny!" Phipps screams.

A harpy has latched on to Lenny's shoulders and is pulling him into the sky. Lenny kicks and squirms, but he can't break free.

Phipps races along the grass below the creature, stumbling under the weight of his arm. When he starts to fall behind, he stops short, then drops to the ground and finds a rock. He launches it at the beast, hitting it square in the back of its head.

"Close your eyes, Lenny," he cries.

He digs deep into his pocket. And I watch as he pulls something small out and turns away just as the harpy looks toward him, renewed rage on its face.

But the creature doesn't make it any farther. It turns instantly to stone, dropping straight toward the earth with Lenny in tow. Lenny is locked in the bird's frozen grip, unable to get out from under its descending weight.

Royce takes off at a sprint. He collides with Lenny just before he brushes the top of the grass. The hit gives them both enough momentum to avoid being crushed under the majority of the stone harpy's enormous weight as it drops to the ground and cracks into hundreds of pieces.

"Lenny!" Phipps scrambles through the grass, knocking away chunks of rock until he finds his brother.

Lenny sits up groggily but seems unhurt besides some cuts where the bird's talons had ahold of him.

Reassured his brother is okay, Phipps starts holding the object above his head and the harpies start dropping. Slowly, the number of harpies dwindles until Hettie severs a talon of one and it flies off alone.

She has blood streaming down her face, but I don't think much if any is hers. Her eyes are wild and her chest heaves as she scans the skies. When it's clear the creatures aren't returning, she wipes off her blade and stomps through the grass and accumulation of twisted feathers. She heads straight to Rhat, who's cradling his arm. Hettie helps him take off his ripped shirt, tearing it into long sheets to wrap around his shoulder.

Across the field, other sailors are patching up scrapes across their scalps and cuts up and down their arms and necks. We don't look like a force ready to take on Dionysus.

My hand shakes as I slide my sword away, and I can't help but notice the green veins making their way to the ends of my fingertips. Despite the heat in the core of my body, my fingers and toes feel oddly numb.

I try not to think about what that means.

"Two men are dead, Captain," a sailor says to Royce.

Royce nods stoically.

I try not to dwell on the sailors who won't be returning home, who died bravely in battle. If I do, it'll crush me. Instead, I think about all the people we're fighting to save.

Hettie rises, helping Rhat to his feet. "I didn't think it was possible to dislike Dionysus even more, but he's going to pay for this."

"We're lucky Phipps figured out how to stop them," Rhat says. He rotates his shoulder around, testing it, but winces with the movement.

"What did you do?" Hettie asks Phipps.

Phipps ducks his head and slips the object back into his pocket, wrapping it in a handkerchief. "I may have taken a souvenir from one of the gorgons. No one will mess with the man with a gorgon eye."

"Did you take anything else?" Royce asks.

"Well—" Phipps says.

"Phipps," Royce says with underlying warning.

"Two eyes. But they're mostly for Lenny. I didn't know what we'd be facing here, and he's not great with a sword yet."

While Phipps might be telling the truth, I also don't doubt he had some scheme to either sell them or put on some sort of show where people paid to see them. But we could deal with that later.

"Could we use them against Dionysus?" Hettie asks.

I shake my head. "If they didn't work on Triton, I doubt they'll work on Dionysus."

"Be careful with them," Royce says. He gazes down to Lenny.

"Aye, Captain." Phipps gives his best salute. Lenny follows suit.

"Let's get out of here before any more of those things show up," I say.

We trudge through the grasses, and Hettie helps me wade through because my feet have gone entirely numb. Once we hit the tree line, she lets me rest for a moment, tilting me against a fallen tree trunk.

I suck in air. It feels like I'm breathing through a layer of water. I close my eyes against the pain racing its way through me, but Hettie's words make me open them again.

"It happened when you were helping me, didn't it?"

"What are you talking about?" I say.

Her eyes brim with tears. "I heard you cry out. On the island."

"It's not your fault, Hettie," I say.

She cradles her forehead in her hands, wiping away the sweat. "I shouldn't have gone off like that. I wanted to kill Dionysus so badly. He caused so much of this, took so much from us, and if I focused on that I didn't have to . . . I didn't have to . . ." she trails off, dabbing at her tears, refusing to let them fall.

"Hettie—" I reach out to her, but she shakes me away.

"No! Ever since my father died, I've been filled with anger. If you're full of anger, you don't have to feel the pain. And I didn't want to feel it—or anything. I thought killing Dionysus would make it all go away. But now—now I'm losing you too."

I open my mouth to tell her she's not losing me, but I look down at the green veins covering the entirety of my hands. But it's not just my veins. My skin has taken on a putrid color, overpowering the golden hue I've grown so used to. My fingers are cracked and wrinkled, like they're shriveling up and dying.

I pull Hettie close to me, breathing in the scent of sweat, sea air, and the sweetness I'd always associated with her. "Oh, Hettie."

"I can't lose you too. Not now," she says, taking a shuddering breath. "I can't do this. Not after—" She turns away.

"You survived that—"

She crosses her arms. "I didn't love him. I hid behind my anger so I wouldn't have to admit that. So I wouldn't have to come to terms with the fact that I wanted him to love me, that now I'll never get that. Now, I'll never have the chance." She shoves her damp hair away from her face, and her eyes soften. "But you—I can still save you. Let me take one of the pegasi and look for a cure—for something to help. Please, this is all my fault. Let me make it better. I can't lose you. I won't."

"It's not your fault. I knew the risks better than anybody." I inhale. "There's nothing that can help now. We won't find Panacea or Hebe in time. I made that choice so we could save Lagonia. And I need you here to help me do that. I need you to be strong for both of us. We can't fail now. Not this close."

She leans against me, breathing heavily across my neck as she buries her head against me, squeezing me tighter than she ever has.

"This is for Lagonia," I say. "We only fail if we don't stop Dionysus. Don't let this be in vain. Be the fighter I know you are."

She sniffles and nods against me.

"And Hettie—" My voice cracks. I'd been trying not to think about this, but there is no way out now. "I need you to look after my father if—if—" I can't finish the sentence.

"Oh, Kora, no."

"He's going to need someone." Tears slide down my cheeks into her hair. "So are you. Promise me you won't hide away. Lagonia's going to need you."

Her eyes are puffy and red as she pulls back to look me in the eye. "I—" Her voice breaks, and she takes a moment to steel herself. She looks like she doesn't want to answer. But after she sucks in a breath, she says, "I promise."

I squeeze her hand. "Let's finish this together."

She wipes her tears away and straightens. She clenches her jaw and stares off into the jungle shadows. "Dionysus doesn't know what's coming for him."

"That's right," I say.

She props me against her side and pulls me farther into the trees, unaware that each heartbeat in my chest is getting slower and slower and slower.

꙳꙳꙳꙳꙳꙳꙳꙳꙳◉꙼꙼꙼꙼꙼꙼꙼꙼꙼

# CHAPTER 26

My vision starts to blur. Shadows jump around the jungle floor, and there's a loud, constant humming in my ears.

A bee floats in front of my face. Maybe that's where the humming comes from. But bees don't belong in jungles. Then again, harpies don't typically belong in fields.

I swat the bug away, but my hand doesn't connect with anything. Yet the bee still lingers before me. I squint and wipe away the sweat from my eyes, wondering if I'm starting to hallucinate too.

I'm about to ask if anyone else sees the bee when Lenny starts pointing to his ears.

The humming gets louder.

When I look toward where I saw the insect, it's gone. I scan the area but can't find anything. Then why is the humming growing louder?

Everyone quiets as the forest reverberates around us.

"Bees!" someone cries.

I turn to see a hoard of bees hurtling our direction. The closer they get, the bigger they get. Their abdomens are the size of my torso. Each of their black legs is thicker then one of my fingers. But it's their stingers my eyes jump to. Their pointed shape looks sharper than any spear.

The bees' clear wings reflect the light coming through the trees as they zoom closer.

Hettie grabs my shoulder, and we stumble through the jungle. Branches and palm fronds slap across my face and snare my legs. Thick vines tangle in front of us like a curtain. I shove through with all my remaining strength, but the vines continue to stretch on for a good long while.

I let Hettie pull me along, but my mind is elsewhere. The bees don't seem to be getting any closer. The one I saw before didn't attack either. I'd thought it was a small, little bee, but what if it had been a monstrous one, only been so far away I'd thought it was small?

I shake my head. None of this is making sense.

Hettie is so covered in perspiration she keeps losing her grip on me. I cling to her shirt, her shoulders, anything I can to stay with her. If she lets go, I doubt she'll be able to get me back up before the bees reach us.

The horde bursts through the vines behind us, knocking them aside as if they were blades of grass.

Two soldiers cry out as they stumble and fall.

But the bees don't swarm them like I expect.

Before I can figure it out, though, the men have regained their footing, and we're off racing through the jungle once more.

My heart pounds in my chest, drowning out the buzzing.

I try to suck in air, but a rattling sound rushes around in my lungs. My eyelids sag. I just want to rest, to sleep.

Hettie's firm grasp around my waist is the only thing that keeps me going. But even her steps are growing shorter and shorter. She gulps in air, heaving for breath.

"Hang in there." She adjusts her hold on me again, and I'm not sure if the words are for her benefit or mine.

Her grip loosens again. As she moves to tighten it, she doesn't lift her foot as high as she should. It catches on a root, and then we're tumbling forward.

My arms barely react enough to do anything to break my fall. Roots dig into my stomach and knees as I land on hard dirt.

"Come on, Kora." Hettie's already on her feet and pulling at my arms.

The bees cloud into my vision as they hover above us. Their wings pound so hard they send the fallen leaves spiraling into the air.

"Just go, Hettie."

A stubborn look crosses her face. "No."

With a strength I didn't know she had, she yanks me to my feet.

We're behind the rest of the crew, but Hettie runs with renewed vigor.

The bees stay just behind us. Never touching us. Never increasing their pace. They easily could've swept in and stung me or carried me off. But they haven't.

Something clicks in my mind. "They're corralling us."

"What?" Hettie cries over the buzzing.

"They're leading us to something."

Hettie risks a look over her shoulder, but then we're crashing through the brush and out into a patch of bright sunlight.

At first, I think we've arrived at another field full of harpies, but there's no tall, dried-out grass here. Only neatly trimmed green grass. As my eyes adjust, I make out long rows. A vineyard.

We've made it. Dionysus's vineyard.

Row upon row of plump purple grapes hang from vines. I've never seen so many grapes in my life. Each one looks delicious, and I realize how thirsty I am.

But Triton's words float through my mind.

I open my mouth to tell the others who've stumbled out of the forest not to touch any of the fruit.

Before the words can leave my mouth, one final sailor stumbles from the jungle and crashes into the nearest row, knocking several grapes to the ground as he catches himself on the vines. Several more grapes fall, rolling into the dirt to rest there.

Seconds tick by. Nothing happens.

I exhale.

But just as I do, vines shoot out from the plant.

They wrap around the man like a snake, pulling tighter and tighter the higher they spiral around his body.

Men rush to help him, but each one is spun into a cocoon of vines as more race out.

Men pull out their swords and start hacking at the vines. But for every one they cut off, two more seem to appear. The vineyard comes to life as branches dart from every row and race toward us.

Next to me, Hettie goes down. She chops at the green stalks with her sword, but another vine rushes forward and snares her wrist, pulling so tight she releases her sword.

I cry out and stumble toward her. Vines scratch against my ankles, twisting their way up my body. I kick at them and lose my balance.

The vines curl around and around and up and up. The rattle in my chest cuts off as the vines constrict, heading for my neck, looping tighter and tighter.

I gasp, but no air enters my lungs.

Next to me, Phipps is on his knees. His arms break free for a second before the vines lash them to his sides again.

"Lenny," he screams over and over again before a vine swirls around his neck, pulling him to the ground.

I catch sight of Lenny next to him. He's wrapped from his thighs to his chest. He wriggles back and forth. But he doesn't appear to be fighting against the vines. It's as if he's positioning himself.

The vines move a little farther up his hips. With unmatched flexibility, he kicks his leg upward, wraps his toes around one of the vines, and pulls. The vine snaps.

That's the last thing I see as rough green vines slither across my face and coil around my head.

The vines scrape against my skin. The earthy scent overwhelms my senses as my nose smushes inward and my lips push against my teeth until I taste blood. The vines compress tighter and tighter. My head pounds. My skull feels on the verge of cracking.

Even if I could suck in air from the slits between the vines, they're wrapped too tightly for my chest to move. My throat constricts. My lungs burn.

And then I'm breathing.

Sunlight streams in above me.

A small, shadowy figure crouches over me, sawing at the vines. There's a crisp snap as each one breaks.

The figure moves. It's Lenny. He has a knife in his hand, slicing through my binds while he uses his feet to snap through the vines that try to tangle him up.

I struggle free from the cocoon, coughing for air, and see

Lenny's already gotten several others free. Phipps works on getting Rhat out while Hettie fights a vine intent on getting to them all. Her hair's come undone, and she looks positively wild the way she swings her sword.

Royce emerges from the next clump of vines and immediately joins the fight to free his crew. A vine slips around his ankle.

"Look out," I scream, my voice barely rising above the noise around me.

Royce falls to his knees as the vine yanks backward, but he doesn't stop hacking through the vines constricting the man in front of him.

I crawl forward. Using as much force as I can muster, I ram my blade down into the vine, pinning it to the ground. The vine thrashes and shakes.

My sword won't hold it long. And even as I watch, more vines shoot out of the cursed vineyard to assail us.

Exhausted, I collapse against the nearest trellis, sending grapes plummeting down. My chest wheezes as I gasp for breath.

More and more vines shoot out toward my friends.

I need to get up. I need to do something.

I pull myself up the trellis, but my legs give out. I stumble to the side, glancing off the next trellis and into the grapes' leafy branches. I reach for them, trying to stand. They rip away from their supports, and I land back in a heap on the ground as the plants tangle above me.

I fling the tattered branches away, and I notice something unusual. These aren't individual plants. This is one long string of grapes hanging from one vine.

"They're all connected," I whisper.

I crawl back toward the battlefield, but a coughing fit stops me in my tracks. I heave in and out as my insides constrict, sending spasms of pain rippling beneath my skin. For a moment, I think my lungs have finally given up, but after what feels like ages, I finally choke in a short breath. Again and again I force air down until I have enough to call out.

"Royce," I cry, the word barely leaving my lips. "Royce!"

Royce slices through one vine wrapping itself around his arm and turns toward me.

"Throw me your coat," I rasp.

Royce gets his arm free and rips off his jacket, tossing it to me.

"Get the men free," I add, noticing two more shapes still wrapped in vines.

He nods and heads back toward where the remaining men are guarded by a string of vines.

Between the numbness in my hands and the unending convulsions shaking my muscles, I have to fumble his jacket around until I find what I'm looking for. Two gold buttons are left.

I touch one, and I feel life well up in me. No, not life. Power.

The gold bounces around inside me, begging to be let go. It gives me energy to scoot my way back toward the nearest vine. I almost don't want to give up that energy when Royce screams, "They're free."

I slam my hand into the grapevine.

The entire vineyard turns to gold in a flash.

The gold rushing from my body feels like it's taking my life with it. I pull my hand away and sag backward.

Somewhere, Hettie is screaming. I lift my eyes enough to see a golden vine, now frozen in place, has her lifted by her hair.

She tries to pull free but doesn't make it far. Eventually she slips a knife from her boot and slices herself free, cutting off several inches of her auburn curls.

All around, men are wriggling free of the hardened vines looped around their torsos and ankles. Once they do, they all congregate around Lenny.

"I told you he could do amazing things with his feet," Phipps brags as the men pat Lenny on the back.

But Phipps doesn't stop patting Lenny. It's like touching him lets Phipps know he's all right.

Royce finds his way to me. His face says everything when he looks at me. I don't look good. Even my vision has started to turn green at the edges.

I try to force a smile. "We're almost there." I hold out his jacket to him.

"Keep it," he says, crouching low and draping it over my shoulders.

He plants a kiss on my forehead. When he pulls back, he looks like he wants to say more. I can see it there, the pain in his eyes—the pain I used to mistake for hardness. He's building his walls back up. The walls I'd thought made him cold and unfeeling so few months ago.

I wish it didn't have to be this way. I wish there'd been another way.

He lifts me gently to my feet, leaning me against him.

I try to take a step but don't get far.

He loops his arm under mine and across my back. "I've got you."

"I know," I say, meeting his gaze. And that look says all the words we don't have time to share.

He gives me one last kiss, anchoring me to him. His lips are light and cool, and I could stay that way forever. But all too soon, he pulls away.

"Let's go get Dionysus," he says.

I nod, and what's left of our crew—stained, bleeding, and limping—moves through the golden vineyard.

"At least we know Dionysus won't be making wine from these any time soon," Hettie says, her now uneven hair frizzing around her face like a lion's mane.

"If he does try," Phipps chimes in, "I hope he chokes on it." The light reflecting off the golden vines shoots through his diamond arm and plays about his face. He grabs a grape with his good arm, but it doesn't come loose from the bunch. He sighs.

Halfway through the vineyard, the ground slopes upward toward a cliff overlooking the ocean. Perched on the edge of the cliff, a stone structure peeks through the gaps in the vines.

I cry out in excitement, but it comes out as a cough. I double over and hack until I spit out green gunk.

I wipe my mouth on the back of my hand, smearing the substance across my skin. It burns, but I ignore it.

"We should rest," Royce says.

"No." I straighten. "Keep going." I need every moment I can get with Dionysus. And right now, I'm not sure how many I have left.

The vineyard phases in and out of focus. Somehow, I keep my feet moving.

At the top of the hill, an open-air pantheon as large as our ship blocks out the afternoon sun. Twisted columns race upward to support a triangular roof. Even steps lead up to an extravagant display.

A table laden with platters of colorful fruits, meat on skewers, and desserts dripping sticky icing down their sides takes up the bulk of the pantheon. At one side of it sits the man who's haunted my dreams for years.

He looks the same as he did in the Oracle's vision, with ruddy cheeks hiding behind a dark auburn beard. But up close, arched eyebrows give his face a mischievous look. So does his smile as he places the cup he'd been drinking from on the table and turns to the figure seated across from him.

"Ha. You should've taken me up on that bet the little humans would make it through the jungle alive," Dionysus says. "You would've won for once."

The second figure turns to stare down at us.

It's Triton.

# CHAPTER 27

Triton's cup clinks against the table as he puts it down. "Ahh, but then you would've had the harpies or the vines or Aristaeus's bees actually kill them instead of leading them to where we could watch them battle it out."

"They're not Aristaeus's bees anymore. They're mine. I won them fair and square." Dionysus's face turns even redder, and I wonder if he's drunk.

"Of course," Triton says, waving his hand dismissively. "You've told me many times—you've won something from every god and goddess. And now all that's left is to beat the Great Oracle herself."

"You traitor," Hettie shouts. She's got her sword out, but as her eyes swing back and forth between Triton and Dionysus, it's hard to tell who she wants dead more.

"I told you not to believe in friendship, that they don't last." Triton takes a bite of an apple, spraying juice down his chin. "And you're a fool if you truly thought I'd want to go against Dionysus. We're gods. We belong together. And we'll exist long after your pathetic human forms are gone." Triton's eyes drag over my green-gold skin. "Which for some of you doesn't look like it'll be long."

"How could you do this?" I say, each word taking effort to get out.

"Because you're all so gullible. You broke me out of my palace, and now I'm free." He spreads his arms wide. "I suppose I should thank you for that. My father never would've let me go without your help."

I sag against Royce, my knees nearly giving out. My whole body shudders, and my stomach seizes inward. I can't take anymore.

"Ah, poor girl." Dionysus picks his goblet back up. It's so big it nearly takes two hands to drink from. "I was hoping to see you here in all your golden glory for a fight of epic proportions. But look at you. Brought down by a gorgon." He shakes his head. "I really don't like seeing my creatures broken—all that power wasted."

"I'm not one of your creatures," I spit, using all the strength I can muster to lift my eyes to meet his gaze.

"I could cure you." He leans forward. His hand goes to the great wooden staff resting next to his chair. Wrapped up and down it are vines ripe with plump grapes.

"How?" Royce's voice sounds out next to me. "How would you cure her?"

"No," I whisper, but Royce doesn't look at me. I'm not even sure if the word truly passed my lips. A constant ringing in my ears is starting to drown out everything else, as if the world is slowly disappearing one sense at a time.

Dionysus grins at Royce. "Didn't learn your father's lesson, did you?"

Royce stiffens. "How?"

Dionysus spreads his arms wide. "By entering into a friendly wager."

"What kind of wager?"

I tug on his arm. I try to tell him to stop, but I start coughing instead. I fight to get my breath back. I can't let him do this.

"Sounds like you don't have much time," Dionysus says, "so I'll make this fast. I'll cure her right now. Then, all you have to do is make it back across the island to your pegasi and leave before the sun sets."

"And if we don't?" Royce asks.

"Then you and those winged horses belong to me."

Royce looks down at me.

I gasp in small amounts of air. I press closer against him. "You can't . . . you can't be considering this."

"I don't want to lose you."

"We barely made it across the island." I pause to catch my breath. "We can't risk it. It isn't worth it."

"It's worth it to me." He cups my face in his hands.

"We should take it," Hettie says, coming up next to us.

I shake my head. "We won't make it." Another coughing fit rips through me, but I wheeze in a breath, fighting for each word. "He . . . he controls everything on this island . . . Too risky."

"Time's wasting," Dionysus calls down. "I need a decision."

"Please, Royce," I pant. "Lagonia is more important. Even . . . even if we made it across, there's . . . there's no way we'd make it back here to find a way to stop Dionysus before the sun sets. You know—" It's hard to get my tongue to move. "You know what the Oracle said about him setting foot on Lagonia." My chest shudders from the effort as I wait for his reply.

Royce stares into my eyes, his eyes so blue I could drown in them. His brow scrunches as he scans my face. Finally, he drops his hands from my cheeks and straightens as he faces Dionysus. "No deal."

"Pity," Dionysus says. "But not a total loss, I suppose. Triton and I will still get a show." He slams the end of his staff into the ground. "Finish them," he calls.

From all around the structure, a handful of men and women stream, followed by a pack of satyrs. They spread out in a line on either side of the stairs leading up to Dionysus.

My vision doubles as I stare at the battle line closing ranks, blocking off the staircase.

"I—I have to get to—to Dionysus," I gasp to Royce as my heart squeezes, taking a moment to restart again.

Royce looks from the stairs down at me, his jaw set. "I'll get you there. No matter what it takes." He rests his hand on my cheek for one moment. One single moment I wish could last forever. Because I see eternity in his eyes. Every moment we've had together and all the ones we'll never get to have.

As a tear slips down my cheek, sizzling where it slides against my feverish skin, battle cries erupt all around. The snarls of the satyrs mix with human roars as Dionysus's force charges forward.

"I love you," Royce says as he pulls his sword. "And I will get you to Dionysus if it's the last thing I do." He presses his lips against mine, and then he's ripping away, pulling me forward into the fray with a battle cry unlike anything I've heard from him before.

A satyr materializes in front of us. Royce doesn't even let go of me as he fights it off. He drives the beast back and back, blocking every attack with his sword. He fights with a determination I've never seen before.

But as soon as the beast goes down, a man saunters in front of us. Smoke escapes from his lips.

Royce stills, hoisting me closer to him. He raises his sword upward.

Our new foe laughs. "And Dionysus thought this would be hard."

The man sucks in a mouthful of air, and his chest expands unnaturally. There's a single moment where I think he might burst, but instead, he exhales.

A scorching blast of fire radiates toward us.

"Look out," Royce shouts, sending us reeling toward the ground. I smash into the dirt, unable to raise my arms enough to break my fall. Royce rolls several feet away. He reaches out to me as he tries to rise to his knees, but a metal foot crashes down on his arm.

Royce roars in pain, reeling back toward the earth. But he manages to wrench his arm free enough to roll to the side and stagger upright.

His assailant's entire body is made up of weapons built into his skin. It's one of the creatures I saw in the Oracle's vision. One hand has been replaced by a sword while the other is now made of an ax. Where his ears should be, two mace balls dangle, their spikes crashing into the daggers that protrude from his shoulders and back. He swings his ax toward Royce, but I don't see what happens next because the man who breathes fire steps before me.

He crouches low and twists his head so it's level with mine. He blows a ring of smoke across my face, causing me to cough and hack.

He laughs and retreats a few feet, once again sucking in an

unnatural amount of air. Then he opens his mouth, and it's like staring at a lava pit. Glowing swirls of red and black rattle around inside, ready to spew forth.

He exhales, releasing the fire directly at me. And just when I expect the pain to hit, something shiny flashes before me.

It's Phipps. He's used his diamond arm to block the flames, sending them splitting to either side of him. And as soon as the man stops spewing fire, Phipps lets out a cry and moves forward, trying to catch the man across the temple with his arm. But it weighs too much, and he's too slow. Giving the man time to duck out of the way.

"Go," Phipps calls to me as he blocks another molten blast so powerful it pushes him backward.

I flop onto my stomach and dig my elbows into the ground, inching closer to the pantheon steps. But every movement I make sends feverish flashes boiling through my body, as if every bit of skin is covered in invisible, raw blisters.

Satyr hooves crash down mere hairsbreadths from my head. Dirt and blood spray before me. I don't stop. I dig my fingers into the earth when my elbows ache too much to keep moving forward.

And then I'm there at the steps, which loom like a mountain above me. At the top, Dionysus sits and laughs, spraying wine down his beard. Triton refuses to look my direction as I claw my way up the first step.

My breath comes out in haggard exhales. I can still barely get any air in. I lean back against one of the pillars flanking the stairs, finally getting a view of the battlefield.

A short, thin, balding man rips boulders from the base of the pantheon wall and tosses them into the fray, not seeming to care if he hits friend or foe. Next to him, a woman with curly brown hair and dark skin disappears. She reappears right in front of one the sailors in the middle of the field who just sliced his blade across the stomach of a satyr. She rams a dagger into the man's chest and then rips it free before vanishing again.

A shadow passes quickly above me as a large bird swoops forward. But it's not truly a bird. It's a human covered in feathers. He plucks pointed brown feathers from his body and flings them downward, catching one sailor in the neck. Hettie manages to get her shield up in time to block most of the arrow-like quills, but one sinks into her thigh. She cries out and rips it free, not even seeming to notice the blood trickling down her leg.

Her eyes follow the attacker's path as he flies over the rest of the crew. The next time the birdman swoops low, Hettie hurls her shield, catching the creature in the head. It drops to the ground, skidding across the dirt and getting crushed under the hooves of an advancing satyr.

Hettie doesn't even watch the man fall because behind her, a woman with olive skin starts to glow. Then there's a blinding flash. I blink over and over again, but I can't see anything.

Screams erupt around me as men cry out that they're blinded.

And then the screaming gets worse. More strangled. And far too often, it cuts off with a gurgle.

When I can finally see, bodies lay on the ground all around me as the satyrs cut them down and more and more of Dionysus's creatures use their powers.

A pair of twins vault forward. They use each other to flip and surprise men from behind as each wields a dagger with dizzying speed. Past them, a woman replicates into several versions of herself and surrounds a group. Another man shoots bolts of lightning from his hands.

Yet another woman shakes the ground around her, sending out mini earthquakes anytime someone gets close.

I spot Royce still facing the man made out of weapons as Hettie darts toward the woman who'd let out the blinding light just as her body starts to softly glow again. Hettie crashes into her and knocks her to the ground.

Rhat tumbles across the middle of the field as a satyr presses its attack. Behind him, a sailor falls to his knees as a satyr's claws rake across his chest. The man slumps face down. Behind him, Lenny has his fingers curled around something. I can't tell what it is until a satyr runs up to him. It looks down, readying a killing blow. But it turns to stone. The gorgon eyes.

More and more satyrs appear. Phipps struggles forward and spins in circles, using his momentum to hit his diamond arm into the temples of the satyrs, making them go limp. But they land on all the human bodies that litter the ground. More people who won't make it back to Lagonia.

The only way to end this is to end Dionysus. I suck in as deep a breath as I can manage and dig my elbows into the stone, pulling myself up the steps. I cry out with the effort of lifting my body over and over again.

The metallic clangs and pained cries of the battle fall away as I put all my energy into making it up those steps. I dig my fingers into every crack, always moving forward. My chest rattles with every inhale, but after what seems like an eternity, I make it to the last step.

I push myself up, and I stare down Dionysus. I crawl toward the nearest pillar and lean against it, facing him.

"Well, well, well," Dionysus says. "This one's still got some fight in her." He shoves off the table and comes over, towering above me, inspecting me as if I were some horse he wanted to buy. He pats my cheek.

I turn away from his touch.

"Should I put you out of your misery?" He reaches for his staff.

"Wait," I call out, the sound raspy and low, as low as my pulse feels.

His hand stalls, and he turns back toward me.

"How . . . how about entering into a bet with me?" I try to get the words out through the pain ripping through my body. I'm surprised my skin hasn't torn open to leak out all the poison flooding my body.

Dionysus clasps his hands. "What are the terms?"

My head falls back against the pillar, yet somehow not having to move any other part of my body gives me the strength to speak. "I'll give you one chance to kill me. If you can't, you'll free my father from every hold the tainted gold and your curse has over him and not harm him in any other way." A small breath rattles through my chest before wheezing out between my dried lips along with my weak words. Words I'd been practicing over and over again in my head for hours.

Dionysus scoffs. "Look at you. You're moments from death."

"Triton . . ." I pause to suck in more air. "Triton told me you only agree to bets you can win. Does that mean you can't? That I've outsmarted the greatest trickster the world has ever known?" I swing my eyes up to Triton, studying his reaction.

"Don't bring me into this," Triton says, rising from the table and stepping back toward the pegasus resting in the shade of the pantheon.

"No, no, stay," Dionysus says. "Stay and watch. The show isn't over yet."

His words draw Triton back. He turns reluctantly away from the pegasus, his arms clasped behind his back. He moves back to the table and leans against Dionysus's chair, watching to see what will happen next.

Dionysus scratches his beard as he studies me.

"Hurry up," I say. "I don't have much time left. You . . . you don't want your friend there"—I nod toward Triton as I pause to get more air into my lungs—"to be able to hold it over you for . . . for eternity that a human girl beat you at your own game."

Triton scoffs. "Of course Dionysus will find a way to outsmart you. I warned you he'd done it to me countless times—and I'm a god." He looks to Dionysus. "Go on, take the deal. Put the poor creature out of its misery, and let's go back to watching the real fight." He takes a grape from the platter resting by Dionysus's seat and pops it lazily into his mouth.

Dionysus's eyes narrow as he looks down at me. "What are you hiding?"

Triton sighs. "She's got a piece of gold in her pocket. She was going to try and turn you to gold when you got close. Can we please go back to the other fight now?"

"Triton!" I cry, the word feeling like it bleeds from my mouth. Or maybe that's my chapped lips ripping open.

He shrugs. "I told you it wasn't going to work. The creatures Dionysus curses can't use his power against him."

My eyes go wide as Triton advances. He wrenches me forward by Royce's jacket, pulling me up into the air. I don't even have the strength to fend him off. He digs around in my pocket, his hand clamping around the golden coin I'd put there—the one Triton supplied when I'd told him my plan last night.

"No." I try feebly to reach for the gold, but Triton discards me, letting me fall back against the pillar. I barely manage to stay on my feet, clinging to the cold marble.

Triton juggles it in his hands, showing it off to Dionysus.

"Don't forget the jacket she's wearing," Triton adds. "Looks like there's still one golden button left."

Dionysus strips the jacket away and tosses it down the stairs where I can't reach it.

I open my mouth to protest, but no sound comes. And when I try to lean toward the jacket, I don't make it more than a few finger lengths.

Dionysus looms over me, a cruel smile twisting across his face. "All right," he says. "Now we have a deal."

"No," I whimper. "No, this wasn't how it was supposed to be. I don't want it anymore."

"It's too late." Dionysus laughs. "You asked for a bet, and I have accepted. There is no breaking it now. A deal has been made, and a deal will be upheld."

There's no shaking of hands to seal the deal. He simply turns around and grabs his staff from where it rests against his chair.

I shake my head. No. No. No.

"I'll give your father your regards when I take over his kingdom."

I push back against the pillar as Dionysus steps toward me, but there's nowhere to go. My eyes flash to Triton, but he makes no move to help me.

My eyes shift back to Dionysus. He pulls back his staff and

cries out something I can't make out. Then he shoves his staff forward, releasing whatever power has built up there.

꙰꙰꙰꙰꙰꙰꙰꙰꙰꙰꙰꙰◉꙰꙰꙰꙰꙰꙰꙰꙰꙰꙰꙰꙰

# CHAPTER 28

I gasp as the staff comes within a handsbreadth of my stomach. But nothing happens.

Confusion clouds Dionysus's face. He gives his staff a shake. The grapes rattle around until one falls off and rolls away, bouncing down the steps to be crushed by a satyr's foot.

"This isn't possible," Dionysus bellows. His lips pull back in a snarl. "What kind of magic is this?"

"I always wondered what it would feel like to hold this," Triton says.

Dionysus whips around.

Triton's there holding a staff that's identical to the one Dionysus holds. Only the one he holds is a little taller, a little sturdier, and the grapes are plumper and don't fall off when they sway back and forth.

Dionysus inspects the staff in his hand. He tears at the vines, ripping them off easily. He strangles his hands around the wood until it snaps and breaks. His chest heaves and his cheeks look like deep embers. "Give me my staff."

Triton pulls the staff closer to his chest, holding it across his body like a shield.

"What are you doing, Triton?" Dionysus rages.

"What someone should've done centuries ago. Preventing you from ruining anyone else's life with your tricks and lies."

"No one gets away with calling me a liar," Dionysus says. He takes a step toward Triton, but I call him back.

"I won the bet," I say. "You have to cleanse my father of the curse you laid on him." My lips tingle numbly, and a nasty taste floods my mouth. I bite my lips together to keep from vomiting. I just need to hold it together for a few more minutes. But I can feel my feet threatening to give out as I slip slowly down the pillar.

Dionysus eyes nearly bulge out of his head.

"You don't want it getting around that you don't honor your bets," Triton adds.

Slowly, Dionysus unclenches his fist. "Fine, but I'll need my staff to uphold my end of the deal."

I look to Triton and nod.

Triton tosses him the staff. Dionysus catches it midair. He raises it to the sky, shouting undecipherable words.

A bright light shoots from the end of his staff. I close my eyes, and for the first time since I can remember, the golden aura marking the locations of each piece of my father's cursed gold doesn't beckon me.

I wish I had time to visit my father and make sure Dionysus hadn't somehow found an accidental loophole in my words. But there's no gold signal to follow to the palace anymore.

I open my eyes.

Dionysus stands in front of me. "Our deal is complete. I cleansed your father, but not you, as your condition isn't part of what I did to him. Didn't think it all through, did you, Princess?

As a result, I'll let you suffer in your golden state for your last few moments. Because now that the deal is complete, I can kill you."

As a coughing fit overtakes me, liquid fire rushes through my body like an unstoppable inferno, starting at my ankle and rising straight toward my heart, and I don't think I'll last long enough to give him the satisfaction.

But Dionysus pulls back his staff, readying his attack.

My knees give out, and I stumble forward, just as Triton shouts my name and tosses me the gold coin.

I catch it, and my hands land on Dionysus's hands wrapped around his staff just as he cries out a curse and sends it shooting out the end of his staff.

He instantly turns to gold.

The light shooting out of his staff cuts off, but not before it blasts through the pillar I'd been leaning against and straight out over the jungle, colliding with the side of the volcano, sending shards of rock flying into the sky.

"I can't believe it worked," Triton says.

"I told— I told you I wasn't one of his creatures. He never gave me anything." Because as soon as Triton told me that Dionysus claimed his creations couldn't use their powers against him, it had set my mind wondering. If anyone was his match, it was someone with part of his curse inside them but not truly *from* him.

But I'd never known for sure.

I rip my hand away from Dionysus. But without something to lean on, I collapse.

My head hits the pantheon's stone floor and ricochets off. I don't feel it. I don't feel anything. My body has gone entirely numb. I couldn't even feel the gold when I'd absorbed it from the coin.

Triton crouches over me. "I'm going to get you to Panacea." He tries to lift me, but I still his hand. It's too late. "Find—Royce—" I sputter.

The inferno inside me rages higher. Every layer of my body burns as if I swallowed lava from Dionysus's volcano.

My lungs sputter for air. I'm not even sure my heart is beating anymore. My body spasms, clenching inward. I curl reflexively into a ball.

Someone clatters up the steps. It's Hettie.

"The few satyrs and that guy who had weapons for arms were all that remained, and they scattered as soon as she turned Dionysus." Hettie drops to her knees next to me and pushes my shoulders back, forcing me to look at her. "Oh, Kora," she breathes. "Don't leave me. You have to stay. We'll find a way to fix this."

I want to reach my hand up to her face, to wipe away the tears slipping down her cheeks, leaving trails in the dirt and blood caked there. But my muscles won't respond.

Royce dashes up behind her. I try to smile, but I can't.

"I'm here, Kora," Royce says. He grasps my hand in his. "I'm here. Stay with me. Please."

My mouth opens. No words come out. A jolt of pain slices through me, threatening to rip me open from the inside out.

My throat constricts. My head falls to the side as I gasp for breath.

"Kora," Royce says, but his words are fading. Everything's fading. Turning a soft shade of green.

The world shakes around me. Or maybe it comes from inside me.

Hettie's shouting something and pointing into the distance, but her words don't make it through the fog in my mind.

My eyelids are so heavy.

I let them close.

"Come on, Kora." Royce shakes me awake again. He grabs his jacket from the steps and tucks it in around me.

Phipps appears behind him. He holds up clenched fists. "I've got the gorgon eyes. We could turn her to stone. Would that save her?"

"It might stop her from dying," Hettie says.

Rhat stares at something in the distance. "She'd be too heavy. I'm not sure we'd get her off the island in time."

"It's worth trying if it saves her," Royce says.

Before they can come to a decision, the world shakes again. But it's not just me. Platters on the table clink together, sending grapes and other fruit rolling across the table. Dionysus's cup rattles off, and I brace, expecting shattered glass to spill over me.

But the cup doesn't break. It rolls toward me.

The glass shimmers iridescently in the light, casting small rainbows on the floor as the sunlight hits its surface.

That's not what catches my attention. The crystal figures embossed on the cup do. A man with a short beard stares at me. Before I can figure out who he is, the cup shimmers. A different face appears—a woman with flowing hair, who I feel I've seen before.

A memory tugs at my mind, but I'm so tired it doesn't want to surface. Instead it swirls around in my mind like the yellow liquid that remains in the still-rolling cup.

The cup rolls to a stop an arm's length from my head.

The figure changes again. The one staring straight at me can be no one other than Triton.

A cup with portraits of the gods.

Hebe's cup.

My heart leaps, sending a pulse of pain through my bones.

What is the cup doing here?

Dionysus and his bets! Triton had said Dionysius won something from each of the gods. It wasn't too far to believe he could've won Hebe's cup.

I beg my arm to move toward the cup. It doesn't budge.

I rotate my head toward Royce. He phases in and out of focus. He and Triton are arguing about something and pointing toward the other side of the island. A sharp ringing in my ears drowns out their words.

"Cup," I try to say, looking toward it, but the word comes out as a gurgle.

Royce turns back to me and grasps my cheeks, forcing me to look at him. His lips move, but the words don't make it through the ringing. He tightens his grip as a tear slips down his cheek.

A shadow falls over me as Lenny peers down, his brow scrunched together.

I peer back toward the cup, but my body still refuses to move toward it.

Lenny's gaze follows mine toward the cup, but before I can try to think of a way to get him to reach for it, shouting erupts, barely breaking through the buzzing in my ears.

"We've got to get out of here," someone yells. "It's about to collapse."

Green fog clouds my vision even more.

I heave for breath. None comes in.

Royce is lifting me, cradling me to his chest. But we're not moving toward the cup. We're moving away from it. Sunlight blinds me as we leave the pantheon behind. I jostle around as he clambers down the steps. The cup gets farther and farther out of reach, disappearing from view as feet stomp down the steps after us.

A moment later, the ground shakes again.

The entire pantheon sways behind us. The pillars rock before falling to pieces. The roof comes down in a loud crash, sending dust, debris, and chunks of gold into the air. Gold?

Dionysus's golden statue bursts into pieces as the roof caves in on top of it.

But any joy at that thought is drowned out by the knowledge the cup was crushed too. My last hope was destroyed.

I'd let out a sob if my body was able. Instead, it gives up. I melt against Royce, my lungs burning and my head spinning. The poison tightens around my heart, strangling it.

Two beats.

*Thump. Thump.*

One beat.

*Thump.*

Then nothing.

# CHAPTER 29

⟩⟩⟩⟩⟩⟩⟩⟩⟩⟩❁⟨⟨⟨⟨⟨⟨⟨⟨⟨⟨

The odd thing about dying is that it feels like coming back to life. My entire body tingles as feeling slowly returns to my toes, then my calves, then my knees. A pleasant sensation gradually works up my body, a comfortable warmth, like waking up under soft blankets. I stretch into the feeling and take a deep breath, surprised by how easy it feels. Fresh air pumps into my body, renewing my muscles.

I open my eyes. A flash of gold sparks through me. No, not through me—all around me. Bright light streams everywhere. It takes my eyes a few moments to adjust.

A peaceful blue sky drifts by above me. But then dark, twisted clouds come barreling into view. Small pieces shoot out of them and fall away. They blast into the ground, sending dirt flying in all directions. The rest of the world explodes. Sounds come rushing in, overpowering my ears.

Royce appears above me. He's talking excitedly to someone I can't see.

But what's he doing here?

I sit up to find we're only a few lengths from the fallen pantheon.

"Oh, Kora," Hettie falls down next to me, pulling me into a hug. "I thought we were going to lose you."

"I thought I died," I reply hoarsely. "What happened?"

Royce shrugs. "Lenny and Phipps nearly got crushed getting this cup out of the pantheon as it fell. But Lenny wouldn't let him leave without it. Something about the way you were looking at it. He wouldn't rest until you had a sip from it." Royce holds up the crystal chalice with the ever-rotating display of faces.

I grab it, surprised my arms respond. "It's Hebe's cup. Dionysus must've won it from her. It's what saved me."

"And right now, I'm glad it did. But we can talk about Dionysus's ill-gotten table settings later," Hettie says. "The whole island's about to blow."

Above her head, the clouds have gotten darker, taking up more and more of the sky. Over her shoulder, the volcano shoots up plumes of smoke that quickly float into the sky. I have a vague memory of Dionysus's curse shooting past me—straight toward the volcano.

"Can you walk?" Royce asks, once again draping his jacket over me as he and Hettie help me climb to my feet.

My body feels so good, I could probably run, swim, somersault, or do anything I put my mind to. It's like all my muscles have been remade. I examine my skin. There's no trace of green veins. I hike up my pant leg. Even the bite marks from the gorgon snake have healed.

"I knew that cup was important." Phipps slides up to me. "But I had a backup plan just in case because I'm always thinking— always one step ahead of everyone else." He pats his pocket where the gorgon's eyes rest.

I grab his hand. "Thank you. You and Lenny." I nod toward Lenny, who raises his arm in acknowledgement.

"Lenny understands eyes like no one else," Phipps says.

I stare down at the cup as the face shifts again. "Maybe if you drank from it, it would heal your arm."

Phipps knocks on his diamond appendage. "I think I'd like to keep it."

Triton stands at the back of the group with the pegasus he'd taken, the one he'd hidden the replica staff on.

"Any idea how this works?" I ask, holding the cup up, just as his face flashes across.

He shrugs. "I'd never seen it before. I haven't spent much time with the other gods. I was too busy having fun with you humans."

I resist the urge to both smile and smack him at the same time. "Thank you," I say, "for helping us humans and keeping up your part of the plan." His performance back on the beach had been so convincing, I wasn't sure if he actually had been fleeing or if he'd stick to the plan we'd come up with to find a way to switch Dionysus's staff out for a replica.

Not to mention I'm glad he was able to get the pegasus we'd let him take to the other side of the island. When I'd first broached the idea as a place to hide the staff, he'd said it was impossible, that he couldn't get a pegasus safely to the far side of the island anymore than he could get us there alive, that it was hard enough to fly to the closest shore. He'd said he couldn't use a wave because the pegasus would no doubt thrash in confusion trying to escape the water, either losing the staff or being killed when the wave hit the island—just like we would be—since the creatures weren't immortal like he was. But I'd pushed him. Even if he couldn't get us all there, there had to be a way he could get one single pegasus to arrive alive with the replica staff in tow.

And after much back and forth, an idea had popped into

my mind, spurned on by the ice dome he'd created around us on Gorgon Island. He could freeze the pegasus in a block of ice, and that way, when it crashed into the island, it wouldn't get injured. After thinking about it for a while, Triton had said it wouldn't work with us humans since we would freeze to death, but since pegasi are born of the sea, they could probably survive the ice casing.

And clearly, it must've worked.

"He got what he deserved," Triton says. He looks back at the chunks of gold amidst the rubble. He props himself on Dionysus's staff, which he must've taken, though I can't imagine why.

"You mean, he was part of your plan to stop Dionysus?" Hettie asks. She stares at Triton critically.

"I'm sorry I couldn't tell you," I say. "I needed you all to believe he'd left. I wasn't sure if Dionysus would be watching us somehow."

"I'm just glad Dionysus didn't twist your bet some other way," Triton replies.

I nod. We'd both been so worried about how Dionysus would spin our agreement against me. I'd had to think so carefully about each word, about what was said and unsaid, what was clarified and what was left open to interpretation. But after realizing how big a predictor the Oracle's tests had been for other parts of our journey, I'd gone back over the test of drinking from the crystal—the one test I didn't think we'd encountered on our path yet, the one I could only assume was meant to parallel facing Dionysus. It made me think about what people infer based on what is actually before them, and I'd used that as my guide in hopes of getting Dionysus to think he was getting the best of me by only cleansing my father and not me. I'd also purposefully left gaping holes in my bet, and he'd fallen right into them in his bid to outsmart me.

"Do you think Dionysus is dead for good?" Rhat asks.

"We shouldn't have to worry about him for a very long time," Triton says.

The ground heaves beneath us as the island shakes. The volcano rumbles in the distance.

"We do have to worry about this island blowing up," Hettie bellows.

The first blast of fiery red lava spills like blood over the edge of the volcano.

"The cliffs," I say, pointing past the pantheon. "We can jump off there." I move toward the steps.

"No," Triton exclaims, grabbing my arm. "You can only leave Jipper where you entered it."

"What?" I cry as another blast of lava shoots skyward, painting the clouds like a mock sunset.

"How do you think Dionysus made sure no one could win those bets about making it off his island before sunset? You can only leave the way you came."

"So we have to go all the way back across?" Royce says, raking a hand through his hair.

"I'm afraid so," Triton says. "And I won't be able to lead you. I also have to leave where I came on. I'll take this pegasus and wait for you on the other side."

"There has to be another option," I say. I stare back across the tops of the trees. They stretch on and on, an impassable sea of green.

The island tosses beneath us.

"There's no other way," Triton says with finality. "You must go. When you get back to the beach, you'll see a small shimmering in the sky or at the edge of the sand. That's where you entered the island."

"Go," Royce calls.

Triton runs toward the pegasus and leaps on.

"Be off before sunset," Triton shouts after us. He wheels the pegasus around and flies it straight toward the cliff edge. I watch as they fly into the air, disappearing as the island speeds onward without them.

A loud boom is followed by an explosion of volcanic rocks. They barrel into the ground around us. We scatter back toward the vineyard, the golden vines a blur as we run past. When we reach the jungle, the giant bees dart above us in a frenzy as smoke hazes over the trees. They appear too preoccupied to bother us, colliding with each other as the smoke thickens.

"This way," Rhat calls from his position near the rear, where he helps keep Phipps and his diamond arm moving.

We tumble through the jungle, tripping over tree limbs and thrashing through vines. Birds cry out and hop along the trees above us, as eager to flee as we are. The heat from the volcano turns the air around us sticky. Sweat soaks my clothes. Even my revitalized lungs beg me to stop and rest, though I ignore their pleas.

We pass through the harpy field, slipping across the streaks of rich red blood that stain the grass.

Next to me, Lenny pants and then doubles over.

I stop to tell him to keep going, but when I turn back, shadows crawl across my body. Everything around me grows darker and darker. My muscles tighten as a storm of ash clouds clog the sky above us, blocking out the sun. The sun that's sinking very quickly toward the horizon. The sun that will trap us here. The sun I can now no longer see, as it's been swallowed by the billowing blackness.

"Come on, Lenny," I say between haggard breaths. I crouch next to him and tug on his shoulders. "We've got to keep moving."

He looks up and nods. He takes a deep breath and starts slugging forward again.

All around me, men are moving slower and slower, their legs fighting to keep pumping forward. Some trip or stumble as they look up to see the darkness pressing in from above. The shadows hang heavily across their faces, highlighting sunken cheekbones and eyes.

We rip through the field and back into the jungle, where the darkness is blinding. Tree limbs scratch and exposed roots trip up our feet.

Murky figures of men fall around me, letting out grunts and groans as they collide with the ground. The heavy sound of them pulling themselves to their feet mixes with my own overwhelming heaves for air.

"Keep your eyes on me," I cry, thankful my skin stands out a little better than anything else in the dark jungle.

I grab Lenny's shoulder and guide him toward the figure in front of me.

It's Royce.

"Which way?" I ask, resting against a tree.

He spins around. "I don't know. It all looks so different in the dark. And that diamond girl is still out here somewhere, along with who knows what else." I can barely make out the whites of his eyes as his gaze searches the jungle for anything familiar.

I shove my hair back where perspiration has pressed it against my forehead.

More men crowd around as we search for the right path.

Every minute we waste could cost our lives. But so could choosing the wrong path. "Royce, the sun is setting. We need to hurry."

"That way," Phipps says. He uses his good arm to point to our right.

"Are you sure?" Royce asks.

"Aye, Captain. I can see a twinkle from one of the diamonds I dropped from my pockets when we were running from that diamond creature."

Hope wells within me.

"Good job," Royce says. "Keep your eyes out for more."

"Now there's a task I'm good at," Phipps says. "I've always had an eye for treasure."

Using Phipps's haphazard trail, we make our way back toward the stream.

"What about the diamond girl?" I ask as we get close to the gurgling water. Amidst the darkness, the diamonds at the bottom reflect the little bits of light they catch, causing the banks to glow unnaturally.

Royce creeps forward, trying to rustle the leaves as little as possible. He leans over the banks. After a moment, he turns around. "I don't see her, but it's hard to tell with all those diamonds glimmering underwater. She could be hiding amongst them."

As he speaks, there's a ripple behind him.

"Royce," I yell as a hand shoots from the water.

On reflex, Royce dives, rolling across the ground and pulling his sword.

The diamond girl rises out of the water, her pointed, angular shape reflecting the small amount of light filtering through the trees. Her fingers spread wide, ready to catch any of us she can.

"Come back for more, have you?" she asks. Her voice is as sharp and hard as her skin.

"I'll distract her," Hettie whispers to me. "Get the others across." Without waiting for my response, she charges forward.

"I'm going to hack you into tiny gems and wear you as a necklace," Hettie says to the creature, twirling her sword around and charging forward.

"Or maybe I'll stop your heart cold," the woman replies. She digs her feet into the diamonds lining the stream, readying for Hettie's attack. She sneers, displaying rows of diamond teeth.

"Quick, Lenny, head that way," I move him forward, keeping my eyes on the creature as I usher him across the river. He leaps across easily. I motion for others to do the same.

The diamond woman tries to wade toward us, but Hettie is there, stopping her at every turn. The woman retaliates by trying to catch Hettie in her grip any way she can. But Hettie moves like a cat. She jumps, she leaps, she arches her back, doing everything she can to avoid the woman's grasp. Every time her sword connects with the jeweled body, there's a tiny flash where the sword transforms from metal to diamond.

Royce joins the fight, making sure the woman is so distracted she can't spare a thought for us.

"Hurry." I motion to Rhat and Phipps.

"Let me go," Phipps yelps. "I'll use this arm to crush her where she stands."

The diamond girl claws toward Hettie's stomach. Hettie stumbles back, rolling onto the ground.

The creature uses the opening to plow toward us.

"Hurry," I cry, throwing up my arms to act as a barrier between the woman and Phipps.

Royce trudges behind the woman, tripping over the uneven diamonds.

I transfer Hebe's cup to my other hand and reach for the last gold button on Royce's jacket.

The woman watches the movement, but she stops short.

"Hebe's cup," she breathes.

Royce's sword crashes into the woman's head. She stumbles forward, not turning to attack back.

Something about her demeanor has changed. Her sneer is gone. "The cup," she says, her voice rising. "Give me that cup." She charges forward faster than before.

I stumble backward as she advances, but I don't get far because the ground around us heaves. Leaves explode into the air and the diamonds in the stream clink together as the soil pulses up and down in shaky waves. I fight to stay on my feet as an inexplicable vibrating thrums through the landscape. It pulses through me, growing stronger and stronger.

Above me, the trees sway and groan. There's a loud tearing sound as several of them rip free from the earth and crash into the ground, sending clouds of debris to clog the already ashen air.

Then the world cracks open with a shattering roar as the island splits apart around us.

# CHAPTER 30

The stream rips in half as parts of the island tear away from each other. Water and diamonds glint and glitter as they disappear down the gaping hole.

I dive toward Phipps and Rhat at the same time Royce does. We roll into the dirt, and I drop Hebe's cup.

The woman pulls herself out of the pile of diamonds she'd been thrown into on the only remaining section of the stream that hasn't fallen into the crack.

Her eyes and mine land on the cup at the same time. She dives for it just as my fingers wrap around it, drawing it back to my chest.

I stagger to my feet.

"No," the diamond woman cries, wedging herself on a small shelf of the remaining stream.

Her voice is echoed by more shuddering as a giant rift separates pieces of the island even farther. Stringy roots stick out of the mud lining the edges, and clumps of dirt fall and disappear into a dark abyss. I don't hear them hit bottom. I lean forward, but there's nothing as far down as I can see. Just utter darkness.

I move away from the edge, from where the diamond woman crouches on our side of the break, ready to grab us if we try to run forward and jump across. But there's no way we can leap that far.

I search for another way out. I scan the trees, but even if we could drag a fallen one and prop it across, the diamond woman is there, waiting.

I stare down the gap. "We might be able to head inward and find somewhere small enough to cross," I say.

Royce nods. He calls to the men on the other side of the gap. "Get to the pegasi. Get off the island before sunset."

Lenny struggles to the front of the group on the opposite edge.

"Don't worry about me, Lenny," Phipps calls. "You go with them. Not all the gods in the world could keep me from getting back to that beach."

Lenny hesitates.

"You've got to go without me," Phipps says. "Go get the pegasi ready for us."

Lenny stands there for a moment before nodding.

The ground quakes, and the gap widens again. The ground under Royce falls away. I pull him back before he can plummet to his death.

"Let's go," Hettie says as soon as the men have been swallowed by the gray haze settling all around us.

We move along the edge of the crack, Hettie and Royce walking backward to watch for the diamond woman's attack.

"Wait," the woman cries. She hasn't moved from the edge of the stream still clinging to our part of the island. "Please."

My pace slows. Something in her voice calls me back.

Her jagged hand reaches forward, but she still doesn't

advance. Her face looks almost human behind all the sharp edges, and if it were, I might just recognize agony on it.

"Come on, Kora," Hettie says. "There's no time." She pulls at my arm as the ground continues to sway under our feet.

But something about the woman won't let me leave. Why hasn't she abandoned the stream?

"Kora, there's no time," Hettie urges.

"Please," the woman repeats.

I hold the cup back, still unsure.

More ground falls away beneath her. She cries out, casting frightened glances into the abyss.

"Please," the woman begs. "My name is Janalisa. I was cursed by Dionysus years ago and trapped here. That cup—if you twist the silver brim, the face will change. If you drink from the cup, it will heal any physical ill. But if you drink from the cup when it shows the face of the god or goddess who cursed you, it can undo curses. Please, don't leave me here. Please undo what he did to me."

Something about the way she says her name—as if it's the first time in a long time, or it's the first time she remembers she has one and was once human—pulls at my heart.

I twist the brim of the cup. Faces flash across the crystal with each turn.

There's another rumble behind me.

I bite my lip. I wish I had more time.

"Kora," Hettie says, "don't listen to her. It's a trick. Let's go."

I hesitate. Because I know that if she's telling the truth, I can't leave her trapped in that state. And I see something in her eyes that once matched my own, the desperation I'd had when searching for a way to get rid of the golden tinge to my skin.

"Hands behind your back," I say.

I dip the cup into a small puddle of water caught in a dip in the bank of the stream, not taking my eyes from her. I twist the brim until Dionysus's bearded face grins back at me from the cup. "Open your mouth."

I pour the water in. It splashes against her teeth and dribbles into her mouth.

She swallows. Instantly, Janalisa's hardened skin melts away to reveal flesh so pale I can trace every blue vein in her body. Long blonde hair tumbles over her thin, bony frame.

She cries out, holding up her hands to inspect them. Then her hands jump to her face, massaging the skin of her cheeks and running fingers through her hair.

Her deep breaths turn into sobs. She collapses onto her hands and knees and into the mud, which doesn't turn to diamond at her touch. "I can feel. I can feel it all." She stretches her arm out in front of her, looking at the mud staining it. She stares down, turning her arm back and forth in inspection.

She rises back to her knees and takes a deep breath. "I'm free."

She's entirely naked but doesn't seem to care. Now that I can see her face, she only looks a few years older than me. Her features are plain and pleasant, with a few freckles dotting the bridge of her nose, cheeks, and forehead.

When she opens her eyes, tears stream down her face. She reaches out to me. "Thank you."

Flaming bits of rock and ash crash through the canopy above us, singeing leaves as they hiss downward. They ignite the brush where they crash.

"Run," Rhat shouts.

"Let me come with you," Janalisa begs as another round rains down.

"All right," I say, praying I don't regret the decision. "Come on. But you can only get off the island where you came on."

"Dionysus throws all his creatures onto the beach when they first get to the island. If they can't make it across to him, they're not worth his time," she says as I pull her upright. "If you were headed to the opposite beach earlier, you likely arrived not far from where he left me."

She wobbles on her feet, as if she's not accustomed to using them.

"I'm sorry," she says as her weight sags against me. "I guess my real feet aren't used to running."

I'm about to offer her Royce's jacket when Phipps makes a show of taking off his shirt and offering it to her instead. His pasty skin stands out amidst the shadows of the forest.

The woman takes the shirt and touches her hand to Phipps's cheek. "I'm sorry about your arm."

"Don't worry, my lady," Phipps says. "We'll get you out of here." He offers her a lopsided grin.

"Enough mooning," Hettie snaps at Phipps as he smiles at Janalisa, oblivious to the island falling to pieces around us.

"This way," Janalisa says as more fireballs rain down from the sky. Royce stays close to keep her from falling as we race along the edge of the gap.

"Are you sure we should trust her?" Hettie asks, coming up next to me as we fight our way through the jungle.

"I couldn't leave her here. And she hasn't attacked us yet."

"Yet," Hettie mutters.

Her words are echoed by a rumbling sound. But this one is

different than all the ones before it. It's not the gurgling roar of the volcano getting ready to spew ash and lava. This is deeper than that somehow, more like a low moan.

"The island is sinking for the night," Janalisa wails, nearly tripping as she turns toward us. "We have to hurry. If your feet are still on land when ocean water touches you, you'll be trapped here forever."

"What do you mean forever?" Phipps calls, breathing heavily. His arm drags down his entire side.

I check the cup, but all the liquid sloshed out while I was running. I should've made him drink from the cup back at the stream. I scan the gap beside us, but the rest of the water and its banks have already fallen away.

"If you're standing on the island when it's sinking," Janalisa explains, "you can never escape. And the way it's looking now, I don't think it will ever rise again."

"Will you be able to get off?" Phipps asks.

Her brow crinkles. "I'm hoping drinking from that cup removed every hold he had on me. But there's only one way to find out."

More and more ash and rock rain down through the trees. A piece burns through my sleeve and scorches my shoulder before I can brush it away. The ash comes down like thick, dirty snow-flakes, clogging the air with the scent of hot dirt.

I pull the neckline of my shirt up and breathe through it.

Next to me, Hettie's hair has turned entirely gray due to the falling cinders.

"There's a giant tree up ahead," Janalisa calls over her shoulder. "It has the biggest roots on the island, so if there's any place the island might still be holding together, it's there. We can use the vines hanging from the tree to swing across."

The ash is starting to pile up around our feet, burning with every step. The air is so hazy I can't tell if the gap has gotten any smaller or if I'm just imagining it has.

Ahead, a massive tree is silhouetted against the glowing volcano. Thick, sturdy limbs reach out in all directions, and from them hang hundreds of vines.

"We might be able to climb the tree and use one of those bigger branches to walk across to the other si—." Janalisa's words cut off as a roar sounds through the jungle.

But this isn't the roar of the island falling to pieces.

A giant shape looms out of the trees around us.

A satyr.

And it's not alone.

Three others drift out of the forest along with the man whose body is made of weapons.

The satyrs bolt forward.

"Hurry, climb," Janalisa says. She staggers toward the vines as Royce rushes to face the closest satyr.

My heart pounds as we burst through the outer layer of vines. They're as thick as my wrists and covered in moss and ash. The vines whack against us from all sides as we set them moving in our rush to push our way toward the base of the tree. But it's obvious from the grunts behind us that we aren't going to make it there in time.

Rhat leaps onto a vine and pulls himself up to a low branch.

"Give me your hands," he yells.

I shove Janalisa toward him, and Hettie grabs his other hand.

Rhat's muscles strain as he pulls both arms upward at the same time until both women can reach the branch he's on.

Phipps tries to climb the vine next to me, but with his diamond arm, he's not making any progress.

"Kora," Rhat calls. He reaches down for me.

"Phipps first," I reply. I toss Hebe's cup up to Hettie and get under Phipps, trying to shove him upward so he can reach Rhat's hand.

Rhat grunts at the effort of trying to pull up Phipps and his arm. I push upward as hard as I can. Slowly, Phipps starts to rise.

But not fast enough. Out of the corner of my eye, the vines start to shake. Then they disappear entirely as a satyr rakes its claws across them, sending each coiling to the ground.

I shove Phipps upward, and he scrambles onto the branch. But it gives the satyr time to advance.

"Kora," Hettie screams. "Look out!"

I duck out of the way just in time to avoid the spiny claws as they rip toward me. The satyr presses forward, bits of ash spewing from its nose as it grunts.

Two other satyrs shadow behind it. They leap upward, trying to get their claws into the branch where Rhat stands with Phipps. They shove vines out of the way and run along the tree branch in the direction of the gap. The satyr in front of me presses forward.

I stumble backward, letting the vines swing closed like a curtain between us.

*Swipe.*

*Swipe.*

More vines tumble to the ground.

The beast's hooves pound into the ground, echoing the groaning of the island.

My back collides with the trunk of the tree. The rough bark cuts into my shoulders.

The satyr dives for me.

I duck to the side.

The satyr crashes into the tree, its claws buried deep in the wood.

I dash around the trunk and find a low branch. I ignore the pain in my stomach as I haul myself onto the bumpy bark.

The satyr charges around the tree and leaps up after me.

I fight my way along the branch, clinging to vines. I climb from one branch to another, ignoring the sharp cuts in my arms and legs. Up and over I climb, swinging under and around limbs trying to get back toward the gap. My chest heaves. My fingers burn from gripping the coarse boughs. I climb onto another branch, but it's not much thicker than any of the vines.

The satyr clambers up behind me. Its eyes burn bright red as it takes me in. For a moment, I can't understand why. Then I feel it. Heat rising up my backside like I've caught fire.

Down below, the gap lights up as thick, black-crusted lava spills its way through toward the edge of the island.

The satyr moves farther out.

I scoot onto a branch behind me, which starts to sag. Then there's a sickening crack as the satyr's claws rip into my perch. The limb tears free, and I plummet downward. I hit one branch and glance off another. Before I can even register pain, I'm falling again.

Searing red streams around me as I spin, catching glimpses of lava spiraling ever closer.

I land on a thick branch. A dull ache radiates through the entire front side of my body. But there's no time to dwell on it, because the limb I'm on quivers as the satyr jumps down on it. Then it creaks as my attacker slides farther out.

I crawl forward. The gap blazes below me, swallowing all the ash that falls into it. Heat waves crest over me, evaporating the air in my lungs and sucking the air from around me.

I blink away the ash that lands on my eyelashes and scan the tree for the others. I don't see them anywhere. There are only empty vines strangling down around me. I grab on to one and pull myself to my feet, turning to meet the satyr.

It charges forward, nostrils flared.

I let it come. Even as the branch bounces and threatens to break, I tighten my grip and stand my ground.

"Kora," Hettie cries from somewhere behind me, the sound muffled by all the ash around us.

Still, I don't move.

When the satyr's hooves leave the branch, leaping for me, I kick off the branch, swinging backward over the gap. The satyr's body follows me, but it doesn't have a vine to cling to. It crashes downward into the lava and lets out an ear-shattering scream as it melts into the red current.

I fly back toward the tree, my feet fighting to gain traction as my fingers slip on the vine. I twist back out over the lava pool. My shoulders burn, and I dig my fingers into the flesh of the vine, causing white sap to leak out.

Finally, I sway back toward the branch. I stretch my foot out and knock ash away to find moss, then pull myself onto the branch, sucking in air.

"Kora," Hettie calls from the other side of the gap. "Use the vine to swing over."

"Be sure to get a running start," Phipps says. "Or you won't make it."

"Where's Royce?" I call into the foggy ash.

"Here," Royce cries, heaving himself up a branch next to me. "Let's get out of here."

I nod and adjust my grip on the vine.

I scoot back down the branch, giving myself room to run forward. I tell myself not to focus on the swirling red torrent spinning in the crack. The one that will swallow me if I don't swing far enough.

I rip my eyes away, focusing on where the lava's glow illuminates the far side I'm aiming for.

"On three," Royce says. "One, two, three—" He runs forward and leaps, swinging far out over the lava toward the other side.

I move with him, but before I can leap, something snags my leg.

"Going somewhere?" the weapon-bodied man asks. His ax pins my pants to the branch while he brings his sword around to swipe at my legs. I pull on the vine, ripping my pants free just in time to leap over his blade.

"Kora," Royce calls. "Where are you?"

The island quakes, and the tree sways violently back and forth. I cling to the vines as they jostle around me, pelting me from all directions. A portion of dirt at the base of the tree plummets into the lava, and the tree jolts downward. My heart goes with it as the tree jerks to a stop.

But then the tree starts to lean. Straight toward the lava. Several limbs sear off as they brush against the unending stream, and small flames lick upward.

The vine I'm clinging to tilts outward. I fly out over the lava, barely keeping my grip as the tree halts. But it won't stay stopped for long. The lava slowly consumes the tree. Limb by limb. Vine by vine. Leaf by leaf, with a crackling quickness.

"Give me Hebe's cup," the man demands. He extends the flat side of his ax like a hand.

"If you want to be cured," I say, "we can help you. We'll give you the cup."

He laughs. "It's not for me. It for Dionysus. When I help restore him, he'll reward me for killing you. He'll give me even more powers."

I shake my head. "I don't have it." Droplets of sweat edge in around my fingers, greasing my palms. I slip farther down the vine as my grip loosens again and again.

"Kora!" someone calls to me again.

The man wraps his elbows around the vines to keep his feet planted on the branch as he leans forward, staring across the island's gap. "Then I'll kill you and take it from your friends instead."

"Get out of here," I scream over my shoulder, not even sure if the others can hear me.

The man edges closer to where I hang.

I risk letting go with one arm. I flail for the other vine, but it's just out of my reach.

I yank my arm back as my body slips down the vine I'm on. I clamp my legs tighter around it.

Bits of lava spit up below me.

The entire tree sinks faster with the added weight of the man moving closer to the pit. The lava bubbles closer and closer. I search for a way out. But the man is blocking the only close branch, and my hands are slipping more and more. I'm out of ideas.

"Kora!" Shouts come from the other side of the gap.

The tree shifts downward.

My knuckles burn as my fingers curl tighter and tighter. My arms start to shake. My feet can't get any traction.

I try to reach for another vine again, but my fingers glance off.

The man laughs, displaying a set of metallic teeth. Then he swipes his sword toward the top of my vine, trying to cut it loose. A small slit appears. The man edges nearer to try again. Near enough I could almost touch him.

Near enough I could turn him to gold. I glance down at the one last golden button hanging on Royce's jacket. It's all I have, but I'll need to let go to absorb it. And my legs are already slipping downward.

The man pulls back his sword, taking aim once more. Just as he swings forward, I grab the golden button with one hand. And then I'm diving toward him. But I don't make it. Instead of crashing into his legs, I crash into the branch he's standing on.

The entire tree flashes gold and careens to the side under the new weight. I try to keep my grip on the branch, but I can't get any traction on the metal. My hands slip off.

I fall and smash into a branch and glance off. I spiral around and around as I plummet downward. The lava rears toward me like a mouth waiting to swallow me whole.

〉〉〉〉〉〉〉〉〉〉◉〈〈〈〈〈〈〈〈〈〈〈

# CHAPTER 31

H eat races through my body. My cheeks flush with warmth. My blood boils.

And then the temperature cuts off with one final blast of heat that soars upward as the entire stream of lava turns a hard, beautiful shade of gold.

I landed on my stomach, and I don't need to roll over to know I absorbed the gold from the tree on my way down. I don't want to move at all. Not only because of the throbbing ache pulsing up my arms, but because I know what'll happen if I reabsorb the gold.

"Kora!" Hettie shouts. She leans over the edge of the crack, sending sprays of dirt down on me. "She's okay," she says over her shoulder. "Get a vine."

She looks back down at me, sending her uneven hair spilling forward. "Hang on. We'll pull you up."

I carefully get to my knees, making sure not to lose contact with the gold and reabsorb it. I contemplate rising to my feet, but as the island trembles, I can't risk being thrown off balance. I scoot toward the other side of the gap, but the trembling doesn't stop. I make it to the wall on the other side just as that part of the island jolts away from the gold.

I nearly tumble into the gap when a vine drops in front of it.

I grab on and in the process crash into the wall of the pit. And then I'm being pulled into the air.

I drag along the dirt until I'm back on solid ground. Once I am, Royce pulls me into his arms. "I thought I'd lost you again."

"You will lose her if we don't get out of here," Hettie chimes in, reminding us again we're still not safe.

She's right. The ground hasn't stopped shaking.

"The man with blades all over him—he's over there somewhere," I say, panting. "He attacked me." I scan the tree branches, but the vines rattle along with the island, making it impossible to track his movements.

"We don't have time to worry about that," Hettie says. "The island is sinking fast."

I scan the tree one last time before I follow the others and dash back into the jungle.

We angle toward the beach. It's amazing how much shorter the journey seems when I'm not overcome by fever and pain.

In no time at all, we burst out onto the sands of the beach. The sky is entirely black with smoke.

Down the beach, the men wait atop their pegasi. They alternate staring between the jungle shadows and the rising tide. But just the fact that they stayed warms my heart. They could've immediately fled, but they didn't. Not even after seeing that half the beach has already been swallowed by the ocean.

The waves dart precariously close to our feet. Janalisa's warning not to let the water touch you rings in my ear.

"We have to hurry," Janalisa calls behind me. "The island sinks slowly at first, but then speeds up the closer it is to being fully submerged."

Up ahead, through the haze of ash, the pegasi are packed

nearly right up to the waterline as the island sinks farther and farther.

"Go, get out of here," Royce calls to the men as we dash closer over the uneven sand. "Go," Royce says again, throwing his arm into the air to encourage them on.

Slowly, the men start taking to the sky and disappear into the smoke.

Two figures stay on the beach with a handful of riderless pegasi as we near.

One is Lenny. The other is Triton.

"Lenny, fly away," Phipps calls as a wave crashes in front of us, cutting us off.

More and more of the sand disappears as the island continues to sink. Only a few arm's lengths of beach remain. And they're disappearing fast.

"Hurry," Triton cries as we get closer.

But we're not going to make it. The water's rising too fast. It slides up the beach in front of us, cutting off our route. Rhat pulls Hettie back before she careens into the tide. She clutches Hebe's cup close, haggard breaths ripping from her chest.

A wave floods into the jungle. Another slices in behind us, and we jump together to avoid being hit.

Triton leaps off his pegasus and plants his feet on the beach. He stares at the waves and raises his hands.

There's a great creaking. And the island starts to rise, water running over the rocks and back into the ocean as it drains. More and more of the beach comes back into view.

But no, it isn't the island rising. It's the water fleeing, pulling away from the island.

"I can't stop the island itself from sinking," Triton says. "I can only control the water."

A small hedge of water grows at the edge of the island, growing taller and taller as the island sinks downward.

We rush forward to the pegasi.

"Go on, get out of here, Lenny," Phipps says, bringing up the rear of the group as his arm drags in the sand.

Lenny guides his pegasus forward, taking with him several of the riderless ones as well. A stark reminder of how many souls we've lost on this island.

"I'll take the diam—Janalisa," Phipps says as Rhat helps him stabilize atop his horse. He turns to Janalisa, motioning for her to get on. "We can race along until you see where Dionysus dropped you off. Then I'll come back and exit."

Janalisa climbs on and scans the sky before taking off farther down the beach.

"Hurry," Triton says, his voice strained and his face red. "You have to get off before the water covers your exit point."

Hettie and Rhat race to mount up.

"Go," Royce calls.

They both kick their heels into their pegasi. Rhat's leaps into the air and disappears in the wisps of black smoke surrounding the island.

But just as Hettie's horse's front hooves leave the sand, there's an explosion, sending a plume of sand up in front of her as something crashes to the ground.

A metal mace.

And a moment behind it is the metal-covered man. He's torn one mace from where it dangled from the side of his head, and he's already ripping at the other, grabbing the chain and breaking it free. He launches it right toward Hettie.

She does her best to get the pegasus out of the way, but she tumbles off the back of the rearing beast and lands on the sand. Looking straight into the face of the metal-covered man.

She rolls to the side just in time to avoid his sword racing toward her.

Across the beach, Triton cries out in pain. Water seeps in around the base of the ever-growing wall of seawater.

"I—can't—hold—it—long—" Triton groans. The veins on his neck stand out, and he has his eyes clamped shut.

"Give me that cup," the man says. He lunges for Hettie.

Royce's sword stops his advance.

"Get the cup out of here," Royce calls over his shoulder without taking his eyes off of the man.

I scramble to help Hettie get her pegasus under control.

The man tries to slice his ax toward us, but Royce cuts him off, swinging his sword in a wide arc.

The pegasus stamps its feet on the beach, prancing back and forth and shaking its mane as the sounds of clanging metal swords echoes all around us.

"Shh." I take slow steps toward it with my arms raised as Hettie approaches from the other side.

But her eyes keep darting from the pegasus to the sky, where her exit point waits. The point that's nearly inaccessible due to the growing towers of ocean.

Hettie sets her jaw. "Calm down, little horsey."

Her voice is anything but calm, and the animal must sense it.

"Shh," I repeat again.

The pegasus tilts its head at me in response.

I put my hands up to its nose, and that seems to do the trick. It lets out a snort against my palm.

"Climb on," I tell Hettie without moving my hand.

Hettie clambers onto her pegasus, and I move out of the way, coming face to face with the wall of water that has grown behind me. It's already far over my head, and more and more water leaks in at the bottom of Triton's wall.

I catch a glimpse of something glimmering in the sky. My exit point. The water is dangerously close to it.

"Get out of here," I say to Hettie, giving the pegasus a swat to make it go faster.

"No," the man cries. He smashes his sword into Royce's and plants a kick to his stomach, sending Royce reeling backward and causing him to crash into Triton.

Triton loses concentration for a moment. The water careens toward us. But at the last second, Triton throws his arms back up. He sinks to his knees, propelling the ocean away from the island. But some of it trickles over the top, filling in the island once more.

The man launches straight toward Hettie's pegasus. I dive to meet him, crashing into him just as Hettie and Hebe's cup vanish through the smoke.

"No!" the man screams as we tumble into the sand.

Before we can rise, the metal-covered man is on me.

He's about to ram his sword through my chest when something glints and smashes into his temple.

I scramble to my feet to find Phipps and his diamond arm there. He knocked the man back so hard he's plastered against the water wall.

Strands of kelp creep out of the water and lash around him.

"What is this?" the man cries, trying to rip them away. More strands loop around his wrists and pull taut, securing him to the wall.

"Phipps, thank you," I breathe just as a shadow passes over me.

I turn, expecting to find the metal man, but it's the mass of water rising higher and higher into the sky.

"Go," Triton calls.

"Don't have to tell me twice," Phipps says, taking off into the sky.

I rush to where Royce is picking himself up off the ground, and together we climb atop our pegasus. I can just barely see our exit point above the wall of water.

"Come on, Triton," I call.

Triton doesn't move.

It takes me a few heartbeats to figure out why.

Water has seeped in around and over the edges of his barrier. He's kneeling in a puddle of water.

"No," I breathe.

"Triton, move the water around you," I say, an odd pitch to my voice. I try to get off the pegasus, but Royce holds me back as the water rears dangerously close to the hooves.

Triton opens his eyes slowly. "I can't," he says. "The water won't move no matter how—how many times I tell it to."

I shake my head.

Pain mars his face. "Go."

"Hebe's cup," I breathe, searching. But Hettie took it to get it off the island and away from the metal man.

My eyes meet Triton's at the realization that it's gone. That his one chance of getting off the island—of breaking the island's curse on him—is gone.

"Maybe I was meant to be the—the hero after all," Triton says. "Tell my father that if you see him."

"Triton, no," I cry as the water rises around him. I glance at our exit point. It's going to be close. I bite my lip. There has to be a solution.

Triton lets out a whistle, and the pegasus next to us straightens. It hesitates a moment before it flies off into the sky.

"I know—" Triton says between gasps, "I have the best muscles you've ever seen—but can't hold this forever." He nods to the wall. "Go. Rule Lagonia like you're meant to." He flashes one last grin before clamping his eyes shut and clenching his hands into fists, giving out a loud roar as he uses everything he has to give us time to escape.

Royce pulls me closer atop our pegasus and kicks it into flight. Water floods onto the island as soon as its hooves leave the ground.

We soar upward, barely clearing the water and rising to where our glimmering exit hole waits. But as we burst through, my last glimpse of the island is water converging over Triton as the entire thing sinks beneath the waves and disappears.

# CHAPTER 32

I'm not sure how long I make our pegasus hover, its wings beating up and down, while watching and waiting for Triton to surface. But he never does.

The ocean waves are calm. There's no hint of what they've taken, of what they're concealing from me in their dark depths. The entire island, volcano smoke and all, has been sucked under. Even the sun has fled, leaving us in darkness.

Only Grax sticks his head out of the water, swimming in endless circles, searching for his friend. After more rotations than I can keep track of, he lets out low moans. They echo hauntingly across the water.

He can't seem to bear to leave, and neither can I.

"Where will the island rise next?" I ask Janalisa.

She's soaking wet from wherever Phipps fished her out of the ocean, and the water running down her face is just another reminder that Triton isn't here to dry us off.

She drops her head. "It goes where Dionysus wants it to. Without him to control it, I'm not sure what it will do—I'm not sure it will rise at all."

Despite her words, I can't seem to tear my gaze away from the waves. Because the thing about waves is that they always continue to toss. And each whitecap sends hope searing through me that this time it's Triton rising from the depths.

I can't get the image of all that water pooling over Triton out of my mind. There'd been the slightest hint of peace on his face, a calmness I never expected as he accepted his fate, welcoming the water washing over him as he would an old friend with arms held wide.

But I just can't accept this is how it ends. We'd dragged him from his prison. We were supposed to set him free, not see him trapped on a cursed island that may or may not rise again.

"There has to be some way to find him, to get to him," I say.

"We only found the island the first time because of him," Hettie says quietly.

"He's gone, Kora," Royce says, rubbing his hand up and down my arm. "The best thing we can do now is head back to Lagonia."

No, the best thing would be to save Triton. But I can't figure out how. How do you find an island that may never surface again? I half think of having Grax take me back to Poseidon, but I doubt I'll make it out of there alive after last time—not after that clam said we'd be drowned if we went back.

The Oracle? Hope dies just as quickly as it came as something inside tells me I'll never find her cave again, the one visit is all I get.

But what other option is there?

Tears prick at the corners of my eyes as I realize I can't think of any. And even if I were to, the men need to rest. And right now, my duty is to them.

So as I wipe away a tear and straighten, I try to remind myself that Triton had chosen this. Just as I'd chosen to go to Gorgon Island and to Jipper. He was ruler of the ocean, and he'd used his power to save us. His friends. To give me a chance to go back and rule.

And I needed to do just that. Because I get it now. Being a leader isn't just about reading journals about how others have ruled or wearing a crown or knowing how to bow or sit or eat the correct way. It's not about knowing whether you should enter a fight or only appear at the back of the battlefield to encourage your troops. Learning from others and following protocols are all little pieces that you can take or leave as you learn what works best for you. But what you really need is to listen to yourself, because at its core, leadership is about making the hard decisions, the ones no one else is burdened with making. Even ones that rip your heart out. Even ones that may cost you your own life—like I'd made when I'd gotten bitten or the one Triton had made on Jipper. Because that's what leaders do. They protect their people by whatever means they have.

And right now, I have to get my crew home before we tire out the pegasi.

I close my eyes and take a few deep breaths, clenching my hands into fists.

What was it Hettie said? You can't feel sadness when you're full of anger, and anger is the only thing that is going to get me through the next few hours.

So, even though it makes my chest ache, I call out, my voice as steady as I can muster, "Lenny, lead us home."

I'm glad for the dark. It hides the tears slipping down my cheeks, the ones even my anger can't keep at bay. I let the wind take the tears from my cheeks and drop them into the ocean. Maybe Triton's out there somewhere. Maybe he knows those tears are for him. For the friend I lost. For the one I still hope to one day see again.

Dionysus must've been headed to Lagonia to either lead the attack himself or to watch it unfold because the island sank only a few hours off the coast. Just as the stars start to fade and the sun sends its first muted rays striking into the sky, the familiar coastline rears out of the water.

The men sit up a little straighter after a long night of flying. They rub the tiredness from their eyes.

Grax leaps in and out of the water below us, fighting to keep up with the pegasi as we quicken our pace.

As we near the cliffs lining the coast, sounds echo out toward us. It's soldiers lining the palace walls, ready for Dionysus's attack. They all point toward us. There are cries for weapons at the ready, until we get close enough for them to recognize us.

"It's the princess," someone cries.

I wave as we soar overhead.

Even though there's room in the courtyard to land, I direct Royce outside the gates to the streets leading up to the palace.

Last time I'd returned, no one had known I'd even gone after my father's gold. This time, I want the people to see that I was victorious. That I can lead them.

"Open the gates," I command, and soldiers rush to undo the defenses they'd put in place. While they work, I spot a riderless pegasus next to me with something strapped to it.

Dionysus's staff.

Triton must've left it there. I reach over and slide it free just as the gates creak open.

A deafening cheer goes up as Royce directs our pegasus through the gate.

The doors to the palace are thrown open.

"Kora!"

A man I barely recognize appears in the doorway. He stands straight and tall. And his face isn't lined by wrinkles or sagged down by the bags under his eyes.

He looks healthy, and strong, and proud.

He looks just like my father always should.

Joy leaps in my heart to see him running toward me. His eyes aren't searching out the gold in the tower. They're on me. For the first time in forever, they're truly on me.

I slip off the pegasus and leap into his arms, and he pulls me close, wrapping his arms around me.

"I knew you could do it," he says, burying his face in my hair and kissing the top of my head. "I knew you could save us all. My brave daughter."

"We all did it," I say, pulling away to find my friends standing around us.

Hettie has her arm wrapped around Rhat's torso. Phipps is letting Janalisa make a big deal about a small cut on his forehead. Lenny has corralled the pegasi and sits atop one like a king. And Royce is standing amidst them all, watching me with a smile on his face.

Behind my father, nobles reluctantly filter out of the doors at the sound of cheering. They give me sidelong glances, studying me. I meet their looks head on, and then straighten my shoulders.

I clear my throat and take a step back from my father.

"Father," I call loudly enough for even the nobles in the back to hear, "I present to you the staff of Dionysus. I have destroyed him and his curse."

People push forward to see.

"He has been defeated," I continue, "and is no longer a threat to our people."

My father smiles down at me. "I accept this token of your victory on behalf of all Lagonia," he says, his voice reaching even farther into the crowd than mine had. "You have our eternal gratitude. Lagonia would not stand this day if it weren't for you."

He turns and holds the staff high above his head for all to see.

And while people are eager to inspect it, there's one more thing I need to do while I have their attention—while I'm their leader.

I take Hebe's cup from Hettie. I hold it high.

"This is Hebe's cup, capable of curing any curse," I say. "And let it be known that anyone who wants to be cured will be welcome here in Lagonia." Because just like with Janalisa, I can't leave anyone cursed by Dionysus in that state if they don't want to be. It is time to rid the world of Dionysus's hold.

"But we'll also welcome those who wish to keep their powers," I say. "We will offer all of them a new start." And I will make sure they are welcomed, whether the rest of the nobles like it or not. They are going to have to get used to those with powers being around, because the more I think about it, I am not going to drink from Hebe's cup. I now fully know my abilities aren't a curse. They're a gift I can use to protect my people—a gift I will need when I take the throne.

Because I am going to lead these people. And not just lead

Lagonia, but make Lagonia thrive. Because my battle was never convincing the nobles I was their leader. It was being their leader regardless and doing what I had to in order to make the kingdom prosper. And I can't think of anything better than inviting in new perspectives and new abilities as we rebuild our kingdom.

Because in the end, many have been lost—and there are still injured men to attend to—but Lagonia survived. And it will continue to survive. Because even if Dionysus managed to survive, he won't win his bet with the Oracle because my father is alive and healthy.

And it's time for us to have a prosperous rule.

Together.

# EPILOGUE

〉〉〉〉〉〉〉❧〈〈〈〈〈〈〈

The early morning waves caress my feet as I walk barefoot along the shore. In the distance, I spot several pegasi taking to the skies as Phipps and Lenny let them out of their stalls for their morning exercise.

Already in the time we've been back, the brothers have made quite a business for themselves. Some pegasi they rent out to travelers. Others they let children pet and ride. And still others delight in putting on a weekly aerial show unlike anything spectators have ever seen.

Phipps uses all the money he makes—not to mention the surprising number of diamonds he was somehow able to keep in his pockets despite running across Jipper—to keep the pegasi living in luxury. The stable he rented out is said to be nicer than the palace. Phipps loves those creatures more than almost anything—just not more than Lenny and not more than Janalisa, if rumors floating around the palace courtyards are to be believed.

I'm not normally one for rumors, but I hope this one is true. Janalisa is a sweet girl who has taken to life in Lagonia quickly. I've appointed her as my liaison to all those with powers and curses, as already many who've been cursed by the gods have come searching for healing from Hebe's cup as news spreads.

Royce has been helping me deal with the influx of people too. He's set up training programs for sailors to join the armada and has started to train both the city and palace guards to ensure we can defend our shores no matter who shows up. He's even created a special unit to train those like me who want to keep their powers and use them to protect others.

As for those with powers who don't want to give them up or use them to defend Lagonia, I've started having the castle support their trades where we can. And thankfully, many others are starting to follow suit. Even Lady Alyona only took a few days to come around to the idea of having dresses made by a young woman with the ability to change the color of fabric just by touching it. And that gives me hope that someday Lagonia might be the most welcoming kingdom of all.

As that thought slips through me, I pause in the sand, closing my eyes and inhaling a deep, heartening breath as the ocean laps at my feet. When I exhale and open my eyes again, several pegasi fly overhead and far out over the waves, dipping and diving after each other. I watch their mesmerizing path for a few moments, but even their ethereal forms can't keep my gaze from slipping to scan the horizon for tall white sails, though I know Hettie won't be back this soon. If at all.

She and Rhat left for his home on the Polliosaian Islands, and I'd understood her need to get away. Even though everyone praised her for her actions saving Lagonia, she needs time. She's fully admitted how her father's death affected her and has finally begun to grieve. And she can do that better away from the castle and the memories it holds, so I'd sent her on her way with my blessing and with instructions to take all the time she needs. Because nothing is more important than for her to heal, and once she does, she can figure out what path she wants to take going forward. And I'll be there to support her, wherever that path leads.

One familiar shape does appear on the horizon, though, eliciting a smile from me and doing a small part to fill the hole in my heart Hettie's absence brings with it.

Grax sticks his head out of the water and swims toward me as he does every morning since we lost Triton—since I've been unable to find a way to reach him.

I pick up a piece of driftwood and lob it as far out as I can into the waves.

Grax swims eagerly after the stick, snatching it from the waves and flopping back through the water toward me.

But once Grax gets to the beach, he stops, his head jerking back toward the waves. He drops the stick, his tail pounding side to side. He looks to the horizon.

I've never seen him act like this. "What's wrong, Grax?"

He looks back at me and then far into the distance behind him, whimpering. He splashes around, sending waves farther up the beach. He starts to swim away, but then turns back and lumbers out of the water, leaning forward to bop me with his snout. I pet his nose, and he rests his head against me for a moment.

Then he darts off into the waves, racing toward the horizon at breakneck speed. I don't know what it means, but as I turn back to the palace, to where Royce will be waiting for me, hope swells in me.

The waves kick up a seashell in Grax's wake, just like the ones I always used to find when I walked the shore with my mother. I smile and slip the seashell into my pocket. Then, I head

back up the beach to start another day as the golden princess—
and future queen—of Lagonia.

# ACKNOWLEDGMENTS

I try not to let a day go by without thanking God for all the blessings in my life, and this book is one of those—along with you, my dear reader, and so many people who made the book possible.

As always, thank you to my loving and supportive family: my parents, Katie, Danny, Pat, Michael S., John, Maggie, Michael K., James, and Mittens. You have been there every step of the way, and I love you more than words can say. Thank you for letting me dream my dreams and helping me make them a reality.

Also, thank you to my extended family who support me and spread the word about my books—especially my aunt Patti Nietch and aunt Mary Alice Farrell. Your support does not go unnoticed. And thanks to all those family members near and far who've come out to support me at my launch parties, especially John and Cecilia Peirce and Margie Palm-Bakner and Kathy Palm Latsha.

To my friends: thank you for being a listening ear and a sounding board . . . and for getting me out of my house when I've spent days on end writing or editing. Your smiling faces and jokes are a bright point in my life. Oh, and thanks to those among you who watch incredibly awesome shark movies with me . . . because all shark movies are awesome movies. Also, a special shout out to Joe Geisinger and Jazmine Patterson for being my keto buddies.

To my agent, Christa Heschke: thanks for being with me every step of the way and for fighting for me and this story. It wouldn't be here without you. Also, thank you to Daniele Hunter for your continued help! You are rock star agents!

To my editors Hannah Van Vels and Jacque Alberta: this book would not be what it is without your guidance and help! Thank you for believing in the story and in me.

To everyone at Blink: this book wouldn't be out in the world without you. Thank you for being such big supporters of my work.

Once again thanks to Eileen Bos, who created absolutely stunning book sculptures for *A Touch of Gold* and *Tiger Queen*. You bring my books to life in such a unique way, and I am blessed to have found you!!! Everyone should go check out Enchanted Couture by Eileen Bos on Facebook.

To all those who prayed for me, especially Christina, Elizabeth Hunter, and my CRHP sisters!

To those who were there day in and day out as my continual "wind beneath my wings": you've kept me flying for another book, and you're an amazing team that I look forward to being a part of: Ashley Zurcher, Laura Goldsberry, Jennifer Goldsmith, Clint Lahnen, Brennan Ward, and Tara Trubela. (As always, please pay special attention to my use of the Oxford comma. Remember to use it wherever you go.) Also to Paul Chen and Melisa Duffy for your help and support.

To amazing fellow authors who blurbed my book for me. I am so honored.

I couldn't write these acknowledgments without also giving a shout out to a few Facebook groups who have been great supporters of my work: The Book Democracy, Page Turners, TBR and Beyond, YA Fantasy Addicts, and Words & Whimsy Book Club. Also to those in NERDFIGHTERIA and in Old Lady Status! Thanks for your support!

To my teachers at Peter Panda Preschool, St. Pius X, Brebeuf Jesuit Preparatory School, Indiana University, and Butler University: thanks for teaching me and inspiring me!

To my street team: thank you for all you've done and for joining me on this journey.

To my 9Round workout friends and trainers, especially John (J-Mac): thank you for helping me take out all my frustrations through kickboxing and for listening to me babble about sharks.

To some of my most devoted fans, Kira, Jordan Edwards, and Valerie Pelchat. Thanks for your continued support!

To everyone who liked my author page, shared my blog, pre-ordered the book, or helped in some other way: you have no idea how much I appreciate it and how much you helped me achieve this dream.

A special thank you to several people who really helped me along the way in so many different ways: Michael and Nancy Uslan, Sandi Patel, Kathy Lowry, Lynn Ratkey, Valerie Scherrer, Jodi Clark, and Julie Timke.

To those shows and musicians who kept me going during those long nights of editing: Taylor Swift, Sara Bareilles, and Hailee Steinfeld, I listened to your songs on repeat more times than I could even count. Thanks for creating great music that continues to inspire me. And thanks to *Law & Order*. You make for great background viewing while I'm writing and editing.

Finally, to you, my readers: thank you for going on another adventure with me. You always inspire me to write more—and to write better—with every fan email you send or kind review that you leave. I couldn't do this without all of you. Stay golden!

CPSIA information can be obtained
at www.ICGtesting.com
Printed in the USA
JSHW031100190620
6253JS00002B/6